OTHERWORLD

A Stoner McTavish Mystery
by Sarah Dreher

New Victoria Publishers Inc.

Published by New Victoria Publishers, Inc., a feminist literary and cultural organization, PO Box 27 Norwich, Vermont 05055

ISBN 0-934678-44-8

Cover Design by Ginger Brown
Author photo by Susan Wilson
Printed on recycled paper

All characters and events in this book are fictitious.

Library of Congress Cataloging-in-Publication Data

Dreher, Sarah.
    Otherworld : a Stoner McTavish mystery / by Sarah Dreher.
        p.   cm.
    ISBN 0-934678-44-8 : $10.95
    1. Women detectives--United States--Fiction. 2. Lesbians--United States--Fiction.   I. Title.
PS3554.R36085   1993
813'.54--dc20
                                                                    93-6977
                                                                        CIP

For Joanna and Linda

CHAPTER 1

"Help me!"

Stoner pressed the receiver hard against her ear. "I can't hear you."

"Help me!"

She motioned to Gwen to switch off the television. The listing of the day's special events at Walt Disney World's Magic Kingdom dwindled to a bright dot and winked out.

"Please," she said, "try to speak up."

The line went dead.

She punched the cradle button—an act she had always considered less than useless, after all when a phone was dead it was dead and there were no two ways about it, abusing it wouldn't bring it back. But people did it all the time in the movies and on TV. Of course, they never said "goodbye" in the movies or on TV, rude. She hadn't sunk *that* low, not yet. But there didn't seem to be anything better to do, so she tapped on the cradle buttons like an idiot.

"What is it?" Gwen asked.

She hung up and lifted the receiver and got a dial tone. "Somebody calling for help."

"We're not even unpacked," Gwen said. She sighed. "Your reputation has finally preceded you."

"This is serious," Stoner insisted. "It was someone on the phone, and she said 'Help me!' twice, and then the line went dead."

Her lover smiled indulgently. "Dearest, this is Walt Disney World. It's full of children. Children enjoy pranks. Most of all, they like telephone pranks. As a species, it's what they do best ."

"I guess so," Stoner said, not the least bit convinced.

Gwen tilted her head to one side and looked at her. "That doesn't do it for you, does it?"

"Not really."

"Well, call the switchboard and see if anyone has placed a call to this room in the last five minutes."

She punched up the hotel operator, who didn't have—or wouldn't admit to having—that information-thank-you-for-calling.

"I guess there's nothing we can do about it," Stoner said reluctantly.

1

"I'm sure you'll think of something." Gwen heaved the largest of the suitcases onto the bed. "Do you want to unpack this, or should I?"

"I'll do it. It's mine." She popped the locks and began tossing her clothes into a dresser drawer.

"Stoner."

"What?"

"Maybe you should hang some of those up."

"It's just T-shirts and stuff."

"Some of that 'stuff'," Gwen said patiently, "is cotton blouses. And cotton slacks. And a silk shirt. Do you know what being stuffed in a drawer will do to them?"

Stoner looked at her helplessly, one hand dripping underpants, the other oozing socks.

Gwen took them from her. "Let me do it. Your idea of organization is one drawer for clean and one for dirty."

"It works," Stoner said.

"I don't think so." Gwen held up a wrinkled, rumpled shirt. She slipped a hanger through its sleeves.

"You really shouldn't do that," Stoner said uneasily. "It's too much like—well, like roles, you know?"

"Roles, schmoles." She looked at Stoner in that brown-eyed, soft, mock-stern way that always made her fall in love all over again. "I adore you. Go check on Marylou. See if she's recovered."

Marylou's room was next door. She knocked.

"Come!" Marylou called.

Stoner peeked around the door.

One of the beds was completely covered with vibrators.

"Marylou, what's that?"

"What's what?"

"The vibrators. What are you doing with all those vibrators?"

"Safe sex," said Marylou. She was eating the last of the cheese and crackers they had been served on the plane as a "snack." Or maybe it was "lunch." It was hard to tell these days.

"I know the travel business is dull," Stoner said, "but you should have told me you were quitting."

"Quitting?" Marylou frowned at her. "Kesselbaum and McTavish is finally an institution. We have a repeat clientele. Next year we might even make a profit, if the building doesn't go condo. Why would I quit?"

Stoner picked up an Eve's Garden special and turned it over in her hands. "So what're you doing? Selling these on the black market or something?"

"I'm not planning to sell them. I'm planning to use them."

"On what?"

"On myself."

"All of them?"

"Not all at once," Marylou said. "Maybe consecutively."

Stoner returned Eve's Garden to its assigned spot and sat on the other, uncluttered bed. "Where's your mother?"

"At a workshop. She left a note." Marylou wiped the cracker crumbs from her fingers and began rummaging in her voluminous tote bag. "Don't you think it's kind of sick having a psychiatric convention at Walt Disney World on Hallowe'en?"

"To tell you the truth, it's the first time I ever realized psychiatrists could have a sense of humor."

Marylou dumped the contents of her tote onto the dressing table and rooted through them. "I know I had something to eat in here."

"Why not call room service?"

Marylou sighed heavily. "If they have room service in this place—which I doubt—the food's probably wretched. Mouse-ke-fries and Mickeyburgers. Made from real mice, no doubt."

"The restaurants in World Showcase are supposed to be good."

Marylou humphed.

"Honest. Remember when the Newtons came here a couple of years ago? They really liked the restaurants."

"True," said Marylou. "But we haven't the slightest idea what kind of standards they have. For all we know, they could make my mother, the Fast Food Queen, look like a gourmet."

Stoner stretched out on the bed, hands behind her head, and looked over at her friend. "I'm glad to see you've gotten over the trip down."

"Gotten over?" Marylou asked, her voice sliding up an octave. "Gotten over? It was the most disgusting experience in my 35 years on this planet. I'll never get over it."

Stoner grinned at her. "I'll bet, right now, there are flight attendants saying the exact same thing."

"It was their decision to do that kind of work. I'm not going to feel guilty. Besides..." She sniffed haughtily. "...I think I conducted myself admirably."

Stoner pretended to give that serious thought. "I guess so. Of course, your behavior during take-off and landing wasn't exactly restrained."

The minute the plane had begun to taxi down the runway, Mary lou had started to harangue the other passengers in a loud and unignorable voice. "You people are all crazy. We are in a long metal tube that can't possibly support our weight. They've locked the doors. There's no escape. Did you see the pilot? I did. I saw him last week on *Unsolved Mysteries*. Are you aware that that very man—if he's even human, which I doubt—personally murdered eight people? Do you know how he did it? He took them up in a private plane and jumped out. Jumped out. Leaving them to perish in the fires of Hell..."

The flight attendant—a bubbly brunette with skin-tight uniform and the only real spit-curls Stoner had seen outside of old photographs in 1950's issues of *Life Magazine*—pounced on her with soothing tones, "There-there-ing" like a mother with a frightened child.

"Do not patronize me, Madam," Marylou snapped. "They are taking us miles into the air, from which we will drop like a rock. I have no intention of being patronized at a time like this."

At that point, Stoner had tried to deny ever laying eyes on Mary lou before in her life—which was difficult since Marylou was sitting between Stoner and Gwen, and it was obvious from various little gestures of affection that passed between the two of them and across Marylou's lap that they would never have allowed themselves to be separated by a stranger.

"It's all right," Gwen said, letting a little of her Georgia accent slip into her speech because this was a Delta flight, and the attendant was probably from Atlanta. "It's her first flight." She patted Marylou's hand, while looking earnestly at the woman. "She's only been out a couple of days, you know."

The flight attendant, whose name tag introduced her as Ellen, a good, steady, reassuring, dependable kind of name, rearranged her face into a mask of professional competence and concern. "Out?" she asked in a voice that didn't quite manage to sound blasé.

"Of the..." Gwen made circles in the air with her hand. "...the...the...you know."

"Oh," said Ellen. "The...you know."

"Nothing serious," Gwen said in a hushed voice. "A little impulse control problem, that's all."

She's going to get us thrown off the plane, Stoner thought. But they don't throw you off of planes. Not at 30,000 feet. Do they?

Gwen fumbled in her purse and brought out a packet of chamomile tea. "If you could just make this up for her, I'm sure she will

4

be fine."

"Well," Ellen said. "If you think so. But we can't have the other passengers..."

"Of course not," Gwen said.

When Ellen was out of ear-shot she turned to Marylou. "If you don't get a grip on yourself right this minute," she said, "I will never speak to you again."

Which had reduced Marylou to a state of mumbling grumble until they began their descent into Orlando International Airport. At which point she announced that they were *now* being hurtled earthward at the speed of light and would never survive the loss of pressure and subsequent explosion.

"What I wonder," Stoner said as Marylou began rearranging the vibrators into a pattern she felt was more aesthetically pleasing, "is how we're going to get you home."

"I'm not going home," Marylou announced. "I'll conduct our business by phone from our branch office in Kissimmee—whatever that is."

Stoner felt mildly annoyed. "This really isn't funny..."

"*FUNNY?*" Marylou shrieked. "Did I look as if I were having *fun?*"

"Sorry," Stoner muttered, though she was still peeved but wanted to avoid an argument.

"I *told* you when we opened the travel agency, I will do everything in my power to help other people—even strangers, even unpleasant strangers—to enjoy memorable and hassle-free vacations. But I will never, ever travel myself. I hate it, Stoner. I really hate it."

Little tears trembled on the rims of Marylou's eyes, and Stoner was a goner. She'd never been able to bear seeing Marylou unhappy. She got up and put one arm around her. "It's okay."

"It's *not* okay." One of the tears gave in to gravity and slipped down Marylou's cheek. "It's bad enough, not being able to do something that everyone else in the entire world enjoys, but the one time I screw up my courage and try, I'm stuck in this God-forsaken, overgrown amusement park full of—of CREATURES, or whatever they call them..."

"Characters," Stoner said.

"I may never get home, and they don't even have room service."

"They must have room service," Stoner said in a comforting way, and handed Marylou a tissue.

"They don't." Marylou sniffled and blew her nose.

Stoner brushed Marylou's hair back from her face. "Sure, they do. If they don't, I'll get you something."

"That's not the point. We're stuck in a hotel that doesn't understand the *concept* of room service. If they don't understand that, God knows what else they don't understand. This place is...is *primitive*."

"Marylou, it's one of the most up-to-date, state-of-the-art resorts and theme parks in the country. Probably in the world."

" 'State-of-the-art',"Marylou grumped. "You're starting to talk like a Yuppie. Reagan and Bush are gone to reap the benefits of twelve years of greed and general nastiness, Yuppies are Out—and *now* you start talking like one."

"I try to stay current," Stoner murmured modestly.

Marylou tossed the damp tissue into the waste basket and finished off the last of the airline peanuts. "Did you see the topiary? God in Heaven."

"Sure, I saw it."

"Sea serpents. Elephants. RATS!"

"I think that was Mickey Mouse."

"We hadn't even reached the hotel, and the place is full of mutants."

"They were only bushes."

"Plants are plants," Marylou declared, "and creatures are creatures..."

"Characters," Stoner said.

"...and anyone who grows plants to look like creatures is sick. We are trapped here at the mercy of SICK MINDS."

"It's a *theme park,* Marylou. Walt Disney World is a *theme park.* Theme parks are like that."

"Yes, and what's next?" She rummaged deeper into the spilled contents of her voluminous tote bag and managed to come up with a tiny box of Godiva chocolates. "Next, I suppose you'll be dragging me off to Dollywood. Or that Jim and Tammy Fay Christian Place."

"They sold the Christian Place."

"Well, I'm sure there are other spots equally appalling." She unwrapped a chocolate and popped it in her mouth. "No, you may not have one of my chocolates."

"I don't do designer candy," Stoner said.

"Quiet. I'm having a peak experience."

She waited until Marylou had finished the chocolate, fascinated

6

as usual by the way a simple piece of candy drained the tension from her friend's face. Sort of like watching someone start to have a heart attack and pop a little nitroglycerine. She wished her own problems were that easy to get rid of.

"I'll never understand," Marylou said as she lovingly folded the foil wrapper and placed it reverently in the waste basket, "how you can face daily life in America on the things you eat."

"I eat pretty much like everyone else," Stoner said.

"And look at what 'everyone else' has done to the world." She sighed. "God, to think I'll never see Boston again! The Public Gardens! The Isabella Stewart Gardiner Museum, the MFA, the Pops! Fenway Park!"

Now Stoner really had to laugh. "You've never set foot in Fenway Park in your life."

"But the *possibility* was there."

"We'll find a way for you to get home," Stoner said. "For now, why not just enjoy it? We have a whole week to relax and have fun."

"Fun," Marylou grumbled. "Surrounded by creatures."

"Characters."

Marylou began unpacking furiously. "I don't know why I let you talk me into this."

"I didn't twist your arm. I didn't hold a gun to your head. In fact, I tried to talk you out of it."

"They offered us rates," Marylou admitted.

"We get offered rates to all kinds of places. All the time."

"Not to Walt Disney World." She drew a sequined black bra from her suitcase and tossed it into a drawer.

Now Stoner really was curious. "Seriously, why *did* you decide to come?"

"No reason."

"I've known you for more than fifteen years. You've never done anything without a reason. Maybe a fucked-up reason. Maybe for a reason you found out later wasn't the reason you thought was the reason. But there's always a reason."

Marylou grabbed a handful of red lace panties and stowed them in the drawer. "All right. I felt left out."

"Left out?" It was hard to imagine Marylou left out. She seemed always to be with someone, or about to be with someone, or arranging to be with someone—out with friends or on dates, visiting clients' homes to look at slides. Marylou was one of those people who make friends effortlessly and without apparent anxiety. Unlike,

7

Stoner thought, yours truly.

"You're always going off to neat places and doing exciting things, because you're not afraid to travel. And I always have to stay home."

Stoner was shocked. "Neat places? That haunted house in Maine? You thought that was a *neat place*? You must be nuts!"

"Well," said Marylou, "maybe not that one."

"I've nearly been killed half a dozen times. Maybe that was exciting, but it wasn't *neat*."

"Not exactly, I guess."

"And for *real* fun and games, try being warped into another century. That's *really* neat."

Marylou help up her hands. "All *right*. So maybe those things weren't fun, but at least things happen to you. Nothing ever happens to me."

Stoner had to admit that was true. Very little did happen to Marylou. Stoner had always rather envied her that. "Well," she said, "something's happened to you now."

"It certainly has," Marylou said in a righteous tone. "And it more than makes up for all the things I've missed. But I still haven't had a mystery to solve."

"Okay," Stoner said, "here's one. A few minutes ago the phone in our room rang. When I answered, a woman's voice said 'Help me.' Said it twice. It sounded like someone in trouble."

"Easy," Marylou said. "She was desperate for room service."

"Marylou, I promise you, in the Walt Disney World Contemporary Hotel, there is room service." She shook her head in dismay. "All I can say is, I'm glad you're bunking with your mother and not with us."

"Ah, yes." Marylou rolled her eyes. "Dr. Edith Kesselbaum, psychiatrist *extraordinaire*. That promises to be a lot of laughs. How would you like to spend a week at the Magic Kingdom with *your* mother?"

A week in Hell, Stoner thought, would be a vacation by comparison. "Your mother's not the same as mine."

"You're only saying that because she was your shrink."

"That isn't true, Marylou. And it was a long time ago. We've gone beyond that."

"Maybe you have," Marylou said. "But don't count on Edith. She takes this therapist business very seriously. Just when you least expect it, she'll lean over to you and whisper, 'How are you *really*?'" She glanced at herself in the mirror. "God, Stoner, why didn't you tell me I was getting so fat?"

"You're not. You haven't gained a pound in three years."

"I've looked like *this* for three years?"

"You look just fine."

Marylou stepped back a couple of feet and rotated, studying herself. "I have to go on a diet."

It made Stoner sad when Marylou started talking about diets. Being Marylou meant loving to eat, and showing it. There was something sensual about the way she ate, as if food were the most exciting, magnificent, utterly elegant experience one could have. It wouldn't be the same if she were thin. When Marylou started talking about going on a diet, Stoner felt as if she were talking about dying.

"I like you the way you are," she said.

Marylou gave herself one more critical look. "Well, then, it's time to reread *Fat as a Feminist Issue.*" She patted her bosom affectionately. "When does your aunt check in?"

Stoner picked up a classic Hitachi Wand and studied it. "Not until later tonight, around dinner time. She's visiting her friends at the psychic camp in Cassadaga."

"Really?" Marylou raised one sculpted, ebony eyebrow. "I'd think that crowd would be a little conservative for her taste."

"They go 'way back. She was a little nervous, though. Isn't sure how they'll take to her conversion to Wiccan."

"Not well, I'll bet. Kind of a hard-core Christian lot, aren't they? But preferable to Jewish Mystics. Now, there's a formidable and terrifying bunch of believers."

There was a tap at the door.

Marylou sang "Come."

Gwen walked in. "Stoner, that call came again."

"Same as before?"

"Well, not really. I mean, a call came, and when I answered it I thought there was someone there—you know, how you just kind of know—but they didn't say anything. I tried to have it traced, but all they could tell me was it came from outside the hotel." She looked at Marylou's vibrator collection. "Planning to have a little fun?"

"Mayhap."

"What do you think?" Stoner asked.

"I think we're not going to see much of Marylou on this trip."

"About the call."

Gwen went to the window and gazed out. "I think it certainly could be a prank, even if it isn't from inside the hotel. We have an

9

efficient phone system here, and about a thousand child-infested acres. If it isn't a prank, there's not much we can do until we have more information, and I haven't the slightest idea how to get it. Do you?"

"No."

"Then I suggest we enjoy our vacation and await further developments."

"I guess so." Stoner went to stand beside her. The room overlooked the swimming pools and the lagoon beyond. Small bright yellow motor boats scampered back and forth like water bugs across the sparkling lake. A few sailboats drifted in the distance. At the center of the lagoon, a motor-driven launch packed with sightseers was pulling away from a jungle island. The October sun, low in the sky, burned through the humidity with a pinkish glare. "What should we do first?"

"I don't know. Marylou?"

"Don't look at me," Marylou said. "I've never traveled before."

Stoner leaned over to Gwen. "I don't think she ever will again, either."

"Come on," Gwen said to Marylou. "This place is magic."

Marylou grumped incoherently.

"Well," Gwen said, "I, for one, plan to give Mr. Disney a chance. What say we hop the monorail and get an overview of the sights? Stoner?"

"Great. Marylou, want to join us?"

"I have just survived a death-defying plane ride, and now you want me to get on a speeding bullet-train. Thank you very much, but I believe I'll wait for Edith."

"You really are welcome," Stoner said, not wanting Marylou to get that fifth-wheel feeling she sometimes got because Gwen and Stoner were lovers.

"Really," Gwen put in.

"In all honesty, Loves, I do need to settle in." She swept her arm in an arc that took in the room, the luggage, and the bed full of vibrators. "Specifically, I have to stow these little items away before my mother arrives."

"Surely your mother's seen vibrators before," Gwen said. "Though probably not so many at one time."

"The Liberated Dr. Edith Kesselbaum is one thing," Marylou said. "Edith Kesselbaum, mother of Marylou, is another. Edith Kesselbaum, mother of Marylou, will be shocked and speechless."

Speechless? Stoner had never known Edith Kesselbaum to be at

10

a loss for words—which was why, Edith had explained to her during her lengthy and successful stint as Stoner's therapist ten years ago, she could never be Client-Centered. "They *sit* there," she had said. "Nodding and reflecting like senile dogs."

"When the Mother Thing is upon her," Marylou explained, "she turns into Donna Reed. It's not a pretty sight." She gave them a little push toward the door. "Go. Enjoy."

"If you get bored," Gwen suggested, "you can always study the room service menu."

"The *WHAT* ?"

Gwen picked the hotel information folder from beneath Marylou's well-thumbed copy of *People Magazine* on the bedside table and handed it to her.

"You," said Marylou as she clutched the folder to her bosom, "are an absolute saint. Don't hurry back."

The Grand Canyon Concourse had a deep, muffled feel to it, like a carpeted ravine. Or Grand Central Station with rugs, Stoner thought as the monorail slid in and regurgitated its load of passengers, who immediately began pushing, shoving, and milling. Tiers of rooms towered 15 stories above the main floor, and men in business suits leaned over concrete balconies, drinks in hand. Somehow, the convention-going look of the suits was incongruous against the 90-foot tile mural of cute, round-headed, round-eyed Indian children. Cute and suits don't go well together.

As a matter of fact, the cute, happy, round-eyed Indian children cast a little doubt on Disney's ethnic sensitivity.

Unlike Grand Central Station or even a carpeted ravine, the place was filled with light and color and air. The monorail, yellow-striped, slipped away like a ghost train though an opening that framed trees and sky like a trapezoidal painting. Or a cartoon of sky and trees. The Terrace Cafe, nearby, was open-aired with a southwestern motif, and you went inside to get your meal, then sat outside—which was really inside—to eat. There seemed to be a lot of outside inside the Contemporary. All part, Stoner suspected, of a Disney plot to scramble your senses and warp you into a world of real/unreal where you couldn't tell the two apart.

Maybe Marylou was right. Maybe it *was* all the product of a sick mind.

Gwen had wandered off. Stoner looked around in a panic and saw her headed for an escalator. She ran to catch up. "What are you doing?"

"I thought we might as well get our World Passports as long as

11

we're here. Besides, we have to go up here to get on the monorail."

"Don't leave me like that!" Stoner panted. "I'm experiencing culture shock."

Gwen slipped her hand into Stoner's. "I'm sorry. I won't let you get lost."

That's right, Stoner thought as she trotted along behind her, Gwen keeps me from getting lost.

And had from the day they had met, in Wyoming, in Grand Teton National Park, when Stoner had been overwhelmed with the beauty of the mountains and the thrill of her first sight of the West, and the just plain knock-out amazing presence of Gwen herself.

CHAPTER 2

There were other lesbians on the monorail. Two of them. Holding hands right in the face of God, Mickey Mouse, and a straight, two-child-two-parent-one-grandparent Traditional Family.

Stoner made eye contact.

Acknowledged.

Smile contact.

Acknowledged.

They exchanged niceties and names.

Pauline was tall, blonde, and looked like an outfielder—not too athletic but able to handle herself on the women's softball level as long as she played on the Feminist team that wasn't into heavy competition. She had eyes the color of the late-afternoon sky reflected in the lagoon—blue shading to purple. She installed aluminum siding for a living and was called "Stape".

Stape's partner—or "friend", as she said, out of deference to the sensitivities of the Traditional Family, who looked a little midwestern—very clean, kind of stiff—was Georgia. Short, tawney-haired, and looked as if she kept score at the round-robin tournaments at best, but was probably a mean catching machine no one dared steal on, even on the competitive teams. George—as she preferred, after her favorite Nancy Drew character—worked for Walt Disney World, but turned slippery when they asked what she did. Stoner suspected she had something to do with security.

Stoner volunteered the information that she and Gwen were from Boston, that she was a travel agent and Gwen taught junior high school history—which brought sympathetic murmurs from Stape and George. Gwen remarked that it was even worse than they could possibly imagine.

One of the Traditional children rolled his eyes and muttered, "Teachers! Gross!"

Gwen smiled sweetly at the parents, who had the good sense to look embarrassed.

"Can't be much of a teacher," Grandma opined. "They let you out in October."

"I'm on accumulated sick leave," Gwen explained, adding

13

pleasantly, I was afraid I'd kill a child if I didn't get away."

The boy looked at her with renewed interest—and possibly respect, "They took me out," he volunteered and indicated his parents.

"Well, good for them," Gwen said. "Is it a special occasion?"

"Motels are cheaper," Grandma grunted. She nodded toward the father and sniffed. "He wanted to save money."

Son-in-law, Stoner thought.

By the time they were crossing the inlet to the lagoon, with the towers of Cinderella's Castle reflecting a pink, Disneyesque sunset—Stoner wondered if it was a *real* sunset, or a special effect—Stape had given them her business card, which also showed their phone number in Kissimmee, and they had offered to get together some evening, and George and Stape would "show 'em the sights."

Daddy Traditional Family pulled his daughter a little closer. Stoner wondered what kind of lurid pictures his Traditional mind was entertaining.

"Most folks miss half of what we have here," George said. "They never leave WDW. Hardly anyone goes to the Tupperware Museum."

"The Tupperware Museum?" Gwen asked eagerly.

George grinned. "You interested?"

"Of *course* I'm interested. How could I not be interested?"

Stoner slouched down in her seat and tried to make herself invisible.

"You oughta see the blue outfits the guides wear," Stape said. "Cute. And they're real nice, too. Ordinary gals, nothing glamorous. Make you feel right at home."

The Traditional women, mother and grandmother, were unconsciously leaning forward a little. Stoner smiled at them.

They smiled back, tightly.

"There's an entire house inside the museum," George said. "Kitchen, dining room, living room, you know. They show you how you can use Tupperware in every room in your house. I'm not kidding. They even have Tupperware baby toys. You wouldn't believe the stuff they make."

"George wants to have a baby," Stape said to Stoner. "I don't know. What do you think?"

Stoner shrugged. "Depends, I guess." She knew a couple of lesbians with babies—boys. A midwife friend had told her most babies born through artificial insemination were boys. It seemed to her the world didn't need any more boy babies. Boy babies tended to grow into boy adolescents. Things were likely to go downhill from there pretty fast.

"They have a whole new line of stuff," George was saying. "For the microwave. They call it Tupperwave."

The Midwest women were practically drooling.

"Have you ever tried it?" Gwen asked.

"Use it all the time. Comes in sections, and you can stack them on top of one another and cook a whole meal at the same time. You have a microwave?"

Gwen shook her head. She and Stoner had discussed it once—now that Gwen had broken with her grandmother over being a lesbian, and was living in her own apartment—and they had both admitted that microwave ovens seemed like the ideal appliance for a small apartment and busy life style. They had also both admitted they were terrified of them.

"You ought to get one," Stape put in. "It'll change your life. Frees you up for other things."

Daddy was now imagining what those "other things" might be. The man was going to have a heart attack if he didn't get a grip on his fantasy life.

"Aren't we *ever* going to get there?" Traditional Daughter whined.

Mommy hushed her.

"I *hate* this place," Daughter groused.

"Oh, you do not," said Grammy.

"Do, too."

They tried to ignore her, turning their attention back to George and Gwen, eager for more appliance gossip.

"They're perfectly safe," George assured her. "Long as you don't do anything stupid, like try to dry your laundry or put the cat in them or something."

"I don't think I'd be likely to do that," Gwen said.

"I'm *hungry*," Daughter fussed.

"You just ate," Mommy hissed.

"Tell you what," Stape said. "You guys come over to our trailer for dinner some night, we'll put her through her paces."

Gwen glanced at Stoner.

"Sure," Stoner said. "Suits me."

"We have some friends with us, though," Gwen said. "We'd have to coordinate."

"Shoot," Stape said. "Bring them along."

Stoner could just imagine Marylou's face when she told her they were going out for a microwaved dinner cooked in Tupperwave. It would almost be worthwhile selling tickets.

"I don't know," Gwen said. "It's kind of a rough crowd."

"I have to wee-wee," Daughter puled.

"Do not," Traditional Son snapped, and poked his sister in the abdomen.

"*Mommy! Davey hit me!*" Daughter's shriek could have awakened the topiary.

"Stop teasing her," Mommy ordered.

Daddy roused himself from his fantasy life long enough to mumble, "Leave the boy alone."

Daughter sniveled.

Mommy turned to Gwen and smiled apologetically.

Gwen smiled back.

"I wonder," Mommy said hesitantly, summoning up great strength of character to address them. "Could you tell me how to find this here museum?"

"Simple," George said. "It's right outside Kissimmee, on 441, just south of the Beeline. If you're going to the airport, just leave a couple of hours early and stop by for the tour."

"They give samples?" Grammy demanded.

"Orange peelers," Stape said. "They work, too."

Mommy and Grammy exchanged determined nods that sent a clear signal to Daddy that he was going to be in deep Midwestern fertilizer if he tried to scuttle *that* little outing.

"What else you got down here?" Grammy asked, suddenly alert to the possibilities of central Florida.

"There's Spook Hill, down by Lake Wales. You can put your car in neutral, sit tight, and the car just moves backward uphill all on its own."

"I seen something about that," Grammy said. "Year or so back, on the CNN."

"I saw that, too," Stape said. "I didn't understand the explanation they gave, though."

"Neither did I," Mommy admitted.

Daddy looked as if he might throw up. Here were his women— *his women*—carrying on with a bunch of...it was disgraceful.

"If it was late winter," George said, "you could see the Black Hills Passion Play. But it's not here now."

"Already seen that," Grammy said with some smugness. "Went to South Dakota for it. I was moved."

"She cried," Mommy offered. "Broke right down and cried at

the nailing up."

"Yeah, it was gross!" Son put his two cents in. "Blood and stuff. Not enough, though."

He lapsed into silence to contemplate inadequate gross blood and stuff.

"The most amazing thing happened," Mommy said. "After He got up there on the cross, dying? A storm comes up right behind the amphitheater. Thunder and lightening and all. We got plenty of thunderstorms back home, but that one scared me right back to Church, being in the midst of the crucifixion the way it was."

"Yes," Gwen said, "I can see where it might have that effect."

The monorail slid to a stop at the entrance to the Polynesian Village Resort. The Family gathered up its assorted sweaters, jackets, stray socks, and upbeat Mickey Mouse shopping bags and squeezed through the doors.

"You girls have a nice trip." Grammy called back to them.

Gwen gave her a wave. "And don't you forget. Tupperware."

"You're from the south?" Stape asked as the doors slipped shut.

"Georgia. Jefferson. But I haven't lived there in years."

Stape thought hard, frowning. "Jefferson."

"Northwest of Atlanta," Gwen said. "It's a tiny place. You might not have heard of it."

"I can't really say I have." Stape glanced at George, who shook her head. "Sorry."

"The only time it ever gets mentioned is if there's a KKK rally there. I think the last one was at least ten years ago. There's some kind of museum of medical technology there now, but I haven't seen it."

They were passing the massive white verandas and red-shingled roofs of the Grand Floridian. Elegant, intricate. Stoner tried to imagine children running through its halls or carousing on its beach, and found it a difficult concept. She tried to imagine herself being comfortable in its Victorian formality. Impossible. Even though the guide books tried to make it sound friendly—just like the other resorts, with shops and ice cream parlors and video game rooms and snack bars. But drop her into a lobby with stained glass domes and chandeliers, and she'd be like a beached dolphin, thrashing and gasping for breath.

Probably because it was exactly the kind of place her mother would love.

Also because she would be aware, every minute of every hour of every day, that she was a lesbian.

Not that she minded being a lesbian.

What she minded were situations that grabbed you by the throat and screamed MISFIT—MISFIT—MISFIT until you wanted to crawl down a crack in the floor.

The Grand Floridian Beach Resort looked like one of those situations.

What some people—even well-meaning people, even some younger lesbians—didn't understand was that being a lesbian was a full-time occupation. You got up in the morning and looked in the mirror, and the woman who looked back was a lesbian. Sometimes you looked at her and wanted to shout with joy. Sometimes you wanted to fall on your knees and thank whatever passed for God in this Universe that you were one of the lucky ones. And sometimes you just wanted to die.

Stoner had, at one time or another, experienced each of those scenarios.

Ever since, with Edith Kesselbaum's help, she had come to honor her lesbianism, she didn't often want to die. But she could still remember when her fear and self-hatred ran so deep it was always beneath the surface, ready to be tapped by a cold look or a rush of love for another woman. Or sometimes the dull depression would just drop on her out of nowhere. Even now she could be thrown back into the old anguish if enough circumstances came together with enough force.

Edith Kesselbaum said that was understandable. "If you put a crazy person and a sane person in the same room," she had once said in the middle of a discussion about dinner, "sooner or later the sane person will go crazy. Likewise, a self-accepting lesbian and a homophobe. The homophobe probably won't have her/his consciousness raised, but you can be sure the lesbian will pick up a little temporary slime of homophobia. It's the nature of things." She examined a polished nail thoughtfully. "Would you rather go out for Burger King, or order a Pizza Hut delivery?"

So sometimes the haters made her crazy, made her turn on herself. She supposed it would always be like that. Like an old injury that aches when the weather turns damp, or a once-torn ligament that can never quite take the strain it used to take before the tear. Growing up in a lesbian-hating family in a lesbian-hating town in a lesbian-hating country had left her vulnerable.

She tried to avoid haters, and to forgive herself when they made her cry.

"Stoner?"

She felt a hand touch hers. Softly, questioningly. She looked up at Gwen. "Sorry. I was thinking."

"It's okay," Gwen said. "We don't have to stay at the Floridian."

Stoner winced. "I hate it when you read my mind."

"I didn't read your mind. I was thinking the same thing. My grandmother would love that place." She turned to Stape and George. "My grandmother hasn't spoken to me since I came out."

"Sucks," Stape muttered.

"My folks were like that at first," George said. "But they came around when they realized they'd never see me again if they didn't." She shrugged. "It was dicey there for a while. But families are real tight down here."

"My grandmother doesn't show signs of mellowing," Gwen said. "I'm not even sure I want her to."

"You want her to," Stoner said.

"I guess." She turned to George. "How is it to work here, being a lesbian?"

"A what?" George asked in mock innocence, and Stape guffawed.

"Oh," Gwen said. "That bad, huh?"

The monorail pulled into the Magic Kingdom stop. Over the Turn-of-the-Century railroad station, the turrets of Cinderella's Castle punctured the evening sky. Crowds of people, treetops, balloons, all jumbled together in a turmoil of color and motion.

Stoner caught her breath. "It's overwhelming," she said.

"I envy you," George said as she gathered up her things. "I wish I could see it for the first time again."

"Try not to do everything at once," Stape advised. "Take a day here, a day at Epcot, then decide what you want to see again." She crammed a visored cap onto her head. "How long you staying?"

"We have reservations for a week," Gwen said.

Stape whistled. "That must have cost you a year's salary."

"Not really," Stoner said. "They gave us special rates, because I'm a travel agent."

"Lucky you," George said. "They won't even give the staff special rates. Well, hey, let us know when you want to come to dinner."

"Or if you need anything," Stape added. "Like aluminum siding."

They pushed out through the right-hand doors as another mob squeezed in from the left.

"Amazing," Gwen said. "We really *are* everywhere."

"Well?" Marylou wanted to know, "are you oriented?"

"Absolutely," Gwen said. "We caught a glimpse of the Magic Kingdom through the trees, met a borderline-appalling family from the Midwest, were totally intimidated by the Grand Floridian, and made contact with two local dykes."

"Sounds like a worthwhile jaunt. You'll be glad to know my mother has returned, looking none the worse for workshops. Aunt Hermione called to see if we had made it—said she already knew it but Stoner preferred to believe she got her information through worldly channels like everyone else, rather than plucking it out of thin air."

Stoner flopped down on the bed. "All *right*, Marylou." She felt overloaded and exhausted. Probably the heat and humidity. Back in Boston it would be drizzling and gray, collar-up weather. The Miseries. Here, it was tropical. Maybe a little too tropical, kind of chest-pressing, soggy, breath-grabbing...

"Incidentally," Marylou said, "I kept an ear out for your phone. No mysterious calls."

"How would you know?" Gwen asked as she peeled off her T-shirt and splashed water over her face. "You probably had all those vibrators going at once."

Marylou chose to ignore her. "However, I do have one bit of excitement to report. We have been given tickets to the Polynesian Revue."

Stoner shoved herself up on one elbow. "The what?"

"The *Polynesian Revue*. At the Polynesian Resort."

"But what does it do?"

"It's food. Polynesian food. And entertainment. Hula dancers. Fire jugglers."

Gwen went to the closet for a shirt. "What's Polynesian food like?"

"I don't know," Marylou said. "But it sounds exotic. And get this. Usually you have to plan months in advance for tickets, and someone just handed them to us. Free."

"Who?" Stoner asked.

"The management. They were slipped under the door to your room."

"Why would they do that?"

"Probably," Gwen said, "we've won a contest as the oddest family in Walt Disney World."

"WDW," Stoner corrected.

Marylou jangled her wrist full of silver bracelets in exasperation. "I can't believe you people. Someone gives us a fabulous, exciting, once-in-a-lifetime experience, and you act as if they've insulted you."

"I'm sorry," Stoner said. "I think I'm tired and cranky."

Marylou plopped down on the bed beside her and tried to tickle her. "Come on, Stoner. You're on vacation. Enjoy."

"For someone who always hated to travel," Stoner grumbled as she pulled herself to her feet and headed for the shower, "you're certainly having a good time."

"I'm getting into it."

"Of course you are," Gwen said. "And I can't wait to see how you take to the monorail."

Marylou screamed and threw a pillow at her.

* * *

The path leading to the Luau was lined with torches, lazy yellow flames oozing smoke into the humid Florida night. The dining area was packed with families, women in halter tops and shorts, men in Hawaiian shirts, children in Mouse ears and Mickey T-shirts.

A waitress wrapped in a brilliantly colored sarong and sporting an orchid in her hair came forward and led them toward their table.

Stoner felt a tug at her sleeve and dropped behind the others.

"Something's not right," Aunt Hermione said. "I feel it."

She glanced at her aunt's worried face and experienced a brief sinking feeling of sadness. Her hair seemed grayer, her wrinkles deeper. The soft, smooth skin of her cheeks had a translucent quality, as if she might evaporate at any minute. Aunt Hermione was aging. "Are you okay?" she asked.

"Of course, dear." Her aunt gave a little laugh. "Visiting old friends is always exhausting. Especially when all their Spirit Guides want to drop in for a chat. At times it's worse than a wedding reception."

Stoner had to smile. "I love you, Aunt Hermione."

"I love you, too, dear. And I'm not about to die, so you can stop worrying about that. Plenty of time for worry down the road."

"Darn it, Aunt Hermione, how many times have I asked you not to read my mind?"

Her aunt shook her head. "I *am* sorry, Stoner. Sometimes I forget. After all, we've never had secrets from each other."

"How could I have secrets from you?" Stoner asked in mock

exasperation. "You and Gwen. You're always poking around in my head."

"Oh, my dear," the older woman said with a little laugh. "You know better than that. As is true of most people, the majority of things that go on in your head are static. Many deep thoughts, of course, an occasional brilliant intuition, and some truly bizarre and stimulating sexual fantasies. But most of the time..." She shrugged. "...static."

"I'm going to kill you," Stoner muttered, her face as red as the passion flowers on the hostess' sarong.

"I really doubt that, but we can discuss it later." She leaned closer and lowered her voice. "Someone here is in danger, Stoner. Real danger."

"Here?" There must be hundreds of people here, crowded around tables, laughing and drinking in the torchlight.

"Not everyone here. Though some of them have interesting, *moderately* dangerous experiences in their near futures." Aunt Hermione pursed her lips in disapproval. "And a few have conducted themselves disgracefully in this life, and might want to take a look at that. But they'll just have to do it again until they get it right, won't they? No, I mean someone in *our* party."

"Who?"

"That's what worries me. I can't run it down. Whoever this person is, she or he is very good at blocking. I sense the intrusion but not the target."

"It's a psychic, like you?"

Aunt Hermione paused for thought. "Not necessarily," she said at last. "Some people of modest psychic ability can learn to block. As a matter of fact, I usually recommend it to such persons. There is nothing worse than having only modest psychic ability. It leads to unwelcome precognitions, flooding by all sorts of floating messages from the astral plane. They're likely to go off in all directions, chasing into the night after souls in trouble—some of whom have already passed over but refuse to accept it. Not much one can do on this plane, of course, but highly disturbing. I recall a young man— several years ago it was—drove himself to distraction rushing about the country on missions of mercy, or feeling guilty if he didn't go, which is just as bad. He reached the point of collapse. I had to insist he take up a practical, down-to-earth sort of occupation. I believe he accepted a position in a hardware store and did quite well."

A waitress went by with a plate of vegetables and dip. Stoner

22

felt hunger like a live thing waking in her stomach. She followed the waitress with her eyes. "Aunt Hermione..."

"Some, on the other hand, just aren't terribly bright. Very hard to penetrate a mind whose contents are merely a low hum. Once inside, what do you have? Not much."

"Aunt..."

"But you take someone with genuine psychic ability, well-developed psychic ability, not like yours which is considerable but dormant...Have I mentioned that my friend Grace is giving courses in psychic development?"

"Yes," Stoner said. "Many times."

"Still not ready. What a pity." Aunt Hermione sighed deeply. "But, as I was saying, you take a person with strong psychic powers, and the ability to block—plus no compunction about how he or she uses his or her abilities...well, anything is possible."

A tray of something that looked like Chow Mein went by. Stoner gazed at it longingly. "I guess so."

Aunt Hermione began moving toward their table. "But what do we have here? A threat. Strong vibrations. Negative energy. Nasty intentions, if you will, directed by and toward person or persons unknown."

Person or persons unknown? "I thought you'd sworn off those late-night Perry Mason re-runs."

Her aunt tapped her arm. "Try to concentrate, dear. What we do know is that this individual is linked to someone in our party. Someone in our party has enemies..."

"Everyone in our party probably has an enemy or two."

"Yes," said Aunt Hermione gravely and she pulled out her chair and sat down. "But of this caliber? Who? And why?"

The eminent Dr. Edith Kesselbaum was resplendent in a black and electric-pink-and-green MuuMuu. She sipped an enormous tropical-looking drink and nodded enthusiastically to a tall, slender, balding man with a Sigmund Freud beard. He moved away as they approached. "Lovely to see you again, John," Edith called after him with a cheery wiggle of the fingers. She turned back to the table and rolled her eyes heavenward. "My God, psychiatrists are the world's dullest people."

Maybe it's Edith, Stoner thought. Someone out to get her. Professional jealousy. Or a dissatisfied patient. "The risk," Edith Kesselbaum had once told her, "is that the higher the patient places you on a pedestal at the beginning of treatment, the longer the fall at the end. It's the Mother archetype that causes the trouble. At

23

first, during the honeymoon period, you're all they ever dreamed of, motherwise, but when you let them down—as you inevitably will." She shuddered. "Well, let's just say it's an experience I hope you never have." She took a sip of her drink. "If you have the good fortune to pass through reality between Heaven and Hell, the visit is invariably brief."

Well, if it was Edith, there wasn't a snowball's chance in Ecuador Stoner'd find out from her. Edith Kesselbaum was about as tight-lipped as a shrink could get. Oh, sometimes she referred to problems she'd dealt with—as an object-lesson or to illustrate a point—but Stoner frequently had a sneaking suspicion she made them up. If not, Edith Kesselbaum was blessed with having been consulted by clients who illustrated every point she had ever wanted to make. Actually it was most likely that Edith Kesselbaum drew her conclusions about life from her clients. A unique approach, one that Stoner had not seen in many therapists.

Not that she knew many therapists. There was that bunch back in Maine, in the mental hospital she had checked herself into to find Claire Rasmussen. They probably didn't count, since they were only in the racket to cover up shady doings. On the other hand, Edith had checked the credentials of a few and found them to be genuine. That was pretty disturbing, people using the mental health profession to line their pockets. Though Edith assured her that sort of behavior wasn't so unusual. "All in the way you look at it, Stoner. Some turn to crime, and some merely charge exorbitant fees. There are those—and I won't name names, though I'm certainly tempted to—who soak their clients for $1.50, $2.00 a minute. All perfectly legit, too. Let me tell you, before I'd let someone pay me $2.00 a minute for *my* pearls of wisdom, I'd better be able to make the blind see and the lame walk, and raise the dead."

A waitress in a grass skirt and little else offered her something called Chicken Pago Pago that looked like leftover Chop Suey. "Thank you," she said quickly, averting her eyes from the woman's bosom, which seemed to be covered only by enormous, mutant, fuchsia hibiscus flowers.

Gwen caught her eye and gave her an understanding, affectionate smile.

Gwen. Maybe the person/persons unknown was/were after Gwen.

Gwen?!

Gwen didn't have real enemies. Other than her grandmother, who hadn't dealt well with Gwen's announcement that she was in

24

love with Stoner, and whom she hadn't seen in nearly fifteen months as a result.

Her ex-husband probably wasn't terribly fond of her at the moment, either, considering that she and Stoner had contributed to his death. But there wasn't a lot he could do in his present condition, and even if he'd reincarnated immediately, he'd still be too young to do any harm.

The same went for Larch Begay, back there in Arizona...

"What?" Gwen asked when she laughed out loud.

"I was just thinking, the people who do you wrong seem to end up dead."

"Well," Gwen said sweetly, "let that be a lesson to you." She sniffed Stoner's plate. "Are you really going to eat that?"

"Sure. Why not?"

"It looks like the flux."

"What's the flux?"

"Diarrhea. And if it isn't diarrhea, it will undoubtedly cause diarrhea."

"Don't be silly." She stirred the food around on her plate. "Look, Edith's eating it."

"Right," Gwen said. "And we all know Edith Kesselbaum has the dining instincts of a goat."

Not Gwen. Not real enemies.

What about Marylou?

How could Marylou offend?

Well, there was always the botched-airline-tickets possibility. People were known to become murderous over botched airline tickets. Understandably. What with air travel these days a matter of increasing risk, cramped seats, crummy meals the size of doll food, flights late or cancelled, and prices higher than cruising altitude—all most people needed to go on a killing rampage was to end up on a wrong or non-existent flight.

But they hadn't botched a ticket in ten years. Either of them. In fact, they should make it the motto of the agency: Kesselbaum and McTavish, Travel Agents, Ten years without a Botched Ticket.

How about her private life, though? Marylou liked sex, and found men useful along those lines. But they were always falling in love with her, wanting a commitment, wanting CHILDREN, for God's sake. Marylou Kesselbaum with children was...was...well, it just wasn't. Some of her ex-boyfriends had gotten a little pushy about it. There was even one against whom she'd had to take out a restraining order. He'd hung moping around outside the Cambridge apartment where Marylou and her mother and stepfather lived. Not doing anything, exactly. Just hanging around. Following her. Gazing up at her window. Writing poetry on tear-stained paper. Finally Max—Marylou's step-father and a retired FBI agent—had declared enough enough and called the cops.

But that had been two years ago. All she'd heard from him was a brief note, six months after the incident, apologizing for his bad behavior and promising to enroll in a men's group to get in touch with the "Wild Man" within. A chilling thought, but it seemed to have cured his obsession with Marylou.

And she doubted that Wild Men stalked the corridors of Walt Disney World projecting dark thoughts into people's minds. They were probably too busy grooving on the Jungle Ride and getting off on the Pirates of the Caribbean.

So what about Aunt Hermione? She'd made a few enemies in her life—not counting her oldest and dearest enemy, Stoner's mother, whom she had dared to defy by taking Stoner in when she was sixteen and a runaway, and refusing to throw her back into the lion's den.

But if someone was trying to harm Aunt Hermione, they wouldn't do it psychically. Anyone who'd spent an hour with her would know they couldn't win that battle.

Which left—drum roll, please—yours truly. Yours truly, who only had to walk down the street to pick up enemies by the dozen. Yours truly, who really only wanted to go through life calmly and simply, no hassle, no complexities, just smelling the roses. She had a family, a lover, friends, and a job. Quite enough to look after in one lifetime, thank you. She didn't need the added aggravation of enemies.

Marylou passed her a drink in a coconut shell. It was the size of a bucket, and topped with enough fruit to decorate Carmen Miranda's hat a dozen times over.

"Am I supposed to drink this?" she asked. "Or save it for breakfast?"

"Whatever you like," Aunt Hermione said. "Though from the amount of rum it seems to be carrying, I shouldn't think it would make a very suitable breakfast. You don't want to experience EPCOT Center through an alcoholic haze, do you?"

"To tell you the truth," Stoner said as she pushed the drink away, "I really don't want to experience anything through an alcoholic haze."

"Yes," her aunt said, "I've noticed you haven't been having

your usual before-dinner Manhattan lately. I didn't want to say anything, but…well, dear, is there a problem?"

Stoner shook her head. "Somehow it just doesn't seem like a good idea any more." It had actually happened, she recalled, one evening at a dance. For some reason she had taken the time to notice how her drink tasted, and realized that she didn't really like it at all. Then she noticed how it made her feel, and realized she liked that even less.

"It seems to me," Aunt Hermione was saying, "people just don't respond well to liquor these days. Thirty years ago I don't believe we had quite so much drunken violence. Do you suppose they're making it differently? Or is it the hole in the ozone layer?"

Stoner thought about it. "Maybe it's genetic."

"It could be the nuclear testing, I suppose."

"Actually," Gwen put in, "I think it's television. Boys see boys getting drunk at sporting events and think it's cool. It gets attention."

"I vote for the hole in the ozone layer," Aunt Hermione said.

Glancing up, she noticed Marylou staring morosely at her plate. Poor Marylou. They could tease all they wanted, but Marylou did hate being away from home. And as unconventional as Edith Kesselbaum was, it certainly wasn't an easy thing to travel with one's mother.

"I think," Gwen murmured in her ear, "a little extra attention is called for over there."

"You're right." She excused herself and pulled up a chair between Marylou and her mother. "So. How's it going?"

"This is absolutely," Edith said, "the most fantastic food I've ever eaten."

Marylou groaned.

For the first time, Stoner took a good look at their dinner. Some kind of salad, possibly shrimp and vegetables, but diced within an inch of its life, every bite identical to every other bite in size, shape and texture. Two varieties of baked chicken in sauce—one clear sauce and one yellow. Chunks of beef, also in sauce…

"Walt Disney World," Marylou grumbled. "Sauce capital of the universe."

Stoner dipped her little finger in each of the sauces and tasted them. They seemed to be identical, smooth and slightly gingery. "How come they're different colors?" she asked.

"Food coloring," Marylou said.

"No."

"Look." She pointed to a swirl of yellow in a river of clear. "They didn't stir that one enough."

"Oh, God," Stoner said. "You're right." She took Marylou's hand. "I'm sorry about this, really I am. When we get back to the hotel, you and I are going on a real food hunt."

Marylou smiled evilly. "You're going to pay for this, Stoner McTavish. For the rest of your life."

"Marylou," Edith Kesselbaum said, "don't pick on Stoner."

"Mother! You're acting like a mother!"

Edith held up one hand in apology. "Sometimes I forget myself. Do you suppose it could be some strange manifestation of displaced counter-transference? Maybe I should see my training analyst again."

"I think it's probably just habit," Stoner offered.

"Nonsense. All behavior is motivated, usually unconsciously." She caught herself and pressed a finger to her lips. "Listen to me, talking like a Freudian. And I thought I'd put all that behind me. It's a cult, you know. Remind me to think twice next time I'm tempted to go to one of these conventions."

"Edith," Stoner asked, "do you have any enemies?"

Dr. Kesselbaum tossed her hair and adjusted the orchid she wore behind one ear. "Not at the moment, but I undoubtedly will before the conference is over. I am only..." She held up two fingers, separated by a millimeter. "...this far from telling someone off. Today we were subjected to one of those touchy-feely group experiences I thought had died back in the '70s. And after that a seminar on managing the business end of your therapy practice, with particular emphasis on dealing with HMOs." She frowned and sucked on her drink. "Sometimes I wonder if anyone does *real* therapy any more."

Drums exploded to a frantic, hysterical cadence.

The lights went out.

Dancers leapt onto the stage, torchlights glistening and reflecting from the dinner sauces.

"Dear God!" Edith Kesselbaum murmured, and turned to watch them, mesmerized.

"You and Edith getting along?" Stoner asked, leaning close to Marylou.

"Fine."

"Did she find the you-know-whats?"

Marylou grinned. "The coast is clear."

"Where'd you put them?" She could imagine Edith going

28

through the drawers, looking for a spare blanket or the phone book or something, and coming across the world's largest collection of vibrators.

"In your room. That's how I found the dinner tickets."

"My room!"

"Sure. If she finds them in there, she'll think your therapy was a complete success." She caught her breath. "I just had a terrible thought."

"What?"

"Suppose we lose the key?"

They looked at each other and began to giggle.

"You know," Marylou said with a little hiccup, "this vacation could be all right."

Stoner pressed her forehead against Marylou's. "You're a great friend."

"Stop it, Love. You're embarrassing me."

Loudspeakers blared out the announcement of the "Knifa Oti", the Samoan Fire-Knife dance.

The drums became frenzied.

The stocky Polynesian men whirled, tossing their flaming batons into the air and catching them without missing a beat.

"Too bad they're boys," Marylou whispered in her ear. "With this act, they'd have the talent section of the Miss America Pageant sewn up."

They watched for a while.

So Edith Kesselbaum didn't think she had enemies. At the moment. Well, she could be right. But...

And how vulnerable was Marylou, really?

She was obsessing. "Marylou, do you have any known enemies?"

"Thousands," Marylou said. "Why?"

"Aunt Hermione thinks someone here is out to get us. And there are those phone calls..."

"Know what I think?" Marylou asked as she took another bite of what she had identified as the real Chicken Pago-Pago.

"No. What?"

"I think someone's out to ruin your vacation."

"Mine?"

"Yours. Someone who knows your fatal flaw is worry. And is attempting to drive you mad by making annoying phone calls and putting thoughts in Aunt Hermione's head. Which isn't difficult, as you know. Aunt Hermione's ability to pick up signals is the envy of

29

every satellite-dish owner in the country."

"But why me?"

Marylou spread her hands in a 'who knows?' gesture. Her silver bracelets jangled. "Could be anything, love."

Stoner frowned. "I don't like this."

"I know. But remember what you're always telling me. If you don't have enough information to reach a conclusion, best to wait until more comes your way, and meanwhile sit back and enjoy yourself."

"I never said that, Marylou."

"You might say it. Probably did at one time or other only you don't remember. Probably will again. Probably in the next few hours. It's the kind of thing you'd say."

A hand appeared from nowhere, wearing a flowered bracelet and holding what looked like a rum-and-coke. "Excuse me. Ms. McTavish?"

Stoner looked up.

"Compliments of that gentleman over there," the cocktail waitress said.

She glanced over. The nearest table was packed with couples. No one was looking their way.

"Which gentleman?"

The waitress scanned the group. "I don't know which person. I'm sorry, but their dinner server took the order and passed it on."

"I don't think..." But the woman was gone. Stoner scanned the other table. "That's odd. I don't recognize anyone in that crowd."

"Maybe somebody just likes your looks. Maybe they have a thing for green eyes."

"They know my name."

"A secret admirer."

"I don't have secret admirers."

Marylou reached for the drink.

"I don't think you should drink that. It might be poisoned or something."

"At Walt Disney World? Don't be silly," Marylou said. She picked up the drink, took a sip and made a face.

"What is it?"

"Rum and Coke. A real lollapalooza. Try it."

Stoner shook her head. "I'd rather not."

"Oh, go on. Just taste it. You don't have to swallow enough to kill yourself."

Cautiously, she tried the drink. It was bitter, with a smoky over-

30

taste. Reminded her of the valerian tea they used to drink for P.M.S. back at the Cambridge Women's Center. "Does it seem all right to you?" she asked.

"Seems fine."

"You're positive?"

"Absolutely. Will you please *relax*, Love?"

One of the hula dancers approached, holding out her hands, inviting them to join her on the stage.

"Come on," Marylou said. She jumped to her feet, flinging her napkin into the yellow sauce.

"You go ahead," Stoner said. "I'm happy to watch."

"Don't be silly," Marylou shouted from the stage. The hula dancer took her by the hips and began swaying back and forth. "You're a great dancer."

"Not tonight."

"Okay," Marylou called over her shoulder, getting into the rhythm and motion, "but this could be the end of a beautiful love affair."

She watched the dancers for a while, and tried to take her mind off of her apprehensions. Marylou was right, of course. There was nothing she could do but wait and see what developed. If she had a nickel for every time she'd had an apprehension that had died on the vine, she'd be rich. She was prone to unreasonable apprehensions. Forebodings that scurried through her mind like squirrels in autumn, rustling dried leaves of anxiety, burrowing into piles of premonition-weeds and pulling out nuggets of sheer terror. Most of the time they didn't amount to anything. This was probably one of those times.

Probably.

CHAPTER 3

The phone rang. The night shattered. Startled awake, her heart racing, Stoner picked it up. "Hello?"

"Help me."

She sat up. "Please, tell me who you are."

"Help me!"

"I can't help you if I don't know who you are."

"I'm lost. You gotta help me!"

Beside her, Gwen switched on the light.

"Who *are* you?"

The voice became very small. "I don't know."

"You don't..." She could make out background noise. A man's voice. Familiar. Couldn't make out the words. She tried to place it. Damn. It was right at the edge of her mind, but...

"*Help me!*"

Stoner rubbed her eyes, chasing away the remnants of sleep. She had to keep the woman—clearly, it was a woman, a young woman, not a child, heavy rural Southern accent—on the line. "Look, I want to help, but you have to tell me more."

She picked up the pencil and pad of paper from the bedside table and scrawled a note. "Marylou's room. Trace call."

"I gotta go."

"Wait!"

Gwen tossed her bathrobe over her shoulders and scurried from the room.

"Please," Stoner said. "Don't hang up."

"I gotta."

The young woman's voice was faint and a little hollow, as if she were down a well.

"At least try to tell me *where* you are."

"I don't know."

What do I do now?

Damn. Can't think.

She kneaded her face. "I..."

Okay. Analogy. You're... Christine Cagney, and Mary Beth's been kidnapped. She's called you on the phone but doesn't know where she is and you say...you say...

32

"Somebody *help* me!"

"All right, all right." She tried to make her voice calm. And you say...damn...you say...Got it! "Look around. Tell me what you see."

"Dark. All dark."

Oh, great. No wonder *Cagney and Lacey* was cancelled.

"Well, there must be *something* or *someone* there. I hear a voice."

"There's a voice, but nobody here."

"Voices don't come out of nowhere. Try to find out..."

"Please!"

Stoner tried to identify background noises. The man's voice went on and on. Lecturing? Explaining? Unintelligible. Who would be lecturing? At this time of night? "Don't hang up," she said firmly. "Okay? We're trying to find you, but you can't hang up."

"They're gonna take me away," the woman said. "I don't want to go. I'm afraid to go."

"*Who's* going to take you away?"

"I don't know. I can't see 'em but they want me."

"Okay, okay. Try not to panic. Take a deep breath and clear your mind." Who *is* that in the background. Damn it, who *is* it?

"I gotta go. Please, I don't wanta go!"

"No," Stoner said firmly. "You can't go. We're going to find..."

The phone went dead.

She dropped the receiver onto the cradle and ran her hands through her hair.

This was one well-planned hoax, or someone was in real deep trouble. Either way, the potential for making her crazy was limitless.

As she started for the door, Gwen came back into the room. She looked a little shaken.

"Did they trace it?" Stoner asked.

"Yes." Gwen hesitated.

"And?"

"Did you keep the person on the line?"

"Sure. Until just now. Seconds ago. Why?"

Gwen looked at her. "I called the operator. He checked and double-checked. I made sure he had the right room number."

"Good," Stoner said. "What did you find out?"

"Nobody was using our line," Gwen said quietly.

She frowned, puzzled. "What do you mean?"

"Nobody was calling in."

"Well, they must have made a mistake. There must be some-

33

thing wrong with their equipment..."

"There was nothing wrong with the equipment."

"If it was a *male* operator, he was probably incompetent."

Gwen took a deep breath. "He wasn't incompetent. He cut into our line. He patched me in so I could hear you talking." She hesitated, then pushed on. "Stoner, you were talking, but you weren't talking to anyone."

* * *

"I know I'm not crazy," she said next morning as she fought a headache over breakfast in the Terrace Cafe.

"Who said you were? Look!" Marylou pointed to something behind Stoner's back. "It's Goofy!" She jumped up and waved. "Hi, Goofy!"

"For Heaven's sake, Marylou." Stoner picked at her scrambled eggs. "There *was* someone on the phone."

Gwen took a sip of her coffee. "I heard the phone, too, Stoner. That much wasn't a hallucination."

"But I know I *talked* to someone."

Aunt Hermione piled bacon and fried potatoes onto her bagel and cream cheese and took an amazingly ladylike bite. "If you would only open your minds just a little—and I mean *all* of you, not just Stoner—you wouldn't have to spend so much time searching for explanations."

Stoner shook her head, which made it pound like a drum. Sinus, no doubt. One day they were fighting the bone-gnawing cold of late fall in New England, the next day suffocating in Florida heat and humidity. It opened her pores, but played havoc with her sinuses.

Or maybe it was last night's Chicken Pago Pago. "I'm sorry," she said, "but I just can't believe spirits make phone calls. If they want to communicate, can't they do it more directly?"

"Ordinarily. But suppose part of the *point* is to make you work. To appear quite mundane so that you learn whatever lesson you're supposed to learn."

"You mean," Gwen said, "kind of like the Medium is the Message."

"You might say," Aunt Hermione said with a litte giggle. "Excuse me for laughing, dear, but that's sort of an in-joke among psychics."

The monorail slid into the overhead station.

"God," Marylou said wistfully, "he's magnificent."

34

Stoner looked around. "Who?"

"Goofy."

"Marylou, he's a *Character*."

"All the better. I like a man with a sense of humor."

"A Disney Character. They come to the Character Cafe at break-fast time to entertain the children."

Marylou heaved a sigh. "What a waste."

"There have been instances," Aunt Hermione went on, "well-documented instances, by the way, though of course one has to know where to look for the documents—of Spirit making use of material objects when it's the only way She/He/It/Whatever can get through. I recall the case of a man who was driving down a dark mountain road late at night. He fell asleep at the wheel. Just as he was about to crash into a run-away eighteen-wheeled semi-tractor-trailer truck loaded with logs, Spirit stepped in and literally yanked the steering wheel from his hands." She nibbled on a bit of jam-covered toast. "Just yanked it right away from him. It saved his life. My, this jam is quite ordinary tasting, isn't it?"

"What do you suppose they do after work?" Marylou pondered.

"Spirit doesn't have working hours," Aunt Hermione said. "It has no conception of time as we know it. The idea of nine-to-five is quite amusing to Spirit."

"I meant the Creatures," Marylou said.

Stoner took another look at Goofy. "It's probably a women. About nineteen years old. And after work she goes home and does her laundry and washes her hair and gets ready for the next day. Or she goes out to teen-oriented discos with her nineteen-year-old friends and they make plans for college and pick up boys with whom they don't practice Safe Sex."

Marylou thought it over. "I think one should try to have a wide variety of experiences," she said at last.

Aunt Hermione turned to look at the Goofy Character. "It does have a nice aura," she said. "Very calming."

"I wonder what it's like to have that job," Gwen said. "I mean, when you put on the Goofy costume, do you *become* Goofy? Does the essence of Goofyhood enter you?"

Stoner looked at her.

"You know," Gwen went on. "Like the Kachinas. When the Hopis put on the Kachina masks, they become the Kachinas."

Stoner tried to think about it, around her headache. Maybe. And maybe Walt Disney Characters were the white man's Kachinas. Gods of Enthusiasm and Entertainment. It was a sobering thought.

Aunt Hermione wiped her mouth daintily and folded her napkin. "I have to be going. I promised some old friends I'd meet them at the Haunted House. Always such fun to see how the average person conceives of Spirit. Quite ridiculous, really, but I suppose a warped conception is better than no conception at all. Will Edith be joining us later?"

"Probably," Marylou said. "I'm supposed to leave a message when we decide where to have dinner. If she can get away, she'll meet us there."

"Grand." Aunt Hermione tucked her glasses into her fanny pack. "Have a pleasant day. Or, as they say in those dreadful, repetitive television ads, 'Have a Disney Day'." She shook her head. "Dreadful." The crowd swallowed her.

* * *

The monorail pulled into the EPCOT station.

"Well," Gwen said, "here we are. Science. Technology. Children. Every teacher's dream." She leaned across Stoner's lap and touched Marylou's hand. "You can open your eyes now."

Marylou screwed up her face. "Are we ON THE GROUND?"

"At the station."

"Tell me when we're ON THE GROUND."

Gwen unlocked Marylou's hand from the cuff of Stoner's shorts. "Okay, follow me."

Two park employees in clean, freshly-ironed uniforms appeared out of nowhere and offered assistance. Gwen waved them off. "We're trying to teach her self-reliance. She's moving to independent living in six months."

The helpful young men moved a respectful distance away but kept a casual eye on them.

The crowd was flowing down the stairs, toward the entrance to the Experimental Prototype Community of Tomorrow. Stoner slipped into the human current and let it take her. Gentle New Age music tinkled around her like wind chimes.

Pretty, she thought, and then for one panic-stricken moment couldn't remember what she'd done with her World Passport. She found it in the back pocket of her shorts and transferred it to her hand. She glanced over her shoulder, looking for Gwen. Losing her World Passport would be bad enough. Losing track of Gwen would be dreadful. They hadn't done any of the things they usually did when travelling or shopping—decide where to meet if they got lost, decide who would stay where she was and who would go looking, what code names they'd use if someone had to be paged...

She was right behind her. Marylou seemed to be moving under her own steam.

They stepped into the turnstile line.

Another employee took and stamped their tickets and told them to enjoy the park. All around people were milling past, funneling toward a central point.

Gwen slipped an arm around her waist. "Well, here we are."

"I really did hear someone on the phone," Stoner said, studying the ground as they walked along. The headache was making her a little dizzy.

"I believe you."

The sun felt warm and soft on her back. "I didn't make it up."

"I know."

"You're sure you didn't hear..."

"Honest."

"It's really crazy, you know?"

Gwen stopped suddenly. "Stoner, look where we are."

She looked up, and caught her breath.

Spaceship Earth sailed high against a pale blue sky. Wisps of gauzy cloud caressed the gigantic silver globe. Massive and delicate, it seemed to hover protectively over the earth.

Stoner felt tears spring to her eyes, and swallowed.

"Magnificent, isn't it?" Gwen whispered.

"Spaceship Earth," Marylou read from the guide book, "is 180 feet high and weighs a million pounds. The sheath is made of triangular panels of anodized aluminum, whatever that is, with a polyethelene core."

"It's an illusion," Gwen said. "This thing is not what it seems at all."

"How can you tell?" Stoner asked.

"I feel it. Can't you feel it?"

Yes, she could feel it. Something unearthly about it, something otherworldly, something...mystical. Despite the music, despite the crowds in constant motion, there was a feeling of profound stillness and silence.

A long line of people stood at the base of the geosphere, snaking between chains in an orderly maze. At the top of the maze, a carpeted ramp led into inky darkness.

"Want to go in?" Gwen asked.

The suggestion seemed like blasphemy. And something else. Something she couldn't quite identify. "Not yet. Can we look around a little first?"

"Well," Marylou announced as she peered at the guidebook, "I know *my* first stop. Earth Station."

"What's that?" Gwen asked.

"Probably the most important spot in all of EPCOT," Marylou said.

Okay, where would Marylou want to go first in this whole gigantic, exciting park? On a ride? Hardly. Ladies' room? Possible, but not likely. Souvenir counter? No. Information?

She had it. "Earth Station," Stoner said, "is where you make dinner reservations, right?"

"Correct!" Marylou bolted through the sliding glass doors and made a dash for the TV monitors.

"Think we should supervise this?" Stoner asked.

Gwen shook her head. "Let her go. I feel guilty enough for dragging her here."

"Yeah," Stoner said. She shoved her hands into her back pockets. "She really hates it, doesn't she?"

"Hard to tell." They found seats where they could see Marylou set to work on a WorldKey Information screen, beginning her browse through the menus of every restaurant in EPCOT.

"One thing we can count on," Gwen remarked. "If we let Marylou pick the restaurants, they may be bizarre, but they'll be good."

"Don't be too sure," Stoner said. "She *likes* some strange stuff, like snails. And smoked oysters."

Gwen grimaced."I don't want to hear about it."

Stoner stretched her legs out in front of her and watched the constantly-changing images on the electronic billboards along the ceiling as they gave grainy previews of what could be found in the various exhibits. Now that they were finally here, she was so overwhelmed by impressions it was hard to think. Light, water, sound, heat—especially heat. Yesterday they had been shivering in Boston drizzle. Today warm air surrounded her, caressing and pressing.

She glanced to her right. Outside, beyond the glass, the park shimmered as if under a film of water. The sun was cruelly white, and pricked her eyes like needles. Objects and people broke into shards of color and motion.

Gradually, she began to make out larger masses. They resolved slowly into palm trees. Terraced flower beds blazing with crimson. Fountains spraying mist into the already-soggy air. Glaring green and white. Shadows as black as coal mines. In the distance, a softly curving building came into view. The facade of the building was brilliant blue, and shaped like a gigantic, stylized wave.

"That must be the Living Seas," Stoner said. She was feeling increasingly fuzzed-out lethargic.

Gwen put on her reading glasses and consulted the guide book. "Looks like. Wow! They have a restaurant surrounded by a fish tank. We can order seafood, and watch them watching us eat them."

"Tacky," Stoner said.

Marylou had given up on the touch-sensitive screens and had summoned the image of an up-beat Disney hostess. Stoner couldn't make out their conversation, but from the look of deadly serious-ness on Marylou's face, they were discussing either the meaning of life, or the relative merits of the French, German, Italian, and Japa-nese restaurants.

"What?" Gwen asked.

"Huh?"

"You seem luke-warm on the Sea idea."

She forced herself to look alert. "No, really. I want to see every-thing. I just don't know where to start."

"Well," Gwen said, "we're right here at Spaceship Earth. That seems a logical..."

Stoner cut her off. "Birnbaum's guide recommends leaving that for later in the day, when the crowds aren't as heavy."

"There aren't any crowds, Stoner. This is October, not the mid-dle of summer."

She felt a funny, anxiety-like tingle along her backbone. "There were some crowds on the way in. Didn't you notice?"

"It certainly looked to me as if the line was moving with deliber-ate speed."

The tingle was growing to a cold itch. "But we don't want to waste time standing in..."

Gwen gave a little laugh. "Pebbles, we have a whole *week* here. Wouldn't you like to stand in line in the sun for a few minutes?"

"Sure," Stoner said. She wanted to be agreeable, in spite of her apprehension, in spite of her pounding head. After all, they were on vacation. She got up. "I'll tell Marylou..."

Gwen grabbed her belt loop and hauled her back down. "Some-thing's bothering you. What is it?"

"Nothing. The Ball would be great."

"The Ball?"

She gestured in the general direction of Spaceship Earth. "The Ball."

39

"Stoner…"

Her anxiety was becoming genuinely uncomfortable. "It's fine."

"It's not fine. You're as white as a ghost. Tell me what's going on."

The trouble was, she didn't know what was going on, except that something about going into the Ball scared her. Scared her a *lot*. "It's dark," she said lamely.

"Sure."

"And weird."

"Weird?"

Stoner nodded.

"Weird in what way?"

"I don't know?"

"Are you having a premonition?"

"I'm not sure."

"A *personal* premonition? Or is it more like the whole thing's going to roll off its base and squash us all, and generations from now people will still be looking at grainy home video films and singing folk songs about the Disney Disaster?"

She managed a weak smile. "Didn't you notice how many people were going *into* the Ball, and no one was coming out?"

"No," Gwen said, "I didn't notice that. But if people were vanishing off the face of the earth at the rate they're going into the Ball, don't you think CNN would have picked up on it?"

"Maybe Disney and Ted Turner are in it together."

Gwen shook her head. "Jane Fonda would never agree to be a part of something like that."

"She could be a double agent," Stoner said. "Maybe that trip to Hanoi was just to throw us off the track. I mean, don't you find it strange that she could get a passport so easily? And why did the U.S. Government let her back in the country…?"

"I knew we shouldn't have gone to see *JFK*," Gwen said with a heavy sigh. "You see twists and turns and conspiracies everywhere."

Stoner laughed. "They *are* everywhere." She lowered her voice to a whisper. "Look around." She glanced over her shoulder as if looking for…"Oops."

People were emerging from a door at the back of the room, a door which, if entered instead of exited, would lead directly into Spaceship Earth.

Gwen grinned. "Gosh, Tinker Bell, it looks like we've found the Lost Boys."

"All right, all right," Stoner said, trapped. "I'll go."

"Stoner," Gwen said, "where is it written that you have to go on each and every ride?"

"But if you want to..."

"If I want to go, I'll go. That doesn't mean *you* have to. You don't have to protect me. You know I hate that."

"It's not that," Stoner tried again. "I just feel as if something's going to happen, and I don't think we should be in there when it does."

Gwen stretched her legs out in front of her. "Well, do you think it'll pass if we wait a while?"

She thought about that. "Maybe." But she had a feeling it had to do with only her, and with knowing. With knowing something she really, honestly, sincerely didn't want to know.

The smile on the face of the upbeat Disney hostess behind Marylou's screen had taken on a waxy appearance.

"I think," Stoner said, "I'd better help Marylou get closure on dinner." She got up and crossed the room and put her hand on Marylou's shoulder. "Time's a-wastin'. Think you can wrap..."

Marylou waved a hand to quiet her. "Hush, Love, I've almost got it." She turned back to the screen. "You're certain we can't reserve for tomorrow while we're at it."

"No, Ma'am," the hostess said for what was probably— knowing Marylou and her total lack of belief in Rules—the twenty-eighth time, "we can only take reservations for tonight. You can reserve up to two days in advance from your hotel room."

"Okay, I say we go with Marrakesh at seven. That's five of us. The name is Kesselbaum, Dr. Edith Kesselbaum."

The hostess suppressed a look of surprise. "*Dr.* Kesselbaum?"

"Dr. Edith Kesselbaum. We're with the psychiatric convention."

"I see." The woman's composure returned, and with it her Disney smile. "May I have your room number at the Contemporary, Dr. Kesselbaum?"

Stoner had to admire the way the young blond woman handled herself. The quick appraising glance, the lining up of the woman she saw in *her* monitor—wild-haired, dressed in gauzy black slacks and revealing blouse, face nearly hidden behind sunglasses and a huge, floppy black hat that tied with scarf-like material beneath her chin and completely obscured her features, and wearing enough jangly silver jewelry to back up a full day's output from the Treasury Department—against her own and the media's view of The Psychiatrist. Do we have a match? Hit or miss? Kook, charlatan, or

41

the Real McCoy? And what might this strange, obsessive woman have in mind with all her questions about restaurants and menus and what was fried in palm oil and what in sesame, and the kind of bread served in each restaurant, and to what extent each item was Americanized—more questions than the Disney people had ever dreamed of, which was a miracle in itself, God knew *they* were an obsessive lot?

Kathi—at least that was her Disney name—found herself wondering as she smiled and nodded and explained, whether she was really meant for the tourist business. Maybe the benefits of her time spent at WDW, great as it might look on her resumé, weren't worth the wear and tear on body and soul. She had been 23 when she came to work this morning. She was at least 40 now, and it wasn't even noon.

"One more thing," the woman in black was saying, "when is the busiest time in the restaurants?"

"Usually between 5:30 and 7:30," Kathi said with a Disney smile. Really, she wanted to scream at this woman. That was exactly what she wanted to do. Scream at her. She didn't care if she was a psychiatrist or not, the woman was a Disney Pain in the Disney Neck.

"Even at this time of year?"

"Yes, Ma'am." What, you think the world comes to a screeching halt when we switch to Standard Time?

"So we can expect the restaurant to be crowded."

"That's right."

"People sitting along the wall in uncomfortable chairs, waiting to get in? Head waiters trying to get you to pass the time in the bar so you'll spend more money and drink too much and not even taste the food, that sort of thing?"

"That sort of thing," Kathi acknowledged.

The woman's eyes were unreadable behind her dark sunglasses. They really were terribly dark sunglasses. Unnaturally dark.

"Well," the Black Hat said, "I suppose it can't be helped. Unless there's another restaurant, not so crowded but of equal quality..."

"All our restaurants are crowded," Kathi said, her teeth beginning to clench.

The other woman who had come up to stand beside the Black Hat, a rather normal-looking woman with mahogany hair and green eyes, tugged at the Black Hat's sleeve. "I think we've taken up..."

The Black Hat waved her away. "I'm almost through, Love."

She returned her attention to Kathi's monitor. "I suppose there are children in these restaurants."

"All of the restaurants in Walt Disney World are open to children, yes."

"And are they well supervised? The children, I mean."

Uh-oh. "They aren't permitted without parents," Kathi said carefully. "Will there be children in your party?"

"Of course not," the Black Hat said. "Do I look like a woman with children?"

"Uh..." the other one said.

"These children who are with their parents, are they permitted to cavort about the restaurant? I mean to say, should the parents prove negligent, is there a designated person who will exercise authority and restore calm?"

Definitely an uh-oh. Carefully rearranging her smile, Kathi reached forward, out of sight of the monitor, and pushed the Security button.

Now the hard part, don't let them get away. "If you're concerned about children, Dr. Kesselbaum, perhaps you'd like to consider eating at another time. Earlier or later? I'd be happy to arrange it."

Black Hat turned to the other one. "What do you think?"

The other one looked tired and exasperated. "I don't care. Just make the reservation and let's get out of here."

"I might be able to suggest..." Kathi glanced down at her reservations monitor as Security's voice came through on her "your ears only" channel. *Hang in there, we're on the way.* Visions of Employee of the Month awards began to dance in her head. "... how about France, Dr. Kesselbaum? There aren't usually many children in France."

Kesselbaum chewed her lip thoughtfully. "France..."

"It doesn't matter about the children," the other one said. "Let's do whatever you already decided."

Nice little routine, Kathi thought. Pretend to want to get away from children, when what you're *really* after...The red light over her video monitor went out, indicating that Security had arrived on the scene.

"Might as well stick with Morocco," Black Hat said.

"Marrakesh at seven? Party of five? Thank you, Dr. Kesselbaum."

"Thank *you*, Kathi. And if I can be of help to *you* while we're here, don't hesitate to call."

43

Yeah, right. Old Black Hat, here, was just the sort of person she'd tell *her* troubles to. Kathi switched off her monitor and signalled to the supervisor that she was taking a rest room break. She wasn't about to miss the fun.

"So," Stoner said. "We're eating in Morocco?"

"We are," said Marylou, quite pleased with herself.

"I hope they have alternatives to goat," Stoner said, half-teasing. "Your mother would hate it."

"They don't have goat. They also don't have many children. Too exotic. What they *do* have, and you will appreciate this, is belly dancers."

Stoner stopped in her tracks. "Belly dancers?"

"Belly dancers."

"Marylou, you know I can't eat with some woman's naked *skin* in my face."

Marylou giggled. "You'll do fine, Love. And I might pick up a few tips."

"Excuse me." A strange-but-vaguely-familiar voice. "I'd like a word with you."

She glanced around.

It was George, from the monorail, walking deliberately toward them. Dressed in khaki slacks and sandals and a loose, cool T-shirt, carrying one of the ubiquitous Mickey Mouse shopping bags and a shoulder bag over one shoulder. Stoner wouldn't even have noticed her in the crowd of tourists if she hadn't called...

"Hey," Stoner said. "How are you? This is a neat coincidence."

George cleared her throat. "Not exactly."

"Are you working?"

"Yep." She nailed Stoner with her eyes. "Want to introduce me to your companion here?"

"Sure." Funny, she remembered George as much softer and friendlier than this. "This is my partner, Marylou Kesselbaum."

The woman took Marylou's hand and shook it, and used the momentum to draw her toward a deserted corner of the room. "Let's talk a minute."

"If this is an arrest," Marylou said, "I'm going to have to see identification."

"For Heaven's sake," Stoner said, trotting along behind them. "This is *George*. I told you, I met her on the mono..."

George took a card case out of her pocket and opened it and showed them the contents. "Security," she said tersely.

Stoner felt herself blush, a reaction she always had in the presence of teachers, cops, nuns, and assorted authority figures. "We haven't done anything wrong."

"I hope not," George said.

"Calm down, Stoner," Marylou said. "Let the woman ask her questions."

That seemed to throw George off balance a little. She pulled herself together. "You just made a reservation for Marrakesh, right?"

Marylou folded her arms. "I did."

"Is that a crime?" Stoner asked with just a touch of sarcasm.

George ignored her. "In the name of..." She consulted a small notebook. "...Dr. Edith Kesselbaum. Are you Dr. Kesselbaum?"

"She's her daughter," Stoner offered.

"Do you mind?" George said sharply. "I'm talking to your friend. I'll have some questions for you later."

Out of the corner of her eye, Stoner saw Gwen stand and start toward them. She motioned to her to stay back.

"I'm her daughter," Marylou was saying placidly. "Or rather, she's my mother. I like it better that way. The other way around sounds so rather infantile, don't you think?" She caught herself. "Excuse me, you probably don't have independent opinions, being a lady *dick* and all."

"Marylou!"

"Oh, hush, Stoner."

"You're going to get us arrested!"

"I'm sure George has a sense of humor," Marylou said, "even if she is a *dick*."

Stoner ran her hands across her face. "Marylou isn't well," she said lamely.

"You made reservations in your mother's name." It wasn't a question, it was a statement of fact.

"That's right."

"Your mother is a guest here at Walt Disney World?"

"That's right."

"Want to give me her room number?"

"I gave it to Kathi," Marylou said. "Surely she already checked it out."

"Want to give it to *me*?" George asked firmly.

Marylou broke into a smile. "I get it. You want to see if I remember, because if I give you a different number you'll know I'm an imposter and up to no good. Am I right?"

"Something like that."

Stoner sighed. "Just give her the number, Marylou."

45

Marylou did. Also Edith's check-in date, her own check-in date and time, and the departure and arrival times and gate numbers of their Delta flight.

"You have a good memory," George said, writing furiously.

"Yes, I do. You have to, in the travel business. People get very annoyed when you make mistakes."

"You're in the travel business?" George asked.

"Didn't Stoner tell you? My goodness, whatever did you talk about on the monorail?"

"I told her," Stoner said.

"Oh, I see. Another test." Marylou turned to Stoner. "What *did* you talk about on the monorail?"

"Tupperware."

Marylou frowned. "How very odd." She shifted back to George. "Would you like to slip away and check out the information I gave you? We don't mind waiting."

George was already checking it out, reading the data into a walkie-talkie that appeared by magic from her shoulder bag. Or maybe the Mickey Mouse shopping bag. It seemed George could move with impressive speed.

"Wait," Marylou said, and touched her wrist.

George stepped away and looked up. Her face was a portrait in caution and wariness. And maybe a little disappointment.

"Oh, dear," Marylou said, "now you think I'm going to confess to some heinous crime, and you just *hate* for Stoner to be involved."

George started to speak.

"I only wanted to give you my mother's departure times and dates, so you can double-check." She snatched the note book and pencil and began scribbling.

George seemed to be about to reach for a magically concealed gun.

"Marylou," Stoner said, "let the woman do her job."

"It's okay." George seemed reluctant to make a scene in the middle of a Disney Day. People were already becoming a little curious.

Marylou handed back the notebook and George reported the information to whomever she reported to on the other end of the walkie-talkie.

"That's a nice instrument," Marylou said amiably. "Very compact. Where'd you get it, Radio Shack?"

"Comes with the job," George said.

"We should get some of those for the travel agency," Marylou said to Stoner. "Then, when you get lost, all I have to do is call you."

"The only time I get *lost*," Stoner said, "is when I'm halfway across the country."

"Or in another century." Marylou turned to George. "Did she tell you about the time she was transported to another century?"

Great. Now, in addition to being arrested for God-knows-what, we're going to be thrown into the local looney bin. "We talked about *Tupperware*," she said.

"I can't believe it," Marylou sighed. "You have had this terribly exciting, not to say *bizarre* life, and what do you choose to share with people on first meeting? Tupperware."

"It was George who talked about the Tupperware."

"In that case," Marylou said to George without batting an eyelash, "I have to say the same thing about you. There's a certain— well, tacky kind of glamor in being a lady dick at Walt Disney World, don't you think? Seems such a waste to talk about..."

"She can't talk about that," Stoner said. "It would blow her cover."

Marylou pursed her lips. "If people weren't so bloody concerned with keeping up appearances," she declared, "conversation would be a lot more interesting."

"I suppose," Stoner said, and wanted to strangle her. They were in serious trouble here, on the verge of being arrested, though it was a little unclear what they'd done wrong. As a matter of fact...

"Excuse me," she said to George, "before we go any farther, maybe you could tell us what we're suspected of. Come to think of it," she made her face as stern as she could, "maybe you'd *better* tell us, or we'll just stop the whole thing right here until we can hire a lawyer. We came here for a vacation, not to be detained and harassed, and this sort of thing does *not* make the Disney organization look good."

George had been pretty much ignoring her, listening into her walkie-talkie. She clicked off and turned to Marylou. "Where's your mother now?"

"At a seminar. Let me think." Marylou knitted her brows. "I believe she said it was called 'New Directions in the Treatment of Bi-Polar Affective Disorders.' Something like that. She wasn't looking forward to it. Want to check it out?"

George wanted to check it out. Spoke into her walkie-talkie. Listened. Spoke again. Waited. Minutes passed. Listened. Nodded.

"Is she there?" Marylou asked.

"She was. She went to her room a few minutes ago."

"Probably bored," Marylou said. "Good thing I ditched the vibrators in Stoner's room."

"Marylou!"

George gave each of them an unreadable glance, and returned to her note-taking. Stoner wondered if she had to report the vibrator remark.

"One final question," George said at last. "Why did you use your mother's name to make the reservations?"

"Because she's a doctor," Marylou said happily. "You get better service."

George stared at her for a moment, and then let her face crack. The professional mask fell away and she burst out laughing. "Lady *dick*." She guffawed. "I've been called a lot of things, but that beats them all hollow."

"I'm terribly sorry," Stoner said.

"Come on," George said, and clapped her on the shoulder. "You just livened up my one thousand and fifty-fifth consecutive Disney day." She turned and waved. "Hey, Gwen."

Gwen stood up. "May I approach?"

George signalled her forward.

"Were you going to arrest them?" Gwen asked.

"Yeah." George tucked her walkie-talkie back in her shopping bag. "The way she was asking about children in the restaurants, we thought we had another kiddie-grab in the making."

"Kiddie-grab?" Marylou squeaked. "Why in the world would I want to grab a kid?"

"People do," George said. "Satanists, mostly. You guys aren't Satanists, are you?"

"No, but Stoner's aunt's a witch."

George looked at her.

"Not like in horror stories," Stoner explained. "It's her religion."

"Religion?"

"Like..." She fumbled for a socially acceptable analogy. "Like the psychics out in Cassadaga."

George seemed to understand, though not to approve, at least not entirely.

"Satanists take children from here?" Gwen asked.

"Sometimes. They can pick up a kid, go into the ladies' rooms, drug the kid, change the clothes, and dye the hair in 20 minutes. Even the kid's parents wouldn't recognize it, unless they left the shoes on. Shoes are hard to switch, they have to fit, and most kidnappers can't plan that well ahead, unless it's a certain kid they're after. So the minute someone reports a grabbed kid, we get the parents to the entrance gates to check the shoes."

"Fascinating," Marylou said.

"Have you ever caught anyone?" Gwen asked.

"Not yet. I sure would like to, though. That kind of thing makes me real mad."

Stoner wondered what George would be like mad. She was grim enough just serious and steely.

"Well, I have to go," George said. "Lost my cover in EPCOT for the rest of the day. Now they'll probably send me over to Disney-MGM." She shook her head. "God, I hate that place. The sun never sets on the fun over there."

"I'm sorry," Stoner said.

George shrugged. "All in a day's work. Don't forget, the dinner invitation's still open." She waved over her shoulder and disappeared into the crowd.

"Well," said Marylou, "that was an adventure. What's next?"

Stoner exploded. "Damn it, Marylou, it wasn't fun and it wasn't funny. You almost got us in serious trouble."

"Don't be silly," Marylou said breezily. "No harm done."

"We came on this trip to have a good time." Her head was bursting. She felt the words tumbling out and couldn't stop. "And we've spent half our time dealing with your hysteria, or your anxiety, or your bizarre behavior..."

Marylou glared at her. "It wasn't *my* idea. You had to push. 'It'll be good for you.' 'It'll be fun.' Well, it's not a whole hell of a lot of fun, and so far I haven't noticed it's very good for me."

"And your clothes! Of course they were suspicious. You look like Mata Hari. Why can't you just be *normal* once in a while?"

"Because I'm *not* normal. Never have been, never will be."

"I suggest we go over to the Land for an ice cream," Gwen said.

Stoner shoved her hand through her hair. "Good, let's see what she can do to humiliate us there."

"Okay," Marylou said loudly. "You want me out of here, there are plenty of places I can go."

Gwen put a soothing hand on Marylou's arm. "You don't have to leave."

Marylou brushed her hand away angrily. "Stoner doesn't want me here, I'm not staying. I'll see you later." She stalked off, then turned back. "By the way, McTavish," she barked, "you'd be a lot more *fun* if you weren't so damned obsessed with superficialities."

CHAPTER 4

Stoner felt terrible. "I hate my temper," she said.

Gwen laughed. "Stoner, you hardly *have* a temper. Most people blow up fifteen times for every time you do." She took Stoner's hand. "Besides, Marylou can be a real jerk. There's nothing wrong with being a little impatient."

"She didn't mean to get us in trouble. She was just being Marylou."

"And sometimes just Marylou is too much for any sane person to handle." She brushed the hair from Stoner's eyes. "Come on, Pebbles, let's get ice cream."

She stood at the railing and looked down at the milling crowd. Food was happening in The Land. Lots of food. All kinds of food. Salads and soups. Baked potatoes. Quiche. Desserts. Picnic tables with brightly colored umbrellas lay scattered like mushrooms around a fountain at the Farmers' Market, while replicas of hot-air balloons rose and fell gently beneath the glass-domed ceiling. The picture was one of calm, light, and health—which was what was intended, no doubt. Though she hadn't been in WDW very long, Stoner had definitely gotten the idea that whatever one experienced was exactly what the Disney folks wanted you to experience.

Except for her anxiety over Marylou, of course. But you couldn't blame WDW for that, unless the brains behind the place had programmed in some bizarre emotional experiences. "Anxietyland, a magical trip through the rocky shoals of friendship, highlighted by a terrifying plunge down the Waterfall of Moods."

"Stop *worrying*," Gwen said as she handed her a chocolate ice cream in a dish.

"I called," Stoner said. "I thought she might have gone back to the room, you know, to console herself with her vibrators. She wasn't there."

Gwen took a thoughtful spoonful of ice cream and worried it around in her mouth. "Probably hasn't had time to get there," she said at last. "Assuming she gets up her nerve to get back on the Monorail alone."

"Probably." The sweet, chocolate taste was overpowering. She'd be jumping out of her skin in ten minutes. "I talked to Edith. She

50

said don't be silly."

"Well," Gwen said, "sometimes Edith gives good advice, and sometimes she doesn't."

"I told her, if Marylou comes in, tell her I'm sorry and please stay there until fifteen after whatever hour she comes in. I'll keep calling until I reach her."

"Sounds good to me."

"I guess there's not much else we can do."

"Guess not." Gwen moved closer, so their arms touched. "Stoner," she said, and pressed her shoulder against Stoner's in a reassuring kind of way, "I know you hate to have anyone mad at you, but it really will be all right. You and Marylou have been friends for half your life. That can't be ruined with an argument."

"I know." Gwen was right, of course. She wished she believed it. She didn't like to argue. Some people found it exciting in a perverted way. Some people didn't believe life was real unless they were fighting. Some people were even aroused by it. People like that scared her. There was danger in anger. The potential for the breakage of things that couldn't be mended. Things like trust. And love...

But she had to agree with Gwen about one thing: there wasn't much they could do about it right now. She finished her ice cream and pushed away from the railing. "Want to take in the boat ride?"

"Sure," Gwen said, and trotted their dishes to the nearest trash container.

* * *

David leaned against the palm tree and ate his popsicle and listened to the birds carrying on overhead. The air was warm and soft, the sky bright and blue. Life was good.

He liked his work. Took pride in it. That was important, to do your work well and to take pride in it. Sometimes he wished his mother could see him now. She hadn't understood what he did and how it made him feel. Not that he blamed her, exactly. She was an uneducated woman, and didn't know about art. Sometimes he felt real bad about his mother, guilty that he hadn't understood about her not being educated and had let her disapproval come between them. After all, it had been up to him to see it. He'd been around. His mother had never been anywhere. Just Baltimore, where they had lived in one tenement or another for most of his growing-up. And Ocean City once, off-season, all they could afford. But by the time he had figured it out, about her education, she was dead. His therapist had helped him to see it wasn't his fault. It was just how life was. The important thing was that he go on feeling good about himself.

But he missed her sometimes. You could have a lot of friends, and a lot of lovers, but you only had one mother.

One of the most difficult things about his work was his curiosity. More than once, he'd wondered about his assignment. It had been hard at first, doing what he did without knowing the reason. But he'd learned to take a professional attitude. It was reward enough, to do the job at hand in the best way he knew. There were only three things that were important to him: do your best, keep clean, and take pride in your work.

And, now and then, an assignment like this one would come along. Something special. Something only he could do.

His therapist had helped him with that, too. David smiled to himself. She was a real special lady, his therapist. He'd been real messed up when he met her. Young, unsure of himself—face it, the word was "dumb." Fresh out of Juvie for a hold-up he'd helped some older guys commit, only when the police arrived they'd run off and left him holding the bag. And the gun. But the parole board got him the therapist, and she'd set him right. Showed him where he'd been used, encouraged him to get his high school diploma through the G.E.D. program. Helped him apply for college correspondence courses. And pointed out how nothing that had happened was his fault.

He'd kept in touch over the years. You did that, with people who meant a lot to you. A card at Christmas, flowers for her birthday, sometimes a letter just because he felt like it. She'd always written back.

His therapist. He liked the way that sounded.

He watched a group of young parents go by with their children, all tanned and happy. David yawned. He was getting bored with Orlando. Nice climate and all, but he missed the excitement of Vegas and the West Coast cities. There were too many children and old people here. Too homogenized. Too easy. His skills were being wasted. Leave this easy stuff to the new men, the ones just coming up, the ones who needed a couple of successes to build their confidence.

Yes, he could do with a change of venue. Maybe, after this assignment, he'd take a trip back to Vegas. See how things were there.

He spotted a man he'd met some weeks back, and dipped his head in greeting. They'd gone drinking together one night after work. They were in the same business, though they didn't talk about it. Nobody talked about this business, that was how he knew the other man was in it. It was like working for the CIA. He was beginning to suspect that other man was in with the Satanists. David had no respect for that. A bunch of loonies, bad as Bible-beaters. You were here on this earth, and you had to make the best of it, not run around trying to get someone else to take responsibility for your life. God or the Devil, it was all the same. When it came down to it, what you had was you, for better or worse.

His therapist said that made him an Existentialist.

Sounded good to him.

Instinct made him look up. The quarry had left the Mexican take-out stand and was coming toward him. David pretended to be immersed in his guide book until she had passed. She hadn't noticed him. Casually, he slipped the guide book into his pocket and sauntered off with his eye on the floppy black hat.

* * *

It was Stoner's first direct experience with the Disney touch, and despite all her vows not to be taken in, she was completely enchanted. The little barge with its rippling striped canvas canopy floated on a canal surrounded by magic. Artists' renditions of roots and seeds and blossoms, cut from what looked like cardboard, seemed to glow in the moist dusk. The canal opened into a tropical rain forest, where birds chirped and lizards darted, catching insects, while a warm mist surrounded them and smelled of earth and vegetation. Then, suddenly, they were in the desert, and the air turned hot and dry. Desert gave way to prairie, and grazing bison, and swarms of locusts racing before a lightning-struck grass fire.

Around another turn and they were floating past a midwestern farmhouse. A giant sycamore stood before a comfortable porch. It was just after dawn, and a rooster crowed at the growing day, while golden light spilled from the farm house kitchen, quickly glimpsed through the open front door. From an upstairs window, a woman waved to them. A little dog, some kind of terrier, yapped a warning, then broke from its rope leash and dashed barking after the boat.

Then through a barn, with displays of farming equipment and stacks of hay. And finally into the growing areas themselves, where tomatoes glowed like Christmas lights, and beans and cucumbers grew from string-supported vines. In a large rotating drum, lettuce gleamed brightly, growing in a simulated gravity-free environment. Everything was lush and healthy and tidy. Aunt Hermione's McTavish Blue Runner Stringless Hybrid Snap Beans wouldn't last a minute in this Eden. The Blue Runners were bred for the squalor, chaos, and carbon monoxide of the city. Stoner could just imagine a single daring carbon monoxide molecule finding its way in here, to be leapt upon and vanquished by the Germ Police.

"That was amazing!" Gwen exclaimed as they slid into the dock and climbed out—helped by the ever-watchful young men in futuristic bib overalls who seemed to materialize out of thin air when needed. "How do they do that?"

Stoner shrugged. "Beats me. I hear there's this exhibit in the Magic Kingdom with all the Presidents. They move around and give speeches. The Ronald Reagan one even falls asleep."

"If it's all the same to you," Gwen said with a laugh, "we'll pass that one up. Eight years of that was enough."

"You know, I can figure out how they get them to move and talk and stuff, but how did they get the dog to chase the boat? I mean, that was a long way to run, and I didn't see a track of any kind."

"It didn't."

"Sure, it did."

"I didn't see it."

"I know it happened. I saw it." She glanced at her watch. "We can't check on Marylou for another 20 minutes. Let's go through again."

The dog didn't chase the boat this time, but one of the bison on the prairie wandered over to the side and looked her in the eye curiously.

Gwen didn't see it.

Okay, this was beginning to make her a little crazy. They couldn't keep going through The Land all day, hoping to catch the same illusion at the same time. The little ditty that accompanied the ride was catchy enough, but she had the uneasy feeling that too many repetitions and it would be like one of those commercial jingles you get in your head and can't get rid of for a week. A week of "Listen to the Land," and she'd be ready for the rubber room. Time to get a friendly Farmer of the Future for a little information.

One materialized on cue. It was a young woman. Stoner made a mental note that WDW was doing its best to be non-sexist, and to be on the lookout for lapses. "Can you tell me," she inquired of Sue (that was her name on the discrete plastic tag), "how the moving exhibits work?"

Sue was prepared. The 'Audio-Animatronics' were driven by computers and motors, with feedback to the main God-computer that could tell you exactly what each one was doing at any precise moment, and if anything went wrong...

Like an Audio-Animatronic Revolution? An Audio-Animatronic Runamok?

...engineers would be on the scene in minutes. In addition, each tiny movement of the figure, down to the flick of a fingertip or blink of an eyelash, could be computer-controlled.

That was what she was looking for. "What I really wanted to know," Stoner said after Sue had run down (or completed her program), "was how they vary the movements from moment to moment. I mean, is the dog programmed to chase every third boat, or every second boat, or is it random or what? And how come the bison walks up to the boat sometimes and sometimes it doesn't?"

Sue looked at her. "Excuse me?"

"Well, I mean, I can figure that much out, I guess. Computers being pretty complex things and all, aren't they? Scary, really, until you realize how stupid they really are. I mean, you have to tell them everything, just the right way, or they don't know what to do. They can't think, is the problem. Of course, do we really want them to?"

Gwen cleared her throat loudly.

"Oh," Stoner said. "Running on again. I do it when I'm nervous. Does this place make you nervous?"

"Not really," Sue said.

Stoner felt incredibly foolish. Okay, press on as if nothing were happening. You're not making a fool of yourself, you're asking for perfectly reasonable, sensible information. Intelligent information, really. "What I really mean is..." She had the feeling this was not going to sound like a request for intelligent information. Or an intelligent request for information. Or whatever. "...how come the dog chased the boat when I was watching, but it didn't chase when Gwen was watching? And how come the bison came over and snuffled me but she didn't see it...?"

Sue glanced around surreptitiously, as if checking for the nearest Security person.

Not again. "They don't do that, do they?" Stoner asked quickly.

"Not that I know of," Sue said in a friendly tone.

"Must have been an illusion, then." Stoner smiled. "This place does funny things to your head, doesn't it?"

"I suppose," Sue said.

Gwen squeezed her wrist to shut her up. "What she means," she said to Sue, "is that the juxtaposition of illusion and reality is so finely tuned...Well, one hardly knows what to think."

"I guess not," Sue said.

"Thanks so much for your help," Gwen said, and yanked Stoner away.

"It really did happen," Stoner said when they were out of earshot. "We both saw it. Or didn't see it. Or one of us saw it."

"I'm sure we did. Or you did, or I did. Maybe Sue did. I don't really care who did, but I think we'd better not attract attention."

"Right. We're probably under surveillance already."

"No doubt. Call Marylou again and let's try some other rides."

* * *

The woman had the constitution of a camel. David wiped the sweat from his face and folded his handkerchief very neatly and slipped it back into his pocket. She'd been eating and drinking her way around the World, and never once stopped at a rest room. Rest rooms were good places to grab someone, though in this case it would have helped if he'd had a female operative with him. Well, actually it wouldn't have helped, since the quarry never went into the rest room.

* * *

Marylou still hadn't come in by the 1:15 room check, or the 2:15, or the 3:15, or 4:15. Stoner kept telling herself not to worry, and worrying. Trouble was, Gwen was beginning to look a little worried, too. It hadn't reached brow-knitting concern, but Stoner could sense a slight wrinkling of energy that told her a Gwen-worry was imminent. Even Edith Kesselbaum had ceased to be reassuring, saying she had known her daughter to get into fits of pique in the past, but certainly never one of this magnitude.

She was beginning to suffer from sun-shock. It made her feel dizzy, claustrophobic, and a little grumpy. There didn't seem to be an empty seat anywhere, in all of EPCOT. What benches there were—and they seemed to be disappearing by the minute—were jammed with tourists or stuck out in the glaring sunlight and heat and humidity, and the thought of sitting on one had all the appeal of being staked to an anthill. Gwen suggested they go back to their room and wait there. "At the very least," she reasoned, "Marylou will show at the restaurant. She'd never get angry enough to skip a meal."

"Especially not one she nearly got arrested for," Stoner added

56

with an attempt at humor that fell flatter then a pricked balloon. They trudged onto the monorail and rode back to the Contemporary in silence.

"Here's a suggestion," Gwen said as she came out of the bathroom rubbing her hair with a towel. "If she doesn't show up at dinner, we'll have Aunt Hermione try to make psychic contact, and if that doesn't work, we'll call George. She ought to know what to do."

Stoner pulled the cold washcloth off her eyes and sat up. "You probably have to be missing for two days before they'll do anything. Like in the real world."

"Well, this isn't the real world." Gwen tossed the towel onto a chair back and ran her hands through her hair. "In case you hadn't noticed."

"Yeah." She couldn't help it, she was always left weak-kneed by the way Gwen looked running her hands through her hair. She didn't know whether it was the hands or the hair that moved her the most. But it was a graceful, sensuous, completely un-self-aware gesture, and she wouldn't have mentioned it for the world, for fear she'd make Gwen self-conscious and spoil it all. Some things, she knew, shouldn't be tampered with. Turning the light of awareness on them would only make them disappear. Gwen running her hands through her hair was one of those things.

Gwen running her hands through Stoner's hair, on the other hand, was equally exciting and something on which she commented at every opportunity.

She forced her attention to the problem at hand. "Do you think George would help us?"

"Why not?"

"We didn't exactly have a friendly time this morning. We made her have to be at MGM."

Gwen stared at her. "For Heaven's sake, Stoner, the woman's a professional. And a lesbian. One of the tribe. Of course, she'll help us. But let's not get bent out of shape yet. Marylou's like a pet dog. She'll come home when she gets hungry."

* * *

David was pleased. The project was going like clockwork. It had been a brilliant stroke on his part to send a drink to their table last night. Pure instinct, and brilliant. The most he'd hoped for was to make a definite I.D. But when they'd *shared* the drink...The way his client had described their relationship, it only made sense they'd get all cozy and romantic on vacation, of course. And now the quarry was even helping out by walking back to the hotel. Walking. When there was the monorail, as easy to get on. It was almost as if she were trying to put herself in his way.

That made him pause. A set-up?

It couldn't be. Nobody knew about this except him and his client, and he hadn't told the client any of the details. That was one of his iron-clad rules. Never tell anyone how you plan to do it, no matter how much they pay you.

No, he was just lucky. She'd probably figured she needed the exercise, after stuffing herself all the way around the World Showcase.

Whatever the reason, it made his job a whole lot easier. A casual approach to ask the time. Then, while she was looking at her watch, he'd slipped behind her and clamped the chloroform-soaked handkerchief over her nose and mouth. Just like in the movies. Easy as that. He glanced around, then ducked behind a hedge and heaved Marylou's unconscious body into the rented wheelchair.

CHAPTER 5

Marylou still hadn't shown up by dinner time. They went to Marrakesh, waited in the promised hard, straight-backed chairs with the promised children cavorting about. They had appetizers. Aunt Hermione and Edith Kesselbaum had drinks. They had dinner.

No Marylou.

The others were concerned, too. Stoner could tell by the way their energy fields had taken on a kind of prickliness. Aunt Hermione volunteered, without being asked, to try to contact Marylou's Higher Spirit—though they would have to wait until after dinner, as it was impossible to attune with belly dancers shoving their midriffs in your face.

Stoner had to agree, and promised herself she'd make every effort to root out a restaurant in WDW that didn't come with entertainment.

If they ever found Marylou, that was. If they didn't—she wasn't sure what she'd do. She couldn't even think about it. Because it was clear by now that Marylou wasn't just trying to make them suffer for being mean to her, or playing a prank. Stoner knew, in her heart of hearts, that something had happened to Marylou.

"If she's doing this to get our attention or to punish us," Gwen muttered over coffee and dessert, "it's time to stop now. We've gotten the point."

Back in their room, they tried to create an atmosphere of quiet attentiveness suitable for Aunt Hermione's meditations. But, try as she might, she couldn't make direct contact with Marylou—not her Higher Spirit, or her Lower Spirit or any Spirits in between. She sent out messages, waited, but got, she said, "Nothing but fuzz."

"Fuzz?" Stoner asked.

"Well, I feel she's somewhere, but..." She tried again. "There's been a mistake, I think."

"What mistake?" Gwen asked.

"I just can't make it out. It has to do with...with music, and...and sewing? No, music and cleaning. That's it, music and cleaning."

Stoner frowned. "Music and cleaning."

"Not terribly meaningful, is it?" Aunt Hermione said apologetically. "Perhaps I can do better later. You know Marylou. She's never been easy to read."

Edith Kesselbaum kept reminding them not to give in to neurotic anxiety. She, herself, she claimed, wasn't at all worried. Marylou was an adult and capable of taking care of herself—probably better than any of them, better than all of them put together, and the important thing was not to Lose One's Sense of Proportion.

Stoner was convinced that Edith was frantic under the surface.

They tried to enjoy the Electric Water Pageant on the lagoon, but even the happy spouting whale and jumping fish and other sea creatures made of sparkling lights, even the cheerful tootling electronic music seemed forced and a little sad around the edges.

It's as if she's died, Stoner thought, and slipped her hand into Gwen's for comfort. Gwen squeezed her fingers.

"We're going to call Security before we go to bed," Gwen said. "it's all we can do for now."

"I know." But she wished she could stop remembering what Aunt Hermione had said last night—there was someone in Walt Disney World who wanted to harm them.

* * *

My God, Marylou thought, now I've gone blind. This is just too much.

She rubbed at her eyes. Bright red sparks swirled across her line of vision. Her eyeballs felt sore.

I can't possibly be blind. I'm a travel agent.

She glanced to the side and noticed a pencil-thin line of light along the ground. A doorway.

She sighed with relief. This so-called vacation was bad enough. She didn't want to spend the next six months running to specialists.

Her head felt as if she'd been caught in a hailstorm without a hat. Sore. Tender. Clear symptoms of food poisoning. I knew it, Marylou thought. There was definitely something a little off about the guacamole.

Well, she intended to report it.

She wondered what would happen if she opened her eyes. Somehow it didn't seem like a good idea. Somehow it felt as if that would be a very painful thing to do.

"Bother," she said, and congratulated herself on coming up with a Winnie-the-Poohism. Stoner would be pleased that she was trying to fit in with the Disney program.

There was a strange sound around her. Sort of a low hum and whooshing, like an air vent.

The surface beneath her was hard. She must be in a First Aid station, lying on one of those steel, functional tables, the kind on which you could bleed to death and not make too much of a mess. She could remember deciding to go back to the hotel, and not wanting to face the monorail so she had gotten out her guide book— Birnbaum, of course—and started off along the road. Someone asked her the time, and the next thing she knew she was here.

That couldn't be right. She must have fainted, but she couldn't remember fainting. In fact, she couldn't remember feeling ill.

Curiouser and curiouser.

What she could remember was...she'd have it any minute now...she could remember...

Being grabbed from behind! A hand over her mouth.

Drugged!

Marylou's eyes flew open. Everywhere around her was darkness. "Excuse me!" she called.

A door opened and someone came into the room. A male someone. He flicked on the light. She had been right. It was very painful.

"For Heaven's sake, turn that off," she said, covering her eyes with her hands. "Are you trying to kill me?"

"Not yet."

His voice had a kind of metallic overtone, as if he were speaking through his nose. Really quite unpleasant. Marylou was willing to bet his wife didn't encourage him to talk about his day.

"At the risk of appearing trite," she said, "may I ask where I am?"

"You may," the man said. "But I won't tell you."

How very rude. "All right, then. What time is it?"

"Night time."

She stretched. "Well, I certainly have had a nice nap. Did you have to pump my stomach? I'm glad I missed it. Are you a nurse?"

"A what?"

"Nurse. This is the First Aid station, isn't it?"

"No, it isn't the First Aid station."

"Okay, I give up." She spread her fingers a little, letting in a gradual bit of light. "You win. Where am I?"

"I told you, I'm not telling."

She sniffed the air. It certainly didn't smell like an infirmary or anything medical. It smelled like...like ironing. "Is this a ride?" she asked. "Because, if it is, I really do have to complain to the management. It's in very poor taste, what with the crime rate and the drug problem and all. Quite irresponsible to make light of, if you know what I mean."

"It's not a ride." He sounded impatient. "You've been snatched."

"Snatched? What is this 'snatched?'"

"Taken. Shanghaied."

"Kidnapped?"

"That's right." He took her wrists and roughly yanked her hands from her eyes. "Now here's what you're going to do."

* * *

Stoner hadn't expected to be able to sleep, but she did. Until shortly before dawn, when someone rattled the knob of their door.

Marylou!

She shoved back the covers and jumped out of bed. She opened the door and peered into the hall.

The hall was empty. "Marylou?" she called in a loud whisper.

No answer.

Puzzled, she turned to go back into her room. That was when she saw the sheet of paper that had been slipped under the door.

She grabbed it up.

"We have your lover," it read. "Await further instructions."

Panic broke over her. First Marylou, now Gwen?

Nonsense. Gwen was in the other bed, sound asleep.

She raced back to the room and punched the light.

Gwen's bed was empty.

The inside of her head turned to white noise. They couldn't have...not without her hearing...

But Gwen was gone.

The phone rang. She raced for it.

"Please, you have to help me!" It wasn't Gwen. It wasn't Marylou. It was—whoever had been calling before.

Something in her broke. "I can't help you," she said angrily. "I don't know who you are. I don't know where you are. Everybody's missing. I have my own troubles."

"Please. I'm so lost."

"Don't you understand?" she shouted. "I CAN'T HELP YOU!!" She slammed down the receiver.

"Was it her again?" Gwen asked.

Stoner looked up.

Gwen stood there, her eyes puffy with sleep, her hair tousled, her pajamas wrinkled in the most endearing way.

Stoner grabbed for her. "I thought they took you."

"Who?"

"The people who left the note."

"Note?"

"And when your bed was empty..."

"I was in the bathroom. What note?"

She showed it to her. Gwen read it, then turned it over. "It's from Marylou. Why did you think someone had taken me when it's obviously from Marylou?"

"Huh?" She took the note. There, on the back of the message she'd read, was another in Marylou's handwriting. "I didn't think to turn it over," she said sheepishly.

"Stoner," Gwen said in a firm voice, "get a grip on yourself."

The message was brief, to the point, and obviously dictated: *Do what these people tell you. They are desperate and dangerous. I am well."* Then, almost as an afterthought, *I miss your sexy body. Remember the Carlyles."*

Stoner grinned. She could see Marylou convincing them these two sentences would prove the note was valid, and not a forgery. What they couldn't know...

"What's to smile?" Gwen asked.

"The Carlyles were some clients we had a few years ago— before I even met you, I guess. These people were so stupid they couldn't find their way from one room of their house to another. They were the only clients we ever had whose luggage always got to the right place while they got lost."

"I see. And the message is..."

"She doesn't know where she is, her captors are stupid, and the food is terrible."

"You got all that from one name?"

"You'd have to know the Carlyles." Stoner rubbed her hands together. "Okay, I'll go tell Edith and Aunt Hermione. Then let's catch some sleep. We have a lot to do today."

"I'm glad to see you've recovered your equilibrium," Gwen said.

"At least I know what I'm dealing with. That's a start."

* * *

Over breakfast they set up a schedule for phone and room coverage. Edith would take the first shift, then go to her afternoon meetings. Since the kidnappers thought it was Gwen they had, it was important for Edith to behave normally. They didn't want the kidnappers getting questions in their heads. Aunt Hermione would cover the afternoon. Stoner and Gwen would contact Stape and George, then see what they could discover by retracing their steps of the day before, while George interviewed park personnel. They would all check with one another at ten past the hour.

"It's amazing," Gwen said as they had a second cup of coffee. "Yesterday you were a wreck. Now you act as if you're enjoying yourself."

"I know." She spread jam on another slice of toast. "I know Marylou's all right. I know our suspects aren't too bright. I know this is about me, so Aunt Hermione and Edith aren't in danger. But the most important thing is, these people don't really know much about me. It gives me an advantage."

"If it's about you, they must know something about you."

"They think Marylou's my lover." She waved at Donald Duck. "That means they've watched us for the past couple of days and come to that conclusion."

"Must have been the fight," Gwen said.

"That means they're working for someone. Someone who gave them a description of me, but not of you. And probably not of Mary lou. Which narrows our list of suspects considerably."

"To whom?"

Minnie Mouse approached. Stoner smiled politely and indicated "no children." Minnie withdrew to search for more traditional couples. "I don't know yet, but it must."

"And for what reason?"

"Revenge, probably."

Gwen looked at her. "Revenge for what? Stoner, how many enemies do you have?"

"We can rule out Bryan." She dug into her hash browns. "He's dead, and he knows Marylou's not my lover."

"True."

"He knew I was attracted to you even when you were on your honeymoon with him and I thought you were straight."

"Bryan," Gwen said with a somber nod, "was a very perceptive man."

"Not any more," Stoner pointed out. "Which leaves us with two possibilities. Millicent Tunes, who is in jail and not likely to do much harm from there. And..." She hesitated.

"And?"

"Your grandmother."

"Ah," Gwen said. "My grandmother is an excellent choice.

Except that she could probably describe me with some accuracy."

"True."

"On the other hand, if we find that Marylou has been kidnapped by some fundamentalist Christian homophobic cult for the purposes of brainwashing..."

"We'll know it's your grandmother." She took a bite of toast and looked up to see George and Stape emerging from the monorail. George signalled to them to come to the platform.

They paid the bill and headed for the escalator, showed their passes and went out by the tracks.

"Pretend you don't know us," George muttered. "You don't know who might be watching."

Stoner nodded and leaned casually against the chain that divided the rows of waiting riders into neat columns. The train pulled into the station, and the attendant motioned them inside a car. He cut off the crowd so that they were alone, much to the consternation of several families who now had to wait for the next train.

"I see rank hath its privileges," Gwen said.

"Safer to talk here," George pointed out. "So what's up?"

Stoner explained as well as she could.

"Wow!" George exclaimed. "You make real serious enemies, don't you?"

Stape laughed deeply. "How many times have I told you, lady? You want to make real enemies, go into the siding business."

"It's Stape's personal belief," George said as she gave her lover's knee an affectionate squeeze, "that people get crazier about their houses than about anything else."

"I don't know about that," Stoner said. "They get pretty crazy about their vacations."

"Hah!" Gwen put in. "You should see how they get about their kids." She thought for a moment. "Maybe people are just plain crazy."

George had taken out her notebook and was making notes. "So you don't know what this is all about, and you don't know where they have Marylou, or who took her or why. You just know they got the wrong person."

"That's right," Gwen said. "They were after me."

George glanced at her. "Any idea why?"

"None."

"It appears to be directed at me," Stoner explained. "That's all we can figure out."

"Seems to me," Stape said to Gwen, "if it's really you they wanted to grab, you ought to lay low. When they realize they made a mistake, they'll come looking for you."

"Probably," Gwen admitted. "But I'm not about to hide in my room like a craven coward."

Stoner realized George and Stape had fallen silent, and were staring at her. She smiled.

They continued to stare in a kind of expectant way. Obviously, something was supposed to happen now, and she was supposed to do it. But she couldn't imagine what it was.

"Something wrong?" she asked.

Stape and George seemed a little shocked at her ignorance. They glanced at one another. Stape cleared her throat. "You going to let her do that?"

"Do what?"

"Get involved in this?"

"If she wants to," Stoner said.

George and Stape looked at one another again. This time the look was definitely disapproving.

"If I'm picking up what I think I'm picking up..." Gwen began.

They ignored her and focused on Stoner. "You're not going to forbid it?"

"Forbid it?" Gwen squeaked.

Stoner had to laugh. "I tried it once. But it's her life, you know? Anyway, she'll do what she wants no matter what I say."

Stape's look was a mixture of pity and disapproval. She nudged Stoner's ankle with the tip of her work boot. "You take my advice," she said. "Get control of that situation before it gets any worse."

She waited for Gwen's explosion. It didn't come. Which could simply mean Gwen was amused. She hoped so.

Gwen was exchanging eye-rolling glances with George. "Butches," she said. "Go figure."

They were coming up on the Ticket and Transportation Center. George took over again. "I'll interview the kids who were on the gates yesterday. See if anyone saw your friend leave. She could still be in the World."

"I certainly hope so," Stoner said with alarm.

"I mean Walt Disney World." She gathered up her shoulder bag. "What are you guys planning to do?"

Stoner realized she hadn't the slightest idea. "I'm not sure."

"I think we should try to figure out where she disappeared," Gwen said. "It might be a start."

George nodded. "Ask the kids running the rides. If anyone saw her, they wouldn't be likely to forget her. Not in that outfit. You want Stape to go with you for muscle?"

Stoner looked Stape over. Muscle? Not likely. On the other hand, if someone was really after Gwen, and if they had discovered their mistake, she really could be in danger. It wouldn't hurt to have another person there. "Probably a good idea," she said.

"Okay, Stape, you keep an eye on things. Better not let on you're together, in case we can flush them out with Gwen for bait. Watch from a distance, but watch carefully. We'll rendezvous at the Energy Exchange in Communicore East at 2 pm. It'll be crowded and we won't be noticed."

"Got it," Stape said.

The train stopped and they got out and let the crowd take them in different directions. Stape disappeared almost immediately. Very professional. She probably went along on George's jobs frequently.

To keep control of the situation, no doubt.

* * *

It seemed to be morning. At least the rumbling and banging and snorting of machinery had a quick, morning pace to it.

Another happy day in Walt Disney World, Marylou thought. I hope, for their sake, they don't expect me to fill out one of those evaluation forms. This is not my idea of a four-star experience.

And, while we're on the subject, they can damn well give me a rebate on my room for last night.

Gingerly, she rolled onto one side, and heard the thin mattress crunch beneath her. She was going to be stiff. Would undoubtedly catch a cold from sleeping on the almost-floor. Plus she was hungry, needed to pee, and probably smelled like a basement.

Stoner no doubt would love this arrangement. Would get off on the thrill and excitement and danger of it all. Of course, everyone who knew her agreed that Stoner McTavish was one french fry short of a Happy Meal.

God, she really was hungry. What would it take to get room service in this place?

There was a tentative tap-tap-tap at the door.

Marylou sighed. As if things weren't bad enough, Creepy-Peepy was back.

She'd heard him in the night, sneaking in to look at her. Did he really think she was going to get up and walk out of there? In the shape she was in? She didn't even know where she was, for God's sake. And there was the matter of that abomination he'd brought her for dinner last night. She'd dismissed it without a taste. If he was going to spend the night prowling and peeking, the least he could have done was bring a snack.

Tap-tap-tap.

Why was he knocking? She was locked in. He had the key. He had no compunction about—as he so elegantly put it—"snatching" her. So why stand on ceremony now?

"Are you awake?" he called softly.

Marylou decided to take an attitude and refuse to answer.

He waited a few minutes.

"You must be awake. Aren't you decent? Is that it?"

Really! "Of course I'm decent!" she screeched. "I'm not the one who goes around snatching people."

"I mean, are you dressed?"

"What, you think I'm skinny-dipping in the pool?"

David cleared his throat fastidiously. "You might be using the…uh…facilities."

"If you mean this bucket you have placed here for my convenience," Marylou said with all the haughty sarcasm she could muster, "no, I am not using, nor do I intend to use these facilities."

"It's all right if I come in, then?"

"Do I really have a choice?"

He was silent for a moment. "Probably not, if you expect to eat."

"I expect to eat," Marylou said. "In case no one ever told you, people die when they don't eat. Or would you like a nice murder charge to add to your dossier?"

"Wouldn't matter to me," David said as he unlocked the door and turned on the light. "I'm a professional."

Marylou looked him over. "Well, you don't dress like one."

At least he had bothered to shave. Last night he had had a serious case of five o'clock shadow. His dark, bushy hair was still unruly, though. In one hand he held a tray covered with a napkin. He smoothed his Bermuda shorts with the other. His plaid camp shirt was freshly starched, his Nikes just scuffed enough not to look new. "In my profession, you have to blend in with the crowd." He looked her up and down. "That's obviously not true in your job."

The change in terminology, the implied condescension didn't escape her. "Trav…" She caught herself. "Teaching is as much of a profession as snatching. Though not as well paid, I'm sure."

David shrugged to show he wasn't impressed, and placed a tray on the floor beside her. "Probably paid as much as you're worth.

What do you teach?"

"American history." She hadn't intended to get any deeper in conversation with him, but the nearness of breakfast made her forget herself.

"Sounds boring."

"Compared to the excitement and glamor of snatching, I'm sure it is." Well, was he going to show her what he'd brought, or was he just going to stand there and stare at her?

He gestured to the tray. "Aren't you going to eat?"

"Aren't you going to uncover it?"

"Jesus!" He grabbed the napkin and swept it away. "You must think you're the Queen of England."

Marylou stared at the tray with dismay. A tiny glass of orange juice, obviously the frozen variety, thawed and diluted. A cup of coffee so lukewarm it didn't even steam in the dampness. And two unsugared, undecorated cake doughnuts that looked like Bess Eaton unoriginals. "This is a meal?"

"What would you prefer, Madam?"

"To the best of my ability to discern, we are somewhere under Walt Disney World. Obviously in commuting distance of World Showcase, where there are restaurants representative of Italy, France, and Norway. Any of which would provide you with food worth eating."

He laughed. "You want me to cater your breakfast?"

"I do." She reached for her purse. "Since your superior profession obviously doesn't earn you enough money for decent food, you may take some of mine." She dug a ten dollar bill from her pocket. "Coffee and pastry from France. Make sure the coffee's hot, no cream or sugar. The pastries should be large, flaky, and filled with a rich substance. If there's any change, get something for yourself. Learn to live."

David wondered what he should do. His client hadn't given him instructions about how to deal with bad behavior. Nor had he been given free rein to deal with it as he saw fit. It created a dilemma. There were several avenues open to him. He could just walk out and let her go hungry. He could give her a good knock to establish his authority. He could ignore the whole thing. He could even kill her, he supposed, though it would be a first for him.

He didn't think his client would go for the killing idea. Obviously, the woman was wanted for some purpose, and that had to do with the other woman, the mahongany-haired one. Some kind of extortion, probably. Maybe torture, revenge, something like that.

"Well?" Marylou demanded, shoving the money at him impatiently. "Are you going get us breakfast, or not?"

This woman was different from other people he'd snatched. He was accustomed to sniveling and pleading, threats and anger, you name it. His profession was a laboratory of human emotion. But he'd never encountered anyone so imperious—yes, that was the word, imperious.

He decided to let it go and see where it took him. "Want any juice?" he asked as he reached for the money.

"Naturally."

David nodded. "Orange okay?"

"This is Florida, isn't it? Of course, I want orange, but only if it's fresh." Marylou picked up her purse and rummaged through it. "And I'd appreciate being shown to a proper rest room. Not some unisex place with urinals and male graffiti." She came up with a handful of tissues and stowed them down the front of her bra.

"You going to cry?" David asked, indicating the tissues.

"I am not. These are for the toilet. Whatever you come up with, if anything, will almost certainly be unclean and inadequately outfitted."

* * *

"I'm curious," Gwen said as they approached Earth Station. "Why didn't you tell them about those other calls?"

"Do you think they're related?"

"Maybe."

"That hadn't occurred to me." She thought it over. "But we started getting them as soon as we got in. Long before..."

"You started getting them," Gwen corrected. "No one else can hear them, remember?"

The whole thing was giving her an eerie feeling. The calls, Mary lou's disappearance, the way the Audio-Animatronics moved for her and not for anyone else. She was no longer so naive that she thought the world was limited to what could be seen, touched, heard, and measured. But sometimes things were just a little too strange for her, and this might be shaping up to be one of those times.

Inside Earth Station, with the crowd milling and the shadows like black holes after the sunlight, she felt at a total loss. They weren't going to find Marylou by wandering all over WDW, hopping on various rides and hoping to bump into someone who might have seen her, and happened to remember her. Marylou was stashed away somewhere, probably out of the park—out of the

70

World—and they couldn't possibly search everywhere in a hundred-mile radius.

She hated feeling helpless.

So she had to do something, however futile. She couldn't just sit and wait for the phone to ring. It would drive her over the edge. Other people might be really good at it. Like some dogs could just wait at the door for hours until you thought of them and let them in. It wasn't a skill she'd ever developed.

It was because she was a Capricorn, Aunt Hermione said. One of the doers and fixers of the world. Maybe.

"I don't know where to start," she said to Gwen.

"It doesn't really matter," Gwen said, "since our behavior is random and meaningless anyway."

Something occurred to her. "Maybe not so meaningless." In fact, the more she thought about it, the more sense it made. "We were here in EPCOT when Marylou disappeared. Maybe they'll make another move if we make ourselves visible."

"Now, there's a comforting thought. What do you figure? They'll grab you this time? Or me? Not that I mind, understand, but the thought makes me a little nervous."

"But we have a secret weapon."

"Right, the Siding Queen." Gwen sighed. "Okay, boss, where do we go first?"

"If I were Marylou, and had just had a fight with me, where would I go?"

"To a restaurant."

"Yeah, but which restaurant?"

Gwen pulled out her guidebook. "We should probably think ethnic. Even under duress, Marylou would never pass up the chance for variety." She leafed through the pages and groaned. "Stoner, every pavilion in World Showcase has a restaurant. Except the American one."

"Great. The one she wouldn't touch with a ten-foot pole."

"Japan, China, Norway, Mexico, England, Canada, Germany…to mention a few. What do you think?"

"I guess we can rule out Morocco," Stoner said, "since we had reservations there for dinner."

"Italy or France?"

Stoner shook her head. "Not exotic enough. We have Italian and French restaurants in Boston."

"We also have Japanese, Chinese, and Mexican."

"I don't think we can count Taco Belle. How many does that

leave?"

"England, Canada, Mexico, Germany, and Norway."

"It's a start," Stoner said.

"If we split up..."

"No! Stape couldn't follow us both." And she couldn't bear the thought of not knowing where Gwen was. Not now. It was just too much.

Gwen slipped her hand into Stoner's. "It was just a suggestion. I really don't want to be separated from you."

Out in the sun, headed for Mexico, she knew they were really only killing time. They could wander around all day and not be approached. On the other hand, maybe they could retrace Marylou's path and get a little closer to where she was being held.

She laughed at herself. What did she expect, that there would be a trail of cookie crumbs leading from the point of abduction to the point of incarceration? That somehow she would just know...

Wait a minute.

Aunt Hermione was always insisting Stoner had psychic powers, if only she weren't too shy to use them. Maybe she could try it now. Maybe it would work. Maybe...

"What is it?" Gwen asked.

"Huh?"

"You're all riled up about something."

Stoner hesitated. It sounded crazy, really crazy. But if she couldn't say crazy things to Gwen without being laughed at, who could she say them to? Wasn't that what love was based on, being able to say things that other people might laugh at? Being safe?

Wasn't it?

"Stoner?"

"Uh...yeah, okay...I was thinking, maybe if we get near the place where Marylou was taken, we might pick up something."

"A lost earring?"

"No, like...well, some sense of what happened."

"Oh," Gwen said. "You mean vibrations. That's a great idea."

Stoner glanced over at her. "Are you teasing me?"

"I mean it." She smiled. "Stoner, my dearest, you're the only person I know who doesn't rely on some kind of intuition. They don't necessarily know it, but most people do it."

"Maybe." She doubted it. There were a lot of people in the world—many of whom appeared regularly on "Nightline" or panel discussions of things like serial killing and the stock market—who would never, ever admit they had reached their conclusions by any but the most logical means. Reason, evidence, experimentation, the Trinity of the Twentieth Century. The intuiters and psychics were relegated to the back alleys of afternoon talk shows.

"Just because they say they don't believe in it," Gwen said, picking up the doubt in her voice, "doesn't mean they don't do it. Most people are downright fools when it comes to understanding their own motives."

Well, that was certainly true. Ask anyone. Ask Edith Kesselbaum, for instance. In fact, there was currently, in this very segment of Florida, an entire hotel filled with people who made a living off the fact that most people didn't know what they were doing, or why.

Of course, a lot of shrinks didn't know what they were doing, either. But she supposed, or they claimed, it didn't much matter. The important thing was that they know what their patients were doing and why. Which probably accounted for the fact that so many of them had miserable wives and delinquent children.

"Okay," Stoner said. "Let's see what we can find. But you have to say if you sense something, too."

"Have you ever known me not to say what was on my mind?"

"Many times."

"Did not."

"You brood about your grandmother all the time, and you never say."

"Do not."

"Do, too."

"Yeah," Gwen admitted, "I do."

They passed over the little bridge that separated Future World from World Showcase. Humidity had turned the sun to white heat, without form or direction. A flock of flamingoes, pink as strawberry ice cream, hung out on the grassy banks beside the backwaters of the lagoon. They grumbled a little, balancing on one leg, and now and then shook off a couple of feathers. Feathers that drifted to earth on currents of windless air. Even the flamingoes looked hot.

"What do you think?" Gwen asked.

"I'm not picking up anything. Are you?"

Gwen shook her head. "Neither was nor wasn't. I wish we'd brought a crystal. Aunt Hermione says they make a good pendulum, for finding answers."

"And people?"

"Possibly."

They had reached the end of the bridge. Ahead of them lay gift stores, an open-air theater, the lagoon, and boat docks. The long boats chugged through muggy waters, carrying riders between the Plaza and Germany or Morocco. A double-decker bus plowed through the crowd, horn honking.

"We have to choose," Gwen said. "Left takes us to Mexico, Norway, and Germany. Right goes to Canada and the U.K. Any hunches?"

Stoner looked around, hoping for inspiration, and spotted Stape chatting with the ice cream vendor on the bridge. She had a hunch there was more being discussed than today's flavors, and that the vendor was a little more than a vendor. Security at WDW came in a variety of forms. Ice cream vendors here were clearly a different breed from the vendors at Fenway Park.

"I have an idea," she said. "Let's both imagine one of those crystal-pendulums in our heads, and see what they say. If we come up with the same answer, it's probably the right one."

"Sounds good to me," Gwen said.

Stoner closed her eyes and tried to make her mind a blank and conjure up a crystal. What she got resembled a lump of coal hanging from a fraying string in the middle of a dim cave. Well, it was better than nothing. She tried to keep herself out of it and let it swing. Slowly, the crystal began to move. Barely perceptible at first. Then a definite motion, almost as if it were caught in a draft. Gradually, the stone rotated and pointed left.

She opened her eyes. Gwen was still concentrating. Stoner waited, not wanting to break her attunement.

God, she thought, she's so beautiful. Maybe she wouldn't stop traffic, but she stops my heart. There aren't enough words in the English language to describe all the ways I love her. Friendship, family, partnership, desire—If we're together for a lifetime there won't be time to explore all the ways of loving her.

"Mine says left," Gwen said.

Stoner brought herself back to the business at hand.

"Mine, too. Let's give Old Mexico a try."

The air inside was cool, the walls of stone and tiled floor a barrier against the steam outside. Stoner supposed there was air conditioning at work, too, but she preferred to think what she was feeling was real. The relief certainly was.

They passed through a small museum, and found themselves on a balcony overlooking a twilight-lit plaza. Directly beneath them was a fountain, and carts offering bright blankets and sombreros, vivid paper flowers, bowls, piñatas and brightly painted animal statues. Trinkets and souvenirs spilled from large baskets. Serapes of brilliant color were draped from vendors' stands. Beyond the plaza, the entrance to the San Angel Inn was a gate set in a high wall. The restaurant was closed this early in the day, but the tables held flickering candles and white linen cloths. Around the wall above the Inn ran a bas-relief mural depicting a Central American jungle, where a distant volcano spewed red light and the illusion of flowing lava. Directly ahead stood an Aztec temple. In the background they could hear the rumble of the volcano, and a wildcat's eerie shriek and roar.

"Oh," Gwen said with a little catch of her breath. "It's lovely."

Stoner had to agree. There was no trace of Mickey Mouse here, no Disney hype. Just coolness and color and soft beauty.

Also no trace of Marylou. No sense of her absence, either. But there was a ride, El Rio Del Tiempo: The River of Time. Rides in WDW tended to be dark things, they had learned yesterday—especially in the Imagination pavilion, with its descent into fantasy and nightmare; and in the Wonders of Life, where they had barely survived a bone-jarring but otherwise disappointing trip through the human body which had caused Gwen to wonder loudly at the exact moment they shot through the blood-brain barrier, why anyone in her right mind would ever want to do that.

El Rio Del Tiempo had the capacity for darkness and hidden pockets and little halls down which someone might be whisked in a flash. They decided to give it a try.

It wasn't crowded. They were alone in their little boat, which would have been neat and romantic under other circumstances, and did offer the opportunity to talk without being overheard, in case someone was following them and trying to overhear.

Leaving the dock, they floated toward a stone underpass decorated with the carved head of a rather unfriendly-looking man. From everywhere and nowhere came deeply intoned words, words in a language nobody probably ever recognized nowadays—except for language scholars and anthropologists and a few tribes hidden for centuries in the mountainous jungles—rumbled from the air around them. Considerately, the disembodied voice translated into Twentieth-Century English to welcome them to his ancient Mexico. A sharp turn, and they were in a grotto, where movies of ancient dances and rituals were displayed on backlighted screens and reflected in pools of water. Then dancing dolls, and a band of musician-skeletons twirling and swirling at the end of strings. Meanwhile, the voice described the coming of the Spanish

75

Conquistadores and other Whites. Dancing skeletons gave way to more dolls, which frolicked and leapt as if they were high on something. Then another grotto, this time with movies of cliff divers and flying dancers suspended from ropes, and speed boats. The voice—which had only a few minutes before been proud and a little threatening, announced the joys of tourism, while overhead a simulated fireworks display burst against black velvet sky.

Gwen nudged her. "Look."

She peered to her right and saw a small alcove, only large enough to hold one boat, with black doors leading to the outside. At night, it would be completely invisible. But now the sun was white bright, and shining directly on that side of the building. A boat could be whisked onto that siding in the dark and disappear before anyone knew what was happening.

It didn't feel as if Marylou had gone that way.

Still, it confirmed what Stoner had suspected—that there were tunnels and passageways, secret entrances and exits scattered throughout WDW. Places where people could appear and disappear in an instant. All part of the backstage work that went on to maintain the Disney illusions. After all, it wouldn't do to have a light bulb burn out or a boat break down and just sit there, a symbol of disorder and failure.

They were near the end of the ride, and now they were passing a plaza where a woman—actually a movie of a woman projected on the wall behind the storefront—ran after the boat and begged them to buy, buy, buy.

Stoner found the whole thing beautiful but depressing.

"I know what you mean," Gwen said. "They were so elegant at the beginning, and by the time the Whites are through with them, they're dehumanized, reduced to dolls, bones, and images on a screen. Do you think it's intentional?"

"Intentional?"

"A subliminal lesson on how we screw things up."

"Maybe not intentional," Stoner said, "but I certainly got the point."

"I'd like to think," Gwen said, "that somewhere in Mexico, whoever designed this exhibit is laughing her or his head off."

"I hope so."

Stoner wondered how they had started off in one direction and ended up at the same point without seeming to turn around or to go in a circle. She hoped it hadn't involved going under the Plaza. She wasn't fond of going under large, dark, heavy things without knowing it. Even less fond of going under them knowingly. Especially since the one thing in Mexico the White Man hadn't reduced to doll-like proportions was earthquakes. Mexico had had some sincere earthquakes in its time, and she wasn't especially eager to experience one. With her luck, she'd be the one the dog found exactly one half hour after she'd breathed her last.

Wait a minute. She was worrying about Mexican earthquakes in Florida? Obviously, for all its dehumanization, the ride had effectively convinced her she was in Mexico.

"It has possibilities," Gwen was saying, "but I didn't feel anything, did you?"

Stoner shook her head. "No sign of Marylou's presence."

"Aunt Hermione must be right. Marylou leaves a very faint psychic trail. Let's try Norway."

Norway was dark and complicated, and offered a hundred hiding places—provided you could convince yourself the Maelstrom was an illusion. Which wouldn't be easy, maybe not even possible. No one in her right mind was going to leap into that raging, sucking water, even if it was recycled, piped in, and only about four inches deep. It made Norway a poor bet for a spot to abduct Marylou Kesselbaum. Assuming you could get her on the ride in the first place. Marylou was about as likely to take a ride into the Maelstrom as she was to—well, to get on their flight back to Boston without heavy tranquillizers.

But Norway did have a wonderful town square at the end of the ride, dim with perpetual twilight, where a sharp, damp breeze blew and the lamps in windows shed a homey glow.

And pastries at the outdoor cafe. Which greatly increased the possibility that Marylou had passed that way. Other people might use their sixth senses for fortune telling or finding lost children or playing the stock market or locating the rest rooms in shopping malls. Marylou reserved whatever psychic ability she possessed for only one thing: pastries.

Germany was a total bust, abduction-wise. No ride, not even a 360° movie. The Biergarten was light and open, and completely extraverted. Despite the tiers of tables on different levels, the impression was that everyone in the room was related in one way or another, and had all decided to eat at the same time. The only way you could be kidnapped from Germany would be through the rest rooms. And they were always crowded, being among the five sets of rest rooms serving all of World Showcase. No waiting, usually, but lots of hustle and bustle and comings and goings and screaming babies and whining children and Satanists busily dying the hair of abducted children.

Come to think of it, how did one go about dying the hair of an infant, here among the crowds. Could you dye an infant's hair without attracting attention? Maybe they had special alcoves, like the changing rooms. With signs on the door: Stolen Infant Disguise Room.

The heat was getting to her. There was nothing funny about stolen children, even if they were cranky children. She could vouch for that. After all, they'd had a cranky adult stolen, and it wasn't amusing at all.

Over by the Refreshment Outpost (which had a sign proclaiming it would someday be the site of the Africa pavilion—as soon as the U.S. Government stopped acting like an idiot over South Africa, though they were too polite to say so), Stape was head-to-head with one of the young men in chino pants and Moroccan-style hats who loitered about waiting for a scrap of litter to hit the ground so they could pounce on it. He was shaking his head. Another dead end.

Something about it annoyed her. She couldn't put her finger on it, but it definitely annoyed her. So much so that she was completely unamused by the slap-stick, slightly lewd performance of the Teatro di Bologna. So much so that Gwen finally noticed her mood and attributed it to the heat, and dragged her into the American Adventure for a break from the sun.

"Oh, great," Stoner said as they seated themselves under a quote from Ayn Rand. "Someone will probably take our picture, and for the rest of eternity we'll be associated with one of the most people-hating women of the Twentieth Century."

"I don't think anybody's going to take our picture," Gwen said reasonably. "But if it'll make you more comfortable, we'll try to find a suitable quote to sit under." She glanced around. "We have Jane Addams over there, but she's occupied. How about Thomas Wolfe?"

"You're being calm and rational," Stoner grumbled. "You know I hate it when you're calm and rational."

"Well, if you can share what's got you in such a foul mood, maybe I can work up a little hysteria."

Stoner ran her hand through her hair. "I don't know. I guess it's Stape. Every time I see her, she's talking to men. I mean, doesn't she think women can help us? Why does it always have to be men?"

Stape was, at that very moment, talking with one of the boys in Colonial costume who had just finished singing bellicose patriotic folk songs on the plaza.

Gwen studied the situation. "I think," she said at last, "it's because 90% of the population is heterosexual."

Stoner stared at her. "What?"

"Heterosexuals pay more attention to people of the opposite sex. So, if you're looking for a woman, your best bet is to ask men if they've seen her. Straight women may notice other women, but they don't study them. Women study men, men study women."

"Did you?" Stoner asked. "When you thought you were straight?"

"I studied women," Gwen said. "It should have been my first clue."

By the time they had finished Canada and the United Kingdom, it was time to rendezvous with Stape. They made their way back to Communicore East and the Electronic Forum.

CHAPTER 6

Stape had news. She stood by the Get Set Jet Game, apparently immersed in a video arcade challenge that involved loading passengers and their luggage onto a plane.

Stoner settled beside her at the Great American Census Quiz, and tried to decide whether she would make less of a fool of herself if she chose Fifty States or Home Sweet Home as her topic.

"We have to talk," Stape said as she began her maintenance and safety checklist.

"Okay." Maybe School Days would be easier.

"Meet me at the Electronic Forum. Don't approach me there. Sit where you can see me, go through the poll, and wait until I leave, then come down front."

"Right."

"I'll arrange for us to meet behind the podium, but don't try to find it yourself in the dark. You'll fall over something and bust your ass."

"Got it," Stoner said. She chose her answer to the first Fifty States question, and was rewarded with a bleep announcing to all within a ten-mile radius that she had guessed wrong.

Stape completed her game within the allotted 60 seconds and walked away, obviously underchallenged.

Stoner allowed herself the humiliation of three more wrong answers, and shuffled back to where Gwen was waiting. "She'll tell us what she found out, but we have to sit through the Electronic Forum first."

"Great," Gwen said happily. "I love quizzes."

The topic for today was Environmental Issues, and they were invited to list them in order of importance. Stoner had always found this kind of questioning particularly annoying, since she couldn't see how one could choose between breathing, eating, and drinking as one's top priority. The last she had heard, you would be equally dead without any of the above.

At least they didn't try to get her to join any organizations or donate money at the end of this one. Not that she'd have fallen for it if they did. She'd long ago learned not to be taken in by opinion polls which were really gimmicks to suck you in and make you feel like garbage if you didn't contribute. Between home and the travel agency, she had been well educated in the various disguises assumed by "gimmies." The large, colorful envelope that cheerily invited you to open it. The official-document ploy. The guilt-trip. The "We're on the White House Enemies List" device. The "You Will Lose a Chance at a Million Dollars—You Have Made It Through Two of Our Three Hurdles" gambit. The dead give-away was the third-class stamp.

In the dim alcove behind the podium, Stape took a small notebook and pen light from her breast pocket. "Okay, here's the poop. Subject was spotted at the following locations, engaged in the following activities: Mexico, Cantina de San Angel, purchased tostadas con pollo, side of guacamole and tortilla chips, chased small children from bench, sat and consumed same —"

"Consumed the children?" Gwen asked. "Or the bench?"

Stape gave her a quick smile and returned to her notes. "Following this, subject continued around World Showcase in a clockwise direction, pausing to purchase kransekake from Kringla Bakeri og Kafe—that's the Norwegian bakery—which she ate except for a few small crumbs she left behind for the birds despite posted warning re same. Stopped next at Lotus Blossom Cafe and bought three egg rolls, which she took onto the double-decker bus."

"I'll bet that's where it happened," Gwen whispered.

"Subject exited bus at the next stop, still carrying egg rolls. Walked back until found seat in the shade at aforementioned Lotus Blossom Cafe. Ate egg rolls. Next stopped at Refreshment Outpost where she purchased a large lemonade. Made one final stop at Yakitori House, consumed one order guydon and two teas."

"I'm glad it was her last stop," Gwen said. "I think I'm going to be sick."

Stoner shushed her.

"I'll say this for your friend," Stape said. "She sure gets around. Foodwise."

"She's known for that," Stoner said. "Is that the last time she was seen?"

"I'm afraid so."

"So she could have left the park, or gone on a ride either here or in Magic Kingdom. Or anything."

"I'd put Magic Kingdom on the bottom of the list," Gwen said. "Marylou's intimidated by children. It's hardly likely she'd seek out their company."

"That still leaves Disney-MGM," Stape said. "Or she could have gone to the Village, or Fort Wilderness…"

"In other words," Stoner said glumly, "she could be anywhere."

"I'm afraid so. I'm sorry."

Okay, where do we go from here? She felt at a complete loss.

"I really am sorry," Stape said. She stared at the ground, her eyes turning down at the edges. She was beginning to resemble Eeyore on a particularly bad day.

"It's not your fault," Stoner said.

"George might come up with something. Someone might have seen her leave EPCOT."

"Maybe," Stoner hoped she sounded encouraged. "The vendors here certainly are observant."

Stape looked uncomfortable. "Well, she kind of drew attention to herself."

Stoner laughed. "Asked the ingredients in every bit of food, and how it was cooked. Right?"

"Yeah," Stape said. "She did."

"At least we know we're talking about the right person," Gwen said.

* * *

"So, tell me," Marylou said as she dealt the cards, "when do I get to meet Mr. Big?"

David rearranged his hand. "Huh?"

"Mr. Big. Your boss."

"My client." Darn, he had lousy cards again.

"Well, when do I get to meet him?"

"I don't know." He was beginning to wish he'd never taught her to play gin. She just kept winning. It made him feel like that poor slob in that old movie, "Born Yesterday." The one that kept losing to the dumb blonde.

Marylou drew a card and discarded something useless. "Who do you work for, anyway? The Mob?"

David looked shocked. "I'm in business for myself."

Marylou shrugged. "I thought we might know some of the same people."

He glanced at her. "Same people?"

"My father has friends in the Mob."

He eyed her suspiciously. "He does, huh?"

She thought it might be a good idea to drop that little hint. It'd either make a connection, or make him nervous. She wasn't going to give him names, of course. Or let on that her knowledge was limited to the few ex-members her stepfather had dealt with during his

FBI days—men who'd fallen out of favor and come running to the Feds to save their tails. But it probably wasn't such a good idea to let him know Max was FBI. It did put them on opposite sides of the street. "He's retired," she added.

"From the Mafia?" David laughed. "You're putting me on. Nobody retires from the Mafia."

"Well, not retired, exactly. More like inactive. Injured in the line of duty. They have an excellent Workers' Compensation plan." Marylou drew the six of hearts, which fit very nicely into her hand. If she could get the four of clubs, she'd be out. "Too bad you don't work for them," she said. "A bright young fellow like you could be a real comer."

"Yeah, well how come a teacher has mob connections?"

"I didn't say I did, I said my father did."

"If you think it's such a big deal working for them, why don't you do it yourself?"

"They don't take on many women."

"Sex discrimination," David said, "is illegal."

"Not any more," Marylou said. "Twelve years of Reagan-Bush took care of that. Where've you been? In jail?"

He hesitated, pretending to study his cards. He didn't want to admit it. It made him feel foolish. But he'd have it on his record for the rest of his life, so he might as well get used to it. "Yeah, but don't tell. It'd be bad for business."

"You can trust me," Marylou said. "My lips are sealed. What happened? Were you set up?"

He thought about lying, but that wouldn't be right. "Oh, I did it, all right. I was just young and stupid. I got caught."

Marylou sighed. "Ah, the foibles of youth. All impulse, no cleverness."

"That's about it," David said.

"Want to talk about it?"

"Nope."

"Well, if you do, my door's always open." She laughed. "Actually, it's not. But you do have the key."

"I already talked about it all," David said. "With my therapist."

"You've been in therapy? How very responsible. I think everyone should go into therapy, don't you?"

"Everyone would," David said, "if they had my therapist."

"Aha." Marylou smiled. Her eyes twinkled. "A little unresolved transference?"

"Mind your own business," David said sharply, and discarded

83

the four of clubs.

"Sorry." Marylou plucked up the card and spread out her hand. "Gin." She picked up her little notebook and pencil and recorded their scores. "The transference thing is not your responsibility. Your therapist should have straightened it out before he let you go."

David thought that over. There was a lot of truth in what she said, but it still made him mad. "How come you know so much?"

"My mother's a therapist." She bit her tongue. Oh-oh. She'd better be careful, or he'd put a positive ID on her.

He was leaning toward her eagerly. "Really? Your mother's a therapist?"

"Didn't you know that?"

"No. You have a mother who's a therapist, and your father works for the Mob?"

"Everyone needs someone to talk to now and then. Even Wiseguys. And so much better to keep your problems within The Family, don't you think?"

"I don't know," he said gloomily. "I never had much of a family."

"I'm sorry to hear that. It must be difficult."

"Yeah." He fiddled with one of the Norwegian cookies he'd picked up for her earlier. "My dad split early on, and my mother's been dead about five years."

She patted his hand sympathetically. It made him feel like crying.

"And so you turned to a life of crime," she said. "You see how these things happen?"

"Nah," he said with a shake of his head. "I was in business before she died." Then he cheered up. "Anyway, your family's in crime."

"Not the whole family, just my father."

"Your mother's a mob therapist."

"Only part time. She has a legitimate practice, too."

David frowned. "I wonder why my client didn't tell me that."

"Well," said Marylou with feigned outrage, "it makes absolutely no sense to me. I mean, if I were to have someone kidnap someone for me, I'd certainly try to trust them a little bit."

Now that he thought more about it, he realized that she was right and he was very hurt. It was a conflicted kind of feeling. The kind of feeling that sometimes made him turn mean.

"So who is it?" Marylou asked.

"Who's what?"

"Your client."

"None of your business," he snapped. Definitely feeling conflicted and turning mean.

"Excuse me," Marylou said. "But it seems to me, if a person's going to be snatched, they have a right to know who's behind it."

"No, you don't have the right. That's not the way the game's played."

"Oh, so now there are rules for this snatching business."

"Of course there are rules," David said. "This is a profession, for God's sake."

"Well," said Marylou huffily, "I am certainly gratified to see that we're playing this by the rules."

"You make me crazy," David muttered.

"Look, I'm sorry I'm not up on the latest etiquette...never having been snatched before. You ought to have a handbook or something, *Hints for Snatchees.*"

He looked at her, his eyes glittering with a cold and slightly demented light. "Just don't get smart with me, okay?"

The silver glint in his eyes scared her. "Okay," she said softly.

"And it's your dern deal."

She picked up the cards and shuffled them and dealt their hands. She needed the jack of diamonds and the five of hearts to win. She'd be willing to bet all the money she had in the bank and her share of the travel agency that his first discard would be one of those two cards. And that she'd draw the other within the first three draws. She was going to win again. It seemed like a really bad idea. Marylou sighed heavily.

"Now what?" he asked impatiently.

"Can't you at least tell me why this is happening?"

"I told you, it's none of your damn business."

"It just seems to me, if a person's going to go to the inconvenience of being snatched—when they came here for a vacation at great personal expense, they should know why they're being snatched."

"Look," he said, "I could kill you, you know."

"I don't think so. If you kill me, you won't have me. And obviously I'm wanted for some purpose, nefarious or otherwise."

David slammed a discard onto the section of floor they were using as a table. It was the five of hearts.

Oh, God, Marylou thought. If I take it, I'll gin in three draws for sure, and he's already edgy. If I don't take it, if I let him win and he finds out, his precious little ego will be shattered. And a man with a shattered precious little ego is a dangerous man indeed. This situation definitely calls for Keeping One's Wits about One.

"I have to go to the bathroom," she said.

"Again?"

"Women aren't like men," Marylou explained in what she hoped was a pleasant and not condescending tone. "We don't have your capacity."

"You had plenty of capacity yesterday."

"I did?"

"I followed you around half the dern day, you know."

"Oh," Marylou said. "You didn't happen to try the guacamole, did you?"

"No. I don't eat when I'm working."

"And a wise decision that is. I was only wondering if you'd noticed anything funny about it. I haven't felt right."

"I drugged you. That's why you don't feel right."

Marylou nodded. "That undoubtedly accounts for it. Unless I'm getting my period, that is."

"Jesus!" David exclaimed. "You're not going to start bleeding, are you?"

Aha. Like most men, he was terrified of menstrual blood. There should be a way to use that to her advantage. "I don't know," she said. "It's close to my time, but I left my date book in my room. And there's the matter of the stress I've been under..."

"You've been under a lot of stress?" he asked, almost kindly.

"Being snatched and all. It really isn't terribly restful. I just hope it's not my month for severe cramps."

"You're going to have cramps? God, lady, don't start bleeding. My mother used to hurt something fierce when she bled. You could hear her moaning all over the house. The only thing that'd help was rye whiskey, and I don't know if I can get rye whiskey..."

"I'll be all right," Marylou said, pathetically and bravely. "They only last a couple of days."

David fiddled with the neck of his shirt. "I thought people like you didn't have anything to do with men."

"Men?"

"My mother always said women had cramps because of how they were treated by men. So I figure, since you don't have anything to do with men, you shouldn't have cramps."

"I see." So his mother was, in her own way, enlightened. It might be the Short Form of enlightenment, but enlightenment nevertheless. This could be very useful. "Your mother was absolutely right," she said.

"So how come you have them?"

"How come I...Oh, you mean because I'm a lesbian."

He nodded eagerly.

Time to bring out a bit of Gwen's history. If he knew anything, and was having doubts, it wouldn't hurt to strengthen his convictions. "I used to be married."

"You? But I thought..."

"We don't always know we're lesbians," Marylou explained. "The culture at large doesn't want to admit we exist, so it conspires to keep us ignorant."

"Uh-huh," he said, looking totally bewildered.

"It's a lesbian thing. You don't have to understand. But I really would like to use the bathroom, if you don't mind." She smiled gently, in what she hoped was a beatific way. "Menstrual pressures do make one have to go."

He jumped up eagerly. "Okay. Sorry."

She smiled again. Blessed him with a smile.

He unlocked the door and stood back. Almost as if he were afraid to touch her accidentally, without her permission.

Well, Marylou thought, that's more like it.

She swept through the door like royalty.

* * *

Midafternoon in Earth Station. The crowds had thinned out a little. It was too late in the day to make dinner reservations, and most people had the rest of their EPCOT visit planned and didn't need Information.

Stoner watched another load of tourists exit Spaceship Earth. She studied their faces. They looked fairly healthy and not terribly shaken. In fact, they seemed to be enjoying themselves.

Which didn't make her feel the least bit better about The Ball. Not the least.

Edith Kesselbaum was probably right. "You see, Stoner," she said frequently when Stoner was her client, and regularly since then, "you're an introvert. That means, what you experience is always going to be more real to you than anything in the outside world. The entire human race can fall down in worship of something, but if you don't like it you're not going to like it."

Which was comforting, since she always seemed to know what she felt—even if it was confusion or ambivalence—and couldn't be swayed by cheap and fickle public opinion. But there were times, like now, when it made her feel terribly foolish and awfully alone. Times like now, when she could watch all those happy faces and know they had come close to something frightening and potentially dangerous, and they didn't even realize it.

Unless, of course, the frightening potential danger was reserved for her alone.

Gwen gestured to her from the telephone.

Stoner went over.

"She doesn't sound right," Gwen said as she covered the mouthpiece with her hand. "See what you think." She turned back to the phone. "Just a second, Edith. Stoner wants to have a word with you."

"What word?" Stoner mouthed as she took the phone.

Gwen shrugged.

"Hello, Edith?"

"Stoner. I was just telling Gwen that things have been quiet here. Very quiet."

Yes, she could hear it. A slight tightness and shrillness in Edith's voice.

"Nobody's called? No notes or anything?"

"Not a thing," Edith said. "I don't suppose you've come up with anything?"

"Nothing definite." She hesitated. "I thought you had meetings or something this afternoon. I thought Aunt Hermione was going to cover the rooms."

Edith took a quick in-and-out of breath.

Hyperventilating, Stoner thought.

"Oh, it's no problem. It would be just too dull for Hermione, here alone."

Stoner doubted that. Aunt Hermione never minded being alone. And, if she did, she could always call some departed spirit in for a chat. She had once spent an entire evening talking with Ghandi, from which she had emerged to say he was a pleasant enough person, but such passivity made her jumpy.

She hesitated, then decided to plunge right in. It would be what Edith herself would do in the same circumstances. "Are you freaking out?" she asked.

Edith gave what sounded like a little squeak. "Not at all."

"Yes, you are. I can tell."

"I'm perfectly composed, Stoner."

"You never were good at covering up, Edith. I knew that even when you were my therapist."

"Aha!" Edith exclaimed. "I suspected at the time that you were watching me instead of focusing on yourself."

Stoner smiled. "Only once in a while. Don't try to change the subject."

There was a moment of hesitation. "Well, all right. I suppose I'm a little concerned."

"More than concerned."

"Frightened. Satisfied?"

"Thank you," Stoner said.

"She's my little girl."

Stoner could swear she heard a sniffle. Edith Kesselbaum? Crying? "She's not a little girl," she said soothingly. "She's a grown woman, and very capable..."

"Oh, she is not capable, and you know it," Edith said. "She's a total flake."

"She can handle herself. I've seen her do it a thousand times. In fact, if I were going to worry about anyone, I'd worry about her kidnappers."

"Fine," Edith said huffily. "I'll worry about the whole bloody world." She caught herself. "Forgive me, Stoner. That was very unprofessional. I hope it doesn't cause you transference problems."

Stoner had to smile. "I think we've worked through most of the transference problems, Edith."

"You must never, ever assume that. If you do, it'll jump out at you when you least expect it."

Edith was back to her old self.

"The thing is," Stoner said, "you really should be going about your business as if nothing were wrong. Remember, they think she's Gwen. If someone's watching you, knowing your name, and they see you upset...well, they'll know they got the wrong person."

"Yes," Edith said. "Your point is well taken."

She hoped Edith wouldn't look at her reasoning too closely. If she did, she'd realize it was absurd to think that anyone with a desire to harm them would be watching them at a psychiatric convention. She just wanted Edith to have something to do, so she wouldn't brood and be anxious. So she'd feel as if she were helping them find her daughter.

Assuming that's what they were doing—finding her daughter.

* * *

Marylou ran water in the dirty, rust-stained sink and looked around the small lavatory. No windows. No other entrance. And

89

the place looked and smelled as if it hadn't been used in years. Kind of a dead, still odor. Very un-Disney-like. Her best guess was that this lavatory, and the room he had her in, had been used while EPCOT was under construction, but abandoned once the park opened.

She hummed the Mickey Mouse Club theme, loudly, and hoped he would take advantage of her absence to look at her gin hand. That was, after all, the point of this little trip, to give him a chance to cheat. Oh, she supposed she could try to escape. But she didn't know beans about escape and survival techniques, and would probably make a mess of it and confuse everyone. Besides, she knew, beyond the shadow of any doubt, that Stoner would find her sooner or later. She was a little sorry she'd behaved like such a jerk this morning—no, she reminded herself, that was yesterday morning, she'd been missing for more than 24 hours, good grief—but she knew that wouldn't keep her old friend from finding her. Certainly she hadn't behaved badly enough to merit being tossed to the wolves.

Had she?

Of course not.

She just hoped Stoner would show up soon. This kidnapping business was beginning to get under her skin.

"Well?" David asked hesitantly as Marylou emerged from the lavatory.

Damn. He'd been standing there all the time. Probably didn't believe in cheating at cards. The situation was turning dicey. "Well?"

"Do you have it?"

Marylou looked at him, bewildered. "Have what?"

"Your..." We waved his hand in a circle. "You know."

"My period?"

David winced.

"Not yet. Any minute, though. I can tell."

He turned a little pale. Or was it green? Hard to tell in this light. It gave her an idea.

"I'm going to need supplies," she said.

He stared at her blankly.

"Supplies. Tampons."

"Oh, Jesus," he muttered.

"You'll have to get them. Tampax. Not scented, not deodorized. Cardboard applicator but not the comfort-fitted kind. They rip the guts out of you."

David groaned. "Don't you have anything with you?"

"I would have," Marylou said reasonably, "if I'd known I was going to be snatched. I certainly would have come prepared if I'd had decent prior notice. But since you didn't see fit to inform me..."

"All right, all right."

"You don't want me to bleed all over this lovely bed, do you?"

"I said all right!"

"I use the Super, not Super Plus." Marylou patted her pelvic bones. "There's nothing flaccid about my vagina. I keep the PC muscles in shape with Jane Fonda."

CHAPTER 7

"Now what?" Gwen asked as Stape trotted off through the crowd, to keep watching and make herself scarce.

Stoner shook her head slowly. "I don't know."

"Discouraged?"

"Frustrated. We've been at this for a whole day, and we haven't come up with a thing. One minute I think we should go back to the room, the next I think I'll go crazy just sitting there."

"I know what you mean," Gwen said. "Listen, I just had an idea. There's one person we haven't talked to, who might have seen something."

"Who?"

"That woman she made the dinner reservations with. The one who called Security on you."

"Possible." She didn't believe it, though. It was just another way of passing the time. Walt Disney World felt more and more like a big, hollow place filled with loneliness.

She looked over at Gwen, and wondered how she could feel lonely with her at her side.

But it wasn't Gwen she was lonely for. It was Marylou, her crazy, irritating friend—the oldest friend she had, the one person she could say anything to, who had been with her through the awkwardness of growing up, the terror of being sent back to her parents, the almost-manic headiness of coming out... The one person in front of whom she could make a fool of herself, and it wouldn't matter. Marylou was familiar. Marylou was comfortable.

Marylou was lost and she couldn't do a thing to help her.

"Don't," Gwen said.

"Huh?"

"Don't get down on yourself."

Stoner raked her hair back from her forehead. "It's just..."

"I know. But we'll find her, Stoner. I know we will." She smiled. "I've always been a little jealous of your friendship with Marylou. Oh, not jealous in the sense of being sad, or wanting to damage it. But it must be wonderful to have a friend who knows your heart."

"Yeah." She shook herself. "Let's do something."

"Okay. What?"

"Beats me," Stoner said. "But as Marylou always says, 'When in danger or in doubt, run in circles, yell and shout.'"

Gwen laughed. "She does? Really?"

"Absolutely."

"You know, Stoner, there's a part of me that feels a little sorry for her kidnappers."

* * *

David was troubled. There was something about this whole situation that made him distinctly uneasy. The quarry, for instance, knew he could and would kill her if provoked. But she went right on provoking. As if she had little or no regard for whether she lived or died. He didn't like that. Maybe she was on some kind of a death trip. If so, he didn't want any part of it.

He shifted the plain brown paper bag under his arm and trudged through the abandoned tunnels. Built during the construction of the park, they had been emptied and sealed behind heavy fire doors. It had taken him many nights of working in the dark to find this one, to find an alternate entrance from above, to move in the necessary supplies. He didn't like to brag, but he had to admit he'd done an outstanding job under risky circumstances. And now he was reduced to fetching tampons. Damn kid at the check-out in the drug store. Looking at him like he was some kind of nut. Smirking. What was so damn funny about buying tampons? People did it all the time, for Christ's sake.

He kicked open a door, not caring if they heard it in the tunnels that housed the behind-the-scenes activities of Walt Disney World. They'd just think it was machinery noise, the way the washing machines and sewing machines and a thousand other machines were always banging away. There was a whole city down here. Like a city of ants or moles or something. It gave him the creeps, the thought of going to work down under the ground, day after day, mending those damn costumes. He knew what he'd do if that was his job—make a nice, weak seam right over old Mickey's crotch, so when he started jumping around like a nut, with all those spoiled brats watching, that old seam'd give way and out would come his little mousey dick, right in front of Minnie and Cinderella and all the rest of those ass-holes.

David checked his watch. Nearly four thirty, and he hadn't heard from his client. What was he supposed to do, snatch the woman, write one puny little note, and spend the rest of his life being laughed at by pimply-faced kids in drug stores?

And why all the secrecy? Why hadn't the client told him who

this person was and what was going on and what they wanted her for? "The lover of the woman with the mahogany hair and green eyes," the client had said, and had gone on to detail the green-eyed one's appearance. But not the lover's. And it wasn't even a very good description. Not good enough so he was certain when he'd spotted her at that Polynesian thing. He'd had to spend his own money buying her a drink, just so she'd turn around so he could confirm the I.D. He should have insisted on some behavioral characteristics. Next time he'd insist on that. He could have made a mistake. Mistakes were a waste of time.

Something was going on, and he wasn't being let in on it. That smelled a lot like being used.

* * *

"Okay," Stoner began in a businesslike way, and couldn't think of anything to say. She cleared her throat. "We've checked out some of the rides, and Stape's talked to vendors and Kathi from the reservations place hasn't seen her and... Well, I guess our next move should be to..."

"To what?" Gwen asked.

"To...uh..."

"Run in circles, yell and shout?"

"Something positive," Stoner said. "Something constructive." She racked her brain. She could feel Gwen watching her, waiting.

"I don't think there's much we can do," Gwen said at last, softly.

Stoner shook her head. "There has to be."

"Well, I read a fair number of mysteries, even if you don't..."

"The plots confuse me," Stoner said.

"... and in all the mysteries I've read, there's never been a suggestion of what to do at a time like this."

"Well, what do they do?"

"Usually," Gwen said, "end the chapter and start the next one the following morning."

Stoner glanced at her. "Are you trying to tell me something?"

"I think," Gwen said, and put her hand on Stoner's wrist, "all we can do is do whatever we'd do if this hadn't happened, and wait for the kidnappers to contact us."

She leaned back against the wall. She knew Gwen was right. She hated this helplessness. Hated it, hated it, hated it.

Unreleased tears, she was reminded, were hot and tasted like metal.

"I know how you feel," Gwen said. "But..."

"You don't know how I feel."

"All right, I don't."

"I'm sorry," Stoner said.

"It's okay to cry, you know."

"No, it is not."

"Sure. Look around. Half the people here are kids. They cry all the time. They'll just think I wouldn't let you go on Space Mountain."

"If you make me go on Space Mountain, I'll never forgive you."

"Listen," Gwen said, "when you agree to let someone love you, you accept certain responsibilities. And one of them is never, under any circumstances, to go on roller coasters."

Stoner had to smile. It cleared her vision a little.

"So what would we be doing right now," Gwen asked, "if Mary lou hadn't been kidnapped?"

She looked over at the line of people emerging from the Spaceship Earth ride. "Probably," she said reluctantly, "going up in the Ball and reviewing the history of communication."

"I thought you didn't want to go up in the Ball and review the history of communication."

"I don't want to. I think I have to."

Gwen sighed in an exasperated way. "The point of this, my dearest Stoner, is to do something you'll enjoy. It is not to terrorize you."

"I don't want to do something I'll enjoy. I want to do something that'll make me feel..."

"Good about yourself?"

"Brave."

"In that case," Gwen said, "the Ball it is."

According to the guidebook, Spaceship Earth was a hollow, magically-engineered marvel that gave the appearance of hovering over the ground, light and buoyant.

According to Stoner McTavish, Spaceship Earth was an eighteen-story solid ball perched precariously on unstable feet and about to roll off and smash everyone in a fifty-yard radius.

The line moved quickly. All too quickly for her taste. Before she even had time to think, for God's sake, they were being shoved into a plastic "time machine" and sucked up into musty-smelling darkness. She gripped the side of the car. They had come at the wrong time of year. They should have come in mid-summer, when the park was full of people and the lines were endless. An hour's wait, that was what she needed. Maybe two. Maybe...

Gwen leaned against her. "I love this," she whispered. "It's so eerie."

Stoner was about to comment on Gwen's mental health when the Voice started up. She caught her breath. "Holy shit," she said aloud.

"Where?" Gwen said, and glanced quickly around.

"The Voice," Stoner said. "That's the Voice!"

"It's Walter Cronkite. He does the narration for this one."

"It's the voice on the phone. The voice in the background. She must be calling from here!"

"In the middle of the night? Do you think they run these things all night?"

"I don't know," Stoner said, "but it's definitely what I heard."

She glanced around. They were leaving Cro-Magnon man muttering in his cave and approaching ancient Egypt. Walter Cronkite faded into a deep voice intoning something that sounded like hieroglyphics. Outside the exhibits, everything was pitch black. But there had to be a way in, or out, or a telephone...

Gwen touched her arm. "Stop bouncing around. You're upsetting the monks."

Beside them, a twelfth-Century Benedictine friar snored over the manuscript he was supposed to be copying.

"There must be a doorway somewhere."

"I'm sure there is, but we won't find it if you get us arrested."

She sat back in the car and tried to be calm. They drifted past scenes of Gutenberg and his Bible, of a Florentine schoolmaster reading Virgil aloud—"at last, something I can identify with," Gwen said of the schoolroom scene—of Renaissance artists at work. Then Michelangelo painting the Sistine Chapel...and suddenly they sped forward, rocketing through space, past printing press, telegraph, telephone, radio, movies, television, electronics, computers...to silence and blackness and a star-filled heaven. At the top of Spaceship Earth, the time machine slowed nearly to a halt.

And there, below, far away and very small, was Earth.

Stoner felt her heart expanding and pounding in her chest. A trick, an illusion, she tried to tell herself. But all the reason in the world didn't stop the feeling of awe.

"All right, Mr. Disney," she whispered. "You win. I believe."

Now they were descending, past a crew of astronauts repairing a shuttle car, past...

The little car came to a stop. Walter Cronkite fell silent.

This is it, Stoner thought. This is what I was afraid of. Spaceship

Earth has broken down, we can't get out, we're running out of air...

Claustrophobia got a good grip on her and started to squeeze.

"Gwen," she said with a slightly-hysterical giggle, "the Earth has broken down. That's it. All gone. Nice to have known you. It was kind of a lousy planet, though. The mental hospital of the Universe. Next time let's go somewhere more civiliz..."

"It's okay," Gwen said.

Dim lights came on, and a very human-sounding voice explained that they were pausing in their journey through time, but would be moving ahead in a very few moments, so please remain seated.

"I wish they'd clue us in on why they stopped," Stoner grumbled nervously.

"Probably to load a wheelchair," Gwen explained. "They don't want to make a big deal of it."

That made sense. And Gwen, being a compulsive brochure reader, had probably picked up one of the guidebooks. Gwen enjoyed what she called, "knowing stuff." Some of the "stuff" she had picked up along the way was truly mind-boggling. She was always coming up with startling and disturbing bits of information. Like the dimensions of the Michigan fungus, reputed to be the world's largest living thing. And the fact that miniscule bugs lived in your eyelashes. And that most people who were allergic to dust weren't really allergic to the dust, but to the feces of dust mites. And...

A red glow caught her eye. She looked ahead and to her left.

They had turned on the Exit signs.

"That's it," she said. "That's how she gets in here." She stood up.

Gwen grabbed for her. "Sit down, for God's sake, Stoner."

She hopped out of the car and slid along the wall to the exit. A door was cut in the black wall. She pushed through, and was nearly blinded by a downpour of light. It was a narrow stairwell. She started down.

Behind her, she heard the attendant's voice, announcing that they were resuming their journey through time.

She'd have to meet up with Gwen at the end. Right now she wanted to follow the stairway and see where it led.

The ride through time had taken them to the top of the eighteen stories. They hadn't descended more than two when the ride had stopped. Which left her trotting down sixteen floors.

At least, she told herself, she wasn't trotting up sixteen floors.

All around her the light was dim. The ground trembled slightly from the motion of the ride going on inside. The drone of Walter Cronkite's voice blended with a low rumble to mask all other sound.

The ride had been claustrophobic. The walk down the stairs was pure suffocation. Walls pressing close on either side. The whole thing vibrating.

Something exploded.

Stoner froze. Okay, this was it. The whole thing was coming down around her ears.

She held her breath.

Nothing happened.

Another explosion, this one not so close.

Hesitantly, she touched the outside wall.

Another explosion, and the wall shuddered.

The Ball was moving.

Get out of here, she told herself frantically. Run.

Her legs wouldn't move. She couldn't catch her breath.

Do it!

Another explosion, and this time she felt the whole structure shake.

Comeoncomeoncomeon.

She forced herself to step forward.

Okay, got 'em moving. Let's make tracks.

One foot in front of the other—and—go!

Suddenly the air was filled with a hissing, swishing sound. Like wind or a waterfall heard from a distance.

Waterfall?

Waterfall.

Stoner laughed aloud. It was raining. Thundering and raining, just like it probably did nearly every afternoon in good old WDW. The rain was pouring down the sides of the geosphere. The explosions weren't explosions at all, of course, but thunder.

Nevertheless, she'd be glad to get out of this oversized golf ball and back to buildings that made sense.

Her running shoes tapped little metallic sounds on the stairs.

She wished she'd counted the exit doors as she ran past. Maybe she'd have some idea of how much longer this would take.

Tap tap tap tap tap tap tap.

Boring.

She must have been in this place for a good fifteen minutes now...

Tap tap tap tap tap tap tap.

Too bad she wasn't going up. It'd be like the Stairmasters at the gym back home.

Tap tap tap tap tap tap.

The gerbil machines.

Tap tap tap tap tap.

Aerobicize!

Tap tap...oops.

She'd nearly missed it. A door in the outside wall, leaking daylight.

And inside, the stairs continuing down.

She hesitated. Gwen would probably be waiting, maybe worrying. She really didn't know how long she'd been in here. She should go out, find her, and come back.

And how would you get back in?

She was willing to bet the door was carefully disguised from the outside. Hidden in the seam of one of the aluminum panels that made up the outer skin of the Ball. Or she could end up on one of the concrete pylons that held the geosphere above the ground. And who knew what that would lead to?

No, better check this out now.

She took a few tentative steps downward.

As a matter of fact, how did she know there was an exit from wherever she was going?

Of course there was an exit. Turn around and go back the way you came. That's an exit.

A few more steps.

Oh, what the hell? Sooner or later she'd arrive somewhere, and if she couldn't get out she'd just keep going until she blundered into some area visitors weren't allowed in and get herself arrested, and she'd be out. Simple.

She kept going.

The light seemed to be dimming. The ride sounds and thunder and rushing water died away. She must be under the ground now.

There had to be an end to this soon. After all, how many stories of underground do you need?

And shouldn't there be a door one of these days?

Deeper.

Things weren't looking promising.

Pretty dim, as a matter of fact.

Real dim.

Nearly dark.

If she were Nancy Drew, now would be the time to take out her always-handy flashlight from her always-handy shoulder bag and shed a little light on the subject.

But she wasn't Nancy Drew, and it was really getting very dark.

She had just about decided to turn back when the steps ended at a gray wall. A gray metal door was set into the wall. The door didn't have a window, or a knob.

Oh, great.

She ran her hands around the frame. Secret button? Trick latch? Or does it only open from the other side?

She pushed against it. Slowly, silently, the door swung open.

She was about to step through when something made her stop. She looked down.

On the other side of the door there was darkness and...nothing.

* * *

David dropped a quarter into the pay phone and punched out his client's number. He'd sat around entertaining the woman for more than a day now, catering to her, bringing her food from every restaurant in World Showcase, it seemed. Been beaten by her in gin. Humiliated by a trip to the drug store for women's sanitary supplies.

He wanted to know what the client wanted done with her, and when, and why.

The client answered on about the hundredth ring.

"What?" The voice was harsh and irritable.

"It's David."

"I told you not to call me here. Didn't I tell you not to call me here?"

"I'm sorry," he said. "But I need to know what you want me to do with the package."

The client sighed heavily. "Hold it until I pick it up. I told you that."

"Yeah, but I was wondering if you'd give me an idea how long that might be."

"As long as it takes."

"I could..." He cleared his throat delicately. "...you know, dispose of it for you."

"I don't want that."

"I mean, if it's what you want done, but you don't want to do it yourself... I understand how these things are. I can take care of it. It's what I do."

"I appreciate the offer." The client's voice softened a little. "I really do, David. But I have other plans."

It wasn't a satisfactory answer, but he sensed it was the best he was going to get. "Well, okay."

"I know this isn't easy for you," the client said.

David chuckled a little. "You don't know the half of it."

"But try and bear with me. Trust me. We've always trusted each other, haven't we?"

He felt himself blush. "Sure."

"So just a little longer, okay, Dave?"

He liked it when people called him Dave. His mother used to call him Dave. Sometimes. When he'd done something to make her happy. And she was sober.

"I'll tell you what," the client said, "I'll drop in tomorrow. That should make her good and nervous, don't you think?"

Since he didn't have the slightest idea what it was all about, he really didn't know. But it seemed like a smart idea to agree, so he agreed.

He hung up and walked slowly back to the holding room.

He should feel better, after talking to the client. But he was still confused.

Sometimes he wondered if his Mom had been right. Maybe this wasn't work to be proud of.

* * *

Stoner leaned against the far wall and waited for the shaking to stop. If she'd taken one more step... If she hadn't caught herself, she'd have fallen into that pool of blackness, and who knows where she'd be now? Falling forever, maybe. Or smashed onto rocks at the center of the earth. Because that sure didn't look like any two-foot drop behind that door. It looked like the Incredible Runaway Journey to Hell.

Nonsense, she told herself. It was just a hole. A very dark hole in a very dark hallway. Nothing to be concerned about, but nothing to mess around with, either. You don't want to go twisting an ankle and end up no good to anyone.

When her heartbeat had returned to normal—or as close to it as she was likely to get before she saw the light of day—she crept back up to the door. It was closed again. This time she pushed at it gently, feet apart, weight on her back foot, giving gravity every advantage.

The door drifted open. There was the darkness again. Bottomless.

It seemed to be moving, swirling lazily, like fog.

Stoner reached into her fanny pack and dug out her wallet. She found a penny and tossed it into the black.

She couldn't hear it hit bottom.

The inky fog went on swirling.

Well, she thought as she put her wallet away and rubbed at the goose bumps on her arms, this is certainly an interesting turn of events, and not one I am particularly drawn to investigate at this time, thank you very much.

The door was swinging shut.

For a split second, she thought she saw the blackness bleed over the sill. It curled around her ankle.

Leaving now.

She took the stairs two at a time.

* * *

"I don't want to hear it," Gwen said angrily. "You made me crazy. I thought you had died or something. There's no excuse for that."

"Honest," Stoner said, "I couldn't help it. I'm sorry. I wasn't gone very long, was I?"

"An hour. An hour, Stoner. And considering that certain members of our party have disappeared, an hour is a very long time to be out of touch."

An hour? It couldn't have been all of an hour. It was only a few minutes, she was certain of that. "Are you sure?"

Gwen gestured in the general direction of outside. "It was raining when I came out of the Ball. Look at it now."

Stoner looked. The sky was clear, the sun bright. There weren't even any puddles. "It didn't seem like..."

"Well, it was," Gwen said.

That little jaunt to the edge of Whatever had been more disorienting than she'd thought. She scrubbed at her face with the heel of her hand. "There's some really weird stuff happening."

"There's always weird stuff happening where you're concerned."

Stoner looked at her. "Don't you believe me?"

"Yes, I believe you. I believe that you are the chosen one to whom all the weird stuff in the Cosmos is going to happen." Gwen folded her arms across her chest. "The point is, Stoner, you have to own up to it and take some responsibility."

"I am responsible..."

102

"I don't mean on an everyday level. I mean you have to admit this psychic stuff, admit it's out of your control, and start working on getting a grip on it."

"So what do you want me to do?" Stoner snapped, annoyed, turning away. "Join a twelve-step program?"

"Oh, stop that." Gwen took her arm and turned her around to face her. "I would like it if you'd let Aunt Hermione's friend Grace teach you a few tricks. Psychic self-defense, at the very least. I mean, if you aren't going to use it, you might as well learn to protect yourself against it."

Stoner nodded. "Okay, I guess I could. One or the other. Something." The trouble was, she didn't know for sure which she wanted to do. Whatever attention she was attracting from the psychic world, it was frightening and annoying—and it made life infinitely more interesting.

"Thank you," Gwen said. "It's a great relief to me."

"I didn't know you were worried."

Gwen rolled her eyes to Heaven. "I never know when you're going to be warped off into another time or space. I never know when Things from some other world are going to attack you. Any day now, I expect you to be possessed by an evil spirit."

Stoner had to laugh. "Don't tell me you believe in evil spirits."

"I believe in evil people. If they have spirits, I'll bet they're not cut from the same batch of dough as Eleanor Roosevelt and Mother Theresa."

And she was willing to bet whatever that was under the ground beneath Spaceship Earth wasn't the Pearly Gates, either.

"Yeah, okay," she said.

"And another thing," Gwen went on, "until you do get this psychic stuff under control, I don't want you running off again."

"I can't promise that. There may be things I have to do. Places I have to go."

"Then you're taking me with you."

Stoner shook her head vehemently. "Where I was today...no, you can't go there."

"And why not?"

"It's too dangerous."

Gwen closed her eyes and curled her hands into fists. "You make me want to scream."

"Why?"

"Because you treat me like a child."

"I don't."

"You do. You're always protecting me." Her voice rose. "Do you know how demeaning that is, Stoner?"

Stoner glanced around. People were beginning to notice. "Please, Gwen, you're attracting attention."

"I don't care. I'll attract attention if I damn well want." She scanned the crowd scanning the World Key screens. "Hey," she shouted.

Several of the WDW guests turned around.

Stoner grabbed her. "What do you think you're doing?"

"I'm going to tell everyone within the range of my voice that you're an overprotective, stubborn..."

"All right," Stoner said. "Okay, I won't do anything without taking you along. But I think this overprotective business works both ways." She touched Gwen's face with her hand. "It's just... I think, if anything happened to you... I wouldn't be able to live, Gwen."

"And you think I would?"

"I guess I don't think about that." She could feel a dampness behind her eyes. "You're a miracle in my life."

"And you're a miracle in mine." Gwen glanced around to make sure no one was watching, then gave her a quick kiss. "But I'll bet this 'I can't live without you stuff' is not politically correct."

Stoner grinned. "That was last year. Who knows what's in now? Cloning, maybe."

"Let's get out of here," Gwen said. "It's a beautiful day, the sun's finally out, and you still haven't told me where you went."

CHAPTER 8

They sat on a bench at the edge of the United Kingdom pavilion, under the sign for the Magic Of Wales shop, and drank lemonade.

"What do you think it was?" Gwen asked when Stoner had filled her in on what she had found under Spaceship Earth.

"Beats me. It might have been anything, or nothing. It was dark down there. Maybe I just misinterpreted what I saw or something."

Gwen thought it over. "But you're certain about the smoke or fog or whatever."

"Yes." She shuddered. "It touched me. On the foot."

Gwen looked down at Stoner's sneakers. "Doesn't seem to have left any residue."

"Just an icky feeling inside. I still feel cold in my bones."

Gwen frowned. "And you dropped that penny and didn't hear it hit the bottom."

"Right, but there could be a lot of explanations for that. Like maybe it just landed on something soft. Or maybe I didn't hear it or..."

"Possible," Gwen said. "But we still haven't accounted for the time distortion."

Stoner shrugged. "I could be wrong about that, too. You know how time flies when you're having fun."

"Ha ha," Gwen said without humor. She looked around. "There's supposed to be a rest room around here. Care to join me?"

"I'll wait for you." The sun felt warm and soft on her skin. She didn't want to move.

"Will you promise me, really and truly and without any reservations, not to leave here?"

"I don't feel like going anywhere, Gwen. Honest." Especially not down long stairwells through the doorway to—whatever.

"All right," Gwen said. "But if I come back and you're not here, it's over between us. I mean that, Stoner."

"I mean it, too."

She sucked on an ice cube and watched Gwen walk away.

The sun really was wonderful. It was a different kind of sun. Not like the steaming, stifling sun of the last day and a half, but a fresh, light sun with soft fresh air. The kind of sun that comes after a cooling rain. Almost like northern sun. She could feel it drawing away the dampness of the dark place. Turning her head up to the light, she closed her eyes. It made her dizzy, the warmth. She felt as if she were floating, relaxing to the hypnotic sound of footsteps on the cobble stone walk.

Gradually, she realized it had become quiet, as if the constant background noise of footsteps and talking and shouting, the chug of the boats crossing the lagoon, the honking of the horns on the double-decker buses—all of it had stopped. She could hear a dog bark, but it sounded as if it came from a distance. The rattle of a cart's wooden wheels against stone. A rhythmic "clop-clop" like a horse's hooves. And geese—it couldn't be geese, it must be flamingoes, but it certainly sounded like geese.

"*Prynhawn da,*" someone said nearby. "*Sut ryduch chi?*"

She opened her eyes.

And found herself sitting on a bench in front of an unfamiliar building. A low, heavy stone building with a wood-shake roof. Two small windows looked out over the street. The window sills were deep and made of stone. It resembled the stores clustered around the U.K. area, but it felt old. Very old. She glanced down the street. A cart, driven by a small pony with large feet, was moving slowly but steadily through the town and into the countryside. Beyond the last building, grayish green rolling hills stretched endlessly under a pale sky.

Dreaming, she thought. I'm dreaming.

"*Prynhawn da,*" said the voice again.

Stoner turned and looked up at the woman. She was short, with wide shoulders and pink cheeks. She wore a dress of soft blue material, and an apron, and seemed to be about twenty-five. The sign that protruded from the building above her head announced that the building was a Dafarn. A bar, maybe. Maybe a restaurant.

"Hi," Stoner said.

"*Mae braf, eh?*" She gestured toward the sky.

Stoner nodded. I'm dreaming. Dreaming in a foreign language. I know I'm dreaming, so I must be lucid dreaming. Lucid dreaming in a foreign language. Lucy in the Sky with Diamonds. Something to tell Edith Kesselbaum about.

"*Ydych chi eisiau tê?*"

"I'm sorry. I don't speak…uh…whatever it is you're speaking."

The young woman smiled. "*Cymraeg.*"

"Right. Kim-rag. That."

106

"Well, I can speak English," the woman said with a heavy sort-of British accent. "But we speak our own Welsh language when we can. A matter of national pride, you see."

"Of course."

"You're American, aren't you?"

"Yes," Stoner said. "But I hope you won't hold that against me. I didn't vote for Reagan. Or Bush. And I wouldn't have voted for Thatcher if I lived in England..."

"What brings you here?" the woman asked pleasantly. "On holiday?"

"Here?" She looked around. "Dreaming, I guess. Where is here?"

The young woman seemed a little puzzled. "You don't know where you are?"

"Well, not exactly."

"This is Twyl. Near Llamonddyfri—or Llandover, as the British call it."

"Yes, that's what I thought." It may be a dream, but she was beginning to feel extremely foolish. Sitting on benches in front of bars or restaurants or whatever in unknown places and not knowing how you got there was a strange thing to do, dream or no dream.

"Would you like a cup of tea?"

Why not? As long as she was dreaming, she might as well carry it through to the Message—which, Edith Kesselbaum was fond of assuring her, would be found embedded somewhere in the dream. And dream messages were to be ignored only at great personal risk, since the unconscious would continue to send them—in more dramatic and attention-grabbing form up to and including award-winning nightmares—until the message was received.

"Sure," she said. "Thanks."

She followed the young woman into the tavern.

The inside of the building was dark. Not surprising considering the few windows and deep sills. The floor was stone, the ceiling low plaster stained gray by decades of coal and tobacco smoke. Large round tables of dark wood, surrounded by dark, straight-backed chairs filled most of the available space. Around the walls ran a high-backed bench like a church pew. The bar was the most cheerful corner of the tavern, and it was only made colorful by the labels on the liquor bottles. The room was deserted except for an elderly, short-necked gentleman whose red-veined nose spoke of too many years of too much drink.

107

The young woman poured tea from a pot that was being kept warm by an ancient electric hot plate. She slid it across the counter. "There you go, Miss."

Stoner perched on a bar stool, wrapping her legs around the rungs.

The old man, slumped over the bar and nursing a beer, looked at her dolefully.

She leaned across to the young woman. "Did I do something wrong?"

"He's been the town drunkard half his life. Injured in a mine accident, he was. Too bad we don't all have such good excuses."

"Yes," Stoner said. She took a swallow of her tea, which tasted a great deal like Aunt Hermione's Earl Gray.

"You look Celtic," the young woman said.

"Scotch, mostly. On my father's side." She held out her hand. "Stoner McTavish."

The woman returned her handshake. "Eleanor Baddam."

"I have a friend who's Welsh. Owens. Gwen Owens."

Eleanor laughed. "A name as common here as Smith in your country." She poured tea into a glass. "You'll want to see the Great Oak of Myrddin Emrys while you're in Wales, no doubt. In Caerfyrddin. Well, sorry to say, it isn't there any more. Only a marker. Cut down to ease traffic. Legend has it, if anyone should destroy Merlin's Oak, great calamity would befall the town. And so it did." She leaned forward and lowered her voice. "Developers. With their blue prints and bulldozers and yellow pencils stuck behind their ears. The worst kind of disaster, wouldn't you say?"

"Yes," Stoner agreed. "I would say that."

"*Diawled.*"

Stoner was willing to bet that was some kind of curse, so she nodded enthusiastically. "Where would you go," she asked, "if you wanted to see something...well, different?"

"To the island of Enlli," Eleanor said without hesitation. "Off the tip of Llyn. It's said the ghost of Merlin lurks there, guarding the Thirteen Precious Curiosities."

"I see." This dream was beginning to qualify for the Fourteenth Precious Curiosity. Though she supposed she shouldn't be surprised. A tourism dream for a travel agent. "What are the Thirteen Precious Curiosities?"

"Let me think." Eleanor blushed a little, in a charming way. "I used to know them by heart. There's the Chair of Morgan Mwynfawr, and the Hamper of Gwyddno..." She frowned thoughtfully.

108

"And the Knife of the Hand of Havoc..."

"That sounds like a good one," Stoner said.

"And..."

"Stoner McTavish!" Gwen's voice cut through the stuffy air. "I asked you to stay where you were."

"I did," Stoner said. "This is a dream."

Gwen took her arm. "It is no dream, and you're driving me to the looney bin."

Stoner looked around. The Dafarn had disappeared. She stood inside a tiny, crowded shop. Tea cozies and pressed wild flowers in frames and jewelry and trivets made from slate lined the walls. Eleanor was there, but instead of tending the bar she was working the cash register, and her name tag identified her as Anna.

Stoner blinked. "I must have walked in my sleep."

"A likely story," Gwen said.

"Unless..." She went to the counter. "Excuse me."

Anna looked up from her money drawer.

"Have you ever heard of the Knife of the Hand of Havoc?"

The woman's face broke into a beaming smile. "Of the Thirteen Precious Curiosities? Have you seen it?"

"Not really," Stoner said. "I only heard of it." As she turned away, she heard herself say, "Diolch."

"Pob hwyl," Anna called, and waved cheerily.

"What was that?" Gwen asked.

"I don't know. I'm not sure I want to know." But she did know she was frightened. She headed for the door. "I need to get out of here."

* * *

Edith Kesselbaum, following Stoner's orders, went to a work-shop on dealing with HMO's, where she delivered a stinging, eloquent diatribe against assembly line medicine and pre-packaged psychotherapy. She was applauded loudly, and dropped from the Harvard Health Plan's list of approved providers.

A group of Aunt Hermione's friends from Cassadaga gathered in her hotel room to meditate, listen, and try to put a light of peace and safety around Marylou. Some of the more traditional Christian mystics also prayed for the soul and conscience of her kidnappers, suggesting that he or she come to Jesus and release her.

Aunt Hermione received a message from one of her Spirit Guides. The message was, "Look for the music," or something on that order. Since this particular Guide communicated intuitively and non-verbally, she wasn't certain those were the right words.

But she was positive she'd gotten the gist of it.

George found Stoner and Gwen wandering aimlessly in Italy and told them Stape had been called away on a job—vandals had cracked a window in "Emma's", a local bar, and she wanted to replace it before it gave the local adolescents ideas. She suggested they meet there at five, before the official opening time, and compare information. Sorry she had to run, but she was on her ten minute coffee break and only had five minutes to make it back to Mickey's Birthdayland, her least favorite spot in WDW and assignment for today ("You haven't lived until you've spent a day tracking down hysterical toddlers in the Mousekamaze.").

Stoner wondered briefly how she had found them so easily on a ten-minute coffee break, then realized they were probably under surveillance. That left her wondering how they had accounted for her time under the Ball. Maybe George could ask the computer. She would be interested to know what it was, and what they called it. Some kind of Land or World, no doubt, in keeping with the overall Theme.

Not having access to a computer herself, she settled for making a mental note to talk it over with George.

* * *

Bored, bored, BORED!

Marylou thought she would lose her mind. If this was what it meant to have adventures, she could see why Stoner had mixed feelings about it. The accommodations were appalling, the food ghastly, and the company...well, spare us even having to talk about the company. In fact, it was her considered opinion that people who went around seeking out adventures obviously had a screw loose. Nuts. A few cards short of a full deck. Elevators don't go all the way to the top. Poco loco in the coco.

She picked at a hangnail—not even a decent nail file, for God's sake, she should have come more prepared—and tried to decide what to do. Making trouble sounded like a good plan, a way to pass the time. She was rather proud of herself for the menstrual bit. That really had him going. Marylou laughed out loud.

Oops! Better watch it. You never knew when Creepy-Peepy would come creeping and peeping his way back. He moved like a cat. Quick, silent, deadly. He wasn't bad looking, if he wouldn't insist on wearing those nerdy T-shirts and terrible baggy shorts. Too much mousse in the hair, made him look like he'd been dipped in plastic, and that "Wall Street" look was no longer in. Of course, he'd been in prison, so he was probably behind the times a little. Ex-cons and ex-nuns all seemed to have holes in their experience.

Clean him up, dress him up, and she might find him attractive—for a sociopath of merely normal intelligence. Not much stimulation intellectually, but physically...

She shook her head. No, he'd probably want to know How It Was every two minutes. She knew the type. From experience.

Marylou looked around the small concrete room for the thousandth time. At least he'd let her keep the light on. Darkness would be unbearable. Nothing to do but sleep. And there was no way you could snooze along happily for three days non-stop, no matter how worn out you were. Was it three days? She didn't think so. She'd gone to sleep twice, but once had been because she was drugged, so you probably couldn't count that as the end of a day...

She picked through the food wrappers and residue. Breakfast had been French. Norwegian snack. Lunch...Italian. She stirred the trash, holding bits of food-stained paper up to the light and sniffing. Well, this was completely and totally outrageous. They weren't even up to dinner of her first full day of captivity!

Trouble-making was definitely called for. Marylou crossed her legs lotus-position style and tried to think. She hummed a little hum, which usually cleared her mind of outside distractions and brought up all kinds of interesting stuff.

The air around her seemed to thicken and grow a little colder. She was tempted to open her eyes, but reminded herself to stay with it until something happened. She hummed a little louder, and concentrated on listening hard to catch the echo of her hum as it bounced off the concrete walls. In a room this small it was subtle, but that made it all the more powerful. She was glad Stoner had talked her into that meditation course at the Cambridge Women's Center. Tricked her into it, really, by calling it a seminar on Stress Reduction—though after this experience she would seriously question why anyone would want to reduce stress. Given that the alternative was the absence of stimulation.

Mind wandering. She lowered the pitch and raised the volume of her hum. Ah, that was better.

If she varied the notes...M.i.c...K.e.y...M.o.u...

Well, really. Stick to one note and vary the volume. Way to go.

Hmmmmmmmmmmmmmmmmmm.

"Who are you?"

Her eyes flew open. "What?"

There was no one there.

111

But she'd heard it. Definitely heard a voice, a woman's voice, asking who she was. "Helloooooooooooooo," she called.

Nothing came back but the quick and tiny echo.

"Helloooooo... ooooo."

Nothing.

Well, if this isn't the pits. Now I'm hallucinating.

* * *

Stape was just smoothing out the glazier's putty as they pulled into the parking lot. Emma's was a square, cement-block building that looked as if it had once been a garage. It had a small picture window covered by drapes with a balled fringe. A lavender door, freshly painted. No name was visible, either on the window or on any sign. The window Stape had fixed was in the door. She stood back to admire her handiwork. "What do you think?"

"Very professional," Gwen said.

Stoner took a closer look and grunted agreement, which seemed to her to be proper butch behavior under the circumstances.

On the hall of the entry way was a large bulletin board bursting with flyers. Most of them pink or lilac, offering Goddess circles, crystal healing, homeopathic veterinary services, polarity massage, a harvest exchange, groups for survivors of just about anything and everything, lessons in the Texas two-step...

Emma's was clearly the local lesbian hangout.

Inside, the room was dimly lit but cheerful. Murals of women of all colors playing, working, picnicking, making love... Small tables with checkered cloths pushed to the sides of the room. A tiny linoleum dance floor backed by a stage just big enough to hold a DJ and equipment, or a small dance combo.

Stoner was willing to bet the Emma of Emma's was Emma 'If I can't dance I don't want to be part of your revolution' Goldman.

Stape exchanged "Yo's" with the bartender, a dark-skinned, bright-eyed Hispanic woman dressed in a paisley vest and skin-tight black pants, and led them to a table.

The bartender, whom Stape introduced as Rita, came over and looked at them questioningly. Gwen ordered coffee. Stoner settled for club soda with lime.

"You from out of town?" Rita asked Gwen.

Gwen nodded. "Boston."

"If you're looking for a meeting, there's a couple posted on the board. Women only, no cajones."

Gwen thanked her.

112

"If you're shy, I can find someone to take you."

"We're fine," Gwen said. "I really don't...do meetings."

"Oh. Well, I figured, on account of the coffee..."

"I just quit," Gwen explained. "Because of my grandmother, I guess. She drinks a little too much, and it seems to have made her intolerant of my..." She shrugged. "You know...lifestyle."

"Bummer," said Rita.

"Maybe I shouldn't blame the drinking. Maybe she'd be that way, anyway."

"Probably," Stoner muttered.

"Yeah, well," Rita said, and returned to the bar.

Stape leaned toward Gwen. "She's flirting with you."

"Who?"

"Rita."

Gwen looked dubious. "Talking about alcohol is flirting?"

"You didn't see her offer to take Stoner to a meeting, did you?"

"She didn't offer to take me," Gwen said. "Not really."

"She was working up to it."

Stoner realized Stape was looking at her. Expectantly. She tried to imagine... Oh, right, this was the time for her to make jealous, threatening noises. She cleared her throat, tried to conjure up some anger—or at least heavy anxiety—but couldn't. Not that anger, jealousy, and anxiety were foreign emotions. She'd had plenty of that in her life, with Agatha, her first real lover. It made her feel worn out and used up. She didn't want to feel that with Gwen, that possessiveness that came from fear and only led to more fear and ultimately to claustrophobia and terrible arguments, nastiness and...

If I ever start feeling that way about Gwen, she decided, I'll just leave town.

"If you want to go to a meeting with her," she said to Gwen, "Go ahead. I can look for Marylou..."

"I don't go to meetings at home. Why should I go to a meeting here?" Gwen reached over and touched her face lovingly. "Stoner, do you feel all right?"

That seemed to satisfy Stape, who nodded—subtly—her approval and picked a bit of glazier's putty off her jeans.

Rita, meanwhile, had put together the coffee and club soda in one big hurry and was back. "Okay," she said as she put the drinks down. "If you change your mind..."

"No go, Rita," Stape said.

The woman shrugged. "Nothing ventured, nothing gained." She sauntered through swinging doors to the kitchen.

"She doesn't mean to be pushy," Stape said. "Went through a nasty break-up in the spring, and she's been a little rancid ever since." She took a swallow of her beer. "Hell, last time it happened to me, I was drunk and horny for a whole year. Made a damn fool of myself, lost a couple of friends, and totalled my pick-up. Ran that sucker right into a tree—booze and drugs, but mostly self-destructive, I guess. They couldn't even salvage the stereo. Only things that survived that crash were me and one Lucie Blue tape, and I was in better shape than the tape."

"I'm sorry," Gwen said. "About you, not the tape."

"It was a long time back," Stape said, and polished off her beer. "Love is hell."

"It certainly is," Stoner agreed. "I hope things are better for you now."

"George is great. Except she's trying to kill me with that microwave. Jesus, I hate that thing."

"Maybe you should let her know that," Stoner suggested.

"Aw, she thinks it's the greatest thing since TV dinners. I can't do that."

Stoner grinned. "Must be love."

"Yeah," Stape said, returning her grin, "I'm stuck on the wench. It's a pitiful situation."

The wench in question was coming through the door, letting in a blast of evening sunlight. She strode to the table and made a grab for Stape's beer. "How many is that?"

"Just one," Stape said a little sheepishly.

George looked at Gwen and Stoner. "That true?"

"As far as I know," Gwen said.

"Okay," George said, and plunked herself down. She leaned over and ruffled Stape's hair. "Not that I care about you, Tough Stuff. But we only have three payments to go on that truck."

Stape turned the color of the camellias in the mural.

"I'm afraid I don't have much for you," George said as she rooted in her purse and brought out her notebook. "The last time anyone saw your friend was early afternoon yesterday, leaving EPCOT."

"She left EPCOT?" Gwen asked. "On the monorail?"

"Through the parking lot."

"We didn't have the car with us," Stoner said.

"Well, she didn't steal one or I'd have heard about it."

Stoner thought hard. "If someone just started walking, where would they end up?"

114

"Just about anywhere," George said. "There's a lot of land around here, and most of it isn't developed."

"What if she was trying to get back to the Contemporary?"

"Make more sense to take the Monorail," Stape said.

"But she's afraid of the Monorail."

"Well, if she turned right coming out of the parking lot," George mused, "she'd end up at the Contemporary, eventually."

"In about a month," Stape added.

"That's assuming she didn't take a right off of World Drive onto Vista Boulevard."

"Where would that take her?" Stoner asked.

"To River Country, Fort Wilderness, or the Village."

"For the sake of Marylou's sanity," Gwen said, "let's pray she went to the Village."

"Marylou's not really comfortable in wilderness," Stoner explained.

Gwen laughed. "Marylou's never even been in wilderness. She'd probably be consumed by a bear."

"Thanks a lot, Gwen. Now I can worry about Marylou being eaten by a bear."

"Not in WDW," George said. "There aren't any real bears in WDW. There's no real anything."

"Except birds," Stape corrected.

"And the ponies," Stoner said.

George turned to her. "Ponies?"

"At the U.K. pavilion..." She caught herself. They weren't ponies. They were dream ponies. Weren't they? She smiled sheepishly. "Sorry. Got it mixed up with something else."

"Probably the Grand Canyon," Gwen suggested.

Stoner kicked her under the table.

"Of course," George went on, "she could have turned left out of the lot, which would take her to the Dolphin and Swan—those are our luxury hotels."

"I vote for that," Gwen said. "Check the dining room."

George shook her head. "Sorry. We already looked into it. No luck. And she didn't stop off at Disney-MGM Studios."

"You might have missed her," Stoner said.

"Our people are pretty observant, and pretty thorough. And, if you don't mind my saying so, your friend is hard to miss."

"It's been mentioned," Stoner mumbled.

George tossed her notebook onto the table. "I'm afraid we have to assume she's somewhere outside the World, or somewhere inside the World and we can't find her."

"What about the tunnels?" Stoner asked.

"It's possible she went in there and no one saw her," George said, reaching for her notebook. "I'll have it checked out. Though, from the direction she was headed in when last observed, it's not likely she'd have found an entrance. And it's pretty busy down there—laundry, maintenance—like a whole city, really." She tried to look hopeful. "But worth a try. Definitely worth a try."

Stoner took a swallow of her club soda and tried to think of a non-self-incriminating way to bring up her next question. She decided on the indirect approach. "How big is WDW?"

"About 47 square miles. 27,400 acres, to be exact," George said. "Not all developed, of course. It used to be forest—palmetto and pine, you drove through it on the way in—and some swamp."

"Did anyone live here before?"

"Not as far as we know. Oh, there are always a few swamp rats in any of these wilderness parts down here. Sometimes whole families going back generations, descended from early settlers or Indian tribes, living God knows how back there with the copperheads and alligators and intermarrying. Nobody knows they're there until the land gets sold and developed, or they're driven out by a flood or hurricane."

"Did they find anyone when they started building here?"

George shrugged. "Not as far as I know, but it was a bit ago—1971 when they opened the Kingdom."

"I guess there must have been tunnels and things while they were building that just got abandoned," Stoner said. "You know— holes and trenches, stuff they don't even bother to fill in."

"Maybe," George said. "But they've never mentioned it, and I think they'd tell us. Kids could find those things and get lost in them. You think that might have happened with your friend?"

"Just considering all the possibilities," Stoner said. How in the world was she going to bring up the matter of Spaceship Earth without admitting she'd committed an illegal act by going where she wasn't supposed to go?

She glanced up at Gwen and signalled "help me" with her eyes.

"What's under the Ball?" Gwen asked abruptly.

"Nothing but air," George said. "It doesn't connect with the ground."

"Are you sure about that?"

"Positive." George looked from Gwen to Stoner and back. "Why? Do you suspect something?"

Gwen put on an innocent face. "Just curious."

"I'm not buying that," George said. "What are you thinking about?"

"Better tell her," Gwen said to Stoner.

She took a deep breath. "Okay. We were on the ride, and it stopped, and I saw an exit sign and went through the door and down some stairs and..."

"Found yourself outside, right?"

"No, I was in some kind of basement or something. It was dark. I couldn't see..."

George shook her head. "I've been up and down those stairs a dozen times. They go outside."

Stoner felt sick. Okay, let it go. You fell asleep again, right? Made a mistake, right? Were boldly going where no one has gone before, right? Had another of those "Stoner McTavish, for your eyes only" experiences, right?

George was looking at her closely. "Stoner, what did you see?"

"Nothing," she said quickly. "I must have been confused, imagination, you know."

"There was something. Come on."

"I went down the stairs," she said hesitantly, "and I know I passed the door to the outside, but the stairs went on, and so did I, and at the bottom there was a...well, a door..."

"And?"

"And I opened it, but there didn't seem to be...anything...on the other side."

Stape was staring at her, open mouthed.

"Did you go in?" George asked.

"No. It was...dark." She folded her hands on the table top. She was damned if she was going to tell them about the fog and the bottomless hole. "That's all."

"There you are," Stape said, a little smugly.

"No, Stape, this is not there you are. This is not necessarily the same thing at all."

Stoner glanced from one to the other. "What same thing?"

"A friend of Stape's was working on some wiring in there..."

"He isn't a friend," Stape said.

"A colleague of Stape's. And he claimed he went down underground, just the way you did. Except what he saw..."

"What?"

George shook her head. "It's nutso stuff."

"What was it?" Stoner said insistently.

George looked at Stape and rolled her eyes in a the-world-is-full-of-loonies-and-I'm-the-only-sane-one-in-it way. "He claims he saw a hole—said the whole area beyond the door was a hole, actually—and that there were clouds or something coming out of the hole."

Stoner noticed her hands were shaking, and hid them in her lap. "Anything else?"

"He says he dropped an electrician's wrench down the hole, and it..."

"Never hit bottom," Stoner finished for her.

George stared at her. "Did that happen to you?"

"Not exactly. It was a penny."

Stape signalled to Rita for a refill all around. George shook her head in warning but didn't object aloud.

"Did he say anything else?"

"Nope," Stape said. "We went and looked for the place, naturally. But there wasn't anything. No stairs past the outside exit. No door. No clouds. Nothing. Not even the big nothing he said was there."

Stoner started to get up. "I have to talk to this guy."

George stopped her. "No good. He's gone."

"Gone?"

"Left the state. Said life was hard enough with the recession, he didn't need Voo Doo complicating his life."

"Is that what he thought?" Gwen asked. "Voo Doo?"

"Something like that."

Gwen grinned. "If it's Voo Doo we're dealing with, no problem. Aunt Hermione can handle that."

"Or one of her friends from Cassadaga," Stoner agreed.

Stape and George exchanged glances.

Oh, boy, Stoner thought. The end of what could have been a beautiful friendship.

"You Yankees are all a little strange, aren't you?" George asked.

Stoner nodded eagerly. "Sort of."

George patted Gwen's hand sympathetically. "Must be a strain sometimes."

"I'm used to it," Gwen said demurely.

"Listen," Stoner objected, "she's just as strange as I am."

"Well," Gwen admitted, "almost."

"I mean, I may have weird stuff happen to me, but at least I don't believe in it. You believe in it."

"Which, Stoner, my sweet, is why is doesn't happen to me."

The evening's entertainment was setting up in the background. Clatterings and grunts as amplifiers were heaved onto the stage. The ripping of duct tape. Someone blew into the mike, apparently liked the sound, and spent a few minutes huffing and "hooaaaaa"ing and "puf-puf-puf"ing.

Stoner glanced up.

A blonde woman of indeterminate age was tuning an acoustic guitar. But not just any acoustic guitar. This guitar was pure white, and shiny as a mirror. And it had "Patzi" written on it in silver sequins that caught the light and threw it like confetti into every corner of the room.

"Nice guitar," Stoner said.

"That's Patzi," Stape said. "She is cool."

"But strange," said George. "Being a Yankee."

The woman was pumping up, tapping the toe of her pure white cowboy boot on the floor, then the heel, making her own drums. She did a little dance, accompanying herself on the guitar, the fringes on her blouse and skirt gyrating wildly.

She was cool, all right. And somehow familiar.

Patzi ran through a few chords, then threw back her head and sang. A couple of bars of Loretta Lynn, strung together with a snatch of Brenda Lee, a little Tammy Wynette, and washed it all down with some early Dolly Parton.

Her voice was familiar, too.

"Great, isn't she?" Stape said, obviously smitten. "Not real up-to-date in her choices, but some kind of voice."

Stoner had to admit it was, indeed, some kind of voice. Deep, lusty, well-travelled, intimate, and definitely bedroom.

And definitely one she'd heard before.

She turned in her seat to get a better look.

Patzi let out a whoop. "Stoner McTavish! I'll be damned, it's Old Home Week."

Stoner couldn't believe it. "Ione?"

The woman put her guitar down and sashayed over to the table. "Call me Patzi, honey. That other woman's long gone." She threw her arms around Stoner and gave her a breath-choking hug. "Damn, it's good to see you. Hey, Gwen!"

Stape and George were looking totally bewildered.

"We go way back," Patzi explained. "We were in the same mental hospital."

"That's nice," George said with infinite politeness.

Patzi flapped her hand at her. "Not that way. Stoner was under cover, looking for a missing nurse, and I was just there because my no-good husband put me there."

Gwen reached back and pulled over a chair for Patzi. "How in the world did you end up here? Like this?"

"Always wanted to be a country-western singer, remember, Stoner?"

Stoner nodded.

"So when old Shady Acres went down the tubes, I just decided, Hell's bells, it's a damn short life. You might as well give it a try."

"That's really great, Ione...uh, Patzi." She wondered how to phrase her next question. "Do you play a lot of...well, women's bars?"

"You mean am I 'in the life'?" Ione/Patzi fluffed her hair a little. "Honey, I am in it. These Baby Dykes love older woman. My dance card's always full."

"I can't believe it," Gwen said wonderingly. "When I met you before you were so, I don't know, so..."

"Mousey," the singer finished for her. "I sure was. It's amazing what divorce will do for you." She sang a few notes of "D.I.V.O.R.C.E."

Stape was still staring at them in slack-jawed awe. "All I can say is, that must be one heck of a mental hospital."

"Sure was, Sweetheart. It was haunted."

"You saw it, too?" Stoner asked.

"I saw it tear itself apart around our ears. And I saw it put back together the next day. You think it was the medication?"

"I don't know," Stoner said. "Did you ever remember all the lyrics to all the songs Doris Day ever recorded?"

"Looked them up. Probably should have just let it go, since my life was coming back together anyway. But by then it was something I knew I'd always wonder about. Listen," Patzi said, giving Stoner a little punch in the ribs with an elbow, "you'll never believe who I ran into. The other night? I was doing a short gig over at the World? The Hoop-de-Doo Review? So there I am relating to the audience, I mean we were rockin' and rollin', honey, and I look up and sitting near the back is none other than Millicent Tunes."

Stoner felt her blood run cold.

"Isn't she in jail?" Gwen asked. She turned to George and Stape. "Millicent Tunes ran the hospital Ione and Stoner were in. She was using it to smuggle gangsters out of the country. Stoner blew her cover."

"She may have been," Patzi said, "but she's out now. Big as life and twice as ugly."

Suddenly a lot of things made sense, and Stoner didn't like the sense they made.

"Hey," Patzi said, "I got to rehearse some before my fans get here. Let's get together later, okay?"

"Sure," Stoner said. Millicent Tunes. Damn.

Patzi pranced back to the stage and started giving hell to her guitar.

"Well, well," Gwen said. "Are you thinking what I'm thinking?"

Stoner nodded slowly. "Now we know what happened to Mary lou. And we know why."

"But she knows Marylou, and from the note it looked like she thought it was me she'd kidnapped."

"Yeah." She could feel the cold fear spreading from her blood to the surface of her skin. If she didn't move soon, she wouldn't be able to. "She had someone else do the kidnapping. But when she realizes..." She stood up. "We have to find her, Gwen. Before Millicent gets to her."

CHAPTER 9

Marylou knew herself pretty well, and one of the things she had always known about herself was when she was getting near the edge of her sanity. That edge, she could tell, was coming up any minute now. What she didn't know for sure was what would happen when she went over it.

This seemed like a really bad time not to know.

She was perfectly capable of doing something that would get her killed, simply to break the monotony. She couldn't stand being bored. It ranked right up there with dark places, terrible food, no sleep, no intelligent conversation, and a score of other horrors indigenous to the present situation.

One of the things she needed to do, and was finding increasingly difficult, was to keep herself under control until someone came to rescue her.

If anyone came to rescue her.

She shook herself. No, you mustn't think that. Stoner will come. She will definitely come.

You see how easy it is to get into negative thinking?

Marylou crumpled a food wrapper in her hand, just to hear sound. But what if she didn't come?

Now that she had thought it, the idea took root in her mind and refused to leave.

What if Stoner didn't come?

What if nobody came?

What if nobody really gave a damn about her?

Maybe she'd been too outrageous her entire life—too self-centered, too insensitive, too zany, too ridiculous, too downright Marylou. Maybe she'd made it impossible for anyone to be a friend, to really love her.

Marylou felt tears come to her eyes. She was sorry. Sorry for every smart-ass remark she'd ever made, every teasing comment. Sorry for every complaint. Sorry about the secret cache of pistachio nuts she kept hidden in her desk drawer so she wouldn't have to share them with Stoner.

For Heaven's sake, Stoner doesn't even like pistachio nuts. Never has.

She really was becoming quite disturbed.

DISTURBANCE was written all over her.

She had to put her mind on something constructive. Like getting out of here. Or staying alive and sane.

Well, not completely sane. No one could go through what she was going through and stay completely sane. Could they?

Maybe she should play with David a little more. She could manipulate him. Easy. He might be a hot-shot kidnapper, but men were her area of expertise.

If there was one thing Marylou Kesselbaum knew how to do, it was to get a man to think he wanted to do something he didn't really want to do.

Marylou sighed. She'd almost welcome a trip on an airplane to break the monotony.

The airplane. That's what had done it. She'd made too much of a fuss and alienated everyone, and now no one was ever going to come and get her. Stoner would hire some fancy, sleazy attorney, have her declared dead, and take her half of the business and all her insurance money. Then she'd split it with Gwen and Aunt Hermione and Edith and they'd all sail around the world, carousing and whooping and congratulating themselves on getting rid of her at last.

The No More Marylou Celebration Cruise.

Even now, they were probably celebrating. Glad to be without her. Going on the rides. Having a better time.

Well, if people didn't like who she was, they could just...

It was her own fault if people weren't close to her. She'd never been able to tell people how she really felt. If people don't know how you feel, they don't know who you are. If they don't know who you are, they can't care about you. Plain and straightforward. No share, no care. Nobody's fault but her own.

She didn't know why she was like that.

She couldn't change it. She was over thirty. You can't change your basic psychology after thirty, it's a scientific fact.

Even her own mother probably didn't like her very much. How could she? How could you like somebody you didn't know?

Damn it, she'd tried to change. All her life she'd tried to change. She didn't want to be a neurotic spoil-sport. But she just couldn't do it. Couldn't make the transition. Couldn't get it together. Couldn't do whatever it was she was supposed to do.

And probably never would be able to. She'd probably never have any real friends.

She knew darn well Stoner was only nice to her because they were in business together. Not to be manipulative, Stoner'd never do that. But just to keep things pleasant. Keep the work environment pleasant.

That's what she was, a Work Environment.

She choked on a little sob.

Well, this was totally ridiculous. Stoner'd better find her before she became completely unhinged. Stoner'd better get that slow-moving, methodical, obsessively thorough Capricorn mind of hers in gear and GET ME OUT OF HERE.

Trouble was, Stoner didn't know boredom would make her crazy.

Stoner probably thought she had all the time in the world to putter around being cautious.

Stoner wouldn't go crazy in this situation.

Stoner would just sit down and think the whole damn thing through, nut by bolt by hair. Then decide on the best course of action. Sleep on it. Look at it again the next day. Run it through in her mind once more to check for snags...

Marylou swore, if she ever got out of here alive, she would kill Stoner McTavish. Do the world a favor. Get rid of the damnable, compulsive, slow moving, irritating...

Fear and loneliness overwhelmed her.

She began to cry.

* * *

"Are you thinking what I'm thinking?" Gwen asked as she pulled off US 192 onto World Drive.

"Probably," Stoner said. She scanned the lawn and bushes they passed. It was getting dark, too dark to see, really—but just in case... "It's the worst possible scenario."

"She wants revenge." Gwen studied the bushes and lawn on her side of the car.

What was that? Stoner peered into the dying twilight. "Worse than that. Marylou was in on the arrest. So she has plenty of reason to want her dead, and no reason to keep her alive." No Marylou, just a topiary Figment.

"And as soon as she finds out it's Marylou she has..." The car started to slip over the center line. Gwen pulled it back into the right hand lane.

Stoner thanked God there wasn't much traffic on the Drive at this time. It was too late for the afternoon crowd to leave, and too early for those who were staying for dinner and Illuminations.

"She'll toss her away like a used Kleenex."

"Probably wouldn't even be interested in a trade."

Stoner looked over at her. "A trade?"

"Me for her."

She couldn't believe it. One by one, all the people she cared about were either disappearing or going insane. She wondered what they'd find when the got back to the Contemporary. Aunt Hermione wandering the halls naked and tearing out her hair, no doubt. Edith Kesselbaum trying to conjure up ghosts by reciting Erickson's Stages of Development, with subcategories. "I can't see one positive thing about that idea," she said.

"Well, there's one thing. I know how I'd be handling it if it were me. God knows what Marylou's doing."

Stoner didn't even want to think about that. "What would you be doing?"

"I don't know," Gwen said. "But if I were there doing it, I'd know."

They were passing through the Magic Kingdom Auto Plaza. Coming up on Vista Boulevard, which would lead to the Village, River Country, and Fort Wilderness. Maybe they should...

No, wherever Marylou was, it was bound to be out of sight. She wouldn't be wandering around in the open unless they'd let her go. Even then, she wouldn't wander. She'd make a bee-line for the nearest phone.

"Know what I think we should do?" Gwen said.

"No, what?"

"Go after Tunes."

Yeah, that made sense. Maybe Edith Kesselbaum had seen her at one of her meetings, if she was hanging out with the psychiatric crowd. Maybe could even find out where she was staying. Maybe someone could follow her.

But who?

Edith Kesselbaum? No, she was much too shaky. And they needed her to behave normally. Because Marylou's life right now depended on keeping Millicent Tunes from finding out who she'd had kidnapped—come to think of it, if Millicent Tunes was hanging around the psychiatric convention, why hadn't Edith seen her? Edith knew what the woman looked like. Edith had helped arrest her.

Maybe Tunes had changed her appearance.

No, Ione/Patzi had recognized her.

But that was at the Hoop-Dee-Doo Revue. Not exactly the kind of place you'd find Edith Kesselbaum. And she hadn't found out exactly when she'd been seen there. It could have been before any of them got to WDW.

Quite possibly, Tunes had planned this from the moment she saw Edith Kesselbaum's name on the convention attendance list. She could have asked a couple of questions, and found out they were all coming to Orlando, and gone out and hired...

"Oh, shit," she said as something even more ominous occurred to her.

"What?"

"I think we've been set up."

Gwen glanced over at her. "Set up how?"

"Well, how did we all decide to take this vacation? Edith was coming down to the convention. About a week after she preregistered, Marylou and I got a call from Walt Disney World Travel Outreach, offering us these really inexpensive rooms at the Contemporary. The only stipulation being that we had to come this week, which, of course, is the week of the convention, only I didn't put that together..."

"It's not your fault," Gwen said.

Stoner kneaded her face with the heels of her hands. "Know what I'll bet? I'll bet there's no such animal as Walt Disney World Travel Outreach. I'll bet Millicent Tunes arranged this whole thing, to get back at us."

"If you want my opinion," Gwen said as she steered the car into the Contemporary parking lot, "the elegant Dr. Tunes has a serious revenge problem."

"Highly motivated," Stoner said.

"And therefore highly dangerous. Do you think it's time to bring in the police?"

"George called them, but they gave her the usual 'Has to be missing for forty-eight hours drill.' Anyway, I have the feeling we'll get further working quietly. What do you think?"

"Oh, I agree," Gwen said. She cut the motor and sat for a moment, jangling the keys. "Stoner, I think I should be the one to follow her." She held up her hand before Stoner could object. "I know what you're going to say. But you can't do it, Edith can't do it. We need Aunt Hermione to keep trying to make psychic contact—and, not to be ageist or anything, at her age she's fine on stamina, but if we need speed she isn't exactly Olympic material."

Stoner hunched down in her seat. "I know."

"I could disguise myself."

"No," Stoner said, "I'll do it."

"You'd just look like you, only in disguise."

"I'm afraid for you." She glanced over. "Please?"

"Stoner..."

"Only if you have to, Okay?"

Gwen drummed her fingers on the steering wheel. "Okay," she said after a minute, "first we'll talk to Edith and see if she's seen Tunes or anyone who might resemble her. With luck, she can come up with whatever name she's using now, and find out where she's staying. Then I'll get on it." She turned to Stoner and took her hand. "I know what you're thinking. I know you hate it. In your place, I'd hate it, too. But it's really the only way."

"Yeah," Stoner said, and slouched out of the car.

* * *

The last reaction she would have expected from Edith was a look of guilt.

"Oh, dear," Edith said.

"What?"

"This is very embarrassing."

"Life is embarrassing," Gwen said sympathetically.

Edith cleared her throat and twisted the bracelet on her wrist. "There is one person—woman who feels, well, familiar, though I haven't been able to place her. I'm afraid I wrote it off as..." She gave a self-conscious little laugh. "... someone I met somewhere and ought to know but can't remember, but I was afraid to approach her because she might be a former client who would be devastated to find that I'd forgotten who she was. You know how it is. No, I don't suppose you do. Anyway, I settled for smiling and waving in a friendly sort of way." She shot a quick, apologetic glance at Stoner. "And, in my vanity—ego, ego, ego—I wasn't wearing my glasses, just the contacts, and I do need to get the prescription changed. Well, I've certainly learned my lesson. Besides, I didn't get that close a look at Millicent Tunes when Marylou and I arrested her. We merely shoved her into a closet and made ourselves a drink. Millicent Tunes had very extravagant taste in liquor."

"Do you think it could be the same person?" Gwen asked.

"It's possible. If so, she's changed her hair color—but then we all do that, don't we? Constantly."

"How about her eyes?" Stoner asked. "She had really distinctive eyes—brown with gold flecks, and kind of dead looking."

Edith shuddered. "Well, really, that is totally disgusting. No, I didn't get a chance to see her eyes."

"That's okay," Gwen said. "I can get in her face."

Stoner went to the window and looked out, over the lagoon. The sun was gone, the last of the twilight fading from the sky. It would be pitch dark in a few minutes. Another night, and Marylou still missing. She hoped she wasn't frightened. She hated the thought of Marylou frightened.

We should have been more sympathetic about the plane ride, she thought. Marylou couldn't help being afraid. And she couldn't help expressing it the way she did. She was just being Marylou. She's always Marylou, just Marylou. And even though she might be a pain in the ass once in a while—like on long plane rides—most of the time it's really comforting, to have a friend who's just who she is.

"I have to get a look at this woman," Gwen said. "Without letting her connect me to you. How do you think I can do that?"

Edith contemplated the problem. "We had name-time, during that wretched touchy-feely workshop I keep trying unsuccessfully to repress. Give me a moment. I might be able to come up with a name."

In about an hour, the Electrical Water Pageant would come tootling and doodling by. Marylou hadn't seen it last night. She wouldn't see it tonight. Marylou would like the Electrical Water Pageant. Either that, or she'd be terrified by it. It didn't matter, she'd be moved one way or another. That was one of the things she loved about Marylou: there was nothing that didn't move her—one way or another.

"It was one of those old names," Edith Kesselbaum said. "An old family name, like you find in novels. Southern or New England. No, wait a minute...there's a dormitory at Harvard, don't ask me how I know, it was a long time ago and I didn't enjoy it, but the name...the name. Elliot, Dunster..."

"Winthrop," Stoner said under her breath.

"That's it!" Edith cried. "Winthrop."

Stoner turned to face her. "Lillian Winthrop."

"Exactly. Hermione must be right, you are psychic."

She shook her head. "Lillian Winthrop is Millicent Tunes' aunt, the one she tried to get rid of."

Edith Kesselbaum tsk-tsked. "And she took her name. How arrogant."

"This is all a game to her. She's leaving us clues."

128

"Meaning," Gwen said, "she probably wants us to be doing exactly what we're doing."

"Except that she wanted you to be the bait," Stoner said. "I really think that's one part of this she's not in control of."

"Marylou seems like perfectly adequate bait to me," Edith said.

"True." But she was even more convinced, now that she knew who the kidnapper was, that Marylou was in tremendous danger. Because Millicent Tunes wanted to hurt Stoner, and hurt her badly. And in Millicent Tunes' mind, it was only Gwen who could cause her pain. Tunes had known back at Shady Acres that Stoner and Gwen were lovers. She had even been a bit jealous. Marylou was only a friend. In Millicent's conventional, twisted mind a friend was expendable, not someone you risked your life for. Therefore, to ensure Stoner's ultimate unhappiness, she had to get Gwen. And that made Marylou just something in the way, to be discarded without a thought. If she hesitated at all, it was to make Marylou suffer as much as possible.

Marylou's life depended on them acting fast.

Without warning, Edith leapt up, flew across the room to her briefcase, and scattered the contents over the bed. "I think," she said as she tore through papers and folders and brochures and business cards, "I can put us ahead of the game. Hah!" She held up a stapled booklet, shook out her glasses and crammed them on her head. "I'll bet she's listed right..." She leafed wildly to the back of the booklet. "Here!" Edith pointed to a listing of conference participants and their local addresses. "Winthrop, Lillian. The Dolphin."

"That figures," Gwen said. "The most expensive hotel in the World."

Stoner nodded. "Millicent always did travel in style."

"If the rest of her taste is like her liquor, she does," Edith said.

Gwen gathered up her things. "Well, I'd better go femme myself up a little and get over there."

"What are you going to do?" Stoner asked.

"Camp out in the lobby. See if I can catch her coming or going."

"There's an awards banquet tonight," Edith said. "She'll probably be there."

"Anticipating an award?" Gwen asked.

"No doubt." Edith consulted her book. "At the Swan."

"Piece of cake," Gwen said. "Borrow your make-up?"

Edith handed her a train case. "You'll be careful, won't you?"

"Of course."

Stoner hated this. It made sense to do it this way. In fact, it was the only way. But she hated it. "How will you know her?"

"Willowy blonde dyed—what color, Edith?"

"Innocuous brown."

"Brown. Skinny woman wearing prison weight. Dead eyes. And probably a name tag."

"Try not to look her in the eyes," Stoner said, trying to be light about it. "She'll turn you to stone."

"Right." Gwen looked around the room. "I need something frillier than what I have. I need to look super-straight. Edith, do you have anything diaphanous?"

"My dear," Edith said as she threw open her closet door, "I always have something diaphanous."

* * *

Stoner paced back and forth, the width of the hotel room, to the bathroom and back to the window. Up and down the narrow runway between the beds. She picked up the phone, but couldn't think of anyone to call, and besides they had to keep the line clear. She turned the television set on, ran through the channels without noticing what was on, flicked it off, then flicked it back on ten minutes later. She glanced out at the lagoon, but couldn't see anything but her own reflection in the darkened window. She wished she could go hang out with Edith, but they had agreed to stay near the phone in their separate rooms, just in case. She wished Aunt Hermione would get back from Cassadaga, but her aunt had gone there to meditate among the other psychics, where the vibrations were high and uncluttered.

At least she could make a quick call to George, fill her in, and ask her to look for any old plans the WDW builders might have around. Not to WDW as it was today, though they would probably be helpful. What she really wanted to see was a map of the workers' tunnels.

Trouble was, when she reached George, she was reminded that tomorrow was Sunday, and the county court house wasn't going to be open for business. But George promised to check around anyway—maybe she knew someone who knew someone who had access to the building and wouldn't object to a little Revolutionary activity.

Well, Sunday or not, Marylou was down there somewhere, and Stoner was going to find her if she died trying.

* * *

David strolled along the edge of the crowd, holding the large paper bag firmly but delicately. He'd really surpassed himself tonight. Chilled leek soup, salmon soufflé with tarragon in a white butter sauce, veal with mushroom sauce from Chefs de France. A nice white wine. And for dessert, trifle from Le Cellier. All of which he had chosen and paid for himself. That should convince her he was no low-life common criminal, but a professional, with professional taste and gentlemanly manners.

The crowd was moving right along, which meant it must be before 9:00, when they'd be shuffling and jostling for spots along the lagoon from which to watch the Illuminations show. He wished he could bring her to see that. He was willing to bet she'd like it— the fireworks, the laser show, the music, the tiny bright lights outlining the pavilions. It must be awful for her, stuck there underground with all this going on just over your head. Last night, he could have sworn he'd felt the vibrations from the fireworks. He wondered if she had, and what she had thought it was.

He had to admit it, he was getting a little emotionally involved with this case. She seemed to like him today, and that made him feel good. She'd even flirted with him a little—not in an "I'll let you screw me if you'll let me go" way, but just a little, and nicely. Maybe it was that menstrual business making her soft and fluffy like a puppy. Maybe it had nothing to do with him. Or maybe her hoity-toity attitude before had been the menstruals coming on. He'd heard plenty about PMS, back in prison when they didn't have anything to do all day long but sit and watch Oprah. Some of the other guys, the rougher ones, would scare each other after lights out, telling stories about bitches with guns and PMS. It was generally agreed among the cons that you didn't want to cross a bitch with that PMS thing.

But they'd had a good time today, playing gin rummy and shooting the breeze. She'd told him about some of her mother's cases—neat, scary stuff involving people with lots of personalities; funny stuff about people with no personality. He secretly suspected she was making it up—therapists just didn't go around telling stories about their clients, not even to their kids, any more than he'd tell stories about his. But she was a gifted story teller. He'd have to remember to tell her that, that she had a gift for story telling. She might want to think about being a writer, if she ever got tired of teaching.

One thing bothered him, though. His client had said she was the red-haired one's "lover," and sure implied she wasn't on the

131

straight and narrow, so to speak. So how come she was flirting with him? Maybe she was one of those women who swing both ways. Or maybe—the thought brought him to a dead halt right in the middle of traffic in World Showcase Plaza—maybe they wanted to have a kid, and she wanted him to be the father.

The idea took his breath away. Him, a father. It made him feel all squooshy and silly, like that guy in "Carousel" singing about his kid Bill.

He put himself in gear. Didn't want her whole dinner to get cold. Casually, he walked to the Mexico pavilion, waited until the crowd was looking the other way, then slipped around back and into the darkness and bushes. Behind the building, where the boats could be taken out and repaired without being seen and ruining the illusion, he found his secret entrance to the abandoned tunnel that led under the Odyssey Restaurant. Glancing around to make sure he hadn't been spotted, he lifted the trap door and slipped inside.

He'd done this so many times now, he didn't even need the flashlight.

Humming under his breath, he crept along the hallway.

A father. He might be a father.

He sure hoped the client wouldn't ask him to kill her.

* * *

One of the bad things about sitting around waiting for the phone to ring is that you get to think. Not just to think, but to think about crazy stuff. Like dreaming you're in Wales and having the characters in your dream speak Welsh. Like being told the name of a tourist attraction in this dream, and having it confirmed in your waking life, in spite of the fact that you've never been to Wales, never read a book about Wales, never even booked a travel itinerary to Wales—and don't have any stray Welsh genes hanging around wherever your genes hang around.

And if you don't like thinking about that, you can think about descending a non-existent staircase and opening a non-existent door leading nowhere through which is seeping non-existent fog.

You can think about Audio-Animatronic dogs that chase after your boat, except no one else on the boat sees it.

And, if that doesn't meet your needs for thinking about crazy stuff, you can think about phone calls from Spaceship Earth, complete with sound effects that aren't really on, and that only you can hear.

You can think about all that fun stuff, and it can lead you

exactly nowhere.

The Hand of Havoc was feeling pretty close at hand.

* * *

Gwen called in around 11:00 to say she had eyeballed Millicent Tunes, a.k.a. Lillian Winthrop, who had gone to her room. Gwen had decided to hang around the lobby of the Dolphin— "Though, personally, I prefer the Swan, more intimate, but qué sera sera"—in case Herself decided to take a little stroll later. She assured Stoner she was perfectly safe, "though I may have gone too far with the diaphanous. Three drunken psychiatrists have tried to pick me up, and I'm sure one of them was a Behaviorist. I should have chosen something with one of those wide, flat Puritan Christian collars they make for women with up-chucking babies. And, no, our quarry hasn't the slightest idea who I am. Didn't even look my way. I'm just part of the scenery to her. Should I be insulted?"

"You should be glad."

"If she leaves, I'll follow her. I'll call you before I go. Be safe, Dearest."

"Be safe, yourself."

"By the way, tell Edith she should get a rebate on that rental car. The air conditioning doesn't work, and the fan belt sounds like a banshee in heat."

She stood there for a moment, idiotically clutching the receiver, as if that could keep Gwen with her, could keep her safe. But the empty dial tone was too depressing. She hung up and sat on the edge of the bed.

Millicent Tunes. She hadn't thought of her in more than two years, though she had given more than a little thought to Gladys Grenier, Shady Acres' favorite sadistic head nurse. Of course, she had assumed that Millicent Tunes was safely behind bars, while old Glad-Ass roamed the world at will with her dutiful and equally sadistic son, Mario. Hell, for all she knew, Gladys and Mario were right here in WDW, tucked away inside Minnie Mouse and Eeyore costumes.

A chilling thought.

But no more chilling than the thought of Millicent Tunes, out of the pokey and hot for revenge.

At least it explained the cryptic message sent by Aunt Hermione's Spirit Guide. What Aunt Hermione had heard as "music" obviously referred to Tunes.

Aunt Hermione breezed in a few minutes later. She'd been in

133

the middle of a meditation, when something told her—as clear as a bell, that something was about to happen, and she'd be needed.

"They didn't happen to mention what it was that was going to happen, did they?" Stoner asked.

"No, and I couldn't get any images." Aunt Hermione shrugged out of her jacket, dug a rumpled and gritty pack of Virginia Slims from her pocket, and set about looking for an ash tray.

"I don't know," Stoner said as she unearthed the ash tray from the same drawer to which she'd relegated the Gideon Bible and which she was using for dirty laundry. "Sometimes I wonder if contacting Spirit Guides is really worth the effort. Half the time they don't tell you much, and when they do it's so obscure it doesn't make any sense."

"That's because you only ask them for help with the minutiae of life," her aunt said as she ensconced herself near an open window and lit up. "They really take little interest in mundane affairs—having a larger perspective. The things that bother us terribly just aren't that important."

"Well, they're important to me," Stoner said. "This is the life I'm living."

Aunt Hermione smoked for a minute and contemplated the sky. "Perhaps," she said, "we should contact one of the more earthly Guides. Someone who's chosen to take a personal interest in the goings-on on the material plane."

"Sounds like a good idea to me. Maybe someone who knows Marylou personally. Or Millicent Tunes' guardian angel—assuming she has one."

"Oh, we all have them, dear. Even the worst of us. It's just that some of us refuse to listen. Very frustrating for Spirit. Imagine being Millicent Tunes' guardian angel."

"What I can't imagine," Stoner said, "is doing anything so awful in this life I'd have to spend the time beyond being Millicent Tunes' guardian angel."

Aunt Hermione put out her cigarette. "It's a choice we make. Some Spirit has chosen to guard her. Well, it's said we all have our uses in this world. For reasons too deep for us to comprehend, that woman has chosen her path. We have to respect that choice, even while we try to stop her."

"Sometimes I envy you, Aunt Hermione." Stoner sat on the bed and wrapped her arms around her legs, resting her head on her knees. "You have such an acceptance of things."

"It wasn't always this way, you know. In my younger years, I

134

thrashed about just as much as you do. I do recommend the aging process. If you allow it to, it brings great peace of mind. At the least, it puts the trivia into perspective." She assumed her meditative posture. Back straight, arms open, palms up. "Now, let's see if I can contact someone to give us a hand with these earthly matters."

Stoner closed her eyes. She heard her aunt take a deep breath, then another...

The phone rang.

Stoner picked it up, and shrugged "Sorry" to her aunt, who only smiled.

"I know who I am," the woman said.

"What?" In the background, Walter Cronkite was holding forth on the wonders of Communication in the modern age.

"Callie Rose. My name is Callie Rose." She definitely had a heavy Southern accent. Not like Gwen's, a slight smoothing out of sounds. Or even George's or Stape's. Callie Rose's accent was thick as molasses, her words slow but run together as if they were all one word.

"And you're in Spaceship Earth."

There was a pause. "I never heard of that."

"It's an exhibit," Stoner said. "In EPCOT Center. In Walt Disney World."

Silence on the other end.

"Callie Rose? My name's Stoner. Stoner McTavish. You're trapped somehow. On a ride. How long have you been there?"

"I don't know," the woman said in a frightened-sounding voice. "A long, long time."

Probably days. The woman was probably starving to death. She obviously stepped off of the ride, maybe even during one of those terrifying, twilight unannounced stops. She'd seen an exit sign, just as Stoner had, and in panic had gone through it and fallen on the stairs. Since then she'd had amnesia—a concussion, maybe—and had been wandering around lost. Sure, that was it. That explained everything.

Except for a few minor details, like why was the ride running in the middle of the night when the park was closed. And, even more fun to wonder about, why was Stoner the only one who heard her?

She tried to brush that aside. "Do you remember getting on the ride?"

"What ride?"

"The ride through Spaceship Earth."

"I don't know what you're talking about," Callie Rose said. Her

135

voice turned a little shaky. "I want to get out of here."

"That's easy," Stoner said. "Just go out through any door. You'll be on the ground, and a security guard will find you."

"I can't do that," the woman said.

"Why not?"

"There's only one door. I'm afraid of it."

Stoner had a distinctly unpleasant feeling. "Why are you afraid of it?" she asked softly, and held her breath.

"There's death on the other side."

Oh, shit. Stoner shook her head. "Callie Rose, which side are you on?"

"I don't know."

"I mean, does the door open toward you, or away from you?"

A brief silence, as if the woman were trying to remember. "Toward."

The other side. Callie Rose was on the Other Side.

Other Side of what?

And how could she get across? If Stoner couldn't cross from her side, how could Callie Rose...?

What the hell was she talking about?

No, this all had a logical explanation. Callie Rose was a tourist who'd gotten lost, trapped in a (nonexistent) tunnel on the opposite side of the (nonexistent) door Stoner had found at the base of the (nonexistent) stairs leading underground from the Ball (which didn't touch the ground)...

Stoner ran her hand through her hair and felt the inside of her face turn cold. "Listen," she said, "try to tell me what you're afraid of."

"The pit," Callie Rose said.

"The pit with the fog?"

"Yes."

There was a hard knot in her stomach. It shifted a little, and made her slightly light-headed. "Do you know what's in the pit?"

"No."

She felt a tap on her shoulder. Aunt Hermione stood beside her, gesturing for her to give over the phone.

"You won't be able to hear her," Stoner said. "I'm the only one who can."

Her aunt took the phone from her hand. "Callie? Listen, dear, this is Hermione..." She paused as if listening. But, of course, that was ridic... "That's right, Hermione. We've known one another before, but you probably don't remember....A long, long time ago.

I've been trying to reach you, but you're hard to get through to, Callie. Now, I know you're lost and feel perfectly wretched, but we can get through this. First we need your help, though. In your travels over there, have you come across our friend, Marylou?... Marylou....Well, perhaps you didn't catch her name. She about thirty-two, chunky build, dark hair cut short, dark eyes....A little disheveled, yes, that's the one." She nodded eagerly at Stoner. "We need to find her, Callie. Yes, it's very important..." She paled.

"What?" Stoner asked.

Aunt Hermione brushed her off. "Are you sure?" she asked into the phone.

"What?" Stoner insisted.

"Callie, try to be calm and pay attention."

Aunt Hermione covered the receiver and spoke to Stoner. "She's very young. A child, really. And very frightened."

"What did she say about Marylou?"

Her aunt ignored her question, turning back to the phone. "Think hard, now, Callie. What makes you think she's dead?"

"Dead?" Stoner squeaked. "She said Marylou's dead?"

"She thinks so," said Aunt Hermione. "But it doesn't feel right to me. I really believe I'd have sensed it if..." She listened, then laughed. "No, Callie, just because she's wearing black doesn't mean she's dead. Marylou likes to wear black....I don't know why, it's just a quirk of hers....Yes, I suppose she's a little different."

She hears her, Stoner thought. Aunt Hermione hears her.

"Callie, can you tell us where she is?...I know, dear, but anything you can tell us would be very helpful." She took the pad and pencil from the table and began to write. "I see. Yes, yes, that's quite good. You've been a big help. We'll be in touch soon. Thank you, Callie."

"What did she say?" Stoner asked as her aunt hung up the phone.

"She's seen Marylou. In the tunnels. There seems to be an abandoned room, a section which was once intended for a work room, I suspect, since there's a rest room nearby. But it didn't seem to her as if anyone had been there in a long time."

"But where is it?"

"She didn't know, poor thing. Callie's time on this plane was quite a long while ago. However, she did describe some landmarks. Maybe we can put them together and come up with something."

Stoner looked down at the rug. "Uh, Aunt Hermione, what does that mean, 'her time on this plane...'?"

137

"Callie Rose has been dead for more than fifty years. Caught between this world and the next. It happens sometimes, when a person is confused by death, or doesn't want to make the decision to go... The source of most, but not all, hauntings, you know. Some hauntings are purely willful and nasty. One wonders how some spirits can be satisfied with being so unevolved, doesn't one? Well, as on earth, so in Heaven, as they say. Or is it the other way around?"

Stoner felt like screaming. "Are you trying to tell me I've been talking on the phone to a dead woman?"

"Crudely put, but yes, that's the gist of it." She consulted her slip of paper. "Water, lily pads—too general. Boats. Where in EPCOT might one see boats?"

"Norway, Mexico, and the whole lagoon," Stoner said. A dead woman? She'd been talking to a dead woman?

Aunt Hermione scratched off boats. "Flamingoes. I imagine they're everywhere, too."

Stoner thought about it. "I don't really remember, but I don't think I saw them everywhere."

"That could be a clue, then." She consulted her list. "There's one more, but it makes absolutely no sense. "A steeple without a spire."

A dead woman was telling them to look for a steeple without a spire. A woman who'd been dead for a long time. More than fifty years. After more than fifty years underground, would she really make a reliable witness?

Not that there were alternatives coming out of the woodwork. A fifty-year-dead woman might be the best they could do.

"Are you thinking?" Aunt Hermione asked.

"Sort of."

"About the task at hand? Or are you questioning the evidence of your senses?"

"All right, all right," Stoner said. "I'm questioning."

Aunt Hermione sighed. "The analytical approach," she said, "was fine in Sherlock Holmes' days. It won't help us now."

Steeple without a spire? She tried to picture the buildings in EPCOT. There was Imagination, the big crystal. It could look like a spireless steeple. The Land might, with its conical shape and truncated lid. The Eifel Tower? No, that was more likely spire without steeple. Callie Rose wouldn't make that mistake. Fifty years ago people knew their spires from their steeples.

She was beginning to feel a little giddy.

Morocco had that tall, steepleish building. And China. And if anything looked churchy, it was the American Adventure. Very right-wing Fundamentalist. And let's not forget the Campanile in Italy. Norway had a genuine church. It had a steeple and spire, but Callie Rose might have missed it. And the Aztec temple that was the Mexican... "There are too many of them," she said.

"Then we'll have to put the clues together in different ways, like those terrible logic puzzles you're always trying to do but never finish and end up throwing across the room."

"They make me feel stupid," Stoner said.

"Of course they do. They make me feel stupid, too. That's why I never try them." She stared fiercely at her list. "This might be something. Steeple without a spire, boats, and water."

"Mexico and Norway, if she didn't see the spire in Norway."

"Steeple, water, boats, and flamingoes."

"Same thing." She hesitated. "Wait a minute. I don't think there were flamingoes in Norway. The water was inside, not outside." Stoner got to her feet in excitement. "Mexico. She saw her somewhere around Mexico." She fumbled around for her shoes.

"Stoner," Aunt Hermione said, "what are you doing?"

"We have to get her."

Her aunt put a calming hand on her arm. "It's the middle of the night. The park is closed."

"Right." She rifled through her brain and came up with an idea. "I'll give George a call. Maybe she can get us in."

"And then what?"

"And then...and then we'll...do whatever needs to be done."

Aunt Hermione shook her head. "You're always talking about having a plan, Stoner. Is this what you call a plan?"

That stopped her short. Okay, maybe she needed to think it through a bit more. But meanwhile she could line George up, and tell Edith. It wasn't exactly good news, but it was news. Callie Rose may have been dead for nearly a hundred years, but she'd given them their first break.

CHAPTER 10

"That was excellent," Marylou said, wiping her mouth daintily on the linen napkin he'd purchased for her at the U.K. pavilion. "You have very good taste, David."

"Thank you," he said.

"I only wish..." she caught herself on the verge of saying "you'd brought some real silverware instead of that dreadful *plastic* trash," but decided not to press her luck. The food *had* been good, though a bit too much of a good thing all at once, one dish tended to distract from another, but the wine had been a decent choice, and it would undoubtedly be tacky to be *too* choosy. Yes, David was definitely trainable. By engaging in simple food-talk, she'd found out enough to know that she was incarcerated in, under, or near Walt Disney World. She'd gotten him to tell her his first name, too. Didn't even have to simper much. She thought it might come in handy. The police would want all the information she could give them, once she got out of here.

If she got out of here.

He was looking at her in a shy, expectant kind of way. Now what?

David wondered if he should bring it up himself, or wait for her to give him an opening. But she might be hesitant, being the woman. The man should probably make the first move.

He cleared his throat.

"Yes?" She glanced at him, head cocked to one side in a most appealing way.

"I hope you won't think this is forward of me..." he began.

Oh, dear God in Heaven, he wants *SEX* ! What the hell do I do now?

"... but, well, you see, I've kind of guessed what you were getting at earlier..."

"You have?" Marylou squeaked in a state bordering panic.

He smiled. She was playing innocent. Probably embarrassed that she'd been so transparent. He took her hand. "It wasn't that you said anything impertinent or anything like that. Please don't think that. There's nothing to be ashamed of. I mean, most men wouldn't even have noticed, but I've always been—well, unusually *perceptive.* So I hope you won't worry about that."

What on God's green earth is he talking about?

"I want you to know right off," he said, "that I consider it an honor and a privilege. And I promise not to interfere with any decisions you make, as long as you let me see it once in a while. I might even be able to help with expenses, when things are going well for me." He laughed a little. "I mean, there is a risk in my line of work. Going to jail and all. I couldn't take a lot of responsibility, but I'd do anything I could, especially if you needed some special thing."

It? What it?

Marylou had a very uneasy feeling. She couldn't put it into words, but somehow, somewhere deep inside—in the general vicinity of her solar plexus—a part of her had a hunch about what was coming.

He was waiting for an answer, or a word of encouragement or something. "You're very kind," she murmured.

David grinned. "So we do understand one another?"

"Of course," Marylou said. "And I find your offer both generous and touching."

"We'll have to wait until this particular episode is over," he said confidentially. "This place…well, it's not exactly *fitting,* is it?"

He was after sex, all right. Well, that was no surprise. Sooner or later, they were all after sex. Young, old, rich, poor, all walks of life—sex, sex, sex until you thought you'd die from the pure unoriginality of it. "No," she said, "not fitting at all."

"And we don't want our child…"

Our child? OUR CHILD?!!

"… getting off to an unlucky start. That was my trouble, you know. I had an unlucky start."

He wants us—ME—to have a child? Me? Marylou Kesselbaum? A child?

She thought she was going to faint.

Marylou forced herself to appear calm. Which wasn't easy with mushroom sauce and white wine fighting for supremacy in her alimentary canal. As a matter of fact, serious curdling was about to take place.

"Did you have an unlucky start, David?" she asked sympathetically through clenched teeth. If she could get him off the topic of *their* child…

He looked at the ground, sadly. "Born on a Wednesday."

Yes, that explained it, all right. "I see."

"'Wednesday's child is full of woe.' That's what she said."

141

"She?"

"My therapist."

Ah, yes, his therapist. His revered therapist. "Well, then," she said, "it must be true."

"She's very smart."

"She must be."

"She helped me a lot."

"I can see that."

"That's why I'm doing this for her."

Marylou's heart stopped. "For her? For your therapist?"

"Ohmygosh!" David felt his face grow bright red. He broke his own rule! "I shouldn't have told."

It's a mistake, Marylou thought. It has to be a mistake. Because, if it isn't, I'm in the worst trouble I've ever been in. Even worse than that time back in college when I went on an M.I.T. fraternity weekend to the Cape with a blind date. At least I could take a bus home from there.

She stifled an impulse to look wildly for an exit. "You can trust me," she said shakily. "After all, we're going to share..." She swallowed to get the mushroom sauce under control. "...something precious."

"You won't tell?" he asked pathetically.

"My lips are sealed. Forever." Which will be more than a metaphor, if what I suspect is true.

He gave a great sigh of relief. This woman might be a pervert, but she was one A-okay pervert. "Thanks," he said. "Dr. T would never forgive me."

Dr. T. Millicent Tunes. He'd been in jail, and so had she. Maybe even done some parole work before, to make her resumé look legit. And, when she was nailed for the Shady Acres scam, Tunes had gone on practicing her craft behind bars—and no doubt looking for the perfect patsy, and having found him, primed him for this...

Oh, God, get me out of this, and I promise I'll keep Kosher for the rest of my life.

But if Stoner gets me out of this, I won't have to keep Kosher.

Come on, Stoner!

David was glancing at his watch. "Uh-oh."

Uh-oh? What uh-oh?

"Told my client I'd check in at midnight. I have to find the public phone," he said. He got to his feet.

This was not a good idea, checking in with the client. Time standing still was a good idea. The only good idea she could think

142

of. "Do you really have to go?"

He smiled. "I'll be back." He moved toward the door.

"David!"

At the panic in her voice, he looked around. "Yes?"

"Uh...don't be long." If I have to fuck him to keep Tunes away, I will. I'll hate it, but I'll do it. Thank God I have condoms in my purse.

"I won't be."

He opened the door.

He started through it.

"Remember," she called after him, "I'm the mother-to-be of your child."

* * *

George and Stape arrived around midnight, carrying some Xeroxed blueprints and a huge set of keys.

"That was quick," Stoner said. "I thought you couldn't get those before Monday."

"Stape remembered someone on her softball team who works in the County Court House. They broke in."

"That's great," Stoner said as Stape spread the blueprints out on the bed. "I'll have to remember to take up softball next spring."

"Comes in handy," Stape muttered. "Only two good ways to meet dykes—softball and bars. And since I'm not allowed to hang around bars any more..." She let the silence become heavy with accusation.

"Don't expect *me* to feel guilty," George said. "You're the one who made a mess of your life."

"Yeah, yeah." Stape searched through the lines and squares of the maps. "Okay, here's the tunnels. George, show me what ones they use now."

George took over, crossing things out with a large Magic Marker. What remained was a series of short, stubby arms that surrounded the perimeter of the active tunnels like rays of sunlight.

There were hundreds of them. It would take days to follow them all.

"Have you ever seen any of these?" Stoner asked George.

George shook her head. "They must have walled them up."

"Not all of them. Marylou's in one."

"How do you know that?"

Stoner shot a glance at Aunt Hermione, who smiled mysteriously. "You don't want to know." She turned back to the blueprints. They made absolutely no sense to her. "Can you find Mexico?"

George pointed it out. One of the little un-crossed-out rays ran from the basement of the pavilion to the edge of a 25-cent-piece-sized circle.

"What's that?" Stoner asked, as she pointed to the circle.

George peered closer. "It must be...Horizons."

"Nah," Stape said. "It's the Odyssey Restaurant."

"I should have known," George said. "Your favorite spot in EPCOT." She touched Stape affectionately. "Which isn't saying much."

"EPCOT's okay," Stape said. "Especially the Maelstrom. You been on Maelstrom yet?"

Stoner shook her head. "Things have been a little hectic."

"You gotta see that," Stape said.

"Don't give it away," George warned her.

"Right. Just don't miss it. It's cool."

Stoner turned her attention back to the maps. She ran her finger down the legitimate tunnel leading under Mexico. "Have you ever been down here?"

George rolled her eyes. "More than I'd like to say. When you draw after-hours duty, you have to go through them all."

"I don't suppose there's a door here."

"A blank wall. Sorry. If that's the place, they must get in another way..." She searched up and down the tunnel way. "But I can't imagine what it'd be."

"They have a toilet in this one," Stape said, tapping the map with her finger.

"That *must* be it. How can you tell there's a toilet?"

"See that drawing? Looks like a short bullet? That's the architect's symbol for toilet."

"Boy," Stoner said with genuine admiration, "you learn a lot of stuff doing aluminum siding."

"Don't learn a shootin' thing doing aluminum siding. Except how to cut yourself twenty-five ways to Tuesday. Want to branch out some day, so I'm taking a correspondence course in architectural design."

"Well, that certainly looks like the place," Stoner said. "But how do they get in?"

"If I was going to go down there," Stape said, "I'd dig my way in from the top."

"Perfect!" Stoner said. "But how could they do that without anyone noticing?"

"If you waited until very late," George explained, "you might be able to work between the patrols. It's really dark back there. And at this time of year, there are a lot of hours of darkness and a lot of time between patrols." She thought further. "You could even do some of the noisier work during Illuminations. Once they get going with the music and fireworks, you can't hear yourself think."

"They must have wanted this real bad," Stape suggested. "That's real shit work." She glanced up at Aunt Hermione. " 'Scuse me, Ma'am."

"That's all right, dear," Aunt Hermione said. "I've heard dirty talk before."

Stoner couldn't resist it. "She's been on Earth at least thirty-two lifetimes, and remembers most of them."

"No shit?" Stape asked, round-eyed.

"The French Revolution," said Aunt Hermione. "Now, there was a time for dirty talk."

"Jeez, Louise," Stape said. "I wonder if we ever ran into each other before."

"Very likely. We do tend to reconnect with the same souls." She held out her cigarettes. "Care for one?"

Stape blushed. "Uh, thanks, but I don't smoke."

"Oh, yes, you do," George said. "At work."

"Huh?"

"You come home reeking of it, Stape."

"You never said anything."

"When I'm absolutely convinced you've stopped abusing alcohol," George said, "I'll start in on the smoking."

Stape mumbled and grumbled and turned back to Aunt Hermione. "Can you read the future?"

"Sometimes. And, yes, you will stop smoking. Don't worry about it."

"If it's all the same to you," Stoner said, "I'd like us to worry about Marylou now."

Stape shrugged. "What's to worry? We know where she is, let's go get her."

* * *

"You're late," Millicent Tunes said.

David glanced at his watch. "Only five minutes."

"We agreed on midnight."

"Sorry." Crim-in-ent-ly. Was she tight-assed or what?

"You know how I feel about lateness."

He knew, all right. Back when he had therapy appointments...man, five minutes late, you apologize; ten minutes, you

145

have to discuss the underlying hostility; fifteen minutes and she's out of there. "I couldn't help it," he said meekly. "There was stuff going on."

"Stuff? What kind of 'stuff'?"

"Well, we had to eat, and..."

She heard the hesitance in his voice and cut him off. "There's nothing wrong, is there?"

"No, everything's fine."

"It doesn't sound fine."

"Really," David said, trying to conjure up enthusiasm. "Everything's under control."

"I'm coming over there," Millicent Tunes said, and hung up before he could reply.

* * *

"Gwen called," Edith said, popping her head into the room. "Subject just left the hotel. She's following." She popped back out.

"Who was that?" George asked.

"Edith Kesselbaum," Aunt Hermione said. "Marylou's mother."

"Exotic looking woman," Stape said.

"She's a psychotherapist," Stoner explained.

"Hey," Stape said, "wonder if she could do anything for Rita."

She was reluctant to leave. Suppose Gwen, following Millicent Tunes, got into trouble and needed her help. They wouldn't be able to communicate. If she started for the Dolphin now, she might intersect with Gwen and they could follow together.

But, of course, that was exactly the wrong thing to do. Chances were they'd miss each other. And, even if they didn't, Tunes might see them together and catch on to the fact that they had caught on.

On the other hand, a lot of time was going to pass while they were out of touch. She didn't like that at all.

Meanwhile, George and Stape and Aunt Hermione were waiting for her to get her stuff together and pile into George's car so they could breeze on over to Mexico and nab the villain in the act. If they were right about where Marylou was, and if that's where Millicent was headed, they'd all end up at the same place at approximately the same time. But if they weren't, if Gwen had to confront Tunes alone, and unarmed...And they knew, or at least had a pretty good idea, that she wasn't working alone. Marylou was probably tied up, or locked in. That mean Gwen would be unarmed and outnumbered.

Inspiration struck. "George," she said, "do you have your walkie-talkie with you?"

"Always," George said.

"Can we get one for me?"

"No problem," said Stape. "I carry one in the truck, for calls from the office. We'll just tune them to the same channel."

"Okay." She went to the closet and pulled down the knapsack she had brought with her for trudging around WDW on a shopping trip and not having to lug a lot of stuff by hand. "Here's what we'll do. Aunt Hermione and I'll go over to Mexico and see if we can find an entrance to the tunnel. You guys head for the Dolphin and try to pick up Gwen's trail. Edith can describe the car to you. Once you find it, stick close. I mean, really close." She dug through her luggage and pulled out a flashlight. "We'll keep in touch by walkie-talkie. If it turns out we're right, and Tunes and Gwen are headed for Mexico, we'll wait for you and all go in together."

"Why don't we just arrest her on the spot?" Stape asked, obviously into the action aspects of it.

"Because we may need to follow her to find our way into the tunnel. Once she knows we have her number, she'll stay a hundred miles away from there. If her cohort's expecting her and she doesn't show up, he or she will undoubtedly try to do something to Marylou."

"He," George said. "I'm betting on 'he'."

"How come?" Stape asked.

"The M.O. feels like a 'he'."

"Yeah, but how can you..."

Stoner felt like pulling hair—her own or someone else's. "Please," she said earnestly, "discuss it in the car." She suddenly realized something. "Oh, shit."

"What?" Stape asked.

"How are *we* going to get into the park? Does the monorail run after the park closes?"

"Not often," George said. "You'd do better to drive. Security will try to stop you at the EPCOT lot and at the gate. I'll call ahead and tell them you're coming."

"Right." This was going to be endless—getting there, identifying herself to the security people...

"I have another one for you," George said. "Could be a problem."

"What?"

"The Dolphin is only about a ten-minute walk from Mexico. You don't even have to leave the area. There's a guard on the bridge leading over, but if she can get past..."

147

"Damn!" Stoner sank down on the bed. It wasn't going to work out at all.

"Excuse me, dear," Aunt Hermione said. She looked up from the blueprints she had been examining. "I might have a solution for us."

They all gathered around.

"George, does this tunnel..." Aunt Hermione pointed to the blueprint. "...have an above-ground entrance?"

George examined it. "Yep. It's one of the ones the Characters use to go from one part of the World to another. They can go in at the Transportation and Ticket Center, or Cinderella's Castle, or..."

"And it intersects with all these other tunnels?" Stoner interrupted.

"Sure does. And I think I get what you're driving at."

"So this would take us right up to the abandoned tunnel, and all we'd have to do is find the entrance. Now, how do they travel within the tunnels."

"Electric car!" George shouted. "Let's do it."

"Give me a moment," Aunt Hermione said, and trotted from the room.

Stoner began madly stuffing items into her knapsack. Flashlight. Wallet for identification. A compass—she'd gotten lost so many times over the years, she never left home without one any more. Tissues—you never know. Briefly considered the handy-dandy metal camping knife, fork, and spoon set she always carried in case she got stuck eating at some fast food place like Kentucky Fried Chicken that supplied only flimsy plastic half-fork, half-spoon items (Gwen called them "sporks," though sometimes "foons" seemed more appropriate), but decided it wouldn't be needed. Rejected check book and keys to the travel agency back in Boston...wait a minute, keys might come in handy, you never knew when one would fit. Added a handful of Jolly Ranchers and hoped she hadn't put in any Cinnamon Fires by mistake. Hikers' first aid kit, yes. Small razor blade knife for clipping grocery store discount coupons, no, yes, you never knew. Hand cream, definitely not. Ticket stubs? Nope.

"Are you ready?" Aunt Hermione asked. She had changed into her dark blue work-out pants and gray sweat shirt and running shoes.

"Ready."

George had the pick-up revved up and waiting. She motioned Stoner in beside her. Stape gave Aunt Hermione a hand up into the open bed. "If you see anyone looking at us suspiciously," George instructed them, "whoop and toss beer bottles. They'll think we're just college students on a spree."

She threw the truck in gear and peeled out of the parking lot. "Reach under the seat," she said to Stoner. "You'll find the walkie."

By the time they'd reached the Magic Kingdom parking lot, she had briefed Stoner on the uses and abuses of walkie-talkies. "Remember," she said as she swung down from the cab, "keep it on that channel. Push to talk, let go to listen. Keep the volume turned down until you're ready to use it. Otherwise, you'll broadcast every bit of static within a 12-mile radius of Orlando."

"Got it." She stuffed the instrument into her knapsack.

"Stoner," George said patiently, "you're supposed to clip it to your belt. That's why it's called a *walkie*-talkie. As in *walkie?*"

"Oh, yeah, right." She looked at her watch. It had already been twenty minutes since Gwen called. They weren't going to make it.

"We'll make it," George said. "Wait until you see how Stape handles those electric cars. Better than bumper cars at the amusement park."

* * *

Marylou could tell he was angry even before he reached the door. The squeak of his sneakers along the floor sounded like rats being tortured. He kicked open the door and strode in.

"Something wrong?" Marylou asked sweetly.

"Aw, she's coming over here."

She felt her stomach seize up in panic. "Here? Why is she coming here?"

"She thinks something's wrong."

Something's wrong, all right. Lots of somethings, not the least of which is the fact that Millicent Tunes is going to get one nasty surprise when she sees me instead of Gwen. Such a nasty surprise, in fact, that she will probably act out in an unpleasant and very dangerous way.

Because I done that lady wrong, David me lad, and that lady doesn't strike me as the forgiving type, no way.

But how do I explain that to Mr. I-Am-A-Professional? "Well, darn," she said as calmly as she could. "I was hoping we'd have a quiet evening to ourselves."

"I don't get many quiet evenings when I'm working," David said plaintively.

"I don't imagine you do." She tried to sound sympathetic.

"Either I work 24 hours a day, or not at all."

Marylou shook her head and "tsked".

"No chance for a normal life."

"No medical benefits, either, I'll bet," she said.

"That's why I can't really take a lot of responsibility for the child."

Millicent Tunes is coming here to kill me, and you're talking about making *babies*? "I understand."

David sighed deeply. "I dunno. Maybe you should think about someone else."

Maybe we should think about some*thing* else. Like getting the hell out of here. "No, David, I think you're just fine. You have brains and good looks. What else could a mother want?"

"I don't know what my mother wanted," he said gloomily, "but I don't think it was me."

"Well, then, she was an utter fool." She touched his hand. "David, David, you've got to let *go* of her. She was wrong about you. She had her own problems. They had nothing to do with you."

He looked at her with such cocker spaniel eyes she was almost moved to pity him. Except for the fact that he had kidnapped her and was holding her here to be slaughtered.

"There's one thing that troubles me a little," she said. She might blow it, but she had to try. It couldn't get any worse. She couldn't get away, death was approaching even as she spoke, and Stoner had obviously fallen through a hole in the Cosmos. "Can we speak openly?"

"Sure," he said. "We don't have any secrets from one another."

If she hadn't been looking death in the face, she might have laughed at that one. "It's about your therapist. Dr. T?"

"I shouldn't have told you that," he said quickly.

"And I promise you it'll go right out of my head as soon as we finish this little chat." She cleared her throat. "She hired you to do this, am I right?"

He nodded.

"It wasn't you who brought it up, was it? I mean, you didn't offer to 'do a job' for her or anything?"

David screwed his eyebrows together and tried to remember. He thought she had...but maybe he had..."I think," he said, "I offered to help her out if I ever could. You know, in a general kind of way."

"And she took you right up on it."

"It was some time later, but, yeah, she got in touch with me..."

Marylou chose her words very carefully. "Has it ever occurred

150

to you that that was just a teeny bit unethical?"

"Huh?"

"To use you to commit a crime. I don't expect you to have memorized the ethical standards for psychiatrists..."

"She's a psychologist," he corrected.

"Okay, for psychologists. But I can assure you, what your therapist is doing is definitely on the edge, if not downright..."

There was a tap on the door.

"She's here," David said, jumping to his feet.

Marylou's heart began beating out the accompaniment to a rap song.

* * *

Stape's driving gave a whole new meaning to the word "careen." Stoner hoped she never had to ride passenger with her in any vehicle whose possible speed exceeded 40 mph.

The tunnels were spotlessly clean, shiny with tile, and filled with echoes. They passed closed door after closed door, with exotic names like "laundry," and "seamstresses," and "costumes," and "make-up, and "dressing room, men," and "dressing room, women." Stoner wondered if Annette Funicello had a private room, or if she was lumped in with "Mouseketeers." It reminded her of being back stage at a theater. Not that she'd even really been back stage at a theater, but it was what she'd always imagined it would look like.

Aunt Hermione was up front, following the map and generally having a ball. It annoyed Stoner a little. After all, this was a very, very dangerous thing they were doing. And here was her aunt acting as if it was nothing more than a thrilling day at the beach. Of course, it could be that Aunt Hermione already knew how it would end, and that there was nothing to worry about. That would be a comforting thought. More likely, she was just experiencing it as one more ride on the roller coaster of this lifetime.

Please, please, please Stoner prayed to whatever gods might be listening. Let us be on time.

They were approaching the outer reaches of the tunnels. Tile walls giving way to concrete. Fewer doors, only "general maintenance."

I'll even pray to the patriarchal gods, she thought, if they'll get us there.

Actually, given the level of technology in WDW, the patriarchal gods were probably the ones to pray to. Oh, Great Microchip, God of the Computer. Great Narrowbeamlight, God of the Laser. God of

151

the Machine, God of Gods...

They rounded a corner.

A blank wall.

Stape slammed on the brakes. The car shuddered to a stop and died. "Looks like the end of the line," she said.

George grabbed the blueprints. "Okay," she said. She pointed to a door in the left-hand wall. "There's a flight of stairs through that door. It'll take you up into the kitchen of the Odyssey. Go out the back door, not through the restaurant. That'll place you almost in the back yard of Mexico. Try not to make too much noise. There aren't a lot of security guards this time of night, but there are some. You don't want to waste time explaining, or maybe get kicked out."

"What about you?" Stoner asked.

"Stape and I will arrange for police back-up."

"Alert the guards on the grounds, too," Stoner said. "They're closer. Is there a way you can do that without broadcasting over the walkie-talkies? We don't want to take the chance of being heard."

George nodded. "There's a code, sounds just like static. It tells them to check in from the nearest secure spot. Then we'll come right back here. Okay?"

"Okay."

"Good luck, guys," Stape said. She spun the car around in a perfect, wall-scraping circle, and tore back down the tunnel.

The stairwell was narrow and dimly lit. Stoner swung her knapsack onto her back, flicked on her flashlight, and started to climb. Part way up, she looked back. "You okay, Aunt Hermione?"

"Just fine." Her aunt, despite her age, despite her smoking, sounded less out of breath than Stoner felt.

"Are you sure?"

"I work out, remember? You don't."

"Oh." She was near the top. A door. She pushed it open, and stepped into the kitchen of the Odyssey Restaurant.

Dark and deserted kitchens at night, she realized, are among the eeriest places on earth. Pale blue light, as if from the moon, flooded the room. Chrome sinks and stoves and various unidentifiable appliances stood silent and hard and menacing. They seemed to sleep.

"Do you see a back door?" she whispered.

Her aunt pointed to her left.

Stoner crept toward it.

"The place is deserted," Aunt Hermione said. "Why are you skulking."

"I don't want to wake the appliances."

Aunt Hermione giggled. "And you think I'm crazy for talking to Spirits."

"I don't think you're crazy."

"Yes, you do. Are we going to stay here and argue all night?"

Stoner sighed and continued on to the door. She pushed it open and prayed she hadn't set off any alarms.

There may have been moonlight in the kitchen, but it didn't come from any moon. Outside, the night was black as tar. Even the faint lights from the pavilions seemed closed in on themselves. The darkness in between was viscous, heavy.

The top of the Aztec Temple was like a pale, flickering candle. Pink sandstone barely visible over the jungle vegetation. They started toward it, picking their way through the undergrowth.

The silence was unearthly. The birds were quiet. Even the waves on the lagoon seemed to be asleep. She glanced back, toward Spaceship Earth. The massive sphere hovered over EPCOT like an approaching planet. The aluminum triangles that made up its skin glowed pale pink and blue and purple against the velvet blackness of space. A tiny crescent moon floated above it, small as an eyelash against the leviathan's mass.

Spaceship Earth appeared to smile. And wait.

Aunt Hermione touched her shoulder. "It's all right," she said. "It doesn't mean you any harm."

"I know," Stoner said. But she wasn't so sure.

She turned back to Mexico.

They pushed forward until the back of the building came into view. Bushes and shrubs nearly hid the exit. A couple of boats bobbed gently in the backwater stream that led out of and back into the pavilion. Stoner held back, crouching behind a thick-trunked palm tree, Aunt Hermione in her shadow.

No one in sight. No sound.

And no hint as to where the tunnel entrance might be. If there was a tunnel. With an entrance. And it was the right one.

She wondered if it would be safe to turn on her flashlight. Without it, they were going to have to crawl around on the ground and feel for a door. And who knew what kind of other things were crawling around on the same ground?

Stoner shuddered. She recalled a time, when she was a child, when the thought of scooting around on a dark lawn filled with small alive things would have given her a shivery thrill. Not any more. That was probably what growing up meant. You changed

153

your attitude toward small alive things in the dark. Or maybe you just changed your attitude toward fear.

She realized she was killing time, not wanting to step into the open. And time was the last thing they had to kill. She turned back to Aunt Hermione. "Let's go."

They circled the clearing, quickly checking the walls of the Temple, pressing and peering.

Nothing. But she hadn't really expected to find anything there. She was sure the entrance would be in the ground.

Unfortunately, the ground was pitch black and open. As soon as she turned on her flashlight, they'd be visible to anyone walking over the bridge or along the pathway. Groping seemed to be the way to go for the moment.

Stoner got down on her hands and knees and felt her way along the grass, working from the outside of the circle in. Just like they told you to in those lost-ball-in-the-field questions on kids' I.Q. tests. Or was it from the inside out?

The grass was damp and icky with congealed humidity. It soaked through the knees of her jeans and the toes of her sneakers. Really unpleasant.

Something live squiggled out from underneath her hand. It was slimy.

Worms, she told herself. Nothing but worms. They can't hurt you. You used to keep them in your pockets, remember?

Goddess, I was a disgusting kid.

She sensed something ahead of her in the darkness. A lump of darker darkness inside the already very dark darkness. She couldn't make it out.

Approach or withdraw? I'm open to suggestions.

It didn't seem to be moving. If it was just a rock or an old tree stump or something, she was going to feel pretty silly.

And if she didn't quit futzing around and take a few risks, Mary lou was going to be pretty dead.

She reached out toward the object. Touched it hesitantly.

It was firm but soft. And warm.

It was a human body.

CHAPTER 11

Two days, more or less, of careful searching hadn't unearthed any magic ways out of here. She wasn't about to find one in the few frantic seconds she had left. Still, Marylou did a quick scan of the walls, hoping to notice a crack she'd overlooked that might be a door, an unevenness of cement that might hide a window. That voice she had heard yesterday—was it only yesterday?—where had it come from? Or was it only her mind playing tricks, a figment of her own imagination?

The quick, sharp tap of high heels on cement. Millicent Tunes for sure. Who else but the elegant Tunes would visit a prisoner in a cement tunnel cell wearing high heels?

May she develop shin splints.

If I suck in my cheeks, pull my hat down over my face, maybe she won't recognize me.

Sure. She'll think I'm who I'm supposed to be, Gwen.

I look about as much like Gwen Owens as...as...well, as nothing.

The doorknob turned. Slowly.

Oh, for Heaven's sake, cut the dramatic tension and get on with it.

The door opened.

Millicent Tunes stepped into the room, a superior smile on her face. Her cold, hard eyes circled the room, came to light on Marylou, and froze.

"You!" she gasped.

"Surprise!" Marylou said. She forced a grin. "I see you still have a flair for a turn of phrase."

Tunes whirled around to confront David. "What the *hell* are you up to?"

"Huh?"

"Are you trying to pull a fast one?"

David peered around Tunes' shoulder, as if expecting to see an empty room, or a stranger in Marylou's place.

"Well?" Millicent Tunes demanded.

David frowned. "Well, what?"

"What did you do with her?"

155

"She's right *there*." David pointed to Marylou. "Where you told me to put her. Look, I think we should talk about this. I've had some second…"

Millicent Tunes struck her forehead. "I can't believe it!"

"You think *you* have problems," Marylou said. "You should try it from *my* vantage point."

David was looking from one to the other in a completely bewildered way. "I don't get this."

"*You got the wrong one!*" Millicent screeched, grabbing David by the collar. "*You stupid, idiotic, insignificant little man!*"

"Now, just a damn minute," Marylou said. "That is very unprofessional behavior, even if you weren't his therapist, which I happen to know you were. I won't even go into the ethics of *that*. But, leaving ethics aside for the moment, this man has done his level best to carry out your instructions. It's not his fault if you were vague, ambiguous, or otherwise unclear."

"Oh, shut up," Millicent said.

"I will not," said Marylou, really angry now. "There is *never, never* an excuse for rude or abusive behavior."

Tunes took a pistol from her purse and tossed it toward David. "Kill her," she ordered, and started from the room.

David caught the gun and looked at it. "I have my own piece," he said. "A lot better than this one. This is a Nancy Reagan Special. It might be okay for the bedside table, but…"

"I don't *care* whose gun you use," Millicent barked, snatching her gun and returning it to her handbag. "Just *kill* the bitch."

"Excuse me," Marylou said. "I really do have to object to your language. I was led to believe at one time that you considered yourself a feminist. Well, let me assure you that calling another woman a *bitch* is certainly not femin…"

"If you don't shut your mouth," Millicent Tunes said to her, "I'll kill you myself."

Okay, Marylou told herself, settle down. With David you might have half a chance. With *this* walking frustrated, premenstrual mess, you're dead meat. "Sorry," she said, and—just to release any built-up and potentially dangerous inner tension—muttered "Politically incorrect" under her breath.

"What are you waiting for?" Tunes demanded of David.

"I want to know what's going on."

Millicent was turning pink with rage. "It's none of your business what's going on. I told you to kill her, so kill her."

"I don't know…" David began.

Millicent Tunes turned all sweet and reasonable. "David," she said in a cajoling voice, "you know you have a problem with follow-through. We discussed it in your therapy. You get yourself into things, and then have trouble finishing them."

He began to turn the color of a particularly vivid sunset.

"Especially with sex, but also in your business ventures..."

His eyes were taking on that glittery look.

Marylou didn't like the looks of it. He was about to go toxic, and that was the last thing she needed. She needed him to be reachable, and capable of functioning in a directed manner. She cleared her throat. "If I may try to shed some light here..."

"You may not," Tunes snapped.

"Let her talk," David said in an unexpectedly firm voice.

Millicent Tunes was startled into momentary silence.

"Thank you," said Marylou. "You see, David, my friend Stoner was instrumental in..." She hesitated. David probably wasn't going to be real positively impressed with this. But it was the only chance she had. Treat him with respect. It might give her an edge over Tunes. "She was instrumental in having Millicent Tunes arrested for using a mental hospital as a front for helping hardened criminals to escape from the country. People with money. Lots of money. People who would have been invited to dinner at the White House under the Reagan-Bush administrations. She wouldn't have lifted a finger to help you or me. Oh, no. Millicent Tunes was in it for herself and herself alone, right from the start."

"Oh, for God's sake," Millicent said with a heavy sigh.

David drew his larger, more business-like and professional gun from a shoulder holster, cleverly concealed beneath his sweat shirt. "I told you," he said through clenched teeth, "I wanted to hear this."

Marylou had never been so glad to see an instrument of violence in her life. "That's a very impressive piece," she said. "I hope you have a permit for it."

He jerked the barrel of the gun a few millimeters toward her. "Are you going to finish this up, or not?"

Oops. "Well, apparently," Marylou went on quickly, "Dr. Tunes has been brooding over her arrest, holding a grudge even though it was she who was in the wrong from the start. Very neurotic." She thought for a moment. "Of course, Stoner did present herself in an untrue light, so she may have a teeny right to resent it, but certainly not to this extent."

Now David was pointing the gun at *her*. "Are you going to take all night?"

"No, no, of course not. Well, apparently she—Tunes, that is—has been hell-bent on revenge ever since. So she arranged to have you kidnap me—or, rather, Gwen Owens—knowing this would make Stoner terribly anxious and unhappy. But she didn't do an adequate job describing Gwen, so you got me instead."

"You said grab the lover," David said to Tunes, puzzled.

"And you didn't, did you?" Millicent Tunes sneered.

"They were *acting* like lovers," he said. "All cozy and kissy at the Luau, and then they had a fight in the Communicore…"

"Sometimes people who aren't lovers have arguments," Tunes said. Her voice was heavy on the sarcasm.

"Not like this," David said.

"That's true," Marylou put in. "This was the kind of argument lovers have. Or very old friends."

He scowled at her. "Then who *are* you?"

"My name is Marylou," she said. "Marylou Kesselbaum. But, other than that, everything I told you was the truth. And I didn't exactly lie about my name, did I? I just let you go on thinking what you were thinking, that's all. Hardly the same as *lying*."

"*Now* do you know what you wanted to know?" Millicent asked.

"What were you going to have me do with the other one?"

"Wait until that McTavish woman arrived, and kill them both, of course."

"Of course," said Marylou.

"Wait a minute," David said. "When I said I'd do this snatch, you didn't say anything to me about *killing*."

Millicent Tunes shook her head wearily. "If it's *too much* for the little man, I'll do it myself."

Marylou couldn't be certain, but she had the feeling calling David a Little Man wasn't a real good idea. Maybe it was the tight white line that was forming around his mouth…

"But you had to get the wrong one," Tunes went on. The woman was relentless. "You'll have to take care of all three."

David seemed to grow more uncertain.

Marylou decided to take advantage of the opening. "Honestly," she said. "First you hire the man under false pretenses. Next you give him inadequate information with the result that he can't do his job properly through no fault of his own—and David's a man who takes pride in his work. Now you want him to make up for your mistakes."

Millicent reached for her gun and levelled it at Marylou. Her

158

choice? If I keep quiet and she doesn't kill me right away, help might arrive. On the other hand, help hasn't arrived so far, and there's very little reason to believe it will do so in the next ten minutes. If I do talk, I might be able to convince David to help me. After all, David and I do have an understanding of sorts. Besides, talking feels a lot better than not talking. "If I may say one more thing..." she began.

Millicent Tunes cocked the pistol. Her finger tightened on the trigger.

* * *

"Watch it!" Gwen whispered.

Stoner nearly laughed out loud with relief. "Gwen?"

"You were expecting maybe Eleanor Roosevelt?"

"I was expecting Millicent Tunes."

"She's gone to earth," Gwen said. She patted the ground.

"When?"

"Ten minutes ago. Maybe less. Certainly not more."

Stoner rocked back on her heels. "You found the entrance?"

"I'm sitting on it."

"Why didn't you say something? We've been looking everywhere..."

"I was afraid we'd attract attention. Besides, once you lose this trap door, you can spend the rest of your life looking for it. You should have seen Old Tunes crawling around on the ground."

Stoner grinned. "I wish I had."

Aunt Hermione was coming toward them, padding across the grass.

"How did she know we're over here?" Gwen asked. "Are we talking that loud?"

"She intuits it. Kind of like a dog." She felt excited, almost high. They were about to find Marylou. Granted, there could still be some danger involved. Probably would be. Probably genuinely risky stuff. At least they weren't working in the dark any more—figuratively, that is. Literally, it was extremely dark. Darker than dark. But they knew what they were up against, knew *who* they were up against, and knew they were up against it. And *that* was something she could deal with. Something real, something concrete. Not unknown voices and cryptic messages and nonexistent stairwells and bottomless holes... "George and Stape have gone for the police," she said.

"Good," Gwen said. "I was beginning to feel distinctly unarmed and vulnerable."

"I guess we should wait for them."

"Probably," Gwen said.

Aunt Hermione tapped her on the shoulder. "Stoner," she said in a low tone, "something tells me we'd better get down there, and fast."

* * *

"Wait a minute," David said. He took hold of Millicent Tunes' wrist. "We need to talk about this."

She brushed him off and turned her attention back to Marylou. "Get up."

"She's gonna have my baby," he said.

"Your *what?*"

"Baby. Child. We made arrangements..."

Millicent shook her head. "Fool." She gestured at Marylou with the gun. "I said, get up."

Marylou looked at her calmly—she hoped. "You're planning to kill me, aren't you?"

"I certainly am."

"Whether I get up or not. I mean, if I don't do as you say, you'll kill me right here and now. On the other hand, if I *do* do as you say, and get up, and we go somewhere, you'll kill me there, right?"

"Correct."

"So why should I bother? It's all the same, isn't it?"

"Gonna have my baby," David muttered.

Millicent cocked her pistol again. "I'll count to five..."

"I've never understood that," Marylou rattled on. "You see it all the time, in movies and TV shows...not Real Life, certainly, my experience of Real Life doesn't include daily exposure to violence and murder, only TV and movies. A person is about to kill a person, and they start giving orders to the killee, and the killee just blindly and obediently carries them out. Does that make any sense to you?"

"As much sense as *you* do," said Millicent Tunes.

Marylou frowned. "Too bad. I was hoping you could explain it—having a much closer connection to crime and violence than I, that is."

"Get up," Millicent said again.

David was looking at something up in the corner of the room, near the ceiling. "Dr. Tunes..."

She wished she could look. It appeared to be something unnerving. But she had to keep her eyes on the pistol. The pistol was definitely where the action was.

160

"Dr. Tunes...

Tunes shot him an angry glance. "Will...you...please...stay...
out...of...this?" she demanded through clenched teeth.

I should have done what she said, Marylou thought. If I were
standing now, I could make a lunge for the pistol.

"But there's..."

Millicent Tunes' arm flew up like a spring, catching David in
the side of the face with the barrel of her gun. "I *told* you to *shut up*."

"Well, *really*," Marylou said.

David exploded. "Bitch!"

"ALL YOU DAMN TRASHY YANKEES GET OUT OF MY
HOUSE!" The voice was loud and thickly Southern and very, very
angry.

Stoner heard it, sidling along the tunnel wall. A familiar voice.
One she'd heard...She glanced back at Aunt Hermione.

Her aunt nodded and mouthed "Callie Rose."

David pulled his gun and fired into the corner. Whatever he
had seen had disappeared.

"What the hell is the matter with you?" Millicent Tunes bel-
lowed. "Do you want the whole world to hear us?"

"If you're interested in my opinion...," Marylou said, and
caught herself. She wasn't certain, but she thought she heard—
through the confusion and echoes—the sound of footsteps. Running footsteps. Familiar running footsteps coming closer. Stoner
hadn't forgotten her. Stoner didn't hate her. She wanted to cry from
sheer joy and relief.

Not now. We have to *think* now.

Get their attention so they don't hear her coming. Give Stoner
the advantage of surprise from the rear.

"Look!" she shrieked, and pointed to the opposite corner.
"There it is!"

David and Millicent swung around, backs to the door, guns
ready.

Stoner skidded to a halt in front of the open door. There were
three people in the room. Two of them had guns. The other was
Marylou.

What to do?

The flashlight in her hand drew attention to itself.

A long shot, but they weren't exactly rich with choices. She nodded to Gwen, pointing her in the direction of Millicent Tunes.

Gwen nodded.

Silently, in unison, Stoner and Gwen counted to three on their fingers. They threw themselves forward.

Millicent Tunes turned.

Gwen rammed her head into Tunes' midsection.

Tunes went down.

"Huh?" David said, and started to turn.

Stoner swung the flashlight as hard as she could. His head jerked to one side as she smashed him in the temple.

The impact threw her off balance. She went fell on one knee. Pain surged up her leg.

A gun went off with a sharp "crack."

David regained his footing and headed for the door. Millicent Tunes scrambled to her feet and ran after him, shoving Aunt Hermione to one side and into the room.

"No point in running," Aunt Hermione shouted. "The cops are already here."

The door to the concrete room slammed shut behind them.

There was a sharp metallic sound like a key turning in a lock.

The lights went out. "Uh-oh," Marylou said.

Stoner touched her knee. It felt as if someone were driving an ice pick behind her kneecap.

He shot me, she thought. But there wasn't any blood. And hadn't she felt the pain *before* she heard the gunshot?

It was very dark in here.

"Well," said Marylou, "I certainly am glad to see you. Figuratively speaking, that is, since we have no light and the switch is on the outside of the door, which is locked. Trust me, I'm an authority on this place. Are the police really on the way?"

"We hope so," Stoner said. "Is everybody okay?"

"I'm fine now," Marylou said. "And yourself?"

"I think I broke something. Aunt Hermione?"

"Right here, dear. Insulted, but not damaged."

"Gwen?"

There was no answer.

"*Gwen!*"

No answer.

Maybe she'd gotten through the door after them. Maybe she was pursuing them down the hall, and they'd meet up with the police and Gwen would bring them back here and get them out...

She had a feeling that wasn't the case. "Gwen?" she asked again in a tight whisper.

No answer.

No, she thought, no, no, no...

She pushed herself up onto her knees. She didn't care how much it hurt. She scurried across the floor, feeling ahead with her hands.

And touched something wet and sticky.

"Oh, God," she said aloud. "Someone find the flashlight."

Frantically, she ran her hands over Gwen's body, searching for her wrist, her carotid artery, anywhere she might get a pulse. There seemed to be blood everywhere. Warm, thick...the room smelled of salt and metal.

"The *flashlight*!" she shouted.

"I have it," said Aunt Hermione. "Just a second."

"God, I think she's dead."

Marylou gripped her shoulder. "Don't panic, Stoner. This is no time to lose your head."

"I don't need platitudes! I need help!" Beneath the stickiness of her fingers, she could feel Gwen's neck, her artery, a slight throbbing. A heart beat. But it could be her own heartbeat. She could be choking Gwen to death.

She forced herself to sit back. "Where the hell is the *flashlight*?"

A faint yellow glow cut a circle in the darkness. "I'm afraid it's damaged," Aunt Hermione said.

It would have to do. In the sickly light, Gwen lay on her stomach, twisted and broken looking, like a doll that had been dropped from a great height. A thick pool of blackness was growing under her.

Holding her breath, terrified, Stoner slowly turned her over.

The blackness was all over her left side. Through the pale light, she could see it growing, like a gigantic amoeba. Desperately, she grabbed the flash light and shone it close to Gwen's shirt. Now she could see the blood pumping. From her heart? Her lungs?

Gwen's face was white, almost phosphorescent.

Through her panic she thought, blood stops pumping when your heart stops beating. She isn't dead. Dying, but not dead. Oh, God, ohGod, ohGod.

She felt Aunt Hermione's hand on her head, firm, encouraging.

Go to another level, she thought, and felt herself turn cold. Her emotions turned off. Her practical side kicked in.

She handed the flashlight to her aunt and shrugged out of her knapsack. "First Aid Kit," she said sharply.

Slowly, carefully, concentrating only on her fingertips, she slipped her hand beneath Gwen's shirt and followed the trail of blood to its source. There it was, just below Gwen's shoulder, a

163

chewed-feeling chunk of flesh like hamburger. Warm liquid pulsed over her hands. Not her lungs or heart, but the bullet had struck an artery—she slipped her hand over Gwen's shoulder to her back; the skin beneath was unbroken—and was still inside her.

Okay.

First, stop the bleeding.

"Bandage," she barked, and reached behind her. Marylou pressed a large square of gauze into her hand. She clamped it over the wound and pressed.

The blood went on pumping.

Stoner pressed harder.

Gwen gave a little moan.

"I'm sorry," Stoner said. "I know it hurts, but I have to do it."

The blood was still flowing. She took Gwen's hand in her free hand. It was limp and soft feeling, as if her skin and muscles were being drained of their tone.

I'm losing her!

She clamped down on the wound with all her strength.

Damn it, close!

Gwen whimpered.

She forced herself not to hear, not to let it penetrate.

The flashlight seemed to grow dimmer.

Stop the blood. She repeated it over and over to herself. Stop the blood, stop the blood, stop the...

The flow died to a trickle.

Either the bleeding was drying up, or...

She fumbled for a pulse. It was still there—thin, stringy, but still there.

Stoner held on.

The light was growing dimmer, shadows creeping back to reclaim the room. In a few moments...

"Antiseptic," she said. "And tape. Get it out and put it where you can find it by touch. We're going to be in the dark any minute."

"There are painkillers in here. Should we give them to her?"

"What are they?"

A pause while Marylou held the package up to what little light there was. "Anacin."

That figured. About as useful as an umbrella in a hurricane. But it might be better than nothing. "Do we have water?"

"Some wine left from dinner."

Stoner laughed a little hysterically. "That's great, Marylou. This is the perfect time to be elegant." She looked down at Gwen. Her eyes were closed, her lips parted slightly. Stoner held one hand above her mouth. Tiny puffs of warm air drifted out. "I think she's unconscious."

"Good," said Marylou.

"Not particularly."

"If I were in her place, I'd want to be unconscious. To tell you the truth, I'd just as soon be unconscious right now."

Stoner shook her head. "I'm not sure why, but it's supposed to be unhealthy."

"Well, should we try to wake her up?"

"I don't know." She glanced toward the door. "We're locked in, aren't we?"

"I'm afraid so," said Aunt Hermione.

"Try it, anyway."

Her aunt went to the door and rattled the knob. "Locked."

"Maybe George and the cops will get here soon," Marylou said.

"*If* they caught Tunes and that guy. And *if* they told them where we are."

"David might," Marylou said.

"David?"

"The guy. We have kind of a relationship."

The light faded.

"I wish my mother were here," Marylou said.

"I know what you mean," Stoner said. "I almost wish *my* mother were here, Goddess forbid."

"Yes, but *my* mother's a doctor."

"She hasn't practiced in years."

"I'll bet she'd know how long it's safe to leave someone unconscious."

It was irrelevant, really. Gwen needed more than just being conscious. She needed real help, and real help depended on someone finding them. Soon.

The light went out completely.

Stoner sat back on her heels, one hand still holding the bandage against Gwen's shoulder. Her knee hurt like crazy, sharply. She wanted to scream.

"Do you think anyone would hear us if we screamed?" she asked.

"I doubt it," said Marylou. "I certainly tried."

A twinge of guilt cut through her pain and panic. Marylou had been through a terrible ordeal, and in all the confusion no one had even asked how *she* was. "Are you all right, Marylou?"

165

"Fine. It wasn't the worst experience of my life, not compared to some blind dates I've been on. Of course, this one couldn't really be gotten out of with a phone call and a taxi, could it? How did you know where to find me?"

"You know that voice, right before we got here? The one yelling about Yankees?"

"Yes, I think she was here," said Marylou. "A mere wisp of a thing. I suspect she saved my life."

"She's a spirit. Disembodied."

"I thought as much," Marylou said. "Not that I necessarily believe in such things, but whether I believe in them or not, I am grateful."

Stoner felt someone touch her arm.

"Dear," Aunt Hermione said, "we really must do something about Gwen. I'm getting a very strong feeling she's…well, separating."

"Separating?"

"Her soul from her body."

Stoner could feel it, too. The energy in the room diminishing, as if being drawn out by a magnet. Flowing, dispersing…

"Don't you leave me," she shouted. She grabbed Gwen's face in her hands. "Do you hear me, Gwen? *Don't leave me!* "

She was still going.

"This isn't how it was supposed to be, Gwen. Damn it, you can't leave me. You promised, Gwen. Remember? We're going to go through lots of stuff and get old together and sit on the porch and rock and reminisce and argue about irrelevant details…" She could feel the tears streaking down her face. She let them fall. "Come on, Gwen. Please don't leave me. Please."

Aunt Hermione reached a hand across her shoulder and waved something in her face. "Try this, Stoner. It'll probably be more effective than guilt."

She took the small packet containing the cloth capsule. Ammonia. Good. Tearing open the packet, she crushed the capsule and waved it under Gwen's nose.

"Breathe," she muttered. "Damn you, *breathe.*"

Gwen took a shallow breath, then another. She jerked backward as the fumes stung her nasal passages.

"Okay," Stoner said. "Now stay with me."

And do what? she wondered. Nobody was coming to rescue them. Either Tunes and the man Marylou called David had escaped, or they were keeping mum. They probably had already

166

hired a slick lawyer, who was advising them not to admit to anything, not to mention this tunnel until the trial. After all, the four of them were witnesses.

But what about George and Stape? They knew what was happening. They knew about the tunnel. Had David and Tunes caught them, too? Or were they crawling around in the dark, looking for the trap door?

Nobody was going to get here on time.

Gwen whispered something. She leaned closer.

"I'm sorry, Stoner."

"No, Gwen. There's nothing to be sorry for."

"I messed up."

Stoner gripped her hand. "This isn't over yet. We'll get you out of here."

"I don't think so."

"Trust me." Sure, trust me. Look how wonderfully effective I've been so far. "Gwen?"

There was no answer. Stoner lowered her head close to Gwen's. She was still alive, but she'd slipped into unconsciousness again.

It wasn't going to work. There was no one coming. And even if the rest of them were rescued, it would be too late for Gwen.

She tried to imagine life without her. She couldn't. From the moment they'd met—before that, even, from the moment she'd seen that blurred, poorly constructed Instamatic picture of her, looking awkward and completely lovely—she'd known she had to have this woman in her life, one way or another. They could be lovers, or friends, anything. Anything so this funny, gentle woman with the fawn-colored hair and deep brown eyes that drew you in, this woman with the laugh like velvet and a touch that was both strong and soft—anything to have her there. Life couldn't be the same without her. Never the same again.

Gwen was dying, and there was nothing she could do to help.

"Aunt Hermione," she said in a choked voice. "She's going."

"Just a minute, dear," her aunt replied. "I'm talking to someone."

"I *need* you, Aunt..."

"Quiet," Marylou said. "She's getting an idea."

There was a silence. Stoner couldn't think of anything to say. It was over.

"I see," she heard Aunt Hermione say. "Well, it's worth a try."

Her aunt crawled forward, crushing the remains of an ammonia capsule under her hand and sending up a weak wave of fumes that momentarily overwhelmed the smell of blood.

"I have a suggestion," Aunt Hermione said. "If we can get to Callie's side, it might keep Gwen alive until help arrives. Kind of a state of suspended animation, such as Eastern Mystics use."

"I don't know…"

"Of course you don't. Nobody *knows* anything, really. But we can try."

Yeah, they could try. Right now she'd try anything. She'd settle for conjuring up the Virgin Mary and begging her to ask her Beloved Son to take care of it. She'd go to church for the rest of her life. Hell, she'd even make a pact with the devil if she had to. It was crazy, but it was something.

"What do we have to do?"

"Nothing."

"Nothing?"

"That's right," her aunt said. "And that's going to be extremely hard for you. We have to do absolutely nothing."

"We're doing nothing now."

"We're doing a great deal now. We're talking, and thinking, and intending. We're holding the cells of our bodies together. Our internal organs are functioning at break-neck speed. We have to let go of all that and…well, drift. Cast ourselves on the Cosmos."

"That doesn't make any sense," Stoner said. She wondered if Gwen was still breathing, or if…

"Because you're *thinking*. If this is going to work, you must absolutely stop thinking. Imagine you're…well, letting yourself drop off to sleep."

"Maybe if we all had a bit of wine," Marylou suggested.

"No wine. Too unpredictable. We could end up anywhere."

"I get it!" Marylou said. "It's like *Star Trek*. We're going into the transporter."

"Yes," said Aunt Hermione, "that's a good analogy. Why don't you go first?"

"Okey-doke. See you on the other side."

Marylou grew silent. It was quiet in the room. Very quiet. It seemed to turn a shade cooler.

"She's over," said Aunt Hermione. "Now you, Stoner."

She tried to imagine a blank mind and couldn't.

"Stoner," her aunt said. "Look over my way."

She turned in the direction of her aunt's voice.

Aunt Hermione slapped her hard across the face.

Startled, she went blank.

She came to lying on her back, on the ground. The earth was rich and crumbly beneath her. The air was sweet with the odor of orange blossoms. Warm sunlight poured down, caressing her skin.

Stoner opened her eyes. Aunt Hermione was kneeling above her.

"I'm terribly sorry I had to do that," the older woman said. "But it was the only way to stop you thinking. An old Zen trick."

"You didn't hurt me." She sat up. Her face didn't hurt. Her knee didn't hurt. Nothing hurt.

They were in the middle of an orange grove. Straight lines of trees extended in every direction. Perfect trees with deep green leaves and bright fruit and soft white blossoms.

"Where are we?"

"I'm not certain," Aunt Hermione said. "Wherever Callie wanted us to be, I suspect."

"Gwen?"

"Right here," said a velvet voice behind her.

She whirled around. Gwen was sitting on a patch of grass, her back against an orange tree, arms around her knees.

"I have never," Gwen said with a laugh, "experienced a ride like that." She looked down at herself. Her dress was spotless. "Looks as if they did the laundry on the way."

"There isn't any 'They'," Aunt Hermione explained. "I suspect you're dressed as you last perceived yourself."

"Well, I wish I'd perceived myself in a more everyday way," Gwen said. "I feel like a down right fool in Edith Kesselbaum's clothes."

Stoner reached for her. "You're okay? You're really okay?"

"I seem to be," Gwen said, taking her hand.

She was going to be all right. Stoner felt her heart grow huge. Gwen was all right. At least until they went back. Maybe, when they went back, Gwen would have...

But if they didn't go back, if for some reason they couldn't go back, she'd happily stay here forever, if it would keep Gwen alive. Wherever Here was.

And where was Marylou?

She turned to Callie Rose, and saw her for the first time.

She was about sixteen. Painfully thin, with stringy long dark hair. Her dress was a faded calico, the kind of clothes she'd seen pictures of in magazines. Made by hand, from old feed bags. Stoner guessed she was from a poor family, in the Depression.

"Hi," she said. "I'm pleased to meet you at last. My name's

169

Stoner McTavish." She offered her hand.

The woman took it tentatively. Her fingernails were torn and bitten. "Pleased ta' meet you. Are you going to get me out of here?"

"Either that or you'll have plenty of company. Have you seen Marylou?"

"That other Yankee?" Callie Rose asked. "That loud one? She went off eating." She turned to Aunt Hermione. "You said you'd get me out."

"And we will, Callie, as soon as we figure out how."

Stoner stared at her aunt. "Aunt Hermione..."

"Now, Stoner," the older woman said, "I'm sure it's just a technicality. I haven't actually *done* an exorcism before..." She turned to Callie Rose apologetically. "Sorry, dear, I know it's an ugly word. Would you prefer I use something less emotionally tainted? 'Removal,' perhaps?"

"I don't give a dern," Callie Rose said sullenly. "Long as you do it."

Aunt Hermione patted her hand. "Thank you, Callie. Now, I haven't actually *done* a removal or whatever, but I have assisted at a few, and I think I can remember most of the details. Quite simple, really. It's the intention that counts."

The air suddenly turned cooler. A breeze came up. In the distance they could hear a rumbling sound, like boxcars rolling slowly along a track.

Stoner shivered. "I know it's irrelevant, but I really wish I knew where we were. I thought we'd just kind of hover around inside the tunnel or something. Outside, at the very least. I feel like a character in 'The Wizard of Oz.'"

"Oh, I'm so sorry," Aunt Hermione said. "I know you hated that movie. Callie, have you any idea where we are?"

The young woman shook her head. "I was just all of a sudden here. I don't understand this place at all, and I don't like it. It gives me the heebie-jeebies."

Which is nothing, Stoner thought, compared to the impact you had on me. "Wherever we are," she said, "I think we'd better get back to the tunnel before they find our—uh—bodies. They might haul us away and we'd never reconnect."

"I agree," Aunt Hermione said. She reached up and plucked an orange and stripped away the skin. She popped a juicy section into her mouth. "One thing certain. Wherever we are is real. There's nothing imaginary about the taste of this."

Stoner tried one. The flavor was spectacular. Tart and sweet and sharp. She thought she could almost touch it.

A dark cloud crept over the edge of the trees, wiping out the blue sky like a painter covering blue with black.

We'd better find Marylou and get to shelter.

A loud, rasping warning alarm split the air. They must be warning the pickers.

"Marylou!" Stoner called.

"Over here." Marylou broke through the trees, scarf waving. She had taken off her hat along the way. Her face was flushed from running. "We have to get out of here," she panted. "Something really bad is headed our way."

"Oh, Marylou," Stoner said indulgently. "It's only a storm. We probably won't even get wet, since we're not really in body."

"Not the storm, idiot." Marylou looked back across the rows. Her pants legs flapped like flags in the gusting wind. "This is a...a..." Her words caught in her throat as the tip of the flying saucer rose above the trees and tilted downward, heading directly for them.

CHAPTER 12

"Hit the dirt," Marylou shouted, and made a dive for the base of the nearest tree.

Fascinated, Stoner stood in the cleared center of the row of trees and watched the object approach. It was a large white vehicle, straddling five rows of trees. Long arms protruded from its sides. It was spotlessly clean and new looking, and somehow very familiar.

"You idiots!" Marylou shrieked. "It's gathering samples. Do you want to end up in a Martian laboratory?"

"I don't think we're in any danger," Stoner said. She looked back to where Marylou, Aunt Hermione, and Callie Rose huddled together under the tree.

"Excuse me," said Marylou, "but I don't think you are someone whose judgment I care to trust on the subject of danger."

"Stoner's right," Gwen said. "There's something about this thing. We've seen it before."

Callie Rose was clinging to Aunt Hermione, her eyes round and dark as plums. "I hope it comes to you soon," Aunt Hermione said. "This child is terrified."

She thought as hard as she could. Something about the smell of the place, and approaching storm, the siren...She had it. "Horizons," she said.

Gwen snapped her fingers in recognition. "Right. We're inside the Horizons ride."

"And that machine is one of the robotic pickers."

"That," said Marylou, "is disgusting. Robotic pickers. And just *what* does it robotically pick?"

"Oranges."

Marylou looked down at the orange in her hand, shrieked, and tossed it away. The picker tilted to the side, sent down a mechanical arm, and plucked the orange from the ground.

"I think this one's on clean-up patrol," Gwen said. "I hope it doesn't read us as litter."

The robot seemed to study them for a minute, then began emitting a high-pitched "beep", which set off ear-splitting alarms in every direction.

"Maybe not litter," Stoner said. The robot continued to hover

over them, as if guarding against their escape. "But it definitely reads us as intruders."

"What do you suggest we do?" Gwen asked.

"Stay where we are. I think someone will come to see if there's a short circuit in the exhibit."

"Okay," Gwen said. "But has anything strange occurred to you?"

"Like what?"

"For starters, if this is just a ride, how come the orange was real?"

"Uh..." Something told her she had a hunch about that, and she didn't like it. She shrugged. "It's Walt Disney World."

"Very informative," Marylou muttered.

The ground trembled a little—real ground, too, she noticed, and the orange trees were definitely real—as if someone were running toward them through the real-trees orchard. She looked around quickly. They'd better split up. If they were about to fall into hostile hands, they had to make sure one of them could get out and find help. And it couldn't be Gwen. If she went back into her body, she was dead within minutes.

"Marylou," she said quickly, "get out of sight."

"No way," said Marylou. "I'm not being separated from this bunch again."

"I'll do it," Aunt Hermione offered.

Good. Aunt Hermione could move between worlds pretty efficiently, if need be.

Stoner nodded.

Her aunt took Callie Rose by the hand and slipped away into the grove.

The running footsteps came closer.

A woman burst through the trees. She was in her late twenties, a brunette, and wore a bright yellow jump suit. She was carrying what looked like a compact walkie-talkie, but didn't appear to be armed.

"Hi," Stoner said cheerfully.

The woman looked them over. "Who in the world are you?" she asked. She didn't seem hostile, just bewildered.

"My name's Stoner McTavish. I'm a travel agent. From Boston. This is Marylou Kesselbaum. And Gwen Owens. We were visiting EPCOT and made a wrong turn somewhere..."

"Visiting what?"

"EPCOT Center. Walt Disney World."

173

The woman shook her head. "I never heard of that."

"Can you tell us where we are?" Gwen asked.

"Mesa Verde." The woman held out her hand. "I'm Elaine, by the way."

Gwen shook hands with her. "You work here, then?"

"I manage the orchards."

"I like your harvester."

Elaine grinned. "Thanks. I designed this one myself." She reached up and patted its mechanical arm. The robot seemed to wriggle, like a pet dog.

"Did you say Mesa Verde?" Stoner asked. "Mesa Verde, Colorado?"

"Colorado?" The woman cocked her head to one side as if puzzled. "I haven't heard that term in years. Not since History classes back in school."

Uh-oh, Stoner thought. Here comes trouble. "Oh," she said.

Elaine turned back to Gwen. "You have an accent," she said.

"A little."

"I never heard an accent before. I've read about them, but I always wondered what it would really sound like on a real person. The language discs always sound so…kind of put on, don't you think?"

"Well," Gwen said, nodding, "I reckon they have to be precise."

"Reckon!" Elaine clapped her hands. "That's *wonderful*. Where'd you learn to talk like that?"

"Back home," Gwen said. "In Georgia."

Elaine laughed. "Come on, stop teasing."

"Really. I'm serious. I grew up in Georgia."

"There hasn't been any Georgia in 150 years. Not here in the former United States, not in the old Russian Territories." She stopped and stared at them, startled. "Oh, my."

"Excuse me?" Stoner asked.

"You're from Nova Cite, aren't you?"

"Nova Who?"

"You've been cryogenized."

"I've been called a lot of things," said Marylou huffily. "But never cryogenized."

Yes, that would work. Stoner nodded enthusiastically and signalled for Marylou to be quiet. "That's right. They froze us back in…the early 1990's."

"Before the War, then," Elaine said.

Stoner shook her head sadly. Damn, she'd hoped there

174

wouldn't *be* another war. "There was a war?"

"Sure was," Elaine said. "That's why we don't have states any more. Or countries, either. Most of the world's population was killed off, so there weren't enough people for boundaries to make sense. Then, when they started rebuilding, they decided overpopulation and boundaries were what caused the trouble in the first place." She looked at them sympathetically. "You really *are* lost."

"Totally," Gwen said.

"Tell me," said Marylou, "what's the food like now?"

"Marylou, for Heaven's sake!" Stoner said.

Marylou turned to her impatiently. "Well, I don't see *you* showing any natural curiosity. This is the opportunity of a life time."

Elaine laughed. "The food's okay. What did you have in mind?"

"Do they still cook Kosher?"

"I'm afraid not. Ethnic cooking sort of went out with the boundaries."

"In some cases," said Marylou, "it's a small loss."

They could be here for weeks, months. The things they could learn, to take back to their own time.

The trouble was, in their own time they could be discovered any minute. And if they were discovered *there* while they were *here* …

"Listen," Stoner said, "this is fascinating, but we have to get back to, well, somewhere, and we're kind of in a hurry…"

Elaine raised an eyebrow. "To Somewhere?"

"Actually," Gwen put in, "to Orlando. That's in Florida, or what used to be Florida."

"Well, that's no problem. You're almost there."

Of course. Just because they had traveled through Time didn't necessarily mean they had gone through Space. On the other hand, getting home through Time was probably going to be more complicated. The last time she'd tried it, she recalled, she'd had absolutely no luck whatsoever.

Sometimes Stoner wished she didn't lead such an interesting life.

"You can take one of the Shuttle vehicles," Elaine said. "They're quite efficient." She smiled. "Especially by 20th Century standards, I imagine." She turned and began walking away. "Just follow me. You can tell your other friend to come out now, too."

"Your sensors are very thorough, aren't they?" Gwen asked as Marylou went to fetch Aunt Hermione and Callie Rose.

"Yes. All our technology is efficient." Elaine sighed. "Sometimes I wish we could just muddle along, the way your generation did."

Gwen laughed. "Should we be insulted?"

175

"I hope not," Elaine said.

There was a sound behind her. Elaine turned, glanced at Aunt Hermione, started to turn away, did a double-take, stared, and gasped. "A crone!" Falling to her knees in front of the older woman, she took her hands and kissed them. "Honored one."

"Blessed be," said Aunt Hermione. She bent down, took Elaine's face in her hands, and kissed her gently on the lips.

"Blessed be," Elaine said. She got up, shakily. There were tears in her eyes. "I don't know what to say to you. I...we...You can't know how we long for the Crones."

Aunt Hermione smiled and nodded. "We do know, those of us who have traveled forward."

Elaine moved closer to her. "You've learned how to go forward?" she asked in a low voice, as if she were asking for dangerous information.

"A few of us have. It seems to come with increasing age."

"Oh," Elaine said sadly. "Then we'll never..."

Aunt Hermione smiled. "Never say 'never', child. Remember, in the Craft, anything is possible."

Stoner looked at her aunt with admiration and amazement. She might be only 5'4" tall, wearing navy blue sweat pants and a gray sweat shirt that used to say "B.U. Athletic Department" about 50 washings ago, but she looked as regal and wise as any High Priestess. In fact, it was as if all the High Priestesses from whom she was spiritually descended stood behind her adding their blessings and power to hers.

"Life is difficult for you here, isn't it?" Aunt Hermione asked.

Elaine nodded. "There are so few of us, and all of our traditions and herstory have been destroyed. Many of the old names are lost, and most of the ancient chants. Sometimes we seem to be nothing more than a pale imitation of what used to be."

"And we," said Aunt Hermione with a gentle smile, "sometimes think we are only a pale reflection of what is to come."

"Can you stay for a while?" Elaine asked shyly. "We have so much to learn from you."

Aunt Hermione shook her head. "I'm afraid not. We're not certain what our time frame is, but if we're late getting back...well, it could have serious consequences."

Elaine looked at the ground. "I understand."

Aunt Hermione drew inward to look for inspiration. "I may have a partial solution," she said. "Do you still celebrate Samhain?"

Elaine's face was blank.

"Hallowe'en?"

"I don't know what that is," Elaine said.

"That doesn't surprise me," said Aunt Hermione. "Even in our time, there were those who wanted to make the holiday illegal. Places where school children weren't allowed to make the decorations in the schools. Ignorant fanatics thought Hallowe'en was a celebration of the Devil." She sighed. "It was our highest holy day. I believe some of those behind the movement realized that." She thought deeper. "The Eleventh Lunation?"

"Yes!" Elaine said excitedly. "We know that one. The Festival of the Ancients. We'll be celebrating in a few days."

"Well, when you do, call on Hermione's sisters. We'll try to come through to you." She chuckled. "There are enough Crones in my coven to satisfy the hungriest of you."

"We will," Elaine said. Her face was shining. "But I do wish the others could have met you. It would mean so much to them."

"You'll have to give them my love," said Aunt Hermione. She reached inside her sweat shirt and drew out her silver necklace and pentacle. "And this for you." She handed it to Elaine.

The woman's eyes filled with tears again. "I'll share it with them all. We'll cherish it." Quickly she unzipped a pocket in her jump suit and tucked the necklace away. "If I'm caught with it..." she said apologetically.

Aunt Hermione nodded. "The more things change, the more they stay the same, don't they?"

Something beeped. Elaine reached into a pocket and pulled out a device that looked like a miniature Walkman without headphones. "0174 here," she said, turning slightly to face back the way she had come. In the distance, an observation tower stood out against the darkening sky.

A man's voice came from the device. "Is there trouble out there?"

"Some visitors from Nova Cite. They seem to have gotten lost. Can you call them a shuttle?"

"Will do. How many?"

Elaine counted heads. "Four."

"Five," Stoner said. She looked around for Callie Rose, who was nowhere to be seen. "There was a young woman with us."

"Funny," Elaine said. "She didn't show up on the sensors."

"That's Callie for you," Aunt Hermione said quickly, and laughed. "Always playing tricks."

"Didn't show up on the...?" Marylou began.

177

"Marylou," Aunt Hermione cut her off. "You were with her last. See if you can find her."

"When we get inside," Elaine said as Marylou trotted off down the row between the orange trees, "I'd be grateful if you didn't mention about..."

"Don't worry," Stoner said. She looked around at the orange grove. "It's a beautiful place. Too bad there isn't more tolerance."

Elaine nodded. "In some ways we haven't come far since you went to sleep. I hope you weren't counting on miracles."

"Not really," Stoner said.

"We've made some strides, of course. Mostly scientific and technological. For instance, we have no disease. We're immunized from birth."

Stoner felt a twinge of guilt. "I hope we're not carrying germs you haven't counted on."

"Not unless you've done some interstellar travel."

"I doubt it."

"Well, we don't have to worry about anything that ever was or is on earth."

"Not even cancer?"

"Nope. No disease, and no pollution."

Marylou and Callie Rose emerged into the open. Elaine waved them forward and started toward the tower.

"Then why don't you have any older people?" Gwen asked.

"Our immunization process doesn't last beyond the age of fifty or so. Oh, once in a while someone will live to almost sixty, but usually they die before then. I suspect there's something in the process itself that kills us." She gestured toward Aunt Hermione. "To meet a real Crone...It's a breathtaking experience."

"I don't understand," Gwen said. "If you know you won't live beyond fifty, why do people go ahead with the immunizations?"

Stoner thought she could answer that one. Like late-Twentieth-Century America, this culture—whenever it was—was age-hating.

"It's done to us at birth," Elaine said. "And we're told such terrible stories about old age and diseases in your time, no one really dares to object."

"But you must have rebels," Gwen said. "There must be small groups of people hidden away somewhere. It's a very large world."

Elaine shook her head. "Our sensors would find them." She frowned thoughtfully. "Though they didn't pick up your young friend."

"Callie Rose has—an unusual electromagnetic structure," Stoner said quickly.

"I wish we could learn from her. Secretly, of course."

Of course. If the authorities, whoever they were, found there was someone who could elude their sensors, they'd want to get rid of her before others learned her trick. The future, it seemed, would be free of every kind of pollution but pollution of the mind.

But there was no getting around the beauty of the place. The scent of orange blossoms and ripening fruit was heavy on the air. Even in the gathering darkness of the storm, the orange fruit stood out like Christmas lights. Apparently, in the future it was left to ripen on the trees, a definite improvement over present practices. She wondered if they had solved the problem of tomatoes. The thought of real, red tomatoes with genuine taste year-round—instead of the pink plastic variety, too soft to use as tennis balls and too bland to eat—came as close to a miracle as she ever hoped to get. "What are your tomatoes like?" she asked.

Elaine laughed. "Not like the ones you were used to. We've heard stories about them. When an entertainer is a complete failure, we call him a 'Twentieth Century tomato.'"

"And wisely so," Gwen said.

But something was missing. Stoner could feel it. She made her mind loose and hoped it would come to her. It did. "I don't see any bees," she said.

"No," Elaine said. "All our pollination is done by machine."

"My folks kept bees," Callie Rose put in. "Had a big old hive out in the dead pine. Pa used to say that was how come we had us the best garden for as far as you could row in half a day." She giggled. " 'Course, we had the *only* garden for as far as you could row, half a day or whole day. What he liked best was how the corn came out. Made the best squeezin's in the swamp."

"Squeezin's?" Elaine asked.

"Moonshine," Gwen explained. "Liquor."

The observation tower was fully in sight now. A small crayon-blue vehicle, looking like an overgrown bullet, hovered above the ground near a door. A man in white jump suit stood beside it.

"Hold it right here," Marylou said sharply, grabbing the back of Stoner's shirt and snapping her to a halt. "You expect me to ride in *that* ?"

This time Stoner was ready for her objections. "Either that or stay here," she said. "But before you decide, remember: there's no ethnic cooking in this place."

Marylou jutted out her lower jaw and glowered. "Dirty pool."

Elaine had approached the man and was engaging him in conversation, glancing back toward them now and then. She seemed to be having an argument. Finally her back stiffened and his sagged, and he stomped away.

"Men," she said, and rolled her eyes. "He insisted on taking you himself. Said you wouldn't know how to work the hover craft. These things were designed so even a child could fly it. You just follow the instructions on the screen. But try telling that to Mr. Self-Important."

"How'd you talk him out of it?" Gwen asked.

"The old fashioned way. Pulled rank."

"We appreciate it," said Aunt Hermione. "He might have asked too many questions. And we might have given him too many answers."

"I figured." She held open the door.

Marylou slid into the back seat. Callie Rose rushed to sit beside her. Stoner had the feeling a friendship was developing between the two of them. It didn't surprise her. Their temperaments were similar.

"I'll drive," Gwen said eagerly, and jumped into the seat behind the computer console. She glanced at Stoner. "Unless you have your heart set on it."

"Go ahead. You like computers better than I do."

"Love them," Gwen said. She stretched her fingers excitedly.

"I'm computer illiterate," Stoner explained to Elaine.

"And phobic," Marylou added.

"What's a..." Callie Rose began. Marylou cut her off with a jab to the ribs.

Gwen tapped the computer screen and an electric motor began to hum. "All aboard."

"Thanks for your help," Stoner said as she slipped into the back next to Callie Rose. "Maybe we'll run into you again sometime."

"I hope so." Elaine leaned toward Gwen. "The F1-key brings up the map. Just key in the coordinates and sit back."

Gwen gave her the thumbs-up.

"World War II, right?" Elaine asked with a delighted laugh.

"Right," Gwen said. "Kilroy was here."

"Bundles for Britain!"

"Keep your powder dry!"

The computer beeped and displayed, "Do you wish more time? Touch 'Enter' for 'yes,' 'N' for 'No.' "

"Just like those darn ATM's back home," Gwen muttered, and

punched 'Enter.'

Elaine offered Aunt Hermione her arm and helped her into the front seat.

"Thank you, dear," she said kindly, "but I'm not quite senile yet."

"Do you mind if I ask," Elaine began, blushing wildly, "the other women will want to know, how old are you?"

"Seventy-three years," said Aunt Hermione with just a touch of pride. "And looking forward to another ten." She pulled the door shut. "Merry meet and merry part."

"And merry meet again," Elaine said. She touched the pocket in which she had hidden the necklace. "Blessed be!"

She waved, and kept on waving until she was only a speck in the distance.

"Okay," Gwen said, and keyed up the map. "Next stop, EPCOT Center. We hope."

* * *

Gwen half turned in her seat. "What in the world is going on back there?"

Marylou and Callie Rose had their heads together, whispering and occasionally breaking out in giggle-fits.

"Nothing," said Marylou.

"Nothin'," Callie Rose said.

Stoner leaned forward. "They're teaching each other dirty words."

"Honest to God," Gwen said with a slow shake of her head. "This is worse than my Junior High class back home."

There was more whispering and giggling.

"Betcha don't cuss like that in front of your class," said Callie Rose.

"And I'll bet you don't carry on like that in *your* school, either," Gwen retorted.

"Shoot, no," Callie Rose said. "I'd be in hot water for sure."

"What I want to know, Marylou," Gwen said over her shoulder, "is why you're not screaming and trying to jump out of this thing."

"Simple," Marylou replied. "We can't possibly be hurt, because none of this is real."

"Whatever gets you through," Gwen muttered.

Stoner wished she could be as certain as Marylou. It felt all too real to her. Real, and confusing, and impossible.

Callie Rose and Marylou had gone back to punching each other and giggling.

"You know, Marylou," Gwen said, "you've missed your calling. You should work with children."

Marylou shrieked.

Callie Rose laughed out loud.

Stoner glanced forward at Gwen, who was watching their progress on her computer map. She was pale, paler than she'd been before. Dark smudges above and below her eyes gave her a hollow look. "Gwen, are you feeling okay?"

"A little tired."

This isn't working, Stoner thought anxiously. We've slowed it down, but she's still dying. "Aunt Hermione..." she said.

Her aunt reached back and took her hand. "We're doing the best we can, Stoner."

That wasn't good enough. Not good enough at...

Gwen leaned over to the window and looked down. "We're here, folks."

Walt Disney World lay below them, glistening in the sun. There were the turrets of Cinderella's Castle, and Spaceship Earth, and the monorail, and the Contemporary, and...

Something was wrong.

Stoner rummaged through her memory and retrieved it. It had been dark when they'd left. The deep of night. And even if they had moved through Real Time, it would only be dawn now. Not high noon. And that wasn't all. Everything below them was *too* bright, *too* colorful, *too* vivid. Like...like a cartoon.

Of *course* it looks like a cartoon. This is Walt Disney World. And it *could* be daytime. You don't *really* know how long you've been gone. And those certainly look like real people scampering about down there. Don't they?

"Where would you like to land?" Gwen asked. "I'm open to suggestions."

"We should probably get as close as possible to Mexico," Aunt Hermione said. "That's our nearest landmark. Can you handle it?"

"No problem," Gwen said. "I haven't watched all those reruns of *Star Trek* for nothing. I can certainly land a shuttle." She touched a flashing box on the computer console. The vehicle seemed to slow, and slid toward the ground.

"This is quite a ride," Marylou said. "Every kid in the park is going to be whining to go on it. By the way, we didn't find out where we drop off the car."

"There's a button here marked 'Return.' It probably sends it back to where it came from."

"Back to the barn on its own, just as horses used to do, before the automobile," Aunt Hermione mused. "Comforting to think progress has come such a long way."

The ground was moving toward them at a steady clip. A fast, steady clip. Spaceship Earth loomed in front of them, a wall of aluminum panels reflecting sky and trees and water.

We're going to crash, Stoner thought wildly. "Gwen, *turn!*"

Gwen held up her hands. "With what? This thing doesn't have a steering wheel."

Any second now..."The stick."

"No stick, either. I knew there was something I should have asked Elaine."

If she reached out the window, she could touch the side of the Ball, and they were still coming closer. Stoner pushed Marylou's and Callie Rose's heads down, and leaned forward to protect her aunt. "Cover your head!"

The shuttle veered, tilting sideways, its belly only inches from the wall. It turned a barrel roll and skirted the equator, reversed directions, shot over the top, and soared into the sky.

"Dern show off," Gwen said, peeking from between her fingers.

Stoner sat back in her seat. "Are you sure you can't control it?"

"Apparently I can order it to land, which I did, after which the computer's superior and obviously more playful intelligence takes over."

They were still climbing, up into the sky. The light grew brighter, whiter. Wisps of cloud and mist flew past the windows. She could feel herself grow lighter, lighter until she was floating. She grabbed for a seat belt and strapped herself down. Remember what Marylou said. None of this is real.

The sky turned black. The shuttle broke the earth's gravity and soared into space. Stars and galaxies and novas rushed toward them. They soared through the Milky Way like a bird flying through a comet's tail. Through her window she could see a space station, rotating slowly and silently in the darkness.

It's the ride again, she realized. The Horizons ride. There's the time-lapse movie of the growing crystals and...

Oh, God, here comes The City!

The shuttle changed direction, tilted downward, and rocketed toward the ground. It was dusk again, and they were headed for New York. The sky darkened and lights came on. Came on and came at them. The shuttle soared over roof tops, streaked between buildings. Spun itself at the walls of skyscrapers, to rise at the last minute like a daredevil Phoenix. The Chrysler building streaked past. She could see people inside the upper floors, looking up, startled as they hurtled overhead. She felt her heart pounding. It's just a ride, just a ride, just a ride…

Someone was screaming.

She realized it was all of them.

Then, with a bumping and banging and shifting of gears, the shuttle slowed. The console lit up.

"What'll it be?" Gwen asked. "We can land on the desert or under the sea, or in the space station…" She stopped and looked again. "Or inside EPCOT." She punched the screen with one finger. "EPCOT it is."

The shuttle gave a little shudder, turned, and shot off into the darkness of space.

Headed for home, Stoner hoped. Shortcut. Past Andromeda, Deneb, Antares. Just a shortcut. A secret shortcut. The fastest way home, really. Everything is relative, just ask Einstein, just ask…

Her mind trembled on the brink of hysteria.

A large structure appeared, outlined by tiny lights, suspended in the black, rotating slowly on its axis. They drew nearer. The structure resolved itself into a space station, the lights into windows.

"Uh-oh," Stoner said. "You must have pushed the wrong button."

"I didn't." Gwen gritted her teeth. "This bloody thing has a mind of its own." She pounded on the console. "A deranged mind, at that."

"There are no deranged computers," Aunt Hermione said placidly. "Only deranged computer operators."

Gwen glared at her. "I think you're enjoying yourself."

"Of course I am," the older woman said. "This is an adventure. There's nothing to be afraid of."

"You believe in reincarnation," Gwen muttered. "There's *never* anything to be afraid of if you believe in reincarnation."

"I suppose that's true." Aunt Hermione frowned thoughtfully. "I never looked at it that way."

Stoner glanced over at Marylou. She seemed to be doing all right. True, she and Callie Rose were holding hands in a kind of desperate way, but at least she wasn't whimpering. "You okay?" Stoner asked.

"Fine," said Marylou. "None of this is real."

"I think it is," Stoner said.

184

"It is *not* ! My reality says this is not real, and what *my* reality says is real for me."

Stoner decided not to pursue that line of argument. Besides, they had nearly reached the space station, and were slowly circling. A door in the side of the structure slid open, and they slipped inside.

"Welcome to Brava Centauri," came a booming voice from a public address system. "All passengers for the express shuttle to Jupiter and the outer planets please follow the yellow arrows to launch port C. Those going on to Venus, Mars, and the neighboring moons please follow the red arrows to Spacebus terminal B. Those remaining on Brava Centauri follow the blue arrows straight ahead to the main terminal."

They all looked at each other. "Now what?" Gwen asked.

"I think," Stoner suggested, "We should go to the terminal and see what we can do about getting back to Earth."

"Good answer," Marylou shouted in her best imitation of a contestant on "Family Feud."

They started forward. The blue doorways led to a long gray, sterile hall, with mysterious, unmarked, locked doors on either side. Just like the airline terminals back home. And, if they were indeed in space, the locals seemed to have solved the 0-gravity problem. Stoner dropped behind to talk to Gwen and Aunt Hermione.

"How are you doing?" she asked Gwen, regarding her closely.

Gwen smiled, but her smile was grim. "A little better. I seem to have gotten a second wind."

"You look awfully pale."

"Of course I'm pale," Gwen said testily. "I'm in spirit."

"A bite to eat might be a good idea," Aunt Hermione suggested.

"Yeah." Stoner looked around. There didn't seem to be anything like a restaurant on this space station. And she had the feeling they weren't getting any closer to the terminal...

All of a sudden, the word "terminal" took on a different meaning. Terminal, as in final, the end, ultimate...

Just a word game, but something told her she was right. That wherever this hallway led, going to the end of it wasn't a good idea. Not a good idea at all.

"Aunt Hermione," she said, "do you sense something wrong?"

Her aunt closed her eyes for a second. "Yes. Ahead of us."

"Me, too." She reached forward and tugged at Marylou's shirt. "Listen, we think there's a problem up ahead. So let's keep our eyes

185

open for a side door or something."

"Whatever you say," said Marylou breezily. "Problems are *your* reality, after all."

She moved more carefully, testing every door they passed. All locked. The end of the hallway was easily visible now, with corridors leading to the right and left. A blue arrow pointed right to "Main Terminal."

So they should go right.

If they could believe the sign.

Well, they were out of side doors. Not that she'd trust them, anyway. If one *did* open, they'd probably find an empty room with a table and a bottle with a label that said "Drink me."

So they had to take their chances with the choice-point at the end of this runway. That's what it reminded her of, those experiments back in Psych. 101 where you put a starving rat in a T-maze, and at the end of one arm is a food pellet, while at the end of the other arm is an electric grid. And if you make the wrong choice—zing go the strings of your life.

Now, really, wasn't she taking all this a little personally? This was, after all, Walt Disney World—or a reasonable facsimile thereof. WDW did not exist to destroy, maim, terrorize, or otherwise harm happy guests.

Except that she sincerely believed they had left WDW behind a long time ago. These places might *look* like WDW. They might *sound* like WDW. They might even *smell* like WDW. But they were definitely *not…*

They had reached the end. Everyone stopped and stood there, waiting for her to make a decision.

Why me? Why doesn't someone else make the decisions? Someone like…Marylou.

Oh, sure, that would be really smart, letting Marylou call the shots. Marylou doesn't even believe it's real.

Aunt Hermione? But *she* thinks all of life is one big amusement park, anyway. It doesn't matter to Aunt Hermione which ride they go on. And, until Stoner had gotten a lot older, or evolved through a few more lifetimes, it was still *very* important to her which ride they went on.

Callie Rose was young, confused, and couldn't make up her mind whether to be dead or alive. She doubted that Callie Rose would use the world's best judgment.

Which leaves Gwen. Gwen's sensible…except for the time she'd married that man they'd had to kill…but she wasn't looking very

186

well. In fact, she was looking very not well. Stoner suspected Gwen needed to keep her energy as close to her life processes as possible.

So there we are. Left up to good old Stoner.

She took a deep breath and stepped into the cross bar of the "T". She glanced quickly to the right. It looked like a normal, everyday airport terminal. Fast food stands, gift store, news stand. Ticket counters. It was tempting. Very tempting. But...

It felt too good to be true, like a trap.

She looked closer. Something strange about it. Something...shimmering. Shimmering as in dissolving. The wall, behind the Delta counter (Delta Airlines? In outer space?), turned porous-looking. Holes appeared. Black holes. And, here and there, stars.

Definitely not in that direction. She took a few steps down the left corridor. There was a closed door at the end. With an identifying sign that read "Greenhouses."

It gave her an idea. "Aunt Hermione, do you think there might be something in there that would help Gwen? Some kind of healing herb or something?"

Her aunt gazed at the door as if she might find inspiration there. "Possibly, assuming it's not filled with Martian kelp or some such."

"You'd recognize herbs, wouldn't you?"

The older woman sensed what Stoner was thinking, and patted her arm. "I may have had a hard time learning them initially, but I'm fairly sure I know what I'm doing now. At least I know which ones to avoid, so I'm not likely to kill her. And, if I find myself totally unsure, I can channel an ancient herbalist."

"Right."

Well, at least the decision was made. Motioning to the others to stay behind her, Stoner forced herself to stride down the hall and open the door.

She wasn't sure what she'd expected. Anything, she supposed, except what she actually found—a real greenhouse. Built like a dome, with glass walls, glass overhead panels, some of them shaded, some open to a pale blue sky beyond. Water trickled from overhead pipes or sprayed in a fine mist from ducts in the floor. Plants grew in tidy rows of what looked like a Styrofoam and sand mixture, which Aunt Hermione said was a popular rooting medium—something like vermiculite. Basically, it was a hydroponic set-up, and managed to support a startling variety of greens, cucurbits, brassicas, and good old tomatoes. Even luffa sponges seemed to be thriving.

"The Land," Stoner said. She turned to Gwen. "Remember? This is part of the Listen to the Land ride."

Gwen looked around. "You're right. That means we should be able to..."

"Find our way out," Stoner finished for her.

Callie Rose was wandering up and down the rows, her jaw slack with amazement. She saw Stoner watching her, and blushed. "Had a lot of these things back home," she said. "But these people don't have bug trouble like we did." She bent down and plucked a couple of ferny leaves. "Even got dill weed. And rough sage. We always stuffed the Thanksgiving turkey with that."

Aunt Hermione's face lit up. "Callie, when you lived back in the swamp, did your mother teach you medicinal herbs."

"You mean the Bible herbs? 'Course. Everybody's got to know that. We didn't have no fancy doctors 'n hospitals 'n stuff like that."

"What did you use for thin blood?"

Callie Rose thought very hard. "Mostly molasses and sulphur. Always had plenty of molasses around. We grew our own cane. But sulphur was hard to get, 'ticularly in bad years when we didn't have much to barter."

"In those years, what did you have?"

"Well, I recall times we'd settle on Kayann. And Life Everlasting. That was a good one."

"Kayann?" Stoner asked.

"Cayenne," said Aunt Hermione. "Red pepper. But I don't think I'd recognize Life Everlasting. Callie, do you see any around here?"

Callie Rose trotted off down a row of low plants and came back almost immediately with a bunch of tiny yellow flowers and three pods of bright red dried peppers. She pushed them at Gwen. "Take as much of these as you can," she ordered. "First one, then the other, and back again. That way you'll be able to keep more down. Black cohosh is good, too, but it tastes awful and makes you see things."

"Thank you," Gwen said, "but I'm having my fill of seeing things." She nibbled on a flower.

"What does that taste like?" Stoner asked.

"Green. And sort of bitter."

She looked around. "Has anyone seen Marylou?"

"I think she's looking for spinach," Aunt Hermione said.

"I saw something else good down there," Callie Rose said, and trotted back down the row.

Gwen was very carefully eating a red pepper. It made her eyes water.

Peppers, Stoner thought. Herbs, greens. It wasn't going to work. They had to get out of here, and get out now. Not that she was really certain where they were that they had to get out of. It looked like The Land, but it didn't. There was that strange, too-vivid, cartoonish look about it. But even if is really *was* The Land, they still had to get out, and then to find where they'd left themselves. And after that to get themselves out of *there*, and...

It looked hopeless.

CHAPTER 13

"I think we'd better get moving," Stoner said. Gwen did look a bit better, though it was obviously a tenuous better.

The question was, get moving to where? Not back to the terminal, certainly. They knew what lay in that direction. Terminal lay in that direction. Forward would take them—presumably—onto the Land. She tried to remember whether there had been anything terrifying or life-threatening or otherwise unsettling on that ride.

She sensed Gwen at her side, and slipped an arm around her.

Gwen leaned into her. "Stoner," she said in a low voice, "I don't think I can do this."

Fear gripped her. "Do what?"

"What we're doing. I just want to lie down."

"You can't, Gwen."

"I know, but I want to. I want to so much I don't really care."

She turned Gwen to face her. "You have to hang on, Gwen. Please."

Tears leaked from Gwen's eyes and slid silently down her face. "I'm really trying, Stoner. I'm just so tired."

Stoner pulled Gwen's face down onto her own shoulder so she wouldn't see her panic. "It's going to be okay," she said softly, stroking Gwen's hair. "We'll get out of here."

Gwen shook her head and put her arms around Stoner. She tried to embrace her but she was so weak… "I'm sorry," she said. "I'm really sorry."

"You have to hang on," Stoner said desperately. "Please, just a little longer."

Gwen looked up at her and forced a smile. "That's…what you said…before."

"Well, I mean it." She looked around. "Marylou," she ordered, "help Gwen. And don't let her pass out."

Marylou came forward and slipped an arm around Gwen's waist. "Pass out on me," she said to Gwen, "and I'll never cook anything but Kosher for you for the rest of your life. It'll be Passover at least once a week. Think about it."

Gwen managed a weak laugh. "Not Kosher."

"Kosher."

190

Okay, let's... Stoner counted noses. Callie Rose was missing. "Aunt Hermione, can you find Callie Rose?"

"I'm here." The girl ran toward them carrying a handful of gnarly roots. "This is good stuff."

Aunt Hermione took the roots and sniffed them. "Horseradish, ginger, and ginseng. Callie, you're a genius."

The young woman seemed to blush. "I was always good at findin' stuff. That's what my Granny said."

Aunt Hermione thrust the roots at Marylou. "Have her eat these as we go along. Not too fast. We don't want her to choke."

Gwen looked down at the roots. "You're...trying...to kill me," she said.

"Shut up," Marylou ordered, and thrust one of the roots into her hand.

Follow the canal. That seemed like the best bet. If they went in the direction of the current, it should bring them out at the ride entrance.

Are you serious? Nothing in this place is the same as it is in Real Life. We could come out anywhere.

Well, so what? It was better than nothing, wasn't it?

Besides, the Land was beginning to get on her nerves. The sun was too sunny, the greens too green, the glass too clean. No bugs. No litter of leaves beneath the plants. Viney things growing politely on perfectly symmetrical vines. Leafy things forming neat, compact heads. Interplanted vegetables and herbs doing what they were meant to do and sticking to their own allotted square foot of artificial soil. A place for everything and everything in its place.

Water bubbled and sang in the concrete canal. Clear water. Perfect water, of course, just like everything else here. Cartoon water. And beside it a perfect footpath, just wide enough for two, no loose stones or thrusting roots, no unevenness.

She trudged on ahead of the others, Marylou and Gwen behind, Aunt Hermione and Callie Rose bringing up the rear. According to her calculations, it should take them about three minutes to reach the end of the ride. From there, they could leave the building, circle around the Communicores, cross the bridge, and end up behind Mexico. Do-able, definitely do-able.

Except that they didn't reach the end of the ride in three minutes. They didn't reach the end of the ride at all. Hugging the canal, the path wound through more greenhouses, a fish farm, an area where seeds were being sprouted in plastic jars...and suddenly they seemed to be in a tunnel below ground. In dim light they could see roots. Thousands of roots. Giganti roots. Smooth roots and knobby roots and hairy roots and twisted roots. Transparent roots through which oozed a clear, thick, viscous fluid.

We're at the *entrance* to the ride, she thought. I must be leading us backward. But if we were going backward, we wouldn't be at the entrance, would we?

Some of the roots were growing. Slowly. With a kind of creaking sound.

It's a good thing this place is so sterile. I'd hate to run into a giant nematode.

A squawking, whistling noise caught her attention. The air turned warm and misty. It smelled of rotting vegetation. Now they were above ground again, in a jungle where water dripped from trees and gigantic dragon flies hummed like helicopters. Ferns drooped over the path. But it was still visible through dim light.

She glanced back. Gwen was still walking, mostly under her own steam, chewing on a bit of root. Marylou, silent for probably the longest consecutive run of minutes in her life, was dripping with sweat and gasping for air. It reminded her that she was having a little trouble breathing, too. Probably ought to slow down. In her anxiety, she was undoubtedly setting a daunting pace. "Everyone okay?" she called, hoping she sounded up-beat.

"Don't ask," Marylou muttered.

Aunt Hermione waved almost cheerfully as a monkey swung down from a tree and landed on her shoulder. If they hadn't been in Serious Trouble, Stoner thought, Aunt Hermione would be in her glory here. It was the Arnold Arboretum and the Boston Horticultural Society all rolled into one. Unfortunately, they were in Serious Trouble.

The jungle began to thin out. The light grew brighter and more intense. Very intense. Searing. The ground underfoot changed from green mossy stuff to sand. The air dried. The heat grabbed them in its fist.

Right. This is the desert section.

It was silent. Completely silent, except for a faint hissing as the light breeze moved the sand. Stoner looked around. The canal had disappeared. The jungle wasn't behind them any more. Ahead stretched nothing but sand and sky and searing sun. It seemed to go on for hundreds of miles in all directions.

Hundreds of miles.

And no Lawrence of Arabia in sight.

The heat sucked the energy out of her. She just stood and

192

looked at that endless expanse of sand and sun, and knew they weren't going to make it. Certainly Gwen wasn't going to make it. She didn't dare look back at the rest. She didn't want them to see that she had almost given up. She didn't want to see that they had given up.

Keep going. That's all you can do, just keep going.

Stoner forced herself to place one foot in front of the other and move. She hoped her stride looked self-assured and jaunty from behind. She had the feeling it looked exactly the way she felt—like some old half-dead prospector staggering across the desert in crazed search of gold.

Maybe, if she left the path and climbed a dune, she could see the other side of the desert. She motioned to the others to keep their places, and set off toward the highest looking one. Sand slid out from beneath her feet as she tried to climb. On all fours, she managed one and a half steps forward for every one back. This was nuts. She wasn't going to see anything, and would wear herself out trying. But she kept going. Mostly because she couldn't think of anything better to do.

Story of my life. Half the things I do, I do because I can't think of anything better to do.

So how is that different from anyone else? Isn't that what we're all doing, and calling it "life?" One day you look around and here you are, and you just go ahead and do it because you can't think of anything better.

She stumbled and landed face-down in the sand. Pushing herself to her knees, she made the unfortunate mistake of licking her lips. The grains of sand established themselves gleefully on and under her tongue, and scattered at random throughout her mouth.

That's what you get for trying to mix sand and philosophy.

She worked her tongue around and tried to get the worst of them out. What she really needed was to rinse her mouth. But, of course...

Of course. Even the jungle drippings had long ago dried from her clothes.

God, Gwen must be in agony.

She made herself glance back.

Marylou had taken off her hat and put it on Gwen's head. With Edith's diaphanous dress, it made her look like someone from the turn of the century. Ensemble by Kesselbaum. All she needed was a croquet mallet to complete the picture.

Actually, she looked pretty good like that. A little out of place, considering the circumstances. But if Stoner had tried to wear those clothes, she'd have looked as if she were in drag.

WHAT ARE YOU DOING? YOU ARE SUPPOSED TO BE GETTING US OUT OF HERE.

Right. Sun stroke, that's what it was. Causes inappropriate behavior.

She pushed herself to her feet and struggled the last few yards to the top of the dune.

Nothing but sand to the east.

Sand to the south.

Sand to the west.

Sand to the...Wait a minute. There, on the horizon, a subtle change in the topography. A kind of raggedness...

... and clouds. Definitely clouds. And mountains and...

She squinted.

... something moving?

Bison!

Yes!

They were approaching the Prairie.

Which, with the locusts and stampedes and grass fire, was not the world's most hospitable place. But it beat this one. And after the prairie came the farmhouse. If they could reach the farmhouse they could rest, and maybe get a glass of water. There might even be people there, who could help them out of this mess. The way Elaine had helped back there on...wherever it was they'd been.

Half running, half sliding, she came down off the dune. "We're almost there," she said to Gwen. "The Prairie. After that the farmhouse."

"What about the fire?" Gwen asked.

She had thought about that herself. Those of them who were healthy could outrun it. But Gwen? "It'll be all right," she said with what she hoped was true conviction. "We can get away from it easily."

Gwen smiled weakly. "You're a terrible liar, but I love you anyway."

"We have to try, Gwen."

"I know. It'll be an adventure. Kind of like eating roots."

Stoner touched her face. "Are they awful?"

Gwen covered Stoner's hand with hers. "A great incentive not to get sick." She looked at the ground. "Stoner, I hate to be a pain, but..."

"You could never be a pain."

194

"I'm starting to feel cold."

It was happening too fast. She didn't know where they were, or how they'd ever get back to where they'd left themselves, and even if they did there probably wasn't enough time left, and...

"We have to go," she said to the others. "Aunt Hermione, give Marylou a hand with Gwen. Just over this next dune is a prairie. There will be a fire. We have to outrun it if we can. And there are animals, bison. We can expect them to stampede ahead of the fire. So, whatever happens, keep moving. Aunt Hermione, give me your sweatshirt." She pulled off her own. The sun seared her unaccustomed skin.

"What about me?" Marylou asked, starting to remove her filmy blouse.

Stoner shook her head. "Too wispy." She took one shirt in each hand and started to run down the path. "Try to keep up with me."

The sand was changing under her feet, becoming less powdery, more gritty. Single sprouts of grass appeared. Then tufts. Long blades whirled in the breeze and cut circular patterns in the sand. Pebbles, then stones. The grass grew thicker and more luxuriant.

She sensed someone beside her and glanced over.

"Lissen," Callie Rose said, "what's wrong with her?" She gestured back toward Gwen.

Stoner slowed to a jog. "Someone shot her."

"Well, I certainly know *that*. I was there. But she's actin' funny. Keeps talkin' about feelin' cold an' weak an' stuff. Don't look good, either."

"She's dying. That's why we have to get out of here."

The girl was silent. Thoughtful.

"Why do you ask, Callie Rose?"

"'Cause I felt like that one time. Do you think it has to do with...I mean..."

She doesn't know she's dead, Stoner thought.

She really didn't want to be the one to break the news.

"I think I can explain it," she said. "Later, okay?"

"Yeah."

They picked up the pace a bit.

"What cha' doin' with them shirts?" Callie Rose asked.

"There are bison over there. We may have to scare them off."

"Buffler?"

"Yes."

"Shoot, I can help with that. I scared enough spooked cows back home."

"That's okay, Callie Rose. It's too dangerous."

"Geez," the girl said. "I never seen such a bunch of people for not lettin' a body do nothin' to help."

Stoner realized she was right. Back when Callie Rose was alive, children were expected to do anything they were physically able to do. It might have been child exploitation, but at least they had some self-esteem. What the heck? The girl probably knew more than Stoner did about such things. And the chances of her getting hurt or killed were minimal, since she was already dead.

"You're right," she said. "It's just how we are. I'd be glad for your help."

They were running full-out in prairie grass now. Stoner stopped to catch her breath, and looked back. Gwen and Marylou and Aunt Hermione were moving much more slowly, but at least they were still in sight.

On the western horizon she could see the first thin trails of smoke. "Get ready," she said, and tossed Callie Rose a shirt.

"One thing I don't get," the girl said as she wrapped a sleeve around her hand and whirled the shirt over her head. "How come you knew this was gonna happen?"

Stoner shrugged. "Just a guess."

"Did'n' sound like no 'guess' back there."

"I don't know how to explain it."

Callie Rose knit her eyebrows together. "They was a old colored lady? Back home? Lived alone 'way back in the swamp. Folks said she could conjure bones. That how you do it?"

"Not exactly." The others were nearly close enough now to see the fire. And the fire was close enough for them to see the flames. Stoner eyed it uneasily.

" 'Fraid they'll put the Juju on you if you tell?" Callie Rose asked sympathetically.

"The what?"

"Juju. The VooDoo hex."

"I don't believe in VooDoo hexes," Stoner said. "It's just a different religion from ours, that racist people try to make you think is primitive and evil."

"Well, I believe in it. We got us folks back home been sickened by that VooDoo stuff." She put her hand on Stoner's arm. "Hear that?"

She listened. A sharp, high-pitched yapping sound. Prairie dogs, giving the alarm. "It's coming."

"Sure is." Callie Rose took a step forward and placed herself between Stoner and the fire. "Y'all get ready to run."

Stoner ran back to where Marylou and Aunt Hermione plodded along with Gwen sagging between them. Gwen seemed to barely be putting one foot in front of the other. She was quickly reaching the end of her strength. "We have to hurry," Stoner said as she relieved Aunt Hermione and slipped Gwen's arm over her shoulder. "The fire's coming."

Aunt Hermione grabbed Stoner's sweat shirt and trotted forward to give Callie Rose a hand.

"How are you doing?" Stoner asked Marylou.

"If this is a dream," Marylou said in a weary and frightened voice, "I think it's time to wake up."

The ground beneath their feet began to tremble.

* * *

"You *shot* her," David said.

Millicent Tunes made a gesture of frustration and dismissal. "She was in the way." She turned her back and reached for the steel rung ladder that led from the tunnel to the hatch above.

David caught her ankle. "*Wait* a minute. I have something to say."

The woman tried to kick his hand away but he held on. She decided to try charm. "David, dear, I can see you're upset, and I care very much about your feelings, but we have to hu..."

"Oh, don't give me that," he said roughly. "You don't give a damn about my feelings. You know it, and I know it."

My God, the stupid little neurotic. Of all the times to start *whining...*"I don't know what kind of sick attachment you've developed for these people, but let me assure you..."

"No," David barked. "You're not going to deflect me with that. We had an agreement and you broke it."

Millicent leaned against the ladder in a pose of weary boredom. "Would you like to explain that?"

"In the first place..." He held up one finger. "You failed to give me a complete outline of your plans. Breach of trust. Two..." He held up a second finger. "Your description of the subject was inadequate. Three..." And a third. "Any use of weapons is assumed to be the option of the person who is responsible for the majority of the project. Everyone knows that."

"Knows what?" Millicent Tunes smirked a little. "I don't even know what the hell you're talking about."

"Easy. It's my gig, I get to do the shooting."

197

"Okay," the woman said, spreading her hands in a gesture of surrender. "You win. Go back there and shoot anyone you want."

He glared at her. "I don't want to shoot anyone. The point is not shooting. The point is respect."

"Respect?"

"For my work."

Millicent gave a lilting laugh. "But, David, dear, your work isn't respectable."

* * *

"Damn," George said. She swung her flashlight in a circle over the grass. "It has to be here. Stape, give me the map."

Stape handed it over. George peered at it. The trouble was, the perpetrators had burrowed into the tunnel from somewhere back here. They weren't using an old entrance that would be easy to find. There *were* no old entrances. The nearest one was under Mexico, and it had been walled up for years.

"Sweet Thing," Ed said, "I think you've been imagining things."

George glared at him. "How many times have I told you, don't call me 'Sweet Thing?'"

"Only a coupla hundred. I got a whole Park to cover. Can't spend all night here."

"But I heard something down there," George argued. "A sound. Like a gun shot. Stape, you heard it, didn't you?"

Stape shook her head. "Sorry. But I was busy with the map."

"I'm not saying you didn't hear something," Ed said. "But, Glory, gal, it could've been anything. A car backfiring. Jet breaking the sound barrier. Maybe one of the flamingoes passing wind."

"It's not a laughing matter," George said snippily. "My friends are in danger."

"Well, that might be, Sweet Thing. But I can't pull any more of my people over here on your evidence. You know that." Christ, now she was pouting. He couldn't stand how pitiful she looked when she pouted. He wondered how Stape lived with it. "I'll let you keep Tom and Frenchie, and we'll keep this channel clear on the Talkie." He shrugged. "Best I can do, Darlin'."

"Someone was here," George said a little desperately. "You can see the grass all smashed down."

Ed Garr peeled a stick of gum and popped it in his mouth. He chewed thoughtfully for a minute. "Naw, probably just them damn flamingoes." He turned and began walking away. "Damn pink birds cause enough damage to the grass, you might as well run a herd of buffalo over it."

The herd was getting nervous. Spooked. Kind of shuffling their feet and swinging their heavy heads side to side like big brown sacks full of grain. Even standing in place they made the ground shake, just lifting one foot and putting it down. When they started to run...

Callie'd never seen a herd that size. Never seen a herd of buffler at all, though she'd seen pictures of them in books at school, before her folks stopped letting her go to school on account of there were government men snooping around. They couldn't risk one of the kids saying the wrong thing into the wrong ears. If the government men ever sniffed out their still, they'd kill them all first, and ask questions later. She knew that was for-sure true. She'd heard it from a cousin who was also a cousin of someone it'd happened to.

They were starting to move now. Just a little, but you could tell they were tensing. Callie took a good grip on the shirt in her hand.

There wasn't a chance in hell—'scuse my language, Lord—she'd be able to turn those beasts once they started running for good. Not turn them back toward the fire, anyway. But maybe she could turn them enough so those other folks could get through. She liked those other folks, the old lady and the strong one and the pretty one and the funny one. Especially the funny one. She wished she could spend more time with her. But she probably couldn't. Not if this was going to turn out the way she figured it would—once those buffler started moving, Miss Callie Rose was a goner.

She didn't like the way the pretty one looked. Pale. Sick. She'd felt that way, too. Right before she fell asleep and woke up trapped in this dern-fool strange place.

Maybe she'd been VooDoo'd, too, that pretty one, the one they called Gwen. Maybe someone'd gone to that old Witchin' man back in the swamp and had a curse put on her family, like those trashy Russells had on theirs. Heck, maybe Gwen was even part of Callie's clan. Wouldn't that be a hoot 'n a hollar?

She could see the fire on the horizon now. Black clouds of smoke rolling like wild horses across the ridge.

That other one, the one they called Stoney or somethin', had tried to tell her there wasn't anything like VooDoo and Witchin' men. Leastways, that was what she *thought* Stoney'd been trying to say. Talked funny. Like a teacher. Using big words and long sentences. She was okay, Callie guessed. A Good person. But she was in for some big surprises if she didn't start changing her way of thinking about curses.

Well, here they came, big as life and twice as mean. The ground started bouncing, so hard Callie thought it'd shake the teeth loose in her head. Comin' on, fast, too. She could almost look the lead cow right in the eye.

"You guys hustle it," she shouted to her new friends. "These monsters'd as soon run you down as look at you."

They probably couldn't hear her, but they got the point. Stoney turned her piece of Gwen back over to the old lady and pushed them along. They all started running, best they could. Reached up with her. Passed her. Kept on going down toward the river.

Good idea, the river. If it didn't stop the herd, it'd slow them down. And they for sure needed slowing down. They were close now. So close she could smell them. So close she could nearly read their minds. And the ground was hopping like an old busted-spring bed. Enough to make you sick.

Callie faced the herd again. Now they were so close she could feel their breath. And running like wild fire.

Callie waved her shirt. She swore.

A cow and her calf thundered toward her. She whistled.

They kept coming.

The herd noise was too loud for them to hear her now. They were too scared to think. All they could do was run. Just run and run and run until they wore out.

The calf bumped her, throwing her off balance.

The herd came on.

She went down.

Glancing back as she ran, Stoner saw her disappear beneath the ocean of brown hooves and backs.

Oh, Goddess, I hope I made the right decision.

She felt a sickness deep in her soul.

I left her to be killed.

"You did the right thing," Aunt Hermione shouted over the din. "There was nothing to gain by trying to save her. Callie has been dead for a long time."

Stoner nodded, but Aunt Hermione's words didn't help. Didn't change the fact that she *had* made a decision, had decided to sacrifice Callie Rose for Gwen. Realistically, given a second chance, she would probably make the same choice again. But that didn't mean she felt good about it.

They were at the water now. A shallow river lined with syca-more trees. The ground shook, the air was thick with dust and the thunder-sound of hooves. Grit filled her mouth and clogged her nose and scoured her eyes. She looked around wildly. The bison were coming on. Flowing like water, a torrent of fur and hooves. She could smell their fear. Trees wouldn't stop them. Nothing would stop their panic-stricken flight.

They had to get out of the stampede's path. They had to get across the river.

How? There was no boat, not even a floating log.

She jumped into the water and pushed her way along the bank, fighting the current, searching for something, anything...

She could swim. Aunt Hermione could swim. Marylou could probably swim, though they'd never really discussed it...after all, Marylou was hardly the type to go to the YWCA pool, and believed beaches were made for sunbathing and picnicking, not for swimming...

You're prattling, she told her mind. Stop it.

They could all be Olympic Gold Medalists, and they wouldn't be able to get across the river with that current, not with Gwen hanging dead weight between them.

It wasn't going to work. They couldn't save Gwen. They couldn't even save themselves. They were going to die here. And she didn't even know where they were.

She stood in the shallows, soaking wet, the current grabbing at her legs. "I'm sorry," she whispered. "I tried. I just couldn't..."

Something made her look up. Marylou stood on the bank, waving her arms and pointing upstream.

A small, roofed, open boat floated toward her.

She threw herself into the middle of the river, arms flailing, swimming wildly toward the boat. She had to make it.

The boat floated closer.

Now the prow was almost even with her, but it was still too far away to touch.

Stoner swam harder. Her arm and leg muscles screamed in pain. It was passing her. In a few seconds...

With a grunt she propelled herself forward, one last frantic kick with her legs, one last frantic push with her hands.

Her fingers touched wood.

Nothing to grab onto.

She felt the boat sliding away beneath her hands.

It was past her, drifting away. Their last chance. Their only chance.

Gone.

Stoner coughed up water and sputtered.

Exhausted, she felt herself sink beneath the surface.

And that was when she saw it.

A rope, trailing out behind the boat, and almost out of reach...

Almost, but not quite.

She grabbed the rope and wrapped it around her wrist. It caught, and she was pulled downstream. The momentum brought her to the surface.

Hand over hand, she dragged herself to the boat, reached over the edge, and pulled herself up.

She was too weak, too tired. Her arms slipped. She fell back into the water.

Taking a deep breath, she brought all of her concentration to a point, for one last try.

She gripped the side of the boat.

She pulled.

This time she made it.

She fell into the bottom of the boat.

She wanted to lie there forever, but there wasn't time. She was passing the others. They huddled on the bank, while the bison herd thundered nearer.

Stoner grabbed the rudder and gave it a hard push to the right. Slowly, the boat came around, the current carrying it now toward shore. Within seconds she felt the bottom scrape on sand. She held it steady.

Aunt Hermione and Marylou slipped and slid down the bank. Gwen had stopped even trying to walk. She looked unconscious. Unconscious, or...

They tossed her into the boat like a sack of flour. Aunt Hermione swung in behind her, Marylou gave the boat a shove and jumped aboard. The current caught it.

Back on shore, the bison milled and snorted, stopped by the water. Shoving and jostling, they slammed into trees, uprooting even the oldest and largest. Trees under which Aunt Hermione and Marylou had been standing with Gwen only a few seconds ago.

Then, as if nothing had happened, they turned and moseyed back to the prairie, grazing as they went. As the dust settled she could see, torn and trampled into the dirt, Aunt Hermione's sweat shirt.

There was no sign of Callie Rose.

CHAPTER 14

Stoner fell to her knees beside Gwen's motionless body. She felt desperately for a pulse. She looked up at her aunt. "Is she...?"

"She's alive," Aunt Hermione said. "But barely."

Stoner pounded on the side of the boat in frustration. She didn't know where they were going. She didn't know what to do. They might float like this for hours, drifting through wilderness, while Gwen...

"For Heaven's sake, calm down," Marylou said. "This is only a dream."

Stoner turned on her in a rage. "It is NOT a dream. It's real. Very real, and Gwen is dying."

Marylou looked as if she'd been slapped. "You mean...?"

"It's not a dream," Stoner repeated, a little more gently.

"And Gwen is..."

"She might."

"Callie Rose?"

"She's been dead for about fifty years," Stoner said.

Marylou turned around in a circle, looking at the river, the riverbanks, the boat, Aunt Hermione, Gwen. Taking it all in. Trying to make sense of it. "Well," she said at last. "It's beyond my comprehension."

Gwen was breathing, softly, gently as a breeze. But it wasn't an easy, resting kind of breathing. It was a letting-go breathing.

Please, Stoner begged her silently. Hang on, Gwen. Please, hang on.

Hang on for what? The were stuck here, floating down a river at the river's very own pace—which had turned leisurely, almost deliberately leisurely. As if the river itself were trying to keep them from getting where they had to go.

Which was?

Back to where they had come from, she supposed. To their bodies. Maybe George and Stape had found them by now. Maybe there were police there, and EMT's and ambulances and...

But she didn't know how to get back. She didn't even know where they were. Some place that was EPCOT but not EPCOT. Some place that was EPCOT made real.

She recalled what Gwen had said about the Characters. "When you put on the Goofy costume, do you *become* Goofy? Does the essence of Goofyhood enter you?"

If so, the essence of EPCOThood had entered them all. And they were stuck here, in EPCOT/not-EPCOT.

She understood now what had happened to Callie Rose. Years ago, when she died, she had somehow gotten caught between Is and Isn't and Was and Wasn't. Between living and dying.

Except that Gwen wasn't caught between living and dying. Gwen was dying.

Stoner looked down at her, knowing Gwen was in the last few minutes of her life. And she couldn't even talk to her. Couldn't say goodbye. Couldn't even cry. There was nothing she could do but watch her breathe, and cherish every breath, and pray for the next one. Just one more, Gwen. Just one more.

Someone touched her. "Stoner."

She looked up.

"It's time to move her," Aunt Hermione said.

Move her? We can't move her. There's nowhere to go...

The boat had stopped. They had drifted to shore and were bobbing in the shallows, the boat's wood scraping against a dock with a soft squeaking noise.

Beyond the dock stretched a lawn with a gigantic sycamore. Beyond the sycamore was a house, two-storied, made of weathered wood, with a front porch. Beyond the porch an open door led to an entry hall. In a kitchen beyond the hall a kerosine light burned. Behind the house, the sun was rising. A small tan, long-haired dog lay curled up asleep at the base of the tree, tethered by a rope.

She knew the place.

Marylou scrambled from the boat and tied it to the dock.

"Can you lift her?" Aunt Hermione asked.

Knees bent, Stoner slipped one arm beneath Gwen's shoulders, the other under her knees. She tried to stand, but Gwen's unconscious weight was too much. She shook her head.

Aunt Hermione slipped to Gwen's other side. "We can do it," she said. "Just give me a second." She took a deep breath, held it, drew in a little more, held it, then exhaled slowly. She repeated the action, then again, until she had drawn seven breaths. She smiled. "The Seven Breaths of Artemis," she said. "Very invigorating. It takes you to another plane. Rather like LSD without the side effects. Now..." She slid her arms under Gwen, grasped Stoner's elbows, and lifted.

204

Gwen's body felt as light as a pillow between them. They carried her to the side of the boat and placed her gently on the dock.

For the first time, Stoner noticed how chilly the air was without her shirt. The kind of damp chill that comes at dawn in the summer, rising from the ground and smelling of soil, mixing with the warm air to make the leaves rustle uneasily in the gray dawn light. She tried to remember where she had lost her shirt. The last time she could recall having it was when the bison were coming toward them. She supposed she had left it behind with Callie Rose.

Aunt Hermione was shirtless, too. Her milky, almost translucent skin was goose-bumpy. Her naked breasts were still round and firm as a young woman's. She noticed Stoner watching her, and smiled. "I'm sure we'll find something to wear inside. Personally, I enjoy going sky-clad, even under these circumstances. But I know you find it disconcerting."

They bent again and lifted Gwen and carried her toward the house. The little dog followed as far as his rope would permit, then sat back on his haunches and complained. As they reached the porch, the front screen door opened.

"Hey," said Callie Rose. "I thought you'd never get here."

* * *

David's eyes glittered dangerously. Tunes was respectful enough of his work when she wanted something from him. But, when push came to shove, she was just like the rest of them. He was tired of being treated like trash. The only person who'd been halfway decent to him since he got out of prison had been the woman he'd snatched. Sure, she'd let him think she was someone she wasn't, but that was to be expected. That was part of how you played the game. It just showed she understood what was going on, and had an appreciation of what it involved.

Saying she wanted to have his baby was probably a lie, too. He was sorry about that. It would have been fun, although if he was really honest with himself he had to admit he was beginning to find the responsibility daunting. So he was a little relieved, at the same time that he was disappointed. The fact that she'd done that, played him along—well, that was part of the process, too. At least she never tried to put him down. And he'd never even told her how he felt about being put down. Not like he'd told Tunes, a hundred times at least. Christ, he'd even *paid* her to understand him, and what good did it do?

She had turned her back on him again, and was starting to

205

climb the metal ladder. She wasn't even afraid of him. It made him furious. It made him want to call her names he'd never call any woman, names only crude, brutish men used.

"Are you coming?" she snapped, not even having the decency to look around.

He didn't answer.

She had reached the top of the ladder, and pushed against the trap door. It wouldn't give. She pushed again, harder, muttering angrily.

David just stood there and watched.

"What's the matter with you?" she barked. "Give me a hand with this."

He started up the ladder until, by reaching up, he could just touch her foot. He wrapped one hand around her ankle. "Fucking bitch," he said, and gave her a yank.

Millicent Tunes tumbled from the ladder and hit the cement floor hard. She sat up, rubbing one elbow. "What the hell has gotten into you?"

David drew his gun.

* * *

"Geez," Callie Rose said, "I've been waitin' and waitin'." She held the screen door open while they carried Gwen inside.

Marylou stared at her. She shook her head. "Not real," she said.

The interior of the house was cool and dark. Ahead of them was a staircase, leading to a landing with high windows and a window seat, then turning to continue to the second story. To the left a formal-looking parlor with stiff furniture. On the right a door led to a small bedroom, outfitted with a metal bed painted a chipping white. A hand-made quilted comforter of bright colors lay on the bed. A rough dresser held a deep china wash bowl and matching ewer in a faded, cracked tea rose pattern. Curtains made from burlap grain bags hung at the window.

Callie Rose let the screen door go with a "bang." The dog yapped.

"Best put her down there," she said, and pointed to the bed. "Looks about done in."

"That's about it," Stoner said as they lowered Gwen gently to the bed. Aunt Hermione wrapped the quilt around her. "Is there anyone else here?"

"Not so far as I can tell," Callie Rose said. She looked at them and gave a little laugh. "You folks don't look half decent. What'd

206

you do, swim the river?"

"Close," Stoner said. "How did you get here?"

Callie Rose shrugged. "Just showed up. There's some shirts ought to fit you in that closet."

Stoner held Gwen's hand. It was cool, but not cold. It didn't feel dead. Not yet.

Her aunt tossed her a soft, faded hounds tooth checked shirt. "I hope, when we return, we return to our own clothes," she said. "It's taken me years to get that sweat shirt just right."

She found it comforting that Aunt Hermione believed they'd return. That she didn't know what condition they'd be in was *not* comforting.

Gwen's breathing seemed a little deeper. Or maybe it was her imagination. Stoner shook herself. She had to stop just standing around staring at Gwen and worrying. It wasn't helping any of them, and it wasn't getting them back.

Maybe they should just hold hands and see if they could go back the way they came. Except that Gwen had been conscious then. What if they made it, and she didn't? They'd never find her in *this* free-time, free-space world.

"Well," said Aunt Hermione as she buttoned her red flannel man's shirt. It hung down below her knees and made her look like a Christmas elf. "I'm going to make us a pot of tea and ransack the cupboards. We might find something for Gwen."

"She probably needs blood," Stoner said abstractedly.

"No doubt about that," said her aunt. "But we don't know her type, and we don't have any way to get it in her."

Stoner looked at her. Why hadn't she thought of it before? She's A$^+$, like me. I could give her some.

But how? How would we get it from my body into hers?

There had to be a way. She'd seen it a thousand times, in movies. People were always rigging up ways to give blood in the wilderness, or in the wreckage of airline crashes, or on capsized luxury liners. This situation was a thousand times better than those. Wasn't it?

So what do we do?

Tubes and hollow things for needles. And how do we get it to run from me into her?

"What are you thinking so hard about?" Aunt Hermione asked.

"Blood transfusions."

"The trouble is," the older woman said, "I do believe it's the body we left behind that needs the blood."

She was right, of course. No matter how you looked at it, the only way to save her was to get back there, and get there in a hurry.

Which brought her back to the original question—how to manage that. After all, it wasn't as if they were accustomed to warping back and forth like...

But one of them was. Her heart started beating fast. They might be able to do it.

"Callie Rose," she called.

The young woman popped her head into the room. "Yeah?"

"You've been going back and forth for a long time, right? Between one world and the next?"

Callie Rose shook her head in bewilderment. "Huh?"

"I mean, well, you're dead, but you're not dead. You go back and forth between the worlds, right?"

"I ain't dead."

"Sure, you..." She felt a tap on her shoulder.

"She doesn't know that," Aunt Hermione said in a low voice. "I think that's been her problem all along. She died, but hasn't accepted it. That's why she hovers between two realities, as it were." She cleared her throat. "If you don't mind a bit of advice, perhaps I should be the one to break it to her. I'm much more comfortable with this sort of thing than you."

"Be my guest," Stoner said. "It's beyond me. But hurry."

Her aunt went toward the girl. "Callie, dear, I need to ask you a few questions. Do you mind?"

"Huh-uh."

"Now..." She took one of Callie Rose's hands between hers. "Do you have any recollection of your home?"

"Sure," Callie Rose said. "It's back in the swamp. Folks call us Swamp Rats, but we ain't. We been homesteadin' in there nearly a hundred years." Her eyes glistened. "Got all kinds of stuff, too. Big house, us kids even have a separate bedroom, sugar mill, chickens. We grow our own corn and things. I can butcher, good as any man. You all come over to dinner some Sunday, we'll serve you up a spread you won't forget, and all of it grown right on our land." She gestured toward Stoner. "That other one can come, too, even if she *is* peculiar."

"We'd like that very much," Aunt Hermione said. She smiled at Stoner. "Wouldn't we?"

Stoner nodded. "Sure." For God's sake, get on with it. Time is doing bad things here. As in Running Out.

"That other lady can come, too. She's fun." She glanced down at

Gwen. "And this one. She doesn't talk much, but I'll bet she's nice."

"Just one thing worries me," Aunt Hermione said. "I've always heard the swamp is dangerous."

Callie Rose shrugged. "Ain't too bad, if you know what snakes to stay away from. Like the difference between a safe coral snake and one that kin kill you, you gotta know what you're doin'. And the 'gators, they ain't real friendly. And sometimes them government men come sniffing around."

"Your father makes his own liquor, does he?"

Callie Rose clapped her hand over her mouth and her eyes got big. "I ain't supposed to talk about that," she said.

"Your secret is safe with us," said Aunt Hermione. "Did you know whiskey is legal now?"

The girl wrinkled her nose. "Nah."

"It is. And has been for some time. You see, dear, you've been away from home for a very long time."

"I know. I got lost. I know I'm real close, but I can't find it. I never got lost before. They did something to the swamp, didn't they?"

"Yes," said Aunt Hermione. "They did."

So that was it. Sometime after Callie Rose's death, Disney had bought and drained the land. And now she couldn't find her way home.

"Tell me," Aunt Hermione said. "What's the last thing you remember before you got lost?"

Callie Rose frowned and screwed her face up tight. "My Ma sent me out to see Granny Conjure."

"Why was that? Was someone sick?"

"Couple of the kids come down with something, burning up and coughing like the Devil had them 'round the throat. Couldn't breathe, none of our remedies helped none. We figure it was Old Cornstalk Man put some kind of spell on us."

"Old Cornstalk Man?" Stoner asked.

"That's what we call him, on account of when he walks it makes a noise like dried corn stalks in the wind. Like he's stuffed with old corn huskin's. Like a old scarecrow, only he ain't no scarecrow. He's a VooDoo man..." She lowered her voice to a whisper. "Likes to steal the breath out of little babies. Leans over their boxes and just sucks the breath right out of them. I know it's true, too. He done it to my baby."

Her baby? She wasn't more than twelve or thirteen. A child. "You had a baby?" Stoner asked.

Callie Rose nodded and beamed with pride. "I sure did. Prettiest little boy, 'til Old Cornstalk Man took his breath. Just a little thing. Wasn't even baptized yet. Put him to bed just fine. Old Cornstalk Man came in the night and next morning he was gone from us." She looked at Aunt Hermione in a sad and frightened way. "You think my baby went to Heaven? Weren't baptized."

"I'm sure he did," said Aunt Hermione. "In fact, I happen to know there's some very, very special places in Heaven for babies like yours. Jesus knows it wasn't your baby's fault. Or yours, either."

"Boy," said Callie Rose, "I sure am glad about that. I been worried."

"After you went to find Granny Conjure, what happened then?"

"I dunno. It was a bad night. Big storm. Bad wind blowing through the trees." She chewed her lip and thought harder. "I kinda remember something...Yeah, something fell outa the sky and hit me. Something like a old tree branch. Hit me real hard. Knocked me down, I remember that. 'N I got all dizzy and lay down for a minute, and when I woke up everything was funny."

"Funny?" Stoner asked.

"Different. I know I did a bad thing, laying down for a minute when they was waitin' on me at home. But I felt real bad, like I was gonna lose my supper, and I couldn't think right, and it's perilous to travel the swamp at night if you're not thinkin' right."

"It seems to me," said Aunt Hermione, "that what you had was a concussion. A hard hit on the head. That's why you felt dizzy and sick. And it must have caused bleeding inside your head."

Callie Rose's eyes grew very large and dark. "Bleedin' in my head? That can't be. Thing like that'd kill you."

Aunt Hermione looked hard and calmly into the girl's eyes. "We think it did kill you, Callie. That's why you can't find your way home."

"Passed on?" Callie Rose asked.

"Well, part way, anyway," Stoner said. "You seem to have gotten stuck along the way. Maybe it was the concussion."

Callie Rose turned that over in her head. "Nah, that wasn't it. I think a 'gator et me. I got knocked out, then et by a 'gator. That's how come nobody come and found me. Wasn't anything left to find."

"You don't seem very upset," Stoner said, "about being dead."

"I gotta get used to the idea first, don't I?" The girl shrugged. "Doesn't seem much different from how it was before. Now that I know where I am, anyhow."

That was encouraging. If Callie Rose knew her way around here, maybe she could help them find the tunnel. "You know where you are?"

"Sure. I'm jest about home, 'cept the world moved on."

"I mean this place, this world."

The girl shook her head. "It's all mixed up to me." She brightened. "I seen *you* before, though. When you come through on the boat. You and her..." She pointed to Gwen. "And a bunch of folks."

She *had* seen them. When they'd been on the Land ride. The figure waving from the upstairs window had been Callie Rose. And she had made phone calls from Spaceship Earth. And somehow gotten from the prairie fire to this house. Obviously, Callie Rose had some way of transporting herself.

"Please," Stoner said, "think real hard. How do you get from one place to another around here?"

The girl just looked blank.

"There must be *some* method. Callie Rose, Gwen's life might depend on it."

"You ain't passed on, then?"

"Not yet. Like you, we're stuck."

"And this ain't Heaven?"

Stoner wanted to scream. "It certainly isn't. Do you think all these terrible things would happen in Heaven? Do you think we'd be in this mess in Heaven?"

"I dunno," Callie Rose said, seeming to draw into herself.

Stoner knew she was scaring her, but she couldn't stop herself. She was frightened, and angry, and it was all just too much. "What in God's name makes you think this place is *Heaven*?"

The girl looked at the floor and scuffed her bare foot along the boards. "Count of the old Granny there." She looked quickly toward Aunt Hermione, then away.

"She's not an old Granny," Stoner said. "She's my aunt."

Now it was Callie Rose's turn to get angry. "Is, too," she shouted, and stamped her foot. "She's a old Granny and a Conjure Woman. I heard that lady say so back at the orange farm."

Aunt Hermione reached out and patted Callie Rose's arm. "I'm not that kind of a witch, dear. I can't make things happen like your Conjure Lady."

"So how come you met that other one?"

"I'm not sure," Aunt Hermione said. "She must have asked for me to come, Spirit to Spirit. But here on this plane...well, here on

211

Earth I'm just as helpless as you are." She looked hard into Callie Rose's face. "You do know something, don't you, dear?"

Callie Rose blushed and stared back at the floor.

Aunt Hermione stroked the girl's hair. "Please, Callie. Our friend needs our help very badly, and we need yours."

She glanced up. "You gonna put a spell on me if I don't tell?"

"Of course not."

"She doesn't do things like that," Stoner said.

"If I tell, you'll make me go, won't you?"

"It's time for you to go, Callie," Aunt Hermione said with a smile.

"An' then I won't have no old Granny no more, and no friends neither."

Aunt Hermione pulled the girl onto her lap and hugged her tight. "You'll have lots of friends on the other side. Your parents are there, and your baby, and all your friends from before..."

"But no old Granny," Callie Rose said with a sniffle. "I never had no old Granny."

"There are lots of old Grannies on the other side," Aunt Hermione said, and rocked her a little. "And I can come and visit you sometimes, too."

The girl looked up. "You can?"

"Yes, I can. When I'm sleeping, or meditating, I can go right to where you are for a short visit. All you have to do is come and get me."

"That funny lady, too?"

"I don't know about that. Marylou may not have the temperament for travelling to the Spirit realm. But, you know what?" She pretended to whisper in the girl's ear. "You can come and visit her, and scare the be-Jesus out of her."

"Yeah?" Callie Rose giggled.

"Aunt Hermione," Stoner said, appalled.

"Oh, hush, it'd do Marylou good. She's much too Earth-bound."

To be perfectly honest, she did rather like the idea of Marylou being haunted by the spirit of a young woman. Marylou would probably like it, too.

"Well, okay," Callie Rose said. She got up. "I'll show you how to go. But it ain't fun."

* * *

"Get up," David said through clenched teeth.

Millicent Tunes laughed. "This is absurd, David. We have to get

212

out of here, and we have to do it together. I don't know what you think you..."

"I want your gun."

"People might be here any second. We don't have time for games."

"Yeah?" he sneered. "You had plenty of time for games before. When you were my therapist, getting me to do this job, lying to me. Lots of games, *Doctor* Tunes."

"David," she said reasonably, "we can sort this out later. There are transference issues at play here, maybe even..." She choked on the word. "... a little counter-transference. I'm certain we can..."

He cocked his pistol. "I don't know what those words mean, and I don't care. I'm pissed. Do you know what *that* means?"

"Of course, I..."

"It means you're in big trouble, Doctor Tunes."

She started to get up.

"Down!" he snapped.

"All right, David. You have the power for now. What do you want me to do?"

"First, hand over your gun."

She did. "Now what?"

Trouble was, he didn't *know* now what. They were here in this tunnel, with just two possible exits, going through the falsely boarded-up door into the working tunnels, where he didn't attract attention in the day time but surely would at this hour of night, with nobody there except security and laundry people. Or climb out this exit to the park overhead—the exit he'd dug himself, late at night, over months of time, risking getting caught night after night—yeah, he had to admit it, glad to do it for *her*. Damn. He was a fool, all right. Impressed by her education and looks and professional manner. Superficial shit. Should have known better. Should have remembered what his mother always said, "Don't judge a book by its cover, Davey. All that glitters isn't necessarily gold."

Well, this book sure wasn't gold. This book was pure, unadulterated S.H.I.T., pardon my French.

And he was stuck with it. Stuck in this lousy hole in the ground with this...this...*unspayed female dog*.

They were going to get caught. He'd bet money on it. And it was back to jail for him, probably for the rest of his life. Jesus, the rest of his life watching afternoon talk shows.

The worst of it was, he'd probably be tried with *her*. They were in it together. A pair. His name linked to hers forever. Next thing you knew, some Bozo'd come sniffing around wanting to write their story. And she'd talk. Boy, would she talk. He could tell just looking at her that this dame would do anything for a buck. So there'd be a book, and paperbacks in all the airline terminals, with their pictures on them—lousy pictures, too, all grainy and fuzzy, he could bet the farm on that—and a TV mini series, with reruns during summers and holiday weeks. They'd make up some cute name for them, like the Orlando Two. Only worse. Some Disney World kind of name, like Mickey and Minnie Louse, the Louseketeers, the...

He kicked at the ladder. He was going to be stuck with her forever. He might as well *marry* the broad. Or shoot himself through the head. One was as about as good as the other.

"I'm waiting," she said sweetly. "Tell me what to do, big man."

His mind was a complete and total blank.

He'd never been clever. He'd known that his whole life. Responsible, but not clever. He was going to have to be clever now.

"Walk," he said.

"Where?"

"To the room."

"And what do we do after we get there?"

He didn't know, but he figured the walk would buy him a little time. Maybe enough time to think what he'd think if he were clever.

* * *

They stood at the entrance to the cellar stairs. The steps were old and splintery. The space at the bottom was black. More than black, hollow, pulling blackness, like the darkness left behind when color has been sucked away. Like a vacuum, trying to draw them in, to drain their strength to feed its own emptiness. They'd made a crude stretcher for Gwen out of the quilt. Stoner tightened her grip on it. Aunt Hermione held the other side. Callie Rose stood one step down, ready to lead the way. Behind them in the kitchen, Marylou was putting the finishing touches on a sandwich of home-made bread and home-made jelly she found in a cupboard, all the while chanting "Not real, not real" in a sing-song voice.

"I'm afraid," said Aunt Hermione, "Marylou is—as you young people put it—losing it."

"She'll be all right. She has to handle things in her unique way. Actually..." Stoner went on as she peered into the darkness, "... maybe her approach isn't such a bad idea."

"This part's easy," Callie Rose said cheerfully. "Wait'll you see
214

that thing they got over where the man talks all the time."

She was referring to Spaceship Earth, of course. And the Pit that didn't exist at the bottom of the stairs that didn't exist, in the tunnel that didn't exist. "I've seen it," Stoner said. "I hope we don't have to get involved with that."

"Me, too," Callie Rose agreed. "Always looked like the Way to Hell to me. I never had the nerve to try that one."

Well, they might as well go. Stoner nodded to Aunt Hermione and together they took a step down the stairs.

The darkness rose like water to meet them, lapping at their feet and ankles. It was cold. Not musty basement cold, but sharply cold. Like the inside of a frozen food locker. Like a winter night. Like the water in a January pond.

"Marylou," Stoner called over her shoulder as the cold rose to her knees, "are you with us?"

"Right behind you," Marylou answered, and embellished it with a few choruses of "Not real, not real." She thrust her sandwich forward into Stoner's line of vision. "Want to try this? It's truly excellent."

"No, thanks. I'm not hungry."

"You really should eat something. It's no wonder you're hallucinating."

"I'm not hallucinating," Stoner said firmly. "This is really happening."

"Suit yourself." Marylou returned to her mantra.

They were waist-deep in cold now. And darkness. Stoner strained to see, to make out anything—a work bench, a shelf, a window, a crack of light anywhere.

Nothing.

Callie Rose had come this way before, she reminded herself. It couldn't be as bad as it looked. Besides, they really didn't have a choice.

Somehow not having a choice didn't make it any easier. In fact, it put her back in all those old childhood "not-having-a-choice" situations—like doctor and dentist appointments, and the first day of school, and endless vacations in the family car touring Civil War battlefields, with no one to talk to and her parents fighting in the front seat. Helpless, miserable, impotent situations.

Even Aunt Hermione seemed shaken. She was quieter than usual, and though Stoner couldn't see her face, she could feel her energy. It wasn't optimistic energy.

"Stoner." She heard a whisper behind her.

215

"Yes, Marylou?"

"Was this part of the ride when you went on it before?"

"No."

"Should we be afraid?"

"Callie Rose doesn't think so."

"That's right!" Marylou said with a sigh of relief. "I forgot. Silly me."

Stoner felt a flash of sympathy for her friend. "Silly you," she said with a little laugh.

"Don't get lost," Callie Rose called from up front.

Don't get lost? How can we not get lost when we've been lost from the minute we warped into this dimension?

She took a tighter grip on the blanket.

There was no way she could tell where she was now. The darkness was so complete, so unremitting it seemed to be not just around and above her, but beneath her feet. The darkness ate sound, and thought, and only motion seemed real. She knew Aunt Hermione was beside her. She could feel the tug on the blanket-stretcher when they drifted out of step with one another. It was comforting, and she was tempted to miss a step now and then just to be reminded of her aunt's presence. But she was afraid of jerking the stretcher.

After a while it seemed that she was being carried forward farther and faster than by her steps alone. She felt off-balance. She might fall. She...

She felt someone near her. "This is the scary part," Callie Rose said. "But it's okay. We'll be somewhere pretty soon."

"Where do we come out," she asked.

"Sometimes one place, sometimes another. Wherever it takes us."

"You mean you can't decide where to go?"

"I never could," the girl said. "That's how come I was so scared when I talked to you. You probably aren't scared at all."

"I'm scared," Stoner said. "Very scared."

"You're joshin'."

"No, I'm really scared."

She felt Callie Rose take her free hand for a moment. "Well, I never woulda thought you'd be scared of anything." Then she was gone, presumably to lead the way.

I know, Stoner thought wryly. Nobody ever expects me to be scared. They always think I can fix things, or do the stuff that needs to be done, or make the decisions...

Only Gwen really knew the truth.

She wanted Gwen to talk to her, to hold her...wanted it so badly it was an ache in her stomach. She missed the sound of her voice, and the way she'd suddenly reach out in a crowd and touch Stoner's hand and whisper, "I love you," for no reason at all and completely unexpectedly. They always laughed together—nobody had ever made Stoner laugh the way Gwen did. She wanted to laugh with her now. She wanted to play Scrabble with her, or sit beside her and read. She wished...

Stoner felt the tears begin to squeeze from her eyes. She wanted Gwen to be alive, and warm and talking—not this cold, silent...*thing*...she was carrying along in a blanket. This wasn't Gwen. Gwen had gone away somewhere. Gwen was...

...dead.

She stopped in her tracks. "Aunt Hermione?"

"Yes, Stoner?"

"I think Gwen's..."

"No, dear, it's this darkness, whatever it is. It plays with your emotions. I can't tell you how many horrors I've been reliving."

"Really?"

"Really. Sometimes there are disadvantages to being in touch with one's past lives."

"I'm sorry," Stoner said. She had to find out if Gwen was still alive. "I'm going to put her down a minute. I want to check her pulse." She started to lower her side of the blanket.

"No!" Aunt Hermione pulled up on her side.

"What?"

"I don't mean to frighten you, but there's nothing beneath us."

"What?"

"Beneath us. Nothing."

"But what are we walking on?"

"Whatever you're walking on is all there is for you, and what I'm walking on is all there is for me. Do you understand?"

She understood, all right. This was like one of those dreams where you have to go from one place to another. It's terribly important, though you don't know why, and the only way to do it is by crossing bottomless chasms on two by fours which are only attached to the ground on one end, and things are always sliding unexpectedly so your whole body jerks and almost wakes up but doesn't, and if you make it across there are deep, narrow underground tunnels you have to crawl through with the earth threatening to fall in on you any second and...

She hadn't had dreams like that in a long time. Not since she'd had the good sense to run away from home at the age of sixteen.

"I didn't want to tell you," her aunt said. "It's quite a terrifying thought, isn't it?"

Just to make sure, Stoner eased one foot out to the right and felt...nothing. Okay. Now we just keep on going as we were before. Nothing happened then, nothing's going to happen now. Keep on going, and trust to instinct. Little kids do it all the time. They climb to dizzying heights. They cross fallen trees over rushing streams. They don't think about it, they just do it.

So just DO IT.

She was completely frozen.

The darkness seemed to close in tighter, while the space around her grew more empty.

She made an interesting discovery: it's possible to have claustrophobia and agoraphobia at the same time.

"Aunt Hermione?"

"Yes, Stoner."

"I don't think I can move."

"Of course you can," her aunt said, and started forward, dragging the blanket stretcher with her.

Stoner stumbled, then ran a step or two to catch up.

"I think," Aunt Hermione said, "you'd do well to take a page from Marylou's book."

"Okay." She turned her mind inward and began a silent chant, "Not real, not real, not real."

She didn't believe it for a minute.

But she did believe the faint patch of light ahead. It looked like natural light, like maybe the first gray dawn light, or evening on a cloudy day. She didn't care. It was light, and meant they'd be out of this infernal darkness. Then she could put the stretcher down and see if Gwen was...

The light sputtered and winked out, like a candle in a sudden draft.

Another illusion.

Stoner could feel her nerves sparking under her skin. She wanted to give up, to let her mind shatter. She was exhausted, and confused, and frightened, and just didn't care any more.

Let go, she thought. Let go and you won't have to do this. Someone else will take over, or we'll all die—anything, it doesn't matter. All I have to do is let go.

Another smear of gray light appeared up ahead. Another illusion, another tease.

Or was it?

She strained to focus on it, to try to make out something, any-thing that would tell her this time it was real, this time they would find the end of this nightmare. But it was still too far away.

Her legs were shaking with fatigue. Her arms burned and trem-bled with the weight of Gwen's body. Yes, body. She was sure of it now. It was Gwen's body they carried, nothing more.

Gwen was gone. The rest of them weren't going to make it. Even if that small window of light turned out to be the end, they'd never get that far.

Let go now, she thought, just let go. Stop fighting, stop trying, stop…

She heard what she was thinking. Rage flowed through her.

"You son-of-a-bitch," she screamed into the darkness. "You don't beat me this way."

CHAPTER 15

George ran her hands through the grass, feeling for a break in the sod. It had to be here somewhere. She was sure of it. And there was someone down there, too. She'd heard a sound a few minutes ago. A banging sound, maybe distant voices. She didn't care that no one else had heard it. Something was going on underneath her and she didn't need a Gallup Poll to tell her she was right.

She sat back. "Stape?" she called softly.

"Yeah?" Stape crawled toward her through the darkness. Lumbering along on her hands and knees, dressed in her work overalls and tool belt, she looked like a slow, lumpy old bear.

You silly thing, George thought. You're as clumsy as a puppy, and you can't half hear because you pound nails all day. You never remember to put your socks in the laundry hamper, and when you need them we have to crawl under the bed and you have to wear them dirty—or mismatched. You have a memory like a sieve, especially if what you're supposed to remember is errands or groceries. And I know you sneak drinks and cigarettes with Rita in the back room at the club. But, hey, I'm no bargain, either. And I do love you so.

"What?" Stape prompted.

"Did you hear something?" She knew she hadn't, but she just wanted to be close to her for a moment.

"Hell, don't ask me," Stape said. "You know how I am."

George smiled to herself. Stape wasn't stupid. There wasn't anything she couldn't learn or fix or solve or build if she put her mind to it. Their trailer looked like the periodicals room at the public library with all the books and magazines she read. But she was uncomplicated. And, living in a world full of people who seemed to thrive on complication, George found Stape to be as cooling and refreshing as a spring rain. She made George feel safe, made it seem as if this living thing was do-able. Because Stape didn't think about it, she just did it.

"Know what Stoner told me back at the club?" Stape said. "She told me it gets so cold up there where they live the bugs die. They go three, four months out of the year without bugs."

"Maybe we should try moving there for a couple of years,"

George said. Stape hated bugs. She often said the only bad thing about the aluminum siding business was what you ran into when you pulled the old siding off.

Stape gave it a moment of thought. "Nah. People from up north are too nervous. I wouldn't want to get that way."

Behind her she could hear Frenchie and Tom laughing softly. She knew they thought she was a jerk for believing in abductions and underground tunnels. Maybe she was. Maybe it wasn't possible for someone to dig an entrance through from the lawn behind the Mexico pavilion without being seen. On the other hand, if they did it on Tom and Frenchie's watch, they could bring in a back hoe and those two wouldn't notice. They'd be too busy telling make-out stories and trying to believe their own lies.

A sound caught her attention. "Did you hear that?"

Stape put her ear to the ground. She frowned, listening. "Yep," she said after a moment. "There sure is something down there."

* * *

The light didn't wink out this time. Instead, it grew wider and taller. With each step she took forward, it seemed to Stoner the edges were losing their solidity, becoming insubstantial and hazy. What only a few moments ago had looked like a window or door was now a fusion of light and darkness, as if she had been in dark woods and was emerging into twilight.

The tunnel light could be that color, she thought hopefully. Flourescent lamps reflected from gray walls would give off misty light like that. She slowed, feeling the anger that had brought her through the past few minutes giving way to exhaustion. It was solid beneath her feet now, too. Things were looking up. Time to catch their breath and take a head count. She lowered the blanket gently to the ground.

Aunt Hermione was there, of course. And Gwen, still among the living, still on the edge. The chanting, humming behind her must be Marylou. She turned to look.

"I must say," Marylou proclaimed as she strode into the light, "I have a real problem with this ride. It's much too long, and not a great deal of fun. Though I must compliment the Disney organization on their Special Effects. Best I've seen since 'Lawnmower Man.' Do you suppose this is one of those Virtual Reality things?"

"I don't think so," Stoner said. "It's Real Reality."

"Nonsense," Marylou snorted.

"It is." She turned to her aunt. "Tell her."

221

"Excuse *me*," Marylou said abruptly before Aunt Hermione could respond, "but I think you have some nerve, defining my reality for me."

"She has a point," Aunt Hermione said.

"It's the height of arrogance," Marylou persisted.

Stoner didn't feel like arguing. So she had lapsed for a second. So she had thought, if she could get her friend to admit the true terror in the situation, they might have the benefit of one more person's input. They might, for God's sake, be in this together. But if Marylou was going to stubbornly cling to her one-sided view of things..."Has anyone seen Callie Rose?" she asked.

"She was up ahead last time I checked," Aunt Hermione said. She turned inward. "It's hard to tell just where she is now, but I sense she's definitely in the vicinity. I suspect she's looking for the entrance." She studied Stoner's face. "You seem reluctant to go on."

Stoner nodded. "I guess I'm afraid we'll never find the end. We'll just keep going and going, and never get anywhere."

"It does seem that way, doesn't it?"

She was startled. Aunt Hermione having a crisis of confidence? Aunt Hermione, who always seemed to believe they were watched over at all times by a loving and protective Spirit? Who was convinced everything would work out the way their own High Spirits had sat down and decided it long before they were born—just a bunch of High Spirits sitting around planning a trip to Earth. What'll we do this time, gang? I don't know, what do you think? I decided last time. Well, let's see, we've done Fame and Fortune and Fun. I've got it, this time let's SUFFER!

Aunt Hermione sensed her surprise and smiled. "I know it's unsettling for you when I become discouraged, Stoner. It always has been. But, if you'll think back, you'll recall that I always recover."

"I know." She was a little ashamed of herself.

"But, no matter how discouraged we are, I think we should press on."

"Why?"

"Because we have only one other option—to stay where we are. And that seems a particularly unproductive decision."

She had to agree. Carefully, she looked ahead, taking a few steps into the light.

It was mist that had caused the grayness. Mist and steam. They were in the middle of another jungle. But not an ordinary jungle. This jungle had trees as tall as skyscrapers, with canopied branches

222

like monstrous umbrellas. Flowers the size of rooms, and blades of grass reaching into the sky like radio towers. Insects as large as elephants clung to house-sized toadstools. Gigantic ferns caught shreds of low-lying clouds and dripped a constant waterfall of condensing moisture.

The place reeked of rotting vegetation, the peaty, earthy smell of swamp water, and—something else, something familiar but she couldn't quite place it...Sulphur. The air was heavy with sulphur. And heat. Stoner had the feeling she knew where they were. The Energy pavilion. Complete with volcanos, earthquakes, and prehistoric creatures. She didn't like it. Didn't like it at all.

She turned to go back, even at the risk of confronting the darkness with its ability to scramble her mind. But the entrance was gone.

An animal shrieked in the distance.

"Well," said Marylou, "that certainly is dramatic. I wonder where we are now."

"I *know* where we are," Stoner said. "And we really, really don't want to be here."

"I can see why." Marylou wrinkled her nose. "It's downright putrid."

"And dangerous." She started to pick up her side of the blanket stretcher and had an idea. If she could get away for a few minutes—her whole consciousness was tied to worrying about Gwen, and time, and the necessity for hurry. Maybe, if she could put that behind her, she could think more clearly. Because she had the feeling there were Answers out there, just beyond reach but reachable.

She looked over her shoulder. "Marylou, can you help Aunt Hermione carry for a while? I want to scout on ahead."

She moved very carefully through misted moonlight. Bubbling lava oozed in a stream to her right. Good. If she became lost, she could find her way back by following the flow of glowing, molten rock. The shifting fog made vision difficult. She tripped, and crashed into a giant fern.

Damn. She froze, holding her breath, expecting to hear the thundering, earth-shaking pounding of gigantic animal feet.

The jungle was silent. Except for the soft "plop" of molten lava, the drip of water.

To her left the trees seemed to clear a little. Stoner hesitated. She really was afraid to get lost in here. Getting lost in here could mean ending up a little puddle of subterranean oil for the Superpowers to fight over. But she had to find the way out. Of all the places they could have ended up, this was about the worst.

And where was Callie Rose? Had she somehow taken a different turn and entered a different world? Anything was possible. If
they were separated now...

What if she *did* get lost? What if something happened to break
the configuration, all five of them moving together? What if that
meant they'd be stuck here forever?

Still, if she remembered rightly, there should be a way out just
up ahead.

Remember rightly? She'd been on this ride exactly once. There
was no way she'd be able to find the exit, the track the cars had rid-
den on. Besides, there might not *be* a track. Maybe not even a path.

Stoner took herself in hand. It had worked back in the Land.
They had followed the right sequence of events and exhibits, and it
had taken them...here.

"Here" not exactly being the vacation capital of the modern
world.

"Here" being the one, the only, the original Forest Primeval.

If they could make it through here, it would put them just a little bit closer to Spaceship Earth. Which was where, she knew now,
they would find a way out of this. Because Spaceship Earth was
where Callie Rose had called her from, and she was linked somehow to Callie Rose. No, not just "somehow." They were linked
through the Door, or Gateway or whatever it was. In Callie Rose's
case, she suspected the door was the Door through which she had
to pass to move on.

But what about me? What does it want from me? What does it
mean to me?

And why am I so afraid of it?

* * *

"Well, smart boy," Millicent Tunes said as they stood in front of
the door to the holding room. "Now what do we do?"

There was only one thing *to* do. Grab one of them as a hostage,
and play "Let's Make a Deal" with the fuzz.

One thing he knew for certain. He wasn't going to let that pho-
ney-baloney Millicent Tunes decide which one. This time *he* was
calling the shots, and if she didn't like it he'd leave her behind to
rot with the rest of them.

It was quiet in there. Too quiet. Quieter than quiet. It wasn't that
he expected them to be yelling and pounding on the door—they
weren't *that* stupid. But they should be talking, or rustling around

224

or something.

They couldn't have gotten out. He tried the door. It was still locked. Besides, the only way out of here went past the tunnel entrance, and they'd have seen them.

Maybe they'd heard them coming. Tunes' high heels made enough noise to wake the dead. High heels down here. Good God, the woman was an asshole. Too bad he hadn't realized it before, he wouldn't be in this mess, would he? Yeah, yeah, spilt milk.

They might be dead. But there was plenty of air. And Tunes had only fired once. No way it could have gotten them all—unless you believed in "magic bullets" the way those Government turkeys said President Kennedy was killed. And the rest of the country swallowed it. Gobble, gobble.

"Any time you have your thoughts collected..." said Millicent Tunes, sarcasm with an overtone of scorn.

"Shut up!" he snapped. But it had decided him. He had to get rid of Tunes. Two down. What the hell? Grab a hostage, blow the rest of them away, and head for South America.

Which one did he want? He wished he'd gotten a better look at them all together. See who was dressed the best, who might be worth the most in a deal. From what he could recall, none of them stood out. Except the one he knew. That woman had class, he could tell it a mile off. Besides, she was fun.

He reached for the door knob.

* * *

Ed was just finishing up chewing out one of the young security guards he'd caught drinking on duty when the walkie went off.

"We found the entrance," George said. "We're going in."

"Get out of my sight," he snarled at the kid cowering in front of him. "Turn in your gear on the way out."

"But..." The kid said.

Ed showed him the back of his head and pushed the 'All Channels' button on his walkie. "I want back-up," he barked. "Mexico pavilion. All available personnel."

He made a dash for his car.

* * *

There was a breeze creeping through the undergrowth. It rustled the fronds of the giant ferns, and made a whispering sound.

"Stooooo-ney! Stoooo-ney!"

She looked around. "Callie Rose?"

225

She turned to her left and saw her, perched on a gigantic root and grinning from ear to ear.

"I'm glad to see you," Stoner said.

"Me, too." Callie Rose looked out over the jungle. "Ain't this place neat?"

"I'm not sure. Have you seen any animals?"

"Couple. They're real shy, though." She giggled. "They got little baby horses here, no bigger'n our old red tick hound."

"Eohippus," Stoner suggested."How about the larger ones?"

"Yeah, some real monsters. Big and scaly, and one real ugly one with kind of a fan down his back. They don't bother me if I don't bother them. I don't think they see real good."

Stoner hoped that was true. Because, if the way out was the way she suspected, they were going to have to pass right under the noses of a brontosaurus family. Thrilling and funny when you were safely tucked into a motorized vehicle and they were clearly a family of Audio-Animatronics. But in this other world, where illusion and reality had traded places, those cute lizards could crush you just being careless.

"Lookit *that*," Callie Rose shouted, and clapped her hands with pleasure.

A dragonfly as big as an eagle hovered just above the tops of the ferns. Its green body glowed like neon in the mist. Its fluttering wings sent droplets of mist flying through the air like driven rain.

"I never saw a thing so pretty in my life," Callie Rose said, her voice hushed with awe.

After all they had been through, and all they still had to face, Callie Rose could freeze time right here and be enchanted with this moment. Stoner wondered if she'd even been able to do that, when she was younger. Had there been times, when she was a child, that she had been able to lose herself in a golden moment?

"You look all sad," Callie Rose said.

Stoner smiled at the genuineness of her concern. "I was just thinking of my childhood," she said. "I used to worry all the time."

"Shoot, I never worried. Probably how come I had that baby and got myself killed." She slipped down from the root.

Stoner held out a hand to steady her. "Do you have any idea how we get out of here? I've been through before, but only on the ride."

"You mean that path through the trees?"

"Is there a path?"

Callie Rose nodded. "It's kinda scary, though. Once I seen

226

spooks on it."

"Spooks?"

"Lots of 'em. Maybe a hundred or more. Sittin' real still and movin' along in great big church pews." She laughed. "Sounds like I'm really crazy, don't it?"

No, it didn't. What Callie Rose had seen had been tourists on the Universe of Energy ride. Maybe the curtain between this world and the other was thinner in places. Maybe there were spots all over Walt Disney World—or even the entire planet—where that barrier was thin. Maybe it was so thin in places that you could pass back and forth if you knew how.

Maybe the Welsh shop in the Great Britain pavilion was one of those places.

Maybe Spaceship Earth was one of those places. Maybe that was why she felt they could get back to themselves if they could get back there.

She turned to Callie Rose. "Can you find the path from here?"

"Sure," the girl said.

"Is it awful, like that basement we came through?"

"Animals are kinda ugly. Other than that it's okay."

They started back to where she'd left the others. The mist was brightening, turning into a white glare. This must have been how it looked when the sun was high, back in prehistoric times. The cloud cover never lifting, water falling and evaporating and falling again. Everything dripping and glistening and running.

Deep in the jungle an animal roared, shaking the ground. Something shrieked overhead. The earth felt soft and unstable underfoot, as if there were pockets of quicksand everywhere.

"Look," Callie Rose said, pointing to a large mound of brilliant green vegetation. "We got that back home. Call it Trembling Earth."

"Why is that?" Stoner asked.

"I'll show you." The girl scampered over to the emerald hillock and stepped on it carefully. It quivered as if it were suspended in Jell-o. She bounced up and down on it. "C'mon, try it. It's fun."

"No, thanks," Stoner said. "I've reached my limit of fun for the day."

Callie Rose took one last bounce and trotted back to her side. "How come you're always so serious?"

Stoner shrugged. "I guess I'm just like that. And the things that have been happening...well, they frighten me."

"Yeah, like your friend dyin' and all."

"Things like that, yes."

They walked along quietly. Callie Rose was thoughtful. "Bein' dead can't be so bad," she said after a while. "I'm dead, an' I don't mind it much."

"It's being separated that bothers me, I guess."

"Yeah, that'd be bad, bein' apart from someone you love. Know what I miss the most? The way my Ma used to smell when she'd been baking. Kinda brown sugary and spicey." She pulled a blade of grass and split it with a fingernail. "But it'd get stale real fast. What are we supposed to do with Forever?"

"I don't know," Stoner said. "I don't even know what to do with Now."

They had reached the edge of the jungle. Aunt Hermione and Marylou were waiting. They had put the bundle that was Gwen under a fern where it couldn't be seen from above.

"You're not going to believe this," Marylou said, "but while you were gone we were attacked by monster birds."

"I seen those things before," Callie Rose said. "They got wings like tents."

"You weren't hurt, were you?" Stoner asked.

"Just frightened," Aunt Hermione said. "They really were terrible. Pteranodons, I believe."

Stoner hesitated. "Uh...Gwen?"

"No change."

The news could have been worse. It could have been a lot better. "Listen," she said, "Callie Rose believes she knows the way out of here. I think we should go as fast as we can. But we have to be quiet. There are animals in there."

She picked up one side of the blanket. Marylou picked up the other side. Callie ran on ahead. They started down a path leading deeper into the jungle.

* * *

"Hey," Frenchie said. He seemed reluctant to leave the pool of light under the street lamp. "You guys really think this is such a good idea? I mean, maybe we ought to wait for back-up."

"There isn't time," George said. "It's coming down *now*."

"What if they have guns?"

"We'll have to chance it."

"Nope," Tom put in. "No way. There's nothing in my contract about guns. I don't even have a permit."

"If something happens to us, our insurance isn't going to cover it," Frenchie said.

George started to argue, then stopped. She wasn't going to beg. She knew these guys only too well—or guys like them. They liked the glamor of working at WDW, and how it would look on their resumés. But work? Forget it. Especially if it involved danger of any kind. They'd finish their stints here and get a good starting job in some resort or hotel, and five years from now they'd be lucky if they could get hired as a night clerk at the Bide-a-Wee motel.

"Suit yourself," she said, and turned away to help Stape haul up the cover to the tunnel.

* * *

There they were, big as life and bigger. The brontosaurus family. Grazing away on swamp leaves, as placid and gentle as sheep.

The trouble was, they were very, very large, with heads that seemed suspended in the tree tops, and bodies the size of...probably small houses, but in her current state of anxiety they looked to her like football stadiums. The sound of their chewing drowned all other noises. It was like a thousand cows, all ripping up grass at the same time.

Marylou leaned over to her. "This is very impressive," she said in a low voice.

Stoner nodded. "I'm impressed."

The air was warm and thick with moisture and the smell of rotting vegetation. If it hadn't been for the odor, she might have begun to see things from Marylou's point of view. There really was a feeling of unreality about it. It made her think of old, not-very-good movies about cave men. But the odor spoiled it. The odor was all too real. And unpleasant. And the closer they came to the brontos, the more the air was permeated with the essence of Dinosaur Manure.

"Isn't it fascinating?" Aunt Hermione whispered, dropping back to talk with them. "I'd love to see what this fertilizer could do for container gardens."

Stoner sensed a shifting in the animals' attention. Their crunching and munching and grinding had slowed almost to a standstill. She glanced up. One of the adults was looking their way, head cocked to one side in a curious manner. She touched Aunt Hermione and signalled for them to stop.

Marylou looked up and gasped.

The bronto cocked its head farther to the side and eyeballed her.

Stoner had heard that dinosaurs had poor eyesight. Though how anyone could tell that millions of years after the fact was beyond her. But Callie Rose had thought so, too. If it was true, they'd do well to remain very still and hope to fade into the scenery. One thing for sure, they didn't have much of a chance of outrunning them. They could go flat out, and the brontos would be on them in a single step.

"I don't like this," Marylou whispered.

"Welcome to the club," Stoner whispered back.

"Are you sure this is a dream?"

"I'm sure it's *not* a dream."

Marylou shuddered. "I was coming around to that. I wish I hadn't." She gazed up into the brontosaurus' eye. "We're in deep doo-doo, aren't we?"

"I think we are."

The animal lowered its head toward them, still apparently curious. A hank of alga hung loosely in its mouth and dripped water and saliva onto their heads.

"This is really disgusting," Marylou mumbled.

"Quiet!" Stoner whispered. "Don't move." The bronto pulled its neck back and tucked its chin, as if to try to get a better look from a distance. More water cascaded down onto them.

Its mate noticed that it had stopped eating, and craned its head forward to see what there was of interest to see. The two giants made low chuckling noises, as if discussing what they should do. Apparently, they decided they had been seeing things, and turned back to their browsing.

Stoner heaved a sigh of relief and picked up her side of the blanket.

Marylou was still staring up at the creatures, her part of the stretcher resting on the ground.

The unevenness of the blanket rolled Gwen onto her side. She groaned loudly.

"Oh, *shit*," Stoner said as the brontosaurus' heads shot up.

The animals didn't wait to consider the situation this time. They came for them.

Marylou grabbed for the blanket. Stoner looked around wildly for somewhere to hide. She saw a cave up ahead. It would hold them, and the opening was too small for the brontos' heads to fit through. If they didn't go on a rampage and tear it apart...

There was only one problem. The entrance to the cave was being watched over by a large, spine-backed lizard that resembled a hyperthyroid iguana. At best, the dimetrodon was merely basking in the pale sunlight. At worst, it was guarding a nest in the cave.

There really wasn't much point in worrying about it. They weren't going to make it, anyway. The brontos were on top of them, so close Stoner could smell the composty odor of their breath. The nearest creature opened its mouth. She saw its hard-edged teeth, like a double row of yellow tree stumps, flecked with wads of chewed grass.

"Get back, you dumb old lizard!" She heard Callie Rose shout.

Stoner looked around.

The girl was hurling rocks at the dinosaurs. There was no way she could hurt or frighten them, but she was distracting them.

This time Marylou was with her when she grabbed up the blanket and ran.

* * *

George motioned to Stape to close the cover of the tunnel entrance quietly. She could hear voices ahead, angry voices. A man and a woman arguing. Behind her and above, the wail of sirens in the far distance. A lot of long minutes were going to pass before Ed got here with the Cavalry. Meanwhile, she hoped the sirens weren't going to give them away.

Carefully, she peered down the long hallway. Through the gray gloom she could see them, the man and the woman, standing in front of a door. The man drew a gun and reached for the door knob.

* * *

She couldn't believe they'd made it. Across the path, between the trees, past the dimetrodon—which turned out to be sleeping, after all—and through the cave entrance. Brontosaurus apparently was a slow and lumbering sort of beast whose brain didn't process with the speed of light. Kind of like Newfoundland Retrievers. You could almost *see* them think.

They also seemed to be afraid of the dimetrodon, which roused itself and stood and raised its spiney fan. It showed its teeth and hissed. Like cows, the brontos decided it would be more interesting and less energy-consuming to return to their grazing.

The cave was very dark. Only the entrance showed with any clarity, but a faint breeze seemed to be blowing from the rear. Possibly another entrance, though there was nothing to see.

"Are we all here?" Stoner asked.

They were. Even Callie Rose, who had stayed behind briefly to distract the dinosaurs, but announced that she was learning she could move with a good bit of speed and ease by thinking herself from one place to another. She declared it was one of the advantages of being "passed over."

There was one problem. Now that they were in the cave, how were they going to get out? The brontos weren't a problem—even if they walked out the entrance in broad daylight they were probably too far away to catch their attention. But the dimetrodon was awake now, and in a particularly foul mood. There was nothing bovine or Newfoundland Retrieverish about the dimetrodon. At the moment it was pacing back and forth in front of the cave, shaking the ground as it stamped its feet, and grumbling to itself angrily. Every few passes, it stuck its head into the opening and snarled. From the rancidity of its breath, Stoner figured it for a meat-eater. And she figured it figured them for hors d'oeuvres or party mix. It seemed nasty, relentless, and willing to wait a long time for its snack.

The safest bet seemed to be to explore for the other entrance.

She passed the word to the others and walked toward the back of the cave, touching the walls for guidance and going deeper and deeper into the darkness.

It was cold and damp back here. Well, it was damp *everywhere* in this world, what else was new?

There might be bugs. She recalled the giant centipedes she had seen on the ride—cute little things, about the size of horses, with hairy legs and hard armor and sharp little pincers. It would be just dandy to have one of those little mothers come scuttling out of the dark. Just dandy.

To say nothing of what else there might be that she didn't know about. Monster ticks, perhaps. Or worms the size of the Loch Ness monster.

Spiders. That was something to think about. Prehistoric spiders. *There* would be a worthy challenge...

She stopped short, holding her breath. There *was* something back there. Something growling, or humming, something making insect noises. Noises that were almost like words, like a subliminal learning tape. She didn't like this. She wanted to turn and run back to the entrance, where there was light, no matter how dim, and warmth, no matter how soggy—and friends.

But she knew what impossibilities lay in that direction. Whatever she was hearing, if it was something they could get past, it might lead them to the second entrance...

... if it didn't kill them first.

She moved forward, slowly, easing one foot along the ground, carefully picking up the other and placing it very, very quietly.

The growling sound grew louder. Now it was even more like words. She thought she could make them out. Words like "dawn," and "tomorrow," and "launch"...

She recognized the voice. It was human, and it was Walter Cronkite.

* * *

David paused and stepped back. He didn't want to leave Tunes behind him. The woman was capable of anything, especially a sleazy trick like shoving him into the room and locking the door and getting away herself and leaving him to straighten out the mess.

Fat chance.

He waved his gun in her direction. "You first," he said.

* * *

Stape and George slid along the wall, keeping to the shadows. Keeping out of sight. It didn't really make a lot of sense, going into this unarmed. But they had to try. They couldn't just let that man wipe out a bunch of people without trying to stop him. If that was what he intended. If he was only going to take hostages, they'd stay out of sight and let him pass, and let Ed deal with it topside. But if it looked as if he had killing in mind...

George wondered if it had been a good idea to have Ed alert Edith Kesselbaum. After all, it might expose a civilian to danger. But she was Marylou's mother, and in her place George would want to be in on it, no matter what. Better to see the worst than sit alone in silence wondering what was happening to someone you loved. Besides, the woman was a psychiatrist, a doctor. They might need one before the night was over. Maybe she'd be able to help out. Like figuring out what made Frenchie and Tom such jerks.

* * *

The cave grew wider, the sounds of talking louder. They followed the voice to gray light and suddenly they were on a landing on the stairs inside Spaceship Earth. The exit was there, and— Stoner breathed a prayer of thanks to the Goddess—the stairs were there, leading underground.

Callie Rose was holding back, obviously frightened. Stoner couldn't blame her. She was frightened, too. But they were out of options. If anything was going to save them, it had to be this.

The stairs clanged and clattered beneath their feet. Stoner didn't care about being careful now, didn't care if they tossed Gwen around, even if they hurt her. It was her life they were concerned with—pain was something they could deal with later.

They were at the bottom. The door faced them. On the other side of the door...

She yanked it open.

Oily fog oozed and crawled over the edge of the pit.

Stoner drew back.

"We have to do this, Stoner," she heard her aunt say softly.

"You're sure it's the right thing?"

"No, but it's the best hunch we have, isn't it?"

Yeah, it was the best hunch.

Callie Rose came up beside her and looked down into the darkness. "You want me to jump in that?"

"I'm afraid so."

"Well, I ain't gonna do it," Callie Rose said loudly. "I don't care if I have to stay in this dumb place forever. I ain't goin' in there."

"We all have to go," Aunt Hermione said. She took the girl's hand. "It's the only way, Callie. You can't stay here forever, and neither can we. It's time to go our separate ways."

Callie Rose looked at her and started to cry. "I don't know anybody over there. Not like you. Not real friends."

"You'll find a lot of friends. The people are very kind." She pulled the girl to her and embraced her. "Remember, your family's there, and your baby, and all the people you used to love."

"I don't care," Callie Rose sobbed. "I love *you* now."

"Remember, we talked about visiting?"

"That ain't the same."

"No, it isn't," Aunt Hermione said. "But it will have to do until we can really be together." She took the girl by the shoulders and held her away so she could look directly in her eyes. "You know this is the right thing, Callie. You know it's time."

Callie Rose snuffled and wiped her nose on her sleeve. "Yeah. You want me to go first?"

"That would be good," Aunt Hermione said. She leaned close to the girl's ear. "You see, these other women are afraid, and it would help if you could set an example."

"Okay." She moved to the edge of the Pit. "See you in Forever," she said. She pinched her nose shut and jumped.

Aunt Hermione turned inward for a moment. Then her face broke into a gigantic smile. "She's over."

Stoner stood looking down into the dark fog. "If we go through here and she's waiting for us on the other side," she said, "we'll know we made a wrong turn somewhere."

"I think we should be touching," Aunt Hermione said.

They put Gwen on the floor and lifted her from the blanket, holding her unconscious body between them.

"Blessed be," Aunt Hermione said, and pushed.

* * *

David heard the sirens. He was out of time.

He cocked his pistol, twisted the door knob, and pulled.

* * *

There was darkness everywhere, and a metallic odor. Like blood. Pain shot through her knee like a knife.

Light flooded into the room, searing white light.

She was wearing her old clothes.

The silhouette of a man stood in the doorway, holding a gun.

Stoner looked down.

She was holding Gwen's body in her arms.

CHAPTER 16

The man reached back, swung his arm forward. The figure of a woman hurtled through the door and crashed to the floor at Aunt Hermione's feet. The room light went on.

Stoner looked down. Millicent Tunes was propped at an ungainly and graceless angle, one hip on the mattress, one on the floor. She had broken the heel of one shoe; it hung down like an exhausted dog's tongue. Her stockings had runs the size of fireman's ladders.

"My goodness," Aunt Hermione said to her. "You look like something the cat dragged in and wouldn't eat."

"Shut up!" David barked. He tilted his head toward Marylou. "You. Come with me."

"Oh, not again!" Marylou said with a heavy sigh.

"Marylou," Stoner warned. "He has a gun."

"All right, all right." She got to her feet and spent minutes arranging her waist, tucking in her blouse, adjusting her hat.

"The rest of you," he said. "Up against the wall."

"She can't," Stoner spat out furiously, and indicated Gwen's limp body. "She's dying. You..."

"Not me," David said. His glance implicated Millicent Tunes. "It was her."

"And I, for one, am not the least bit surprised." Marylou slipped her arm through David's and cuddled up to him. She batted her eyelashes. "What's up?"

The man reddened, obviously taken off guard. He swallowed. "We're getting out of here."

"Oh, thank God," Marylou said. "I can't *tell* you how tired I am of this dump. Where are we going? Some place with a decent restaurant, I hope. And a ladies' room. I really do need to freshen up."

Be careful, Marylou, Stoner thought. Don't take it too far.

Something was moving behind the man. It looked like...

"Come on, come on," David growled. He kept his gun swiveling, back and forth, ready for action. "I said up against the wall."

Stoner placed Gwen's body gently on the mattress and stood up. There was blood all over her, all over Gwen, all over the dirty gray blanket that covered the make-shift bed. Gwen's body was lifeless, inert. Not even the faintest movement in her chest.

Stoner felt as if someone had turned her to ice and cracked her—her chest, her heart, her mind. She ached with an ache that would never go away. All right, he could do what he wanted with her. It didn't matter. Nothing would ever matter again. "We tried," she whispered, and hoped Gwen could hear her, wherever she was. "We really tried, Gwen. I'm sorry."

Someone touched her hand. She glanced over. Aunt Hermione shook her head, so slightly she wouldn't have seen it if she hadn't been attending. Her aunt's eyes flickered toward Gwen. She gave a little wink.

She saw something. Something I missed. Maybe it isn't too late.

"You, too," David said to Millicent Tunes.

Slowly, resenting every move, the woman got up and stood next to the rest of them. "I suppose you're going to kill us all now," she said in a disgusted voice.

"That's right. Except for her." He gave Marylou an affectionate little squeeze.

"No more than I'd expect," Tunes said, "from someone with absolutely no imagination." She turned to Stoner. "You're so brilliant, why don't *you* come up with a solution for us?"

"You make me tired," Stoner said. There it was again, that movement in the hall, in the shadows. She frowned a little, trying to make out what it was.

Marylou noticed her looking. She raised one eyebrow, asking if there was something there.

Stoner blinked once, deliberately.

"What?" Marylou mouthed silently.

She wasn't willing to bet money on it, but she thought, hoped, it might be George. Keep his attention on us, Marylou, she begged silently. Don't let him look behind.

"David, dear," Marylou said, rubbing against him like a cat, "do you mind waiting while I run to the Little Girls' room? I need to change my tampon."

He broke out into a cold sweat. "Don't talk about things like that," he whispered. "It's not genteel."

It was George, all right. She could see clearly as David leaned down to address Marylou. Not only George, but Stape. And Stape was holding a wrench. Not much of a wrench, but a wrench. She was watching David very carefully, and inching closer.

Stoner made eye contact. With Stape, then with Marylou. Hands at her side, she flashed three fingers.

Then two.

Then one.

Go!

Marylou smashed her foot down on his sneakered instep. David stared at her, his eyes wide with surprise. Holding the wrench in both hands, Stape brought it down on his head with all the muscle she could summon.

He staggered and fell against the door frame.

Stoner went for the gun.

He held onto it, doubled over and rolled, and managed to make it out the door.

"I'll get him," Stoner said. "Hang onto Tunes."

She dove out into the hallway.

"He's *armed* !" Marylou shouted.

Stoner didn't care. He had kidnapped her friend, and was going to let Gwen die. Well, it was her turn now, and she wanted him. She stumbled into the hall just as he regained his balance and began to run down the tunnel. She started after him.

Someone grabbed her arm. Stape.

Stoner shook her off.

"Take this," Stape said, and pressed a hard, square bright red object into her hand.

George reached for her. "I've called Security. They're on the way."

"Let her go," Stape said firmly.

George let her go.

Stoner took off as fast as she could, ignoring the pain in her knee.

He was still in sight, but pulling away fast. He'd gotten too much of a head start.

She could feel the blood pounding in her ears as she ran.

Their footsteps echoed a duet off the tunnel walls.

He seemed to be slowing. She was gaining on him.

He stopped, turned quickly, and fired.

Stoner dove to the floor and felt the bullet ricochet just over her head.

He took aim again.

She glanced down at the object Stape had given her.

A pneumatic staple gun.

Staple gun?

She heard a 'click' as David cocked his pistol.

No time to take careful aim. She pointed the staple gun in his

238

general direction and squeezed the trigger. It was tight, almost too tight for her to fire. She took a deep breath and forced all her energy into her hands. There was a loud 'pop' of compressed air as the spring released. The recoil threw her aim upward.

David dropped his pistol in surprise and grabbed his hand.

Stoner jumped to her feet. She ran to him and kicked the hand gun out of reach. "Hold it right there," she said, "or I'll put out an eye."

Blood trickled between his fingers. He lunged for her, awkwardly.

She grabbed his arm and twisted it. He fell face down on the floor.

Stoner threw herself on top of him. She was dimly aware that her knee was screaming, but she didn't care. She snatched a handful of his hair and pounded his head against the cement. "God damn you," she gasped, as her control gave way. Tears of rage streaked down her face and fell on him. She let them fall. She hoped he'd drown in them. "God damn you, God damn you, God damn you."

He was unconscious, his body limp and heavy, his head flopping like a broken doll's. And still she beat on him. She couldn't stop. Didn't want to stop. Kill him, she didn't care. Because it was all over for Gwen, all over for her, all...

A hand touched her shoulder, firmly but gently.

She looked up.

It was George, and behind her a phalanx of security guards with drawn guns.

"The ambulance is here. She's alive," George said. "We'll take over now."

* * *

Edith Kesselbaum stormed past the Emergency Medical Technicians and into the little room to find the elegant Millicent Tunes, looking slightly the worse for wear, hog-tied with duct tape and dumped in the middle of the wretched bed in which the beasts had forced *her daughter* to sleep. She had half expected Marylou to be prostrate with trauma, mumbling to herself in a corner, or flinging herself about the room hysterically. Instead, Marylou stood calmly in the center of the activity, holding a small but lethal-looking pistol which she kept pointed a few inches from Millicent Tunes' face.

"Hi, Mom," Marylou said.

Edith took a deep breath to calm herself. It might be behavior modification, which she hated, but it worked. "Are you all right?"

"I'm fine."

"You," Edith said, and pointed a rage-trembling finger at Tunes, "have made problems for us for the last time. I will personally see to it that you spend the rest of your life in jail."

"Oh, give me a break," Millicent said wearily. "I didn't touch your precious daughter. It was all David."

"He was working for her," Marylou put in. "She was his therapist in prison."

"Hah!" Edith shouted. "Behavior unbecoming a professional, usury, misuse of therapeutic power. Article 372a, *Ethical Standards for Psychiatrists Handbook.*"

"That shows how much you know," Millicent Tunes said triumphantly. "I'm a psychologist, not a psychiatrist."

"And *I*," Edith topped her, tossing her scarf over her shoulder in an imperious gesture, "chaired the Joint APA/APA Committee to Coordinate and Resolve Outstanding Differences, September through November, 1986. It was a crashing bore, but we got the job done. It's in *your* handbook, Sweetie, in black and white."

Tunes glared at her.

"Your training analyst must be ashamed of you," Edith went on. "On the other hand, it was probably a Freudian, a not-very-bright Freudian, concerned only with the Id. No moral sense."

"I intend to sue you," Tunes said, "for false arrest and bodily harm. I have an excellent attorney."

"We," said Marylou, who had been watching the exchange like a spectator at a tennis match, "have a *Mafia* lawyer."

"Okay," Ed Garr said, coming forward and taking the gun from Marylou, "it's all under control now. Care to come downtown and make a statement?"

"I most certainly do." Marylou put on her hat, tossed the ties over *her* shoulder in an imperious gesture, and marched from the room.

Edith Kesselbaum beamed. "Isn't she wonderful?" she asked Aunt Hermione.

* * *

Stoner hesitated at the entrance to Gwen's hospital room, afraid of what she was about to see.

Gwen was alive, but in Intensive Care. She was going to be surrounded by tubes and monitors and terrible machines.

Her knee throbbed something awful. But after twelve hours of pain killers, she'd had enough. They made her feel unreal, floaty. And Stoner felt a great craving for Reality. Even if Reality hurt.

Well, Reality was waiting for her on the other side of that door. She gulped a breath of antiseptic-smelling air and pushed it open.

Gwen was actually sitting up in bed, pale as the sheets, her eyes like dark wells. Her left arm was bandaged to her side, her hospital gown draped loosely across her shoulder. There were relatively few machines and monitors. Just one counting the drops that flowed through an IV into her hand, and one that purred along counting her heart beats. She looked very small and very vulnerable.

She saw Stoner and smiled. It was just a smile, a little one, but it made the sun shine.

"Hi," Stoner said. She limped across the room and touched Gwen's hand tentatively with one finger.

Gwen wrapped her fingers around Stoner's. "Hi, yourself. I'd embrace you, but I have a hole in my chest."

"That's okay." She felt very shy all of a sudden, here in this strange place.

"What'd you do to yourself?" Gwen asked, indicating Stoner's leg.

Stoner shrugged. "Not much. Tore something or cracked the knee cap or something like that."

"Ought to be on crutches."

"Yeah, well, you know me."

"Yes," Gwen said, looking deep into her eyes. "I know you."

She felt a rush of warmth. "I'd like to kiss you, but I'm afraid I'll fall on you."

"That's okay. I probably have hospital breath." She rubbed a finger over the back of Stoner's hand. "Stoner, I had...the oddest dream."

"Did you?"

"I dreamed we were on the rides...I don't remember which ones...Horizons, I think. And The Land. Except that they weren't rides, they were real."

"Uh-huh," Stoner said noncommittally.

"Was it a dream?"

"Sort of, and sort of not, I guess."

Gwen grinned. "Thank you for clearing that up."

"It's kind of complicated. I'm not sure, myself."

"What happened to everyone?"

"Millicent Tunes and David are back in jail—conspiracy to commit murder, something like that. David was Tunes' patient, you know."

"No, I didn't. How tacky." Gwen reached for her glass of water.

Stoner took it and held it while she drank. "Want to hear something funny? Marylou talked David into suing Tunes for malpractice."

"Please," Gwen said. "It hurts when I laugh."

"She's even getting him a lawyer." Stoner shoved her hair back from her forehead. "I don't know. She'd better watch out. I think he already has a crush on her."

"I have a lot to catch up on."

"It'll keep."

Gwen was beginning to look tired. Stoner knew she should go, but she didn't want to. She didn't ever want to leave her again. "You almost died," she said softly.

"So they tell me."

"If you had...Gwen, I..." Without knowing it was coming, she burst into tears.

Gwen pulled Stoner's head down onto her shoulder and stroked her hair. "I know. I feel the same way."

"I'm sorry. Here you are all hurt, and I'm..." But she couldn't stop. Her crying felt hard and jerky, like rocks being forced from her chest.

Gwen let her go, stroking her and whispering her name.

In a while her sobs melted and smoothed. Stoner fumbled for a tissue and wiped her nose. "You came so close, and I was so scared. I didn't know anything could scare me like that."

"Must be love," Gwen said gently.

"I don't know if it's right, to love someone that much. To need someone that..."

"Pebbles..." Gwen said.

Stoner looked up at her. "What?"

"Shut up."

She kissed Gwen's hand and rubbed it against her own cheek. Her skin felt so smooth, so safe. She just wanted to go on feeling her closeness. For an hour, for a day, forever.

"I'm sorry. I know you're tired, I just need to be near you."

"It's okay, Stoner."

"I don't know what I'd do without you."

"I'm not going anywhere."

Stoner grinned. "I don't suppose you are. Not for a while." She was silent for a moment. "I really thought you were dead," she said at last.

"So did I."

Stoner looked at her. "You did?" She reached for another tissue and tried to repair the ravages to her eyes. "You mean with the lights and the tunnels and all?"

Gwen smiled. "A little, maybe. I felt something. Like leaving my body. And there seemed to be someone there—not like real people, exactly. Kind of like a presence. And I sort of remember saying I had to go back..." She shrugged. "It might have been a dream."

"This whole thing has been crazy. Too much unex-plained...*stuff*."

"Speaking of which," Gwen said as she reached for the water glass, "rumor has it you brought down that man with a *stapler*."

"A staple gun. It just deflected his attention."

"You used a staple gun against a real pistol?"

"It was the best I could do. I had to do something. Besides, it was a very powerful staple gun."

Gwen shook her head. "Did you ever hear of letting the police handle it?"

"I was afraid he'd get away."

"Butches," Gwen said with a weary sigh. "Go figure."

Stoner kissed her.

* * *

"Now," Aunt Hermione said as she finished off the remains of her barbecued spare ribs. "Tell me what you've made of it all."

"All what?" Stoner asked, knowing perfectly well what she meant.

"The things that have been happening to you."

"I don't know." She started to get up. "You want dessert?"

Her aunt placed her hand over Stoner's. "I do not. And neither do you. You know we need to talk about this."

It was mid-afternoon, and the crowd at the Crystal Palace cafe-teria was beginning to fill out. Stoner looked around at the floor, the glassed ceiling, the line of people filling their trays. Every-where but into her aunt's eyes. "Some funny things happened, that's all."

"That is *not* all, Stoner," Aunt Hermione said firmly. "Sit down and talk to me."

She dropped back into her seat and stared at her plate.

"I don't mean to be parental about it," Aunt Hermione said, "but I do feel a little responsible for you, you know."

"Yeah, I know." She felt about sixteen years old, as helpless and frightened as she had felt when she'd run away from home and come to live with Aunt Hermione all those years ago. Her aunt had taken charge for her then, when she was lost. Well, she was lost now. "I don't know how to talk about it," she said.

"Just tell me what's been happening."

She glanced up. Aunt Hermione was gazing at her calmly, patiently. It made her feel a little safer. "Well, when Gwen was dying, well, it was as if we'd gone into another dimension or something…"

"I know about that, dear. I was there."

Stoner grimaced. "That doesn't make me real comfortable, you know. I think it was maybe just a dream."

"I've seen you fretting and worrying and trying to make sense of it—or park it somewhere so you won't have to think about it— for days. You refuse to talk about it, and you won't go near EPCOT Center. Something happened to you there, and it had nothing to do with Marylou's kidnapping or Gwen being shot."

"I've asked you a thousand times," Stoner said, "don't read my mind."

Aunt Hermione sighed in mock exasperation. "You can be such a *brat* at times."

"Okay, okay, here's what happened. It wasn't much, really. We went on the Land ride, and the dog followed the boat, only Gwen couldn't see it. And I saw someone in an upstairs window at the farm house, and that turned out to be Callie Rose. And then I was outside the Wales shop, only somehow I was in Wales…"

Her aunt waited for her to continue. Stoner shrugged. "That's all."

"And what do you make of that?"

She tried really hard to concentrate. She knew what she made of it, but she didn't want to know. Every time she got near it—and she had gotten near it at least a hundred times in the past few days— she pulled back. Because what she got near was like a hot stove, and she knew if she touched it she was going to be burned in ways that would change the way she looked at reality forever.

"You have to face this, Stoner. One way or another. You must believe in it or reject it, because if you don't settle it in your mind, it'll just eat away at you."

There were birds flying over the Crystal Palace. Stoner wondered idly if the park people had to clean droppings off every night.

"I don't know how to settle it," she said.

"Yes, you do."

She felt trapped. "Okay, let's assume—hypothetically…"

244

"Hypothetically is good," said Aunt Hermione.

"Let's say there are two different dimensions of reality, or more, even..."

"I'd say more."

"...like parallel univserses or something. And there are places where the curtain or wall or dividing line or whatever is thinner than in other places. And maybe EPCOT is built on one of those spots, so illusion becomes reality, and reality becomes illusion...or whatever."

Her aunt nodded very seriously. "I believe that's a good explanation. However, if everyone experienced it, it would make headlines. Why do you suppose that hasn't happened?"

"Because..." Okay, this was the hard part. Just get it out. "Because not everyone can see it."

"You did."

"I guess," Stoner said.

"And Callie Rose?"

She glanced up. "What about her?"

"She reached out for you, and you heard her."

"Yeah." Stoner squirmed uncomfortably. "Guess we have a connection through twenty past lives or something," she said flippantly.

"Or she reached you because you were willing to be reached."

"I am *not* willing to be reached," she flared up. "My Goddess, don't I have enough to cope with in the real world?" She could just see it. Calls for help from spirits who couldn't move on. Psychic screams from lost souls. They could expand the agency. Get a new motto. Don't know where you belong? Stuck on the material plane when you were aiming for the etheric? Passed over, but your luggage didn't follow? Call Stoner McTavish, travel agent to Spirit.

"What you do with it is up to you, of course," her aunt was saying. "If you don't want Spirit to reach you, there are ways to protect yourself. But I'm afraid, Stoner, these things will continue to happen to you until you acknowledge them."

She stirred the dregs of her tossed salad and brutalized a shred of lettuce. "That's what Gwen's always saying," she pouted.

"And does Gwen also say that whenever you turn petulant, it's because you're getting close to the truth."

She stabbed a sliced green olive viciously. "Yes."

Aunt Hermione leaned back in her chair. "Well, then, it seems our conversation is completed. Shall we have dessert?"

245

"If I knew what we were looking for," George said, "I could probably be more helpful."

"It's really complicated," Stoner hedged. "I just want to see if something is the way I remember it." Sure, she was really eager to explain to this woman she barely knew that they had—maybe—entered another dimension of Time and Space inside the Horizons ride. Where they had met a woman, who was the living embodiment of one of the Audio-Animatronics and working this very artificial orchard—except, of course, in the Other Dimension it was a real orchard. And this woman had been a practicing Wiccan of the future, who had been given a gift by Aunt Hermione. And said gift might or might not still be in the pocket of the Audio-Animatronic version of the real Other World woman, and...

Right. George would believe every word of that.

"Please," she said. "Trust me. I'm not going to hurt anything."

"Well, I know that," George said. "Do you think, if I believed you were the kind of person who'd hurt anything, I'd have invited you to our trailer for a wonderful micro-waved Tupperware dinner?"

Stoner grinned. "And a fine dinner it was, too."

"It was not," George said. "It was a humiliation. But remember, you knew what you were getting into."

"I did," Stoner said. "But Marylou didn't."

"Wasn't she great?" George said with a giggle. "I've never seen anyone be so polite for an entire evening."

"You would have," Stoner said, "if you'd ever seen me when she takes me out to exotic ethnic restaurants. I hope you didn't mind my setting her up. It was pay-back time."

"I loved it." George unlocked the back entrance to the Horizons pavilion and shined her flashlight along the wall until she found the electrical control panel. She threw a switch and lights went on. "We're in, Ed," she said into her walkie-talkie. "I'll check back when we leave." She stuck the walkie-talkie back into its belt holster. "You should see the lights going on at Computer Central about now. We've just been registered as a major breach in security."

"You won't get in trouble for this, will you?"

"Nah, I'll just let Ed call me Sweet Thing a few times." She led the way to the entrance to the ride. "Where to?"

"The Mesa Verde section."

George started off along the track, past the Looking Back at

Tomorrow exhibits. In normal light, without the black lights and moving vehicles and projected images, the exhibit had a flat, dull, slightly ominous look. Like an amusement park out of season. They crept past the OmniSphere, with its gigantic curved movie screens, silver gray, silent and eerie. Then Nova Cite, and finally the orchards of Mesa Verde.

It was all there. The control tower. The painted backdrop of orange trees. The robotic pickers. And Elaine, or rather her Audio-Animatronic persona, looking out over her grove, wearing the same jump suit.

Stoner hesitated. "How often do they launder these clothes?"

"Not often," George said. "It's pretty clean in here."

"Do you think they've done it since I was here last week?"

"Easy enough to find out." She pulled out her walkie-talkie. "Ed, bring up the cleaning schedule for Horizons on the computer, will you?" She waited a moment. "Okay, when did they clean here last? Uh-huh. Okay, thanks." She turned to Stoner. "They finished up the week after Labor Day, and won't be in again until just before Thanksgiving."

So if the pentacle had been there, it was still there, in Elaine's pocket. She stepped onto the floor of the exhibit and reached out to touch the mannequin. She hesitated.

If she found the necklace...?

She would know that everything she'd been taught about life and the world and space and time was wrong. That this thing called Reality was only a half-truth, no more Reality than a photograph of the ocean was the ocean. And, most of all, that she had a great deal to learn, because what she had learned in her more than three decades here was like kindergarten compared to what still remained unknown.

And if she didn't find it?

Then she wouldn't know for sure. There was still the possibility that what she had experienced had happened, but the necklace hadn't made the trip back. So there was still the opportunity...

But she knew what would happen. Slowly at first, but with increasing certainty, she would become convinced that it had all been a dream, or an illusion, or some shift in her thinking brought on by anxiety. The experience would fade until it was merely odd—and finally not even odd but something that might have happened, but she wasn't sure. And when that happened, the magic would be gone.

She dropped her hand.

247

"Find what you were looking for?" George called.

Stoner turned to her. "I think I did," she said.

* * *

It was their last morning in Walt Disney World. A drizzly, nasty, unwelcoming morning. But after a week of looking at day after day of sunny sameness, they were glad for the change. Edith had offered to spring for breakfast at the Top of the World, but Marylou had insisted on the Character Cafe, which everyone found very puzzling until Goofy appeared. Marylou began flirting shamelessly.

"I must say," Aunt Hermione said to Edith, "Marylou acquitted herself admirably on this adventure. She had that wretched man completely flummoxed."

Edith gazed adoringly at her daughter. "Didn't she? Do you know, when she was growing up, I was so afraid we weren't an adequately dysfunctional family. I could just imagine her turning out as straight and stuffy as a Republican. But she's wonderfully flaky, don't you think?"

"Yes," Gwen said, "I think you can put any fears on that score to rest."

"And she's talked David into suing Millicent Tunes for malpractice. I'll testify on his behalf, of course. Maybe we can get him a lighter sentence, if we can prove undue influence. We offered to pay for his lawyer—he certainly won't see any payment for kidnapping Marylou—but he wouldn't hear of it. A nice boy, really. Quite upstanding for a criminal."

"Are you sure you'll be all right on the flight home?" Stoner interrupted Marylou's waving and smiling to ask.

"No problem," Marylou said. "After what we've been through, USAir will be a piece of cake."

"Don't count on it," Gwen muttered. She was still weak and sometimes in pain, though three days spent lounging in the sun on the shore of Bay Lake had put color back into her face.

"Speaking of cake," Edith said, "our first act when we get back to Boston will be to find the most exotic, rich, difficult-to-make cake we can."

"Chocolate Oblivion Truffle Torte with Raspberry Sauce," Marylou declared.

Edith leaned across the table. "They don't have that at McDonald's, do they?" she whispered to Stoner.

Stoner grinned. "I'm afraid not."

"You don't suppose she'll expect me to *make* it, do you?"

"Not unless she's crazier than any of us know."

Aunt Hermione poured salsa over her omelet. "We'll be back in about three days, more or less. I really think it would be too hard on Gwyneth, to be stuffed into one of those God-awful airline seats. And we'd like to set our own pace."

"You don't have to open the agency until I get there if you don't want," Stoner said to Marylou. "You could probably use a rest, too."

"Isn't he delicious?" Marylou sighed as Goofy finally returned her wave. She turned her attention to Stoner. "Don't worry, I'll have everything under control."

"It's cruise season, you know."

"I *know*." Marylou laughed. "Really, after the experiences we've had, I'd think you'd stop sweating the small stuff and turn your mind to higher things."

"Such as?"

"Parallel universes and such."

"Cruise season," Stoner said, "is the Ultimate Parallel Universe. The bookings aren't so bad, but now we're into changes and cancellations and political upheaval."

"Not to mention hurricanes, volcanic eruptions, and other natural phenomena," Marylou admitted. "Maybe I'll take your advice and close the place down. By the way, Love, do you still insist that was all real?"

"I really don't know," Stoner said. She glanced at Gwen. "What do you think?"

"Don't look at me," Gwen said. "I was unconscious the whole time."

"Oh, of course it was real," said Aunt Hermione. "Sometimes you Doubting Thomases, with your stranglehold on the Material Plane make me...make me...well, make me want to lie down." She caught herself and coughed a little in an embarrassed way. "Forgive that outburst, please. It seems Spirit has totally deserted me this morning."

The monorail slipped into the Contemporary with a low rumble. Stoner watched it with a feeling almost like nostalgia. For all the anxiety and fear, in spite of the frightening things that had happened, she really had fallen a little in love with Walt Disney World. And the management had treated them well, inviting them to stay in their rooms at no charge until Gwen was ready to travel. Giving them passes to the parks. Providing all the help they needed when

Gwen came from the hospital. They'd even offered Stoner a wheel-chair and a personal aide so she could rest her knee, but it made her feel self conscious and she politely refused. Maybe they were only concerned about PR, and maybe they were trying to avoid law suits. It didn't matter. Real or packaged, the place was magic, and would always be magic.

Edith stood up. "Well, we have to be off. Our flight leaves at one, and Marylou insists we stop by the Tupperware Museum on the way, God knows why, but I had to promise or she wouldn't get on the plane." She tapped her daughter on the shoulder. "Time to rein in your hormones, child of mine."

Marylou rolled her eyes. "Mother, *really*."

"Has it occurred to you," Gwen asked Stoner, "that we might be missing out on some very interesting moments by not going with those two?"

"It occurred to me," Stoner said. "I don't think we need that kind of interesting."

* * *

While Aunt Hermione had a farewell meditation with her friends from Cassadaga, Stoner and Gwen decided to Listen to the Land one last time. The little boat chugged along the waterway. The theme song, that would stick in their minds for weeks like a Doublemint Gum jingle, invited them to pretend they were seeds and trust in the loving kindness of Mother Nature. The painted roots and pumpkins and seedlings were only painted things now, lovely but innocuous. The jungle was a true-to-life but mechanized jungle. The desert and prairie behaved they way they were pro-grammed to behave, and the bison did only what the computer ordered them to do. The little dog outside the farm house barked dutifully when the sensors picked up the approach of their boat, and stopped immediately when they were past.

They did seem like a dream, the things that had happened. She could put herself back into the events, and recapture a little of the mystery of it. But her logical, Twentieth Century mind was taking over. It made her a little sad.

Gwen tugged at her sleeve. "Listen," she whispered, and tilted her head to indicate the seats behind them.

Stoner glanced around. A young girl, no more than five, dressed in tiny overalls and tiny sneakers, was looking over the side of the boat in wide-eyed wonder. Her mother was smiling indulgently.

"It was just a dolly, honey. Like your wind-up Mickey."

"No, it was a real puppy."

250

The mother caught Stoner watching her and gave an embarrassed smile. "She's a very imaginative child. Always seeing things nobody else sees. She thinks the little dog chased the boat."

Stoner felt a hard knot in her stomach. "It's very realistic," she said shakily.

The child shook her head decisively. "I saw it, Mommy. I really did."

Other mysteries by Sarah Dreher

Stoner McTavish
Something Shady
Grey Magic
Captive in Time
Lesbian Stages (a collection of plays)